A LONG ISLAND STORY

Also by Rick Gekoski

Conrad: The Moral World of the Novelist
William Golding: A Bibliography (with P.A. Grogan)
Staying Up: A Fan Behind the Scenes in the Premiership
Tolkien's Gown and Other Stories of Great Authors and Rare Books
Outside of a Dog: A Bibliomemoir
Lost, Stolen or Shredded: Stories of Missing Works of Art and Literature
Darke

A LONG ISLAND STORY

RICK GEKOSKI

CANONGATE
Edinburgh · London · New York

Published in Great Britain, the USA and Canada in 2018
by Canongate Books Ltd,
14 High Street, Edinburgh EH1 1TE

Distributed in the USA by Publishers Group West and in Canada
by Publishers Group Canada

canongate.co.uk

1

British Library Cataloguing-in-Publication Data
A catalogue record for this book is available on
request from the British Library

ISBN 978 1 78689 342 0

Typeset in Bembo by Palimpsest Book Production Ltd, Falkirk, Stirlingshire

Printed and bound in Great Britain by Clays Ltd, St Ives plc

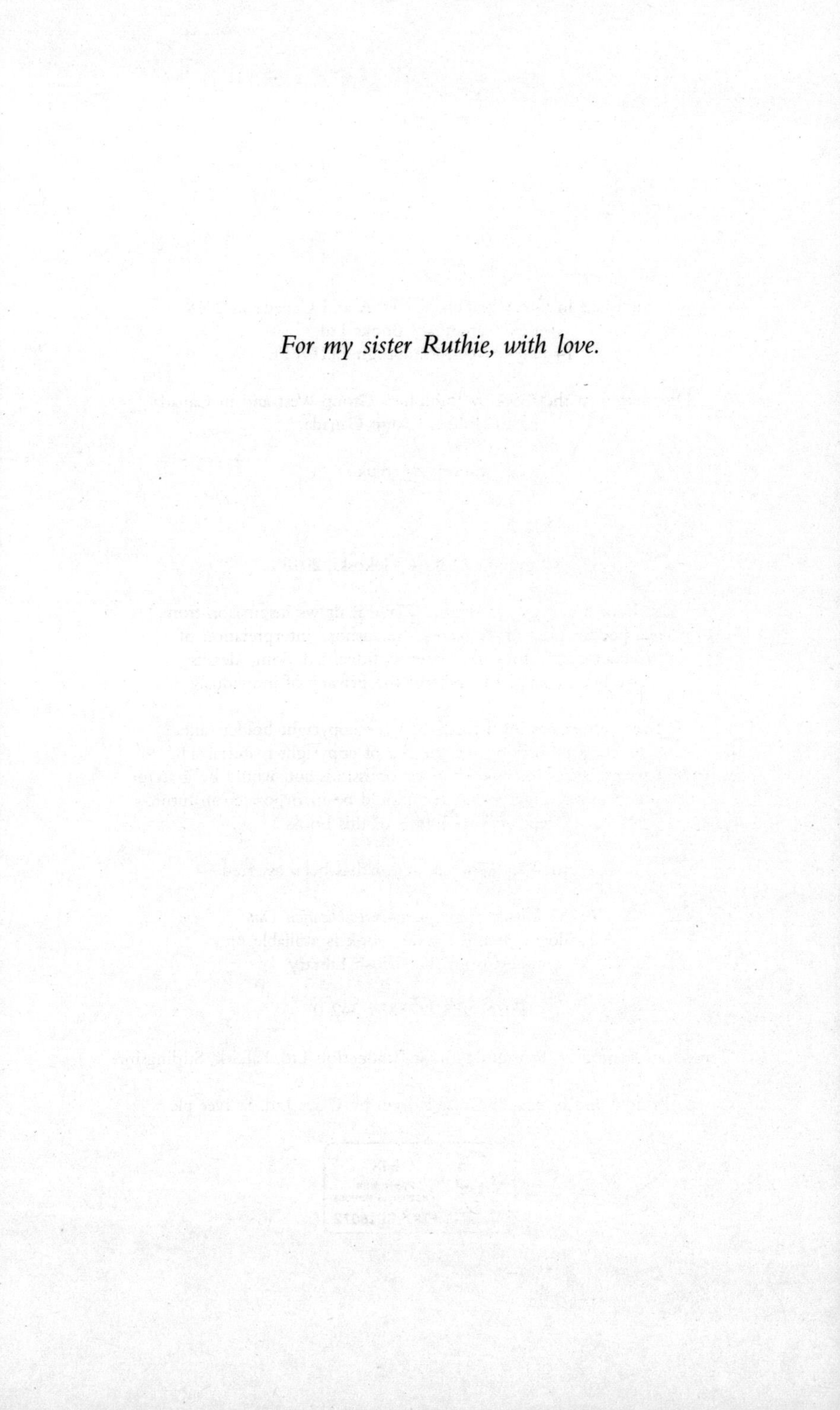

For my sister Ruthie, with love.

'The reason why we find ourselves in a position of impotency is not because our only powerful potential enemy has sent men to invade our shores . . . but rather because of the traitorous actions of those who have been treated so well by this Nation . . . the bright young men who are born with silver spoons in their mouths are the ones who have been most traitorous. . . .

'I have here in my hand a list of 205 . . . names that were made known to the Secretary of State as being members of the Communist Party and who nevertheless are still working and shaping policy in the State Department.'

– Senator Joseph McCarthy, Wheeling,
West Virginia, 9 February 1950

1

Even when her morning started at a reasonable hour her first waking utterance was a groan, followed by a shuddering series of stretches and a string of torporous obscenities. The onset of day surprised her; she resented the imperative to consciousness, as if she had a right to sleep forever, like the dead. Addie turned off the alarm – it was five in the goddamn morning, for Christ's sake – rolled over and covered her eyes with a pillow.

Ben had been up in the night, again. It was impossible to get a full night's sleep, too much to think about, unwelcome plans to be made, worries that could not be resolved. Rather than counting beasts jumping over fences, he preferred to mix himself a double martini. No, not a martini, why bother? In company he would carefully combine one part of vermouth with five of Gordon's gin, agitate in a cocktail shaker, pour over crushed ice. But on his own he dispensed with the vermouth.

He'd been trying to write, sitting at the kitchen table. Not on the typewriter, which made an awful clacking sound, curiously exacerbated in the night-time silence, but longhand on his yellow legal pads, appropriated by the half-dozen from his office at the Department of Justice. *To each according to his needs?* Another Communist lurking at the heart of government! One of 205 reds! Or was it now 57? The number didn't matter, it was as unimportant as the number of metastasising cells in a tumour that threatened to annihilate the lives of so many, of his friends, of himself and his family.

And about this prospect he had nothing to say, nothing to write. It was unimaginable, beyond any language other than brute obscenity. Writing was in his past. It was absurd to try. He was a father of young children, had a constantly demanding job, would have been exhausted even without the additional stress, for these last few years, of constantly looking over his shoulder, being distrusted and investigated. His best friend from law school lost his job in the State Department last year, while other friends and acquaintances, presumed guilty by association, had resigned their positions in university life, in publishing and the film industry.

He had survived, just. Was still employed, could feed his wife and children. But he was exhausted, demoralised and morally compromised. He'd had enough, and twenty-five bucks for an occasional short story was hardly likely to sustain them all.

He'd wanted to be a writer, had always wanted to be one. Had written an 800-page *roman-à-clef* entitled *Nature's Priest* in his late twenties, which prospective publishers praised in one paragraph and rejected firmly in the next. Rightly. The experience taught him a lot: what to leave out, how to separate, to refine, to focus. To make less into more, like Hemingway. He'd honed concentration by composing short stories and had one accepted – what a moment! – by *Story* magazine in 1946. He sent a copy to his parents with a proud inscription, but neither gave the slightest sign of having read it. It was just as well; the portrait of the marriage at the heart of it was depressing and familiar. Addie read it and handed it back with a single sentence. 'Fair enough,' as if she didn't hold it against him. Or perhaps she did.

He finished his gin with a final gulp, put the glass in the sink and went back to the bedroom to fall briefly asleep before the other alarm rang. Addie was snoring unobjectionably, a tremolo that he found oddly attractive, like some sort of wind instrument, reedy and wistful.

'Rise,' he whispered. 'Make no attempt to shine. I'll make the coffee, get things going.'

He got up with the weary steadfastness that was apparently yet another of his irritating characteristics and pulled on his bathrobe. She hunched under the covers, as potent an invisible presence as could be imagined. Her hair bunched on the pillow in a tangled ribbon.

He looked at her form, still and steamy, her early morning smell whispering from the bedclothes to his nostrils. He could have picked her out, blindfolded, in the midst of a hundred sleeping women. On the mornings after they'd made love – not so many mornings now, he'd rather lost interest – the smell was overlain by something sweet and acrid that bore scant resemblance to somatic functioning. Something primal, post-pheromonal, that caught in your throat. He'd once thought it exciting, heady as an exotic perfume left too long in the sun, but now? It didn't exactly disgust him, but he'd smelled better, fresher, and more exciting.

He crossed the hall, had a quick and not entirely satisfying pee, squeezed out the final reluctant drops, washed his hands and took the few steps from the hallway into the kitchen. Get the coffee going, make something for the kids to eat in the car – Becca would only eat peanut butter and strawberry jelly sandwiches, while Jake had been addicted for some months to bologna sandwiches with mustard. At least it was easy. And for the grown-ups? Perhaps some sliced hard-boiled egg sandwiches, with mayonnaise and tomatoes. A few pickles in Saran wrap. And the Thermos of coffee, of course.

No breakfast for the kids, best to lift them from their beds, floppy and warm morning-smelly in their jammies, carry them down to the car however it made his shoulder ache, settle them in the back seat with pillows and blankets. With a bit of luck they might sleep for a couple of hours, kill almost half the journey. A third perhaps. Addie wouldn't have much to say.

Best be on the road by six, miss the worst of the morning traffic, though they would be going against the flow, away from DC rather than into it, north into Maryland, skirt Philly in a few hours, miss the New York rush hour, get to the bungalow for a late lunch. Maurice would soon be at Wolfie's buying half a pound of Nova, herring in cream sauce, egg salad, poppy seed bagels and scallion cream cheese, knishes, dark oily *maslines* and plenty of half-sour pickles. The pantry and freezer would already be loaded in anticipation of their visit. It was a prospect worth hurrying up for, and the weekend at the bungalow would pass quickly enough, until he could return on Sunday evening to the empty apartment, leaving Addie and the kids. He would visit them later, taking the train, but otherwise he was looking forward to the peace, the quiet, no needy noisy children, no needy silent wife – time to spend working and listening to music, more than that certainly, a lot more – with an intensity that rather alarmed him.

She hadn't been asleep, of course. He rarely noticed whether she was or wasn't, unless he wanted something, which he was beginning not to want. She rolled onto her right side, pushed the bedclothes off with a hasty gesture and stepped onto the floor. Turned on her bedside lamp, though Ben had opened the curtains and a dispiriting half-light was making its way gingerly into the room.

She wore her nudity with ease, if not grace. When they'd first become lovers she'd tilted her shoulders slightly backwards when she was naked, throwing her breasts into sharper relief. In later years she had none of the hunched self-consciousness of other women he'd known, breasts retracted. Now her walk was simple, upright, all traces of erotic display long gone.

Young lovers are curious children giggling, peering and peeping, naughty, anxious both to show off yet not to be caught, as if behind a bush with the grown-ups only just out of sight. She and her first boyfriend Ira had laughed when they made love, sometimes stopped to still themselves, perfectly aware that the impulse would abide, carried on, laughed and fucked and cried in mutual release. It hadn't been like that with Ben, not even at first, not so innocent, so pure, so full of wonder. But it had been more powerful, more grown up, and she'd wanted him with an intensity that surprised her. It was gone now, he knew it and seemed hardly to mind.

She pulled the shower curtain carefully, lest the stays on the rail popped again, and shrugged her way into the tub, turning the tap on carefully so as to avoid the downpour onto her hair, not bothering with the ugly rubber shower cap. Not that anything could make it look worse; let it frizz, the hell with it. Poppa Mo had given her a hand hairdryer for her birthday, proud to be up to date on the latest gadgets, but she'd never figured out how to make it work, was certain she'd be electrocuted.

She hated going to the hairdresser's, head stuck in an

ugly helmet blowing hot air, half-listening to more hot air on either side of her, the inconsequential gossip, the babble. It made her hate women, having her hair done. They all loved it, basked and wallowed in the heat like animals. Ugh.

They'd packed the suitcases the night before and put them in the trunk, enough simple clothing and beachwear for the visit, assembled a bag full of puzzles, colouring books and packets of (dangerous) jellybeans, likely to cause discord over who got the oranges, or drew a black. Dr Seuss and *Peanuts*, as well as *Nancy* and *Sluggo* cartoons – but reading in the back seat had to be rationed for the highways, when there wasn't too much sway and things were as stable as you could get with two fidgety kids – Jake was constantly widening his territory, but the little one always had a reliable response up her sleeve. If he offended her sufficiently, she'd say, *'You're Sluggo! That's what you are!'*

The comparison to the ugly, dunderheaded orphan infuriated him.

'Keep it up,' he'd warn, 'and I'll sluggo you!'

The prospect of the car trip – indeed, the prospect of the coming months – filled Addie with an anxiety bordering on dread, though anything was better, even this, than a summer – their last! – in the heat and humidity of DC.

They deposited the children, still fast asleep, dribbling in the corners of their mouths, in the back seat, propped them against the doors, placed pillows behind their heads. Addie brought Becca's Teddo, a slight orange bear with eyes beginning to protrude, the strings showing, and placed it gently beside her. She'd be upset without it, had only just been weaned from sucking her thumb. She was an anxious little girl, vigilantly doe-eyed, focusing first on one then another of the family, though quite what she was watching and waiting for was unclear. Some sort of unexpected disaster, like a jug sliding off a table, which if she could only spot it coming might be averted.

Neither child stirred. Addie placed the back-stick between them, dividing the territory exactly in half. They usually woke within a few minutes of each other. Most mornings, Becca would rise abruptly, rubbing her eyes, looking round the room to orient herself, for she had occasional moments when she awoke from a dream feeling displaced and would begin to cry. On normal mornings, though, comfortable in their small shared bedroom, she awoke alert and cheerful.

'I'm a morning person!' she'd proclaimed. 'Like Bugs Bunny!' She would reach across to Jake's bed and grab him by the shoulder, fingers digging in.

'Wake up, sleepyhead,' she'd say, shaking him until he grudgingly opened his eyes. She loved that moment, it was why she woke first, when she was in charge and he had to do her bidding. In a few minutes things would revert, Jake would rise, enfold his territory, and she would return to her natural place in the scheme of things: on the edges, looking in, vigilant, a solemn freckled owl, unseen, seeing. Darwin would have been proud of her. It was a highly intelligent bit of adaptation.

Her father adored her, held her hand when they were out together, teased her by squeezing her dear little knuckles, gave her little pats and tickles when they were on the couch watching TV, rumpled her hair, could barely suppress a smile when she entered the room, called her freckle-face. It made Addie furious with disapprobation, *not* jealousy, she wasn't worried that the little one would supplant her, take the position as number one girl. Why worry about that? It had happened already. No, what she disliked was the fawning. It made her uncomfortable to the point of nausea.

She'd been her father's favourite, she too, but Maurice

had never debased himself like this at the altar of fatherly love. What could one say, it was all over the place: *Jewish fathers and their daughters.* She'd been given such priority, and been aware of it, but nothing like this. She'd tried to compensate by bonding more intensely with the boy, nothing yucky or overstated, mind you, simply tried to treat him with heightened respect, and interest, and admiration when it was deserved. He seemed not to notice, looked under his eyelids at his father's love affair with his sister, turned away, retracted.

In the back seat the wake-up ritual was unfolding, though they'd been pretty good really, it was almost eight-fifteen. The Thermos of coffee had been shared in the front of the car, half of the egg sandwiches eaten, though it was too early for pickles. They could be a treat later. The kids didn't like them, thank God. Bad for their stomachs, and teeth.

First cigarettes of the day were tapped out of the pack, lit with the Zippo, inhaled greedily, tapped into the ashtray. The first, the best. None of the thirty-odd that would follow had the same freshness, or an equal kick.

Jake had pushed his blanket to the floor, leaned over and moved the stick.

'It's not fair!' he said. 'I'm bigger than she is, I need more room. She's just a squirt.'

'I am not a squirt! Addie! Addie! Make him put it back! I have a right!'

Becca had only recently learned about rights. Negroes had a right to sit in restaurants with the white people! DC was having a major court case about segregation, it was on the TV news, a debate which she had followed as best she could. It was simple really, just a question of what was right and what was wrong. A matter of brown and white, Addie called it. Becca liked that.

Jake didn't care. It was just fine with him, people eating

what they liked where they liked, same as he did. But he wasn't interested. He already had rights. He was bigger, and older. And a boy! He deserved more territory than Becca. He shifted his hip and pushed the stick slightly further towards her side.

In his very occasional spare time, Ben had helped the ACLU pursue the test case against Thompson's Restaurant, a modest segregated establishment close to the White House. One Saturday he and Addie had taken the kids on a moral education trip to see the Negro student protesters, with their signs and angry faces, knowing themselves in the vanguard of a great and just cause. It was a bit frightening for the children, all that chanting and sitting down in front of the door. It wasn't the sort of place they would eat themselves, though that didn't matter. Becca was delighted by it all, everybody should be able to eat together, whenever they wanted. She was pleased when she found that the Supreme Court agreed with her. Negroes have rights! The idea made her feel morally replete. She was promiscuously keen on rights, especially as they applied to her.

In the car, Addie wouldn't even turn round. Took a deep drag of her cigarette, her window only partially open, exhaled with a weary, prolonged sigh, the fug deepening.

'What'd I tell you two! Button it!'

It was a script as predictably fraught as a play by Eugene O'Neill. She kept drifting off, shaking herself as her head slumped, kept awake by the purity of her spirit of opposition. This wasn't what she'd wanted, what she'd planned for, there was nothing sustaining in it. Next to her Ben studied the unravelling road intently. She felt obscurely jealous as he did so, his eyes unwavering as if to avoid looking at her. He rarely did, these days, hardly noticed her at all.

When they'd met at Penn in the thirties, she doing her MA in Social Work, Ben at law school, they had bonded over what looked like common causes. They had passionate sympathy for the poor and the dispossessed, went on marches, picketed here and demonstrated there, made public avowal that things could change for the better, as they were palpably changing for the better in Russia. But it didn't take her long to discover that their similarities were actually a form of differentness.

Ben had read widely on leftist subjects, could quote Marx and refer to Engels, was fascinated by the unwieldy superstructures that supported his new beliefs. But Addie, though mildly conversant with the terminology, eventually found she didn't give a damn about all that verbiage, those fatuous, meaningless categories, all those beardy pontificating men. To generalise is to be an idiot, she'd maintain.

Ben counter-attacked, it was like a war between them. 'You can't run a state on the basis of fine particularities: you need politics, and laws, and a moral creed. You need ideas!'

Ideas? Phooey. What Addie wanted and needed was not *the people*, but people: breathing, suffering, in need of succour. The notion of the workers or the proletariat – the masses – only produced a foggy blob in her mind, whereas she could focus perfectly on a pregnant teenager, an alcoholic or drug addict, a family in need, a child who was being abused or neglected. To care about the people, you take care of people.

While Ben was studying his boring torts (whatever they were), Addie was ensconced in the relentlessly modern, Freudian-based School of Social Work, taking courses that touched her heart, real topics about real people. In Contemporary Love and Marriage, they did a case study on the relationship of D.H. Lawrence and Frieda Von Richthofen, which was a remarkable inclusion in the syllabus, given that he had only died a few years earlier.

'See,' the students were told, 'this is what a working, highly passionate relationship can be,' and by implication should be. Lawrence became a hero to this generation of young women: if only Billy or Joe, or indeed Ben, was burning with such an inward flame! If only Edna or Sheila, or indeed Addie, could respond to that flame, ignite, passionately embrace life in every manner and fashion. Be prompted by the loins, the blood, the bowels – any number of inward bits, the heart even, but not the head! They were bad, heads.

She read Lawrence's poetry to Ben, in bed. Her favourite of his books was *Look! We Have Come Through*, which celebrates Lawrence and Frieda's first years together. Addie would read with appropriate intensity the opening line of 'Song of a Man Who Has Come Through': 'Not I, not I, but the wind that blows through me!'

'I feel like that sometimes, after I eat too many beans,' he said.

She put down the book and turned her back. Passion was no laughing matter.

'Anyway,' he said, intending to provoke this disciple of the wrong kind of beardy prophet, 'they may have come through, but I don't see why I have to look.'

Yet it had been a wonderful period of a few years, in the sunny climes of passionate engagement. And then the rains came, and everything was washed away. The rains were first called Jacob and then Rebecca, like the names of those hurricanes that sweep up the East Coast, buffeting. The end of sleep, and peace, and happiness. That dopey DHL never knew fatherhood, even second-hand, or he could never have talked such tripe. Ben escaped every morning, he wasn't an inmate, just a visitor. She thought, *Well, that was us, wasn't it, fellow travellers, and look at us now!*

No social work jobs for the foreseeable future. Poppa Maurice helped send the children to private school – he regularly supplied brown paper bags stuffed with a surprising amount of money, held together with rubber bands, stacked randomly, ones, fives, tens, twenties, even some fifties, as if released from a cash register at the end of a working day, several working days. But it wasn't enough to pay everyday expenses, it was extra. And so she took a part-time job, when Jake was at school and Becca in nursery, selling *The World Book Encyclopaedia* door-to-door.

She was bright and engaging and actually believed in her product, but her desperation was etched in heavy lines; people wanted to get away from her, sales were few.

'If I had a soul,' she said to Ben after a wasted four hours patrolling the streets of the neighbourhood, 'this would have killed it.'

He was sympathetic. He would have hated that job, couldn't have done it for a second. *Please, Missus, may I have just a moment of your time? I have an offer that will transform the lives of you and your children . . .*

'Thank God for that,' he said.

'Not at all, this is worse. What I do have is a self, and it's killed that instead.'

It was true. She didn't remember who she'd been, in those hopeful spirited sexy days, could hardly recognise the person she now was, save for the clear recognition that she didn't like her.

And as for her world, she detested it. It was intolerably

sylvan in Alexandria, promiscuously treed and bushed, but it was just across the Potomac from DC and the smells wafted across the river. One Sunday, as they were crossing the bridge on the way to an enlightening children's afternoon at the Smithsonian, Ben had looked down at the brown sluggish waters and remarked how polluted the river was.

'Yeah!' said Becca. 'You can even see the pollute!'

You could see it in DC, too. The city landscape was polluted. Shit steamed in the streets. Shits walked the streets (they were called Republicans) and the faecal current swept across America, over the cities and the plains, polluted the rivers and the lakes, crossed the Rockies, stinking and malign. Everyone breathed it, everyone was infected. It was almost impossible to escape.

Ben had a variety of car activities for diverting the children, to get their minds off their struggle for dominance. There was the licence plate game, a singsong, the alphabet game, I spy, tongue-twisters, various simple riddles, though the kids had heard them all by now. Chickens crossing the road? Boring! He amused himself inventing new ones that left him belly-wobbling, giggling like a schoolboy.

'What's the difference between a duck?' he asked.

There was a pause while the children waited for him to continue.

'Do you have any questions?' he asked disingenuously, already beginning to giggle. Addie stared out the window.

Jake was first to respond.

'That's stupid. You can't answer that . . .'

'Why not?'

'You didn't say, the difference between a duck and a . . . *what!*'

Ben allowed a little time to coagulate in the smoky air. Becca leaned forwards: *That was really smart of Jake!*

He half-turned from the driver's seat and looked at each of the children, wisely.

'I'm not giving any hints,' he said, and burst into laughter so protracted that the car began to drift across the lane. Drivers honked furiously. He pulled himself together, straightened their trajectory, wiped his eyes, laughed some more. From the back, you could see his shoulders shaking.

'That's not fair!' said Becca.

'That's not funny!' said Jake.

'Grossman slays Grossman!' said Ben, proudly.

'Again!' said Addie. Ben was unusually animated; it didn't ring true, all this fun. What the hell was there to have fun about? She looked at him sharply. Something was up, he looked shifty and evasive.

'I spy with my little eye,' she said tersely, as the kids began to scan the unfolding countryside, the orange and yellow and brown cars, two-tones, with their chrome and white-walls, the billboards on the side of the road pimping boisterously for Nabisco Oreo Cookies and CANvenient 7Up. More intelligence and wit went into them than into the governance of the whole nation.

'Something beginning with A.'

Jake, reflexively competitive and four years older, looked round the car. Unwilling to miss out, but only just competent, Becca looked wherever he did, in the vain hope that he might miss an A and then she could name it.

'An arm!' he shouted.

'Nope.'

'An ankle!'

Becca scanned her body anxiously.

'Not that either.'

Unwilling to be drawn further into this dangerous body parts inventory, guessing all too easily which one Addie had in mind, Ben joined in.

'There,' he shouted, pointing across the road. 'Amattababy!'

There was a snort of derision from the rear.

'Ben, you can't just make things up!'

'I didn't!'

'Did so! What's a mattababy?'

His shoulders started to shake.

'Nothin', baby. What's a matta with you?'

It was a *brocheh,* Perle reminded herself, such a blessing to have Addie and the children coming, and that Frankie and Michelle and their little ones had settled in Huntington after the war.

'It's a *brocheh,*' she said firmly.

Maurice put down his coffee cup, paused to light his filter-tipped Kent cigarette and place it in the ashtray on the dining table, let enough time go by to suggest unexpressed disagreement, as if he needed to consider whether it was such a blessing after all. You could get *brochehed* half to death during a hot summer with a tiny house full of needy, squabbling, overheated and over-entitled family.

He could hardly have admitted it to his wife, nor entirely to himself, but he was anxious about their imminent arrival, the invasion of a home hardly big enough for the two of them, stuffed for the summer with Addie and her kids, Frankie and Michelle with an uncertain number of babies popping in as fast as they popped out, *Die Schwarze* moping in the tiny maid's room next to the bathroom. The children would be put into the guest room, and Addie – and later in the month Ben, when he joined them in a couple of weeks – would sleep in the back area, which had screens separating it from the porch, and a glass door that could be closed at night, a curtain drawn across. Hardly private, hardly comfortable. A thin partition wall separating the cramped space from the parents' bedroom. He wondered how they ever managed to do it; they gave rare sign of having done so. No noises in the night, no sly smiles in the morning.

No guest ever leaves too early. A month, no, seven weeks this year, of Addie and the kids! They'd be arriving in a few hours, and he was already apprehensive. She was spiky and difficult, had been since her childhood, or at least from those early days when she was supplanted by the arrival of baby Frankie. Perle had adored her son since he first peeked into the world and her recalcitrant displaced daughter had never recovered.

He would make himself scarce. Go into the garage to his workbench, find things to make, or to fix. The fence round the back of the house needed new slats, do the undercoat and painting, put them up next week. There was always something to do at the bungalow. He quite liked Harbor Heights Park, the trip from the city on Grand Central Parkway and Northern State, the slow retreat from his beloved concrete to the occasional pleasures of grass and trees, the mildly alarming rural peacefulness. No horns honking, no traffic, no crowds. It was fine with him, so long as it didn't last too long.

A post-First World War development of summer homes for New Yorkers, the simple bungalows formed a self-enclosed community just ten minutes' walk from Huntington Harbor. It was a promising wooded site, bounded by roads on three sides, unimaginatively divided into lettered lanes. By 1925 seventy units had been sold to city lawyers, engineers, architects, professors, civil servants, builders and small businessmen, anxious to get away from the oppressive heat of the city, to enjoy days on the local beach with their children. Brown's Beach, it was called locally, and brown it certainly was.

Only a few years later, the residents, who had not been warned of the menace of the local waters, signed a petition for an immediate amelioration of their parlous state, complaining of 'a polluted harbor, constituting a menace to health and life . . . with sewage and other disease-breeding material continuously distributed into the waters of the harbor, including the effluvia from cesspools and toilets, making the harbor unfit for bathing purposes or for the cultivation of shellfish'.

Not many of the residents, most of whom kept kosher homes, gave a hoot about shellfish, but the pollution was disgusting, the smell at low tide noxious. The waters were only negotiable at high tide, and grandparents warned of the dangers of getting your head in the water. The children went on frolicking, splashing and ducking. None of them died. The adults donned their swimsuits and paddled. Now and again one of them, swimming in the deeper waters, would encounter an itinerant floating turd, like an organic grenade. Ben called it Perle Harbor.

Becca fought for territory in the back seat, was bored quickly and kvetched, got carsick if she read or ate too much junk. She worried incessantly that they would get lost, particularly if Ben turned off the highway for one reason or another.

'How will we find our way back?' asked the little one, increasingly anxious. 'Is it on the map?' She had a lot of faith in maps, but only Ben could read them. If Addie started unfolding, peering and muttering, tracing various lines with her finger, Becca knew there was going to be trouble and they would end up in fairyland.

'Ben!' she ordered. 'Stop the car! Then *you* can look at the map.'

'I am looking at it just fine,' said Addie, peering down intently, trying to get the damn map to hold still.

'Do you know where we are?'

Addie pointed randomly. 'Here!' she said. 'And we are going – there!' She pointed at a place higher up. 'Towards the North!'

Becca looked outside, at the unwinding landscape of the highway. The North was uphill, like mountains. But the road was flat. They were lost.

The bungalow was at the top of the unpaved Lane L, which had three other houses on it, off Cedar Valley Lane. It was a simple, unheated wooden structure, thrown up by a developer who could hardly produce them fast enough to meet the demand. When Maurice bought theirs for $2,000, in 1939, they were already considered good investments, though Perle worried about the cost.

'Don't even think about it,' he said breezily. 'I'll pay it off.' He would never have said 'we'. She acceded with her own version of good grace: silence, a shrug, acquiescence. Paying wasn't her problem. Morrie would provide, he always did, almost always.

A screened-in front room led into the kitchen, through which was a modest living room, three bedrooms and two simple bathrooms. At the back was a porch, with a gate that led to a small lawn, and a couple of mature crab apple trees between which Poppa could hang the orange striped hammock. The children had to be taught that a gate was not also a swing, except that it was if you wanted it to be.

One day the hinges broke and Becca fell over and skinned her knee. She didn't do that again.

From the very first day, Perle adored the heavenly expanse after the cramped two-room apartment on the fourth floor of the Hotel Brewster, kitchen, dining room and living room together as you came through the door, with a double bedroom and bath. And in Huntington, six rooms! A porch, a yard! She loved furnishing it, choosing fabrics and furniture from the current Sears Catalog, a bedroom suite for only $37.75. That was very reasonable! A red lacquered rocking chair, a few throw carpets, a sofa, some occasional tables: only another $32.40, for them all. She had a few bits and pieces she could spare from the apartment – it was too cluttered anyway – and from the local goodwill shop she bought a dining table and six chairs – eight bucks! – and three sets of used curtains at fifty cents a pair. The empty space soon became a home, if only for the summers. She loved it! A summer was a long time, you could stretch it at both ends as the developers recommended. Residents went to Harbor Heights in the early spring and didn't leave until after Labor Day (for those with children at city schools) or October (for those fortunate enough to stay on for the beautiful fall).

It was a happy period, the two of them in unusual harmony, proud of what they were creating, Perle on the inside, Maurice, the out, members of a professional community of gregarious city residents. They made friends quickly: Momshe and Popshe Livermore (he was the boss of a fancy department store), further up the road Sam and Martha Lowry, and across from them the Cohens (he was named Edwin, but she seemed only to be called Honey). The women became friends, which was a *brocheh,* because it left the men to their baseball, cigarettes and beer, their pinochle games in the evening, while the women schmoozed in the living room.

Maurice had no idea what they talked about. The children, obviously. Clothes, recipes, matters of housekeeping? TV programmes? Who cared, as long as they were happy, and quiet? He would have been surprised by the range of their conversations, would have forgotten to add the topic 'husbands', about whom they were sometimes amused and frequently exasperated. But to a woman they were loyal, occasionally indiscreet, but anxious never to overstep that unspoken line that would make them emotionally unfaithful. They all knew about men, what they were like. No need to say everything, was there?

Sometimes, when the right four could be arranged (which was surprisingly difficult), they would play canasta. Perle was a student of the game, as adept as Maurice at his, but her aggression was not channelled into bonhomie, teasing and patronising instruction. No, hers was the untrammelled thing: she played to win, and when she snapped down her melds, taking the cards from her hand and twisting her wrist as ferociously as if she were trying to remove the recalcitrant lid of a jar of pickles, you could hear the snap as they hit the table, which wobbled under the impact. As did the other players. It was daunting, imperious. No one wished to play with her, no fun in that. Better to schmooze – safer, more relaxing.

And while they talked, they knitted. It was a skill required of the girls of their generation, and during the war they had formed a local group, knitting socks, sweaters and mufflers for the poor freezing soldiers. Afterwards Perle carried on knitting and (a new passion) crocheting, revelling in the freedom to choose her own patterns and colours, to brighten things up with oranges and greens, make sweaters less bulky, socks for more delicate feet, ladies' mufflers to look smart on a winter's night. She knitted at such a rate that the family were swathed in warming garments, begging for less.

The overflow was placed in the cedar chest in the front room, opposite the freezer, which was Becca's favourite spot in the bungalow. When she arrived she'd run up the steps, pull back the lid, put her head right in and take a deep smell. It was heavenly; she couldn't get enough of it, would return several times a day and sniff away happily, like some sort of juvenile junky. Opposite her, Jake would make several trips to the freezer to sneak a Good Humor ice cream. Becca liked them, too. Sometimes he'd share. But he thought the cedar chest was stupid.

When it got just past eleven, the cigarette packs and beer bottles empty, one or another of the pinochle players would suggest that enough was enough, they should settle up. Maurice always won, but the stakes were low, less than five dollars would change hands. He hated having to stop, loved the niceties of play, frequently pointing out the errors of his fellow players, to their intense annoyance. One more round, he'd insist.

'Let's wait till the enemy squawks!' he'd say, shuffling the cards, starting to deal, the air still and blessedly cooler as the night wore on. 'Last round up!'

It had gone quiet in the car, the smoke yellowing and humid. Addie was resting her head against the window, a small floral cushion propping her up. Becca had gone back to sleep in the back seat. Though admonished to shut up, Ben was humming operatic arias, conducting with one hand and steering with the other. Jake was neither reading nor looking out the window, had jellybeans aplenty but was not eating them, had taken out a pad and pencil and was doing some figures. After a time he looked up to see if he could locate an audience.

'Ben?' he said, looking down at his pad.

'What, honey?'

'I am trying to figure it out. Today is July 6th, isn't it?'

'Yup.'

'And Addie says we are going to the bungalow until after my birthday. That's August 25th. So . . .' He paused to count, dividing the number of days by seven. 'So, that's over seven weeks, isn't it?'

'Sure enough,' said Ben lightly. 'It is.'

'How come? We usually only go for a month, right? In August. Why are we going so early this time?'

There was a slight pause. Addie raised her head from her cushion.

'I already explained this,' she said. 'I thought you would remember? This year we get the whole summer at the bungalow. That's an extra treat, isn't it? Who'd want to be in sweaty old Alexandria when they could be with Poppa and Granny and go to the beach?'

He remembered, but he hadn't done the sums. 'A little longer this summer', that was how she'd explained it. It wasn't an entirely appealing prospect. He shared the fiction that he loved it at the bungalow, though he was bored there most of the time, particularly when Ben and Poppa were away. Too many girls! Becca, and cousins Jenny, Naomi and baby Charlotte, with their silly games, dolls and dressing-up outfits. Of course he lorded it over them, got to be conductor of the swinging seats, had first call on the hammock, was the only one allowed on the roof or near the septic tank. He needed boys to talk to about baseball, but even if he found some at the beach they would be stupid Yankee fans. Or maybe the Dodgers or Giants. That was pretty bad too.

None of them had even heard of Mickey Vernon! And what was worse, no one to play baseball with. Not like in Alexandria, where he could play softball three mornings a week in the summer.

But at least there was plenty of time to read, to nosh fruit and jellied candies and ice cream, to go swimming at the beach, or into Huntington for a hotdog at Wolfie's, with sauerkraut and mustard, and a Dr Pepper straight out of the bottle.

The more he thought about it, the better it sounded. But something was wrong, and he could sense the evasiveness in his parents' immobile shoulders, their tones of voice, the inappropriate pauses and emphases. Nothing looked or sounded right.

'Yeah, OK,' he said, 'but I don't get it. Why extra this year . . . Nothing's different, is it?'

From the rear seat, Jake watched as Ben turned slightly to his right and nodded. Addie could do it, she was better at that sort of thing, had more of an anxious child in her, could respond to the uncertainty, get the tone right. He would be too matter of fact, too calm, too reasonable. There's nothing more worrying than being reassured.

It wasn't clear what to tell the kids, or how, or when. They'd avoided the moment until plans were further advanced, to spare them the anxiety of knowing both too much and too little. But the boy was already on edge, and likely to get more so. Becca thankfully was asleep, though she would take the news and accommodate the changes more easily than Jake.

'We're moving, aren't we? That's it!'

His voice was unsteady, and rising in volume. 'I don't want to! I won't!'

Addie didn't want to either.

Leaving Washington, renting an apartment in Huntington on Nathan Hale Drive (God forbid), where Frankie and Michelle lived, the loss of income and status, the dependency on Poppa's random largesse. Removing the children from their happy, progressive school in the Virginia farmlands, enrolling them in the Long Island public-school system with the suburban dopes. How utterly dreadful for them, for all of them. She searched in vain for someone to blame. They'd done nothing wrong, done things well and rightly and justly, believed in what was good. Son of a bitch!

'I'm not going!' said Jake. 'You can't make me!'

At the weekends Maurice worked on the bungalow, made it more comfortable, more attractive, more his own. Dug a flower bed along the southern hedge, planted two hydrangeas and some phlox, installed a double swing at the bottom of the yard, paved an area for a swinging seat for the children, made wooden planters for the side of the house and filled them with red geraniums. He spent most of his time in his workshop in the garage, emerging occasionally to measure this, adjust that or install the other.

Put on the radio, listen to the news – though that was depressing enough – perhaps catch an afternoon Yankee game. Sometimes Jake would wander in and he could teach the boy, who was fidgety and had a short attention span but was greedy for the time the two of them spent together, could teach him how to use a lathe, a chisel, do simple joinery.

Last year he'd taught the boy how to hammer in a nail: took a good piece of sawn-off two by four, fit it into the vise, turned the handle firmly, then told Jake to finish it off with the final twist. The boy tried to show how strong he was, heaved and grunted, got it to move a little, gave a satisfied little smile.

'Good boy!' He passed him the hammer – not the titchy ball peen, a proper hammer with a hefty wooden handle and large head – and a two-inch nail.

'Here you go. Remember what I showed you?'

The boy took the hammer, gripping it halfway up the handle, fearful concentration on his face.

'Not like that, down at the bottom.' He shifted the boy's grip, the hammer sagged slightly from its own weight.

'Now don't just go tap, tap, that won't drive the nail in. You have to hit it. Like Mickey Mantle!'

'Mickey *Vernon*!' said Jake. He was a Senators fan and loved their great first baseman, and though he was stuck with the Yankees for the summer, he didn't like them. Big show-offs! Mickey Mantle! Yogi stupid Berra!

Jake raised the hammer, holding the nail tense against the wood, his fingertips whitening. Poppa took it back from him.

'Let me show you again.' He held the nail just below the top, its point against the wood, raised the hammer, cocked his wrist, drove it three-quarters of the way into the board. He left the rest, handed the hammer back.

'Now you. No need to hold the nail.'

It took the boy three taps, but the head of the nail now rested against the wood.

'Good!'

Knowing he'd been spared, the boy felt patronised.

'I want to do it myself! Let *me* do it!' He gave a girlish pout that made his grandfather's heart contract.

Yet Maurice had adored him from the moment he was born; would have, indeed, once the pregnancy was announced, but it was unclear who exactly was in there.

Might be anyone. Might even be a girl. So he waited, and when the announcement came – from a thousand miles away, for Jacob was born in St Louis – he was quite overcome. It rather surprised him, this genetic fundamentalism. A firstborn (grand) son! What was that old Hebrew word for it? Been a long time since he'd been a member of a *shul*; though he went on Yom Kippur, he could hardly be described as attentive, just attending. Like most of them, going through the ritual but indifferent to it. Atonement? Yeah, yeah.

Bekhor? Something like that. Firstborn: with extra rights to property, to respect. To love. The announcement of the arrival was complicated by the difficulty of using the telephone during the war; even telegrams were reserved for military and industrial purposes. Ben had got round this with lawyerly wit. The ensuing telegram announced the arrival of 'new merchandise with hose attachment'. His following letter gave details, with surprisingly adept cartoonish images of himself, first smoking a large cigar and in the next picture bent over, turning green. It was the cigar, wasn't it? He wouldn't have meant to suggest that babies made him sick.

It would be unfair to claim that it was the hose that Maurice fell in love with; though a no-hose addition to the family would have been celebrated, it would not have been a *brocheh* of the same order. Even before he'd seen the boy his heart had gone gooey at the very thought of him, and his was not a heart that gooed very frequently. And like most babies, Jakie (as he was first known) was rather more loveable in the idea than in the flesh. He was a colicky baby, crying most of the time, red-faced, insistent, what one of *them* would have called a perfect incarnation of original sin.

Maybe it was the difficult birth, the difficult baby. Who knew? But after she tottered home from the days at the hospital, clutching Ben's arm desperately, the baby in a pram gifted by his loving grandparents, Addie took to bed, silent and miserable, smoking cigarettes, drinking coffee, refusing to eat, wasting. Ben fell into the breach. They travelled cross-country by train, to the utter dismay of their fellow passengers, and inflicted the *bekhor* on his grandparents, soon after which Ben, a smile on his face, headed straight back to St Louis – *needed immediately at work*! Addie got herself up and dressed, and spent her days on the porch, gin and tonic in one hand, cigarettes in the other. 'It's a life,' she observed wryly, disbelieving. The drinks made her feel better for a time, then worse.

The indissoluble grandparent-bond with the new arrival was founded then, in spite of the fact that even Perle didn't entirely warm to the bundle of screaming neediness. '*A brocheh*,' she said repeatedly, often enough to convince herself, though Maurice was not so easily misled.

But the baby became a boy and, though still restless and needy, developed charms of his own, of which the major one, in Maurice's eyes, was that he adored his grandfather. Maurice played catch with him, invented games, taught him pinochle, watched baseball on TV, had twice taken him to Yankee Stadium. Poppa Mo adored being adored, as long as it didn't take much time or effort. He was utterly compelling in half-hour bursts, amusing, engaged, delightful. But he soon tired of the very needs that he created.

'First one to fall asleep gets a quarter,' he'd say, resting his head on the sofa and closing his eyes. The children did the same, but never won the quarter. Occasionally he'd give them one anyway in order to be able to ask: 'Friends to the finish?'

They didn't even bother to reply.

'Lend me a quarter?'

He paused for a moment.

'That's the finish!'

His feelings for Jake were archetypally pure, but more ambivalent in fleshy incarnation. He was a spoiled little boy, Addie and Perle constantly giving in to him, all he had to do was insist and he could have anything he wanted, just to shut him up. Still red-faced and crying really, only more subtly.

And so he let him have the hammer: let him, knowing that he was weak-wristed and the hammer too heavy; let him, knowing that it was dangerous; let him, knowing he might well hurt himself. Let him. It would be good for him. He was prone to crying over scratches and poison ivy, stubbed toes, bumps, bruises, frightened of wasps and jellyfish and sounds in the night. His fingers were covered with Band-Aids, his scuffed knees yellow from application of Mercurochrome – he was frightened of iodine. *Ow! It hurts!* No, it would do him no harm if harm it was to be.

It was. The hammer came up, not very far up, and down, not very hard, but it was high enough and hard enough to give the boy's thumb such a whack that, if it couldn't have been heard in the kitchen, the resulting screams certainly were.

Ten years old, making a fuss.

Perle came rushing across the lawn in her apron, waving her hands in her 'It's a disaster' motion, like a marionette operated by a spastic. Jake was lying on the floor holding his hand, screaming, face soaked, snot-ridden. *Making a meal of it,* Maurice thought unsympathetically.

'Maurice! What have you done? How many times have I told you!'

She leant down and lifted the crying boy, who was too big now to carry back to the house but seemed incapable of standing up. Unwilling, really.

'Let me see, let me see!' she said, unwrapping the one hand from the other to reveal the red swelling thumb.

'Don't touch it!'

'Don't worry, my darling,' she said. 'Come with me, we'll put it in cold water and then put a lovely ice pack on it. That'll make it all better.'

She glared at Maurice, who was sheepishly putting his tools away, and propelled the boy gently back to the house, brushing past Becca, lurking to the side, making herself simultaneously invisible and available.

'I'll turn the cold water on!' she said, running back to the house. 'And wake Addie!'

Perle loved to be needed, to make sure the children had everything they wanted, and then to worry after they had it. She spoiled them, and then worried they'd spoil, or worse. Being alive was dangerous. In the meantime *die kinder* needed to be watched over and protected. They'd eat too much fruit and get a stomach ache, go into the water just after eating a hotdog and drown of cramps, fall out of the tree, get stung by a bee or bitten by a dog, get a poison ivy rash, prick themselves on the blackberry bushes. Or get sucked into the septic tank. This was a fiction of Jake's that Perle, who knew nothing of such tanks save what they were full of, curiously colluded in. If you got too close to the septic tank area, behind the garage, the ground would give way and you could fall in! Jake said so, it was like quicksand. Perle never went near it, and Becca wouldn't go into the garage at all – which was, of course, Jake's aim – for fear that the quicksand would reach out and grab her by the ankles, and in she'd go to the most horrible death she could imagine, drowned in poo-poo. Worse than being eaten by the Great Danes up the hill, who howled all night and ate children. At least they were in their cage!

Becca slept for almost an hour, and woke up irritable and thirsty, rubbing her eyes.

'Are we almost there?'

Jake knew she would say that – she was always asking, never satisfied.

'No! It's a long way still. You've got to learn to be patient!'

It was what Addie kept telling her, but Becca had no need to defer to her brother.

'You be patient! I'm hungry and I feel sick!'

It was her trump card. Last year she'd been nauseous on the way to Huntington, vomited copiously in the car, almost missing Jake. Addie had insisted, before they set off, on making bacon and scrambled eggs for the children. Both resisted, but lots of ketchup and extra bacon had solved the immediate problem, and exacerbated the resulting one.

The copious ejaculate, which emerged in a muddy rainbow arc, made the rear of the car uninhabitable, ready for an emergency United Nations task force. Rotten half-digested eggs and red slush with brown bits covered much of the surfaces, and some of Jake's. Fallout was nothing compared to this, just some dusty powder, nothing to it, whatever the consequences . . .

Ben had opened the window, put on the fan for fresh air and, gagging continuously, exited the highway five minutes later in search of a store where he could buy some cleaning materials, and a pharmacy to get something to settle Becca's stomach, all of their stomachs. It took twenty minutes to find one, during which they had to pull over twice for Becca to empty her stomach, and for the rest of them to fill their lungs.

They filled buckets with water, scrubbed and brushed and installed air fresheners, the result of which was that the car smelled like a hospital on a humid day, the air falsified by cleaning odours, underlain by the stench of decay.

Becca knew that none of them wanted that again.

'I ate too many jellybeans. I think I might . . .' She made a retching sound from the back of her throat and repeated it while clutching her stomach.

Jake glared at her. He'd heard that sound before, not when she had actually vomited, which she'd done quickly and without any fuss, but some time afterwards, when she was ostensibly playing in the yard. The first time he'd rushed over to her, to ask if she was sick. She looked sheepish, cleared her throat, walked away. She'd been practising.

Addie had brought a vomit bag from their plane trip to Bermuda the previous Easter and had it ready.

'Here, darling, try to hold on, and if you need to vomit do it in this. It's a special bag. You remember, from the plane?'

'I'm not doing it in a bag! I'll miss and get it all over me!'

'Better than getting it on me!' said Jake.

'I need the bathroom! Hurry!'

It was impossible not to stop, though Addie and Ben suspected, and Jake knew, that there was no danger of a barf.

He looked at his sister suspiciously.

'Becky,' he said, 'is drecky!'

She glared right back.

'Jakie,' she hissed, 'is snakey!'

'Shut up! Now!' said Addie.

*

Everything was a potential source of harm. Particularly Maurice. One day he threw a baseball when the boy had his head turned and hit him on the cheek, the next day he pushed Becca too high on the swing and she began to cry. He let them stay up too late, and the next day they'd be cranky and hurt themselves.

He had no sense of having done wrong, the only wrong was in being there at all, or too often. He should have gone to the city for the day, though he supposedly had the month off. But there were always deals to be done, orders supervised: the rag trade was like that, quiet one moment, frantic the next. Even in the dog days. The sales force – grand name for the eight of them, five of them useless schleppers, God knows why Sol and Molly kept them on – all took a break in August, so if there was anything to be done, Sol would get on the phone, knowing Maurice wanted to say yes.

Perle objected each time. But some opportunities were too good to miss, and when he returned from his occasional triumphs, pockets full of cash, she'd be mollified. Sometimes even more than that. Talk about blessings!

She'd watch him drive off, suit jacket folded on the seat next to him, his shirtsleeves rolled up, arm resting outside the window. By now he had more hair on his arms and chest than on his head, but he looked good going bald, not like the rest of the shrivelled *alter kockers*. Even at sixty-one he was a fine figure of a man, noble-browed, browned, still with that body that had once given her such pleasure. In his twenties he'd played the occasional semi-pro baseball game, to help put himself through night classes in law. Five bucks a pop playing for one of the many New York teams. It came in handy, though more often than not he spent it going to a Yankee game himself – tickets, subway fare, few drinks with the other ballplayers and a meal afterwards.

When Addie and baby Frankie were still at home, he'd find an excuse to go out to the Polo Grounds, catch a Yanks game. They were great years, just after the First War, people with smiles on their faces once again, anxious to get dressed up and get out to one of the new speakeasies that were growing up round the town, desperate for a cocktail, a steak and a dance. They were a heedless crowd and he knew how to work them.

That's how Morrie saw it. He could afford to, he had it all. And them all, most of them anyway. Their friendship, their trust, their business, their favours, occasionally their sexual favours. He was not a philanderer, God forbid, but with a few drinks in him he liked some fun. There was one girl. He met her at the Stork Club, not a waitress or hatcheck girl, nothing tawdry, just the niece of one of his acquaintances, with a taste for mature men. He treated her well, and she didn't ask more than the occasional meal and bottle of hooch, and some pretty clothes. He could supply all of those, and he was a better lover than her young suitors. He made her crazy, for a while.

She was in a compartment, and happy to stay there, part of *that* life, not *this* one. Out of her company, he couldn't think of her. Lying in bed at night with Perle, an image of Flora would have kept him awake for hours. Best to read.

He was a poor sleeper, and glad of it. Even after a few hours' rest he felt fresh in the morning, and managed to read two or three books a week during the nights. History and biographies mostly, but an occasional novel too. Howard Fast perhaps, nothing fanciful, something with a good story that you could learn from.

He had a bookplate designed with a black and white image of books on a bookshelf, with one obviously missing, and glued it into his books: STOLEN FROM THE LIBRARY OF MAURICE KAUFMANN. He liked lending the books to friends in the sly hope that they might forget to give them back and be caught out by a visitor looking casually through their bookshelves.

Worse than getting lost, way worse, was what was coming to them all, and soon! Addie quailed at the prospect, the children caught her anxiety, only Ben was immune from the fear. Even when they were an hour away, the children could see their mother withdrawing, opening a bottle of pills and tossing one in her mouth, swallowing it without even a sip of water. How could she do that?

The threat was called the Holland Tunnel. Not that this particular tunnel was so frightening – they might as well have taken the Lincoln Tunnel, a few miles down the road, or that other one on the other side of the city that they would have to take next.

Addie had explained it to the kids when they were little. The tunnel went under a river – the Hudson River – so you could get to the other side. It was built with extra care, it was perfectly safe, the water that surrounded it couldn't get in. It was dry, it was totally dry! And safe, safe as houses!

Once they had entered the fearsome underwater space, the spooky darkness only partially lit, there would be a terrible hissing of tyres, and Addie and the children would peer out the windows and scan the walls anxiously for moisture because that would mean the tunnel had sprung a leak and they would all drown when it filled up. Unless they kept the windows up! Then the car would just float until they got rescued by the frogmen.

Jake dealt with his mounting anxiety as his father might have, by goofing around. He peered out the window, raised his finger and shouted: 'There! There! It's coming out, it's spouting out! The pollute is coming to get us!'

If Addie could have smacked him she would; instead she punched Ben, who was giggling away.

'Both of you shut up. It's not funny!'

There *was* moisture! Everywhere the walls were wet, drops ran down them. Addie hunched down in her seat and held her breath, Becca began to cry. Your lungs would fill with water, you wouldn't be able to breathe.

Ben tried to explain once again. Outside the walls was dirt, not water. It went under the river*bed*, not through the river itself.

That was pretty stupid.

Ben resumed humming his arias, to soothe them. When they emerged on the other side and began making their way crosstown to the Queens Midtown Tunnel, Addie said she'd had enough and threatened to get out at the next red light. They should go uptown, she said, and take the Triborough Bridge. She trusted bridges: the water couldn't sneak up on you.

She was rather surprised when Ben refused.

'It will take an extra hour almost,' he said. 'It's a schlep, you're going in the wrong direction! And you've already done the hard bit: the East River is drek compared to the Hudson, you can get right under it in a minute!'

Addie looked at the children, who nodded weakly, accepting their fates.

'OK . . .' she said.

'Anyway,' said Ben, 'if we drown I will take full responsibility.'

Becca put her hands over her ears, closed her eyes and hid on the floor.

Though a man's man in most respects, Maurice was genuinely interested in women's clothes, kept abreast of fashion, studied the designs of Coco Chanel and Elsa Schiaparelli – none of your American *schmatas* – and instructed his designers and fabricators to make inexpensive versions of haute couture classics, strong on style and low on quality. He talked fashion with the girls, and unlike his fellows was more interested in getting them into clothes than out of them.

He made a great market for Chanel-style clothes (with Chanel labels!) which he produced off site and off the books. He was a fashion bootlegger, and patrolled the clubs and bars stealthily, insinuating himself into conversations and cliques, making his market. The girls loved him, and they loved his clothes, so airy, so dreamy, so light, they made you feel free. To be, to move, to dance: thanks to Morrie! He hugged them, took their cash, watched their tuchuses sway and their bubbies bounce, freed from the constraints of stays, heavy bras, girdles, garters, their bodies released, no dread demarcation of top, waist, bottom, just one organic unit, freed at last.

There was less to the new dresses than met the eye: they may have been sheer and free-flowing, nothing to them at all, but they were lies, like their owners. *Sheer fabrications*, he would joke, but nobody ever got it. His bootlegged versions never looked quite the real thing. But their new owners weren't the real thing either, it was a fair deal, everyone gained, especially Morrie.

He talked about fashion with such enthusiasm that some of the girls supposed him a homosexual. In fact, he cared about flapper's finery as much as he cared about pogo sticks or flyswatters. If he'd been selling either he would have done so just as knowledgeably and enthusiastically, citing statistics about jumpability and squashability, producing references from satisfied customers. *Two feet in the air! Dead flies galore!* His enthusiasm was for the process, not the product.

He was always paid in cash. He believed in paying tax – the country needed schools and roads and hospitals – but you could take such rectitude to excess. He got away with it. It was the gangsters and bootleggers who attracted the eyes of the IRS – tax evasion brought down Al Capone, you can steal and murder your heart out, but the government has to get a cut – and no one was going to enquire about Maurice Kaufmann and his little sideline.

It saw him through the Depression. When he later bought the bungalow in 1939, he pretended to Perle that it was going to be a stretch. He'd have to work extra hours, burn some midnight oil drumming up business. In fact, he paid cash and spent those extra days and nights on the town, anxious for the next drink, and deal.

He met some swell people. Babe Ruth was round town most evenings during the home stands, tanked up, surrounded by well-wishers and floozies, heedless, with a talent so immense that even a man of his indiscriminate appetites couldn't abuse it. Maurice spent some evenings in his company, even got in a few words one night at the Cotton Club with the Bambino, who never had much to say for himself: 'Hey, kiddo, good to see ya, have a drink!' He was an immortal, but Maurice soon left him to his whores and sycophants. The *Babe*. Perfect! He was a big baby.

Maurice had a hero amongst those Yankees, but it was the catcher, Wally Schang. He wasn't a big shot, you didn't see him drunk and surrounded by girls. You could learn a lot watching him. Sure, he made some errors, but he had a great arm and called a shrewd game. Maurice would sit in a box behind home plate, head cradled in his hands intently, eyes fixed on good old Wally.

Maurice was a catcher too, a good sandlot player, squat and durable, with a reliable glove and a quick arm, a decent hitter, though ponderous round the bases. His teammates called him Sparkplug after the horse in that catchy song that Eddie Cantor sang. 'Barney Google'. It was one of those darn tunes you couldn't get out of your head.

He would be humming it as he reversed the car down the drive, jaunty, already in city mode, remembering his youth. His own man. Sparkplug! Sparkplugs got things started, were the basis of the power to come. And he was faster than a lot of them gave him credit for!

In the car, things went fast, then slow. Not because of the traffic but because of the odd paradoxes of time – time passing quickly and sluggishly, time enjoyed and time dreaded. Addie was no philosopher, she rather despised abstract thought, but there was something fascinating and frustrating about their ride. At first with the kids asleep, as she nodded off with her head against the window, time seemed hardly to exist, the first three hours passed in a jiffy, pleasingly enough so that her bad mood was threatening to evaporate. She could sense a feeling of well-being coming on, tried to stifle it – what did she have to feel good about? – yawned, collected herself.

As soon as the kids were awake any lifting of her bad mood was impossible; she felt worse for having felt better. The ceaseless fidgeting in the back seat was intolerable, the whinging, arguing, the inanity. Children! What a lot of crap they talked, with their Howdy Doodys and Mickey Vernons, how self-referring, how needy of attention they were!

'If you two don't sit still and shut up,' she said firmly, 'there's going to be trouble!'

'What trouble, Addie?' asked Jake slyly. 'You going to

confiscate our jellybeans?' He felt invulnerable in the back seat, well provisioned, territorially secure.

'Yeah,' added Becca, catching the drift without knowing what confiscating consisted of but aware that jellybeans could be problematic. 'What sort of trouble?'

Perle watched Maurice reverse down the drive, waved a limp hand and turned back to the front door. Hers was not a marriage in which she was in the back seat, she was lucky to get in the car at all. Maurice chose the cars, paid for them, polished them over the weekends. He only bought Cadillacs (used), the present incarnation (Ben made that into a pun: that was where Morrie lived!) a black 1948 coupe with plush velour seats and snazzy little fins, made him feel a *macher*. He bought cheap – *I have contacts*, he would brag, and of course they had him – and paid dearly. The cars were always breaking down, rust made its home on their sills, they were expensively and incompetently serviced by that chazzer Bert, the local German mechanic, whose annual holidays were financed entirely by Maurice's follies. Talk about being taken for a ride!

She didn't drive, she was driven. Crazy. Maurice would grudgingly take her shopping into the village, to the A&P, Wolfie's, the pharmacy, waiting in the car, tapping his fingers on the steering wheel. She bought her personals in the city, when Maurice gave her some money.

They didn't educate girls when she was growing up: after the requisite few years at school they stayed at home, learned to cook, clean, knit and sew, kept house in a way that would make the family proud, looked after ageing relatives, did good works and waited anxiously for a prospective husband. There were eight children, the boys bright and ambitious, the girls consigned to helping at the counter in their

Morningside Heights bakery, dusted by flour on top of their own talcum powder, flirting shyly with the local boys when they came in to buy an iced bun.

Maurice Kaufmann smiled shyly at her, seemed to take notice. She wasn't a looker, Perle, but there was something warm and toasty about her, something almost delicious, as if she'd been produced out the back, fresh out of the oven. She was three years older than him, old enough at twenty-three almost to be on the back shelf with the other stale buns, increasingly desperate to find a husband, if only to shut her mother and sisters and aunts up. Anything to get out of that house, and Maurice was a lot better than that. He was something, with his pretty ways and beguiling smile, his willingness to loiter for a moment, make conversation, ask after her.

He was a real catch – going to law school! A good looker! – and she was immediately struck by his quickness and confidence. Every morning, before he'd popped in for his bun and chat, he'd already finished the *Times* crossword puzzle, he was a wizard at that, and he did them with a pen, never had to cross anything out! He'd show her, proud but a little shy, what the hardest clues were and how he'd solved them.

'Capital of Belgium!' he'd say. 'Easy!'

She'd pretend to be astonished.

'You couldn't know that! You looked it up!'

'Never, I swear!'

Most days she neglected to take his money, gave him a quick and rather forward glance as he started to reach into his pockets, shook her head imperceptibly. The first time she did this he started to protest, he was an honourable young man and didn't want to get her into trouble, but he soon fell into line. Those nickels added up, and if he could save a quarter a week, well, that was something. She liked him, that was for sure.

He was equally taken by her, though it was her capacious bosom that first turned his eye and touched his heart. He was curiously reticent in that way, and it was she who had initiated first physical contact. Sitting in the Yiddish theatre one evening, on their fourth date, or perhaps it was their fifth, it depended on whether going out for a cream soda counted, she reached gently across the seats to where his arm was resting and took his hand. Gently, gave a little squeeze. That did it, and things progressed nicely, naturally, and quickly from there to the *chuppah*. She smiled, remembering that day, and night. Afterwards – for years afterwards, until the children were born – he was always desperate to tear off a piece, as she called it, crazy really. She enjoyed it, but enough was enough. After Addie was born she more or less lost interest, but she was an accommodating woman and a good wife, and life was easier when Maurice was satisfied.

Addie! They were so different now, young women – educated, with jobs of their own, outspoken, wanted to be equals with their husbands. Not all of them though, thankfully: Michelle was traditional, a good wife to Frankie, happy in her role as a mother and homemaker. She should maybe have a boy one day, that would be perfect. Knowing her, she would keep trying!

Addie couldn't even cook. No, that was wrong; it was hard to find the right words. Addie wouldn't cook. She could have learned, anybody could learn to cook, but she wouldn't. Was it beneath her, with her fancy ways, her political causes and social work? Perle hoped not, that it was merely a matter of being uninterested, or too busy, food merely something that you took on as fuel. If Addie despised cooking, what did she make of her, her mother? Was it contempt she sometimes sensed in her daughter's tone and sharp looks? She certainly wasn't a girl you shared an exciting new recipe with. Addie looked at Michelle the same way she regarded her mother: sharp, disapproving, superior.

Michelle was a good cook and a wonderful mother. Addie was, what? Did she have to say it straight out, if only to herself? She wasn't, please God, a bad mother, it was unfair even to think that. So what was she? The absence of the right word was alarming. *She wasn't a mother at all.* Didn't think like a mother. Didn't worry or fuss, hardly cared what the kids ate or how they dressed, if they bathed often enough, cleaned behind their ears, washed their hair, got constipated. She liked reading to them, as if they could eat words; they'd taste better than her dinners.

Addie could shape a meatloaf, though she thought egg or onions or breadcrumbs were unnecessary, just add salt and pepper to the deflated football lump in the baking tin before putting it in the oven. Put out the ketchup, heat up some frozen fries in the oven, cut an iceberg lettuce in quarters, mix some Russian dressing to pour over it. She could overcook a steak or a pork chop. Slap together a sandwich on white bread, add mayonnaise or mustard.

Even the kids noticed: 'This is delicious, Addie, did you defrost it yourself?' they'd say, and giggle like Ben. Anyway, that was unfair, not everything needed to be thawed. Sometimes she opened cans or packets as well. But the notion that meals were something carefully assembled, to think about, to take pride in, as Perle took pride in her chicken fricassee, stuffed cabbage and pot roast . . . her chopped liver, egg and onion, fresh challah laden with schmaltz. No, not at all. Addie ate them, made the right noises ingesting and thanking, but she didn't care. She took no pride in eating either.

In the morning she made toast, dark brown and crispy, and scrambled some eggs, which she would crack directly into a frying pan hot with butter, stir quickly with a fork, as globs of albumen floated amidst the overcooked yolk. The kids were fussy eaters, would pick at their plates, though she didn't care if they finished or not. They had recently decided they didn't like eggs, nor indeed oatmeal, which Addie produced in great lumps because she couldn't be bothered to stir the pot. Instead they developed a passion for the new wonder cereal Sugar Frosted Flakes. With a sliced banana! They tried to get Poppa to try it, but he made a face, turned away, disgusted.

How could they possibly understand? Maurice was born in 'the old country' in 1892 – 'the same year as Eddie Cantor,' he'd say proudly, 'only I'm eight months older!' As a child – he didn't remember how old, perhaps nine or ten? – he saw in the new century as a steerage-class passenger on a steamship to America, his mother and older sister with him, their tiny Bolekhov tannery hardly able to support the family. His father would join them later in New York, with the boys. Next year perhaps, or the next. God willing.

He remembered it well enough, the noxious smells that permeated their home and clothes, the rough trappers with their filthy clothes and dripping pelts, the vats of hot boiling water, the drying racks. He wouldn't, perhaps couldn't, talk about it. The children weren't interested anyway, though he told them the story of having been given a soft and browning banana with his on-board supper, and told to peel and eat it. He'd never seen one, threw away the brown soggy fruit and tried to eat the peel. He made a face when he told the story.

'I've never eaten one,' he said. 'They're horrible!'

'But, Poppa, you should try! You eat the middle bit! They're good! We have them with our Sugar Frosted Flakes!'

He made the face again.

'Never! *Oy schtinksi!*'

What do the children know of such things? He remembered the voyage clearly enough, in a series of images and feelings that had become constituent elements of his adult incarnation. The smell of hot iron and machine oil, vomit and urine, rotting sauerkraut and the rancid odour of unwashed bodies, the heat, the constant rolling of the sea, stumbling and tripping on the stairwells and decks, clutching the handrails wet with spray and sweat. It was such a long way from the bowels of the ship to the decks, and he felt so ill during the eleven days of the crossing, that he spent most of his time in his hammock, green and listless, as the ship tossed about like a toy in a hyperactive toddler's bathtub.

What little he could eat and drink came back up soon enough. His mother wiped his face with a filthy cloth and let the older children look after themselves. He was the youngest, and her darling, born some eighteen years after her first.

It was hardly possible to sleep, save from pure exhaustion, after an interminable night kept awake by the deep throbbing of the insistent engines that sounded like they were next door, the snoring of the people around them, the vomiting and moaning, the indescribable stench. A few feet away an elderly man moaned '*Oy vey iz mir*' through the night, '*Oy gottenyu!*'

He shook off the images, looked at the kids, whom he understood as little as they, him. Post-war – post two wars! – children of privilege, everything so easy that it had no value, had not been suffered for or earned. If they had souls, nothing would hone or refine them, they would get sloppy with lack of use. Best just to play, to tease and be teased, to keep away from what they could never understand, please God they would never have to.

They liked teasing Granny, too. Most evenings, when they had meat for supper, one or the other would ask if they could have bread and butter with it.

'Please, Granny, please?' they'd insist. 'It's to mop up the gravy!'

She never caught on, each time explained to them that it wasn't kosher, wondered why they could never remember. Even *Die Schwarze* had learned within a week! That it was a childish joke would never have occurred to her. She was literal-minded, lacked any sense of humour, always asked to have a joke explained to her. Ben, who loved telling jokes, had long ago learned not to tell them in front of Perle.

'Explain it to me . . .' she'd begin, and since no explanation of a joke is funny, was confirmed in her lifelong opinion that they were stupid.

Unlike her mother, Becca wasn't high and mighty, she was low and biddable. The little one was always delighted to help Granny in the kitchen, learned what was kosher and what was treif, stirred the bowl of cake mixture and got to lick the spoon (so did Jake, that wasn't fair!), set the table for dinner, filled the glass dishes full of Jordan almonds and sugar-coated fruit slices, red, yellow, green and orange, and placed them on the side tables in the living room. She sensed that she was already a better woman than her mother, and rather regretted it.

She loved being with Granny and Poppa. You didn't have to make your bed or clean up your toys or unset the table – constant areas of conflict in their apartment – because the Negro girl did that. She had the tiny bedroom next to the bathroom. She didn't come out much, ate her meals in there, listened to the radio, read her magazines. She came out to clean the house, do the dishes and the laundry, wearily do the endless ironing, sometimes babysit if the grown-ups went to town. She never came to the beach, she hated the water, couldn't even swim. She had a friend, Agatha, who worked in a house at the top end of their yard. She couldn't swim either. They knew each other from the city.

The girl was called Ruby, but Poppa and Granny called her *Die Schwarze,* which meant a Negro like on *Amos 'n' Andy* on the radio, but Ruby didn't listen to that, made a face, went to her room and closed the door. Becca had no idea why; it was such a funny programme. 'Ah loves you, Sapphia!' Andy would croon. Or perhaps was it Amos? They both talked funny, the same. Ruby didn't talk like that. She hardly talked at all.

In the back of the car, as they passed through the city and onto the Island, Becca gazed out the window, thought of going to the beach as soon as they got there, it was so hot, and sighed with anticipatory pleasure.

'Are we almost there?' she said.

'Only an hour,' said Addie. 'Just hang on.'

But the kids were bored and restless, had eaten too many candies and drank too much Coke, and were beginning to push and nag at each other.

'I know,' said Ben, 'let's have a singsong!'

Addie looked alarmed. 'We discussed this. No singsongs, you know how it yugs them up!'

A clamour arose from the rear of the car.

'Yug us up! Yug us up!'

The kids had finished their sandwiches and jellybeans,

demanded stops to have a siss, which they didn't really need but used as a way of checking out the service stations for Twinkies and chocolate kisses. They were getting fractious, pushing the stick back and forth in fraught imperial combat.

'I think we need some rules,' said Addie. 'The first rule is no more sisses till we get to the bungalow.'

'What if I have to do a doody?' Jake asked, loving a chance both to make a point and to say a rude word.

'Yeah,' said Becca, 'me too! A doody!'

'And the second rule,' Addie said, ignoring them, already irritated beyond endurance by Ben's constant humming of his arias, 'is no more humming. And NO singing . . .'

'That's so unfair!' interrupted Jake. Ben hummed on. Becca looked perplexed.

'You didn't let me finish! No singing "Doggie in the Window"!'

It was the latest hit, Becca sang it to herself all the time. Once it was in there, you couldn't get the goddamn doggie out of your head.

There was a protest from the back.

'OK,' she said, 'in that case, we can also have "Every Little Breeze".'

On holiday in Florida last year Jake had been smitten by a little blonde girl whose name was Denise. Ben had teased him to the point of tantrum on the way home in the car, singing that popular love song about 'Louise', only substituting the name 'Denise'.

That shut Jake up. If the dreaded Denise was the price of the doggie, goodbye mutt, and as for Becca, merely the incipient rendition of *that* dreaded song (the one that upset her so much) was enough to put the pooch in the kennel.

So Addie didn't need to employ her ultimate threat: that she would sing herself, all alone and loudly, which would have caused shrieks of dismay as the children held their ears and went 'UMMMMMMMM' at the top of their voices. Addie didn't hit an occasional false note, she didn't hit any at all: or more accurately, as Ben had once computed, she hit more or less one in eight. Eight notes in the scale, random success. And that didn't count the sharps (ouch!) or the flats (ooch!).

Ben began his song slowly, voice increasing in volume as the first stanza unfolded. It was their favourite song, and they loved it almost as much as Addie pretended to disapprove of it. It was a potent combination, irresistible.

'OOOOOH . . .' began Ben.

The children joined right in, at the top of their voices.

'Oh my name it is Sam Hall, is Sam Hall, is Sam Hall,

'Oh my name it is Sam Hall,

'And I 'ATES YOU ONE AND ALL

'Yer a bunch of MUCKERS all

'DAMN YOUR EYES!'

The children adored Sam, took him up the scaffold surveying the crowd below, proud to have broken the 'bloomin' 'ed' of his victim'. Becca was never sure who Bloomin' Ed was, and why Sam broke him. Maybe he was one of Sam's toys? But she liked him. She loved singing 'DAMN your eyes', as loud as she could, and then when there was a pause at the end of the stanza she'd repeat it quietly, savouring the phrase. 'Damn' was a curse word and only Addie was allowed to curse, though Becca didn't know what most of her curses – you could tell they were curses – meant.

By the end even Addie was singing lustily and off key; it was impossible not to love dear Sam Hall, to celebrate him.

'And it's up the rope I go, up I go, up I go

'And it's up the rope I go
'And I sees the crowd below
'Sayin' *Sam we told you so*!
'DAMN YOUR EYES!'

Everybody's eyes were getting damned! The following three verses were bellowed at increased tempo, Ben leading the singing with his free hand, waving it like a conductor, Addie with tears in her eyes, laughing. In the lane beside them the family in a station wagon with three surly kids in the back gazed at them, rolling with laughter, singing their hearts out. The parents turned to their kids in the back seat and you could almost hear them recommending such a display of family togetherness. It was a great show! They smiled at Addie through the window. She kept singing. Nothing like an unrepentant murderer to bring a family together, she thought.

They subsided happily.

'Now can we sing "Clementine"?' Jake asked, slyly, looking sideways at Becca.

'No! No!' said Becca. Sam Hall made her laugh, however grisly it was, but Clementine reduced her to tears, every time. The poor old miner, and his poor drowned daughter! She couldn't bear it.

Addie immediately reassured her.

'It's all right, darling, don't fret.'

But it was too late, and it was too good a song, and the sun was at its height, and they were tired and hungry and over-stimulated, all, and they were almost there, they'd come together for a few moments over Sam Hall, there was more fun to be had.

'In a cavern, in a canyon . . .' Ben began.

Becca started to make a noise, tried to suppress it, the kind of sound that dogs make when they want something they are not allowed to have, high-pitched, back of the throat, filled with longing and disappointment.

As they entered Cedar Valley Lane, Addie turned and said, 'Kids, we're here, time to wake up!' They'd knocked themselves out with the one thing and the other, were groggy and uncomfortable, but the magic took over as they turned left into Lane L and peered out the window expectantly. Poppa would be waiting for them! Ben gave a honk as he drove into the driveway and parked in front of the garage.

Perle emerged from the front door of the bungalow, her face a rictus of delight, Maurice behind her, arms outstretched as if he could hug the children from twenty feet away. The kids burst from the back door of the car, raced across the few feet and embraced each grandparent – Becca with Poppa and Jake with Granny. Apportioning their love. Addie smiled to herself as she got out. She'd raised good kids. Ben didn't notice, having given a wave and a cheery hello, was immediately busy unpacking the trunk.

Poppa had painted the house, the geraniums glowed against the fresh white, the table inside would be filled with Wolfie's best; Addie made a resolution to be more positive. It was summer, they were on vacation. Nobody was ill, nobody died. When her mother heard the phone ring, she always muttered to herself, 'So who died?' It was a terrible example to put before her children, this fearfulness, this distrust of life, though God knows she had her reasons. But there was no reason to be like that herself, to presume looming catastrophe. It would be a terrific summer, it could be.

Fat chance. Start as you mean to go on. Be resolutely positive and prepare to be disappointed. Her mother embraced her, rigid as ever, that capacious bosom hardly compressed by the contact. Even in her middle sixties she still had the body of a high school line-backer, squat and powerful, leaning slightly forward, ready for contact, however violent. Add a face that would have given a mugger second thoughts and she was a formidable presence.

She and Maurice were physically alike – perhaps his unlikely initial attraction to her was based on some obscure self-recognition? His pals joked that the thought of him on top of her was more like bricks getting laid than people.

Her hair was always pinned carefully into a bun that looked like a helmet, strikingly silver, stronger than grey, suggesting not decline but power. Her eyes, perched below thick brows, had a surprising authority. Perle looked at people directly, met their eyes until they were uncomfortable meeting hers, summing up. Keeping her counsel, judging. Insolent, almost. She made her friends and family uneasy, her stare suggested not so much intelligence, a quality that she had in abundance and kept to herself, but an inquisitorial intensity.

She knew who was leading who on, whether by the *schnozzle*, the *kishkas* or the *schlong*, knew the fumbling and stumbling, the evasions and self-deceptions, could project light into the dark places of the heart, locate the sharp corners and cut corners, took no one at their own estimation. Nor did she spare herself the same scrutiny. 'I will never die of enlargement of the heart,' she observed almost proudly, nor did she wish to. She felt safe in the depth and acuity of her observations. She knew things, *your* things, but never said so, which made it worse.

'Addie!' she said. Warmly enough, you couldn't fault it for warmth. Could you? Addie hugged her firmly, drew her in, Perle acceded, they kissed each other's cheek.

Their arrival at the bungalow was always timed for lunch:

meeting, greeting, seating and eating went together naturally, and if the initial contact was strained – everyone had been anticipating it for too long, Maurice shopping anxiously, Perle setting the table just so, the family just arrived after a tedious ride, everyone on edge and uneasy – then it was natural, it was ordained, that they should sit down together, right away. No need to unpack, to freshen up, to change into casual clothes. A quick visit to the bathroom was allowed, make sure the children had sisses, washed their hands. Then sit! Eat already!

It was the moment at which Perle came into her own, as they sat and helped themselves, groaning with anticipatory delight. DC had nothing like this, no pickles or chopped liver, nothing worth calling a bagel, nothing so delicious and comforting, and real. This was not merely Wolfie's triumph, but Perle's as well, though it passed too quickly. She had no idea how to talk to children, it made her stiff and uncomfortable. Them, too. They passed the first few minutes loading their plates and answering the usual questions. How was the ride? How are things at school? What are you studying this year?

Fine, good, dunno.

Perle counted to ten, took a deep breath, carried on to twenty. She wasn't so rude and uncommunicative when she was a girl, she'd been brought up properly, respected her many aunts and uncles, parents and grandparents, would never have silently shunned contact, eaten so greedily, taken things for granted. Next thing they'd be asking to butter their bagels! She'd been looking forward so much to seeing them and she was already disappointed. It made her feel ashamed. She never learned.

Maurice, in stark contrast, which galled her, was a natural with the children, made up nicknames for them (Sport!

Freckle-face!), threw them in the air (but not while eating!), tickled them under the table – he called it giving jimjees – teased, wheedled, cajoled, yugged them up until everyone else got cranky.

'Maurice! Enough already!'

He was delighted when Addie came – *Adds*, he sometimes called her – was as warm and enveloping as her mother was stiff and retracted, made sure she sat next to him, squeezed her arm as she ate. He found Ben, seated across the table next to Perle – good luck to him! – a little hard to talk to, though they had the state of the nation to discuss and could play pinochle together in the evenings. Ben had learned the game just to be agreeable, but he was not a man's man, had no interest in baseball, preferred martinis to beer, spent too much time reading. In the daytime, even at the beach, always with a book, or even worse a pad and pencil writing something or other in his minuscule hand – he would never say what.

'Just a bit of work.'

Addie would scowl. Why wouldn't he put it away, join in? He was only going to be there for two nights, for God's sake!

Ben was as stiff with Perle as she with the children, what was there to say? *What are you going to cook? What are you knitting?* He didn't know her, had made little effort, and she'd given up with him. And Maurice? He wondered whether his reflexive dislike – no, not dislike but discomfort – in his father-in-law's presence wasn't to a degree envy. The old man was so vital, jolly and warm, so engaged with people and things and projects, so delighted by food and drink – every meal was pronounced 'best I ever ate!' If he was often full of shit, he was also full of life, and full of stories. His words stuffed the air, all eyes were on him, he was the fulcrum on which the family balanced.

It made Ben feel diminished, and commensurately censorious. Poppa was, it had to be said, but not to anyone in earshot, a bit of a shyster, with his dubious contacts, his nightclubs and hotspots, the regular paper bags of cash that he referred to as *sandwiches*. God knows where they came from. And he, Ben, profited from them, his children went to private school because of them, and each time he promised himself, he tried to promise himself, he failed to promise himself: *This must stop! I am colluding in something shady, probably illegal, am the recipient of a largesse which doesn't bear looking into*. So he didn't look, and felt diminished and humiliated by his collusion. Ate his sandwiches and felt bilious.

'Happy enough with the money!' Maurice always reflected, as Ben – or Addie, it was best left to her – was handed another paper bag.

Maurice soon wilted under the pressure of offsetting the strain of arrival, loaded his plate with egg and onion, some lovely oily black olives, kept his mouth full, which was a way of keeping it shut, and food gradually and blessedly became the centre of attention, which was what it was there for. They had seconds, settled in and began to relax. It was lovely being together, really it was, a *brocheh* with pickles: a mitzvah!

Only Becca ate fitfully, picking at her food, knowing to put only a little on the plate so that she could join the others in demanding seconds. But she hated Poppa and Granny food from Wolfie's. It was greasy and it stank, it made your mouth go all funny, it was hard to get down. Chopped liver? Ugh! Nova? Yuck! Even the egg salad was ruined by all those onions. No, she would restrict herself to a toasted bagel – they never remembered she only liked plain ones! – with lots of cream cheese on it. If she'd felt comfortable or confident enough she'd have asked for some jelly to put on it, but she was shy, and no one else thought of it. Jelly on a bagel?

Addie and Ben didn't mind how little she ate, they didn't fuss about food, but Granny did.

'Becca,' she said, 'you need to eat.'

'I am eating, Granny! What do you think I'm doing?'

Perle looked at her, prim and withheld; she was fresh, that's what she was, she needed to learn how to behave, have some respect. Perle would never have talked to her grandmother like that, would have been ashamed. And punished.

Addie was clenched, a wad of soggy bagel stuck in her throat. She coughed, swallowed, wiped her mouth, wanted to scream. Forty-two days to go.

Sitting opposite, Ben saw the thought pass her face and felt sympathetic, and similarly, only for him the figure was two days. He tried to summon some guilt about his forthcoming release, but felt nothing but relief.

'Can we leave this, Mother? We go through it every year. She's a healthy girl, and she eats what she chooses.'

'Chooses? Chooses, schmoozes, what's a little one like that know about good eating, and growing up strong and healthy? She needs to eat more, that's the end of it.'

Jake, listening and watching intently, loaded his plate with everything that Becca hated. He didn't like most of it either.

Perle beamed at him. *Kineahora* he should eat like a horse and grow into a man.

'Can I be excused from the table?' Becca asked, pushing her plate away.

'Of course,' said Addie. 'Why don't you unpack your suitcase, put the clothes in the drawers? You remember where they are? Then you can play on the swing.'

There was a silence at the table, as Becca left the room, broken only a few moments later when Perle, recapturing territory, observed, 'Frankie and Michelle have invited you for coffee tomorrow. Isn't that nice! I can look after the children while you're away.'

The silence resumed. Jake looked ruefully at his plate.

2

'You're a saint, you know that? Or whatever they call them, a saintess? I don't know how you do it . . .' Michelle smiled in response, stacking the plates in the sink, as Frankie finished his coffee at the kitchen table, still talking, distressed.

'I can hardly bear the thought of it! Trouble, that's what we're in for! There's trouble wherever she goes, trouble in spades . . .'

She dried her hands, walked back to the table, put her arm round his shoulder.

'Don't you worry so,' she said. 'It'll be all right. I'm looking forward to it. Addie and I can do things together sometimes, take the kids to the park, go out for an ice cream.'

He laughed because it was so unfunny.

'The park? An ice cream? My sister? She'd rather clean out the sewers, she hates anything that keeps her away from her films and art and trips to the city to see her crappy friends. Did you ever meet that ghastly, pretentious . . .'

'Frankie! I've met them all!'

'And they were just as dismissive of you as Addie is: just as rude and superior. God, sometimes I hate that woman!'

'Don't, please. It makes it worse for all of us. They're fine,

I don't need them to like me. I can look after myself. After all, I have everything she wants!'

He looked puzzled.

'What? Wants? Wants what?'

'You! A wonderful husband who can't keep his hands off me!'

His sister certainly didn't have a wonderful husband. Ben was all right in his way, amiable and undemanding, but Frankie had never forgiven him his allegiances. His sister had married a Communist, been corrupted by him, made foolish decision after foolish decision. Protest meetings, picketing, petitions! This was the United States, for Christ's sake, and Frankie had served his country proudly. He'd had a quiet war, never seen action – which he did not admit publicly – served his time as a naval dentist at various postings, come home entirely unscathed, having seen no more blood than that produced by a root canal.

But he was a patriot still, living in the greatest country on earth, and he resented his superior brother-in-law with his theories and hoity-toity arguments. After a few early skirmishes they had decided to banish politics from their conversation and soon found they got on fine, playing tennis and pinochle, going out with the children, schmoozing at the bungalow. He was all right, Ben was, just misguided. For a time Frankie called him 'the Red' but Michelle hushed him up. 'Next thing you know,' she admonished, 'one of the children will repeat it, and the next thing you know there will be a scene!'

She was a sensible woman, he could count on her. He rose to come behind her as she worked, pressed himself against her.

'I have a good idea,' he said.

She laughed, and pressed back gently, rolled her hips. 'Later maybe, after they leave. The kids aren't due home till after lunch. But now I have to make some coffee cake, there's just time before they come.'

He wet the tip of his index finger and put it in her right ear, rotated it suavely. She was more sensitive on her right side, ear, throat, breast, big toe. He'd never encountered that before, not that he had a lot of experience, a few rolls in the hay when he was in the navy, nothing really. And he would never have noticed it in Michelle until she showed him early on in their lovemaking. It was odd, and oddly exciting, like playing some sort of organic instrument.

She looked at the magazine spread open on the counter, bent over unnecessarily to peer at the page, shuddered a little, gave a tiny moan.

'Stop it now, there's plenty of time, and what I'm really excited about now is this new Betty Crocker recipe. I had it at Irene's last week. It's yummy!'

Frankie withdrew his finger, unsurprised by her reaction, anticipating the pleasure to come, his head filled with delicious images. Coffee cake? Phooey!

'Oh, for goodness' sake! Why bother? They're just coming for a quick coffee and a look round number 42. I can pop out to the bakery and get some rugelach.'

She paused for a moment to consider.

'No, I'd rather make something welcoming, make the apartment smell nice when they arrive. Maybe you could straighten the living room?'

He was quite prepared to take a sexual rain-check, happy to go out to the shops if necessary, would have chopped nuts manfully for the coffee cake, but the idea of making his apartment sparkle for his sister's visit was unsupportable.

'Come on, honey,' he said. 'The place is already neater than hers ever is. They live in a complete pig sty, toys all over the place, beds unmade, dishes in the sink . . . It's disgusting. If she notices our apartment at all, it'll just be to mock us. Petit bourgeoisie! The hell with her! I'd prefer to make it messy.'

Michelle laughed, measured a quantity of flour, put it aside.

'OK,' she said, 'just leave it. I don't mind, and you're right, she wouldn't notice, and Ben doesn't care. We'll just have coffee and eat this lovely cake, then mooch round to the Silbers' for them to have a look . . .'

'My fear is that they'll like it.'

'They don't have much choice, do they? They'll have to move, they'll have to live somewhere, it's cheap enough, we're here . . .'

'That's what I want to avoid. They could live in Huntington Station, there's new apartments going up there, not very expensive, near the railroad station.'

Michelle paused, unwilling to be too explicit. 'Not a very nice neighbourhood,' she said. 'Maybe it isn't too safe, you know, for the children, or going out at night . . .'

'So it has to be here, then?'

Michelle nodded firmly, unusually decisive.

'It does. Get used to it. You and Ben can play tennis and pinochle, Addie and I can do things with the kids, it'll be fine. I'm looking forward to it! And we'll have a free lawyer!'

Frankie laughed humourlessly. 'And they'll have a free dentist. Who gets the better deal? And who's paying for it when he has to study to pass the goddamn Bar? Paying for months and months. My father, that's who!'

'It's very generous of him. I don't know how he does it . . .'

'Don't ask! I don't either. But he won't be helping us when we have to move to the new office.'

The doorbell rang at precisely eleven, as they knew it would. Addie was casual about time-keeping, as befits a left-wing social worker, but Ben was lawyerly in his habits and already counted the minutes as assiduously as he would soon need to when he set up his private practice. Time is money.

Michelle answered the door, leaving Frankie still reading the *Times,* beckoning him with a bent finger at least to get up.

'Good morning! I'm so glad you could come, this is so exciting!'

She gave Addie a brief hug, and could sense the recoil, and Ben a peck on the cheek. Frankie stood up and waved hello, limply.

'Come in, come in!' Michelle was aware that she was being hearty, talking too loud, could sense Frankie disapproving behind her back, tried to relax, took a deep breath.

Ben came in first, gave his brother-in-law a firm handshake and a slight smile that acknowledged many things, looked round the immaculate room approvingly. There was a comfortable sofa with a chintz cover that hadn't been there last summer. He sat down on it, sighed, sunk into the feather cushions, adjusted his position, crossed his legs, took a deep whiff of fresh cake smell. He'd had only a light breakfast, knowing Michelle would rise to the occasion, would need to.

Addie was embracing Frankie gingerly, the distance between their bodies measured in inches, then stopped starkly still in the middle of the room, as if unsure where she was, and what was expected of her.

'Nice of you to have us,' she said, looked round, joined Ben on the couch, unaware of anything delicious in the air.

Frankie resumed slouching in his chair, ignored the sharp desire to return to reading his newspaper – that'd show her! – and asked neutrally, without any warmth, if they'd had a good trip up to Huntington. Ever the naval officer, he always referred to North as up and the South as down, as if they were port and starboard, and if you confused them you'd be irredeemably lost, torpedoed.

'It was fine,' said Addie, ending the conversation. There was a further pause, which Michelle soon filled with coffee cake and a pot of weak coffee, and desultory conversation.

Plates and cups were soon rinsed and put away; it was time to get down to business.

'Shall we go?' asked Frankie, already heading for the door. 'The Silbers are expecting us and they have to go out soon.' Everyone knew this was a lie, and all were grateful for it.

The Garden Apartments on Nathan Hale Drive had been planned in the late forties, the first tranche up for rent a couple of years later. Though intended as affordable housing for the returning servicemen and their young families, there was nothing barracks-like about them. Each brick block was only two stories – a top and bottom apartment, one or two bedrooms, and each unit had a portico attached to the façade, making it look as if it were an individual house. Between the blocks the lawns had been turfed and maintained, trees were planted, beds of bushes ran along the walls. There were garden benches throughout, somewhere to sit with the paper while the kids played, perhaps talk to the other young parents.

A living community! proclaimed the brochures, but most of the residents regarded their tenure as temporary, until they could save up a deposit on one of the modest split level or ranch houses festooning the Long Island landscape. Only twenty years before, the Island was largely agricultural land. Now, within commuting distance to the city, it was sprawling suburbs, growing as relentlessly as a wart, and as unsightly. Nobody noticed, or, if they did, cared, that this new world was uniform and unlovely, because this fertile generation were desperate to become homeowners, for many of them the first home since their grandparents had emigrated from the old country. To own a house confirmed that one was an American, and to own a house first you lived in a garden apartment.

Harriet Silber had been informed, several times, that Michelle would supply coffee and cake before they came round at eleven-thirty, nevertheless a pot of coffee was on the table, plus a plate of pastries. She'd dressed up, after her fashion: wore a bright green smock with a wide front pocket, baggy dark blue slacks, a casual knotted scarf in bright orange: *I am an artist*, the outfit proclaimed, and a glance round the walls provided the evidence, with numerous paintings in the living room, ensconced in frames that were worth more at a junk shop than the pictures themselves.

Addie had heard of Harriet's avocation, her pretensions, and had already branded her – before ever seeing her work – a *local artist*, a puffed-up amateur who has 'exhibitions' in some high school foyer and offers her daubs at prices that would buy you a good weekend in Manhattan. Addie looked, and, surprised, looked again. The seascapes and family portraits were competent, and – no doubt about it – Harriet cared about paint, in the laying down of colour, the nature and quality of brushstrokes, the depth and sheen of the oil. The pictures demanded a second glance, but did not repay it. A portrait of a young woman was painted in brutal impasto, in bright and unnatural colours, the turquoise hair contrasting with a face in lime green with blue touches. It hurt one's eye. Harriet had looked carefully at German Expressionists and failed to learn from them. But the results were at least arresting. Not entirely bad. Not good.

Michelle glared at the plate of pastries, and Harriet shrugged her shoulders. You don't entertain without offering a little something. It isn't right.

Nor do you visit without partaking. Cups – the third of

the morning for each of the visitors, they'd pay for that – were filled, rugelach chosen, one each. Ben popped his into his trouser pocket when he thought no one was looking. Addie was, and passed hers to him, a little too obviously.

He popped it into his mouth.

'Delicious,' he said.

'I'm sorry the place is such a mess,' said Charlie. 'We're moving in a few weeks and have started packing already . . .'

'Where are you going?' asked Ben, for Charlie was also a lawyer, who commuted to his office in the city.

'Great Neck, there's a new development there, just outside the centre, good incentives for first-time buyers and low mortgage rates. It'll save me an hour a day commuting . . .'

Harriet nodded strenuously. 'You bet! It's going to make such a difference!'

'What sort of difference?' asked Addie neutrally, unwilling to reveal her unease.

'Well, you know we came here three years ago, when our second was born, thought it would be a better life for us all? But it's been hard on both of us . . .'

'Hard? How so?'

'Well, the commute for Charlie. He leaves just as the children are waking up and gets home after they're asleep. That's hard on all of us. But I guess I've never quite found . . . I don't know what the word is? My place? No, not that, not quite. But I just don't feel I *fit* in Huntington . . . I'm more of a city girl really, I love being near the galleries and theatres and shops, the restaurants. The people. Great Neck isn't ideal, not by any means, but it's bigger and closer. More cosmopolitan. Did you know *Gatsby* is set near there?'

Addie did. And Harriet's description of herself was familiar: they were both city girls, and the suburbs were an inappropriate setting for them. Like planting orchids in a sandpit.

She looked round the apartment, the bits she could see from the table: the cramped kitchen, squat living room, the short hallway that led to the bedrooms . . . gazed out the window at the mothers and children in desultory commerce in the morning sunshine.

Awful. Just awful. They had similar accommodation in Alexandria, but DC was just a short ride away. They could use it, expose the children to it, make them aware that there was more to life than . . . *this*. This new home, that they could be moving into in a matter of months. She looked across the table at Ben, who smiled back automatically, in a sort of daze. Him? He wouldn't mind, he had his work, and his writing, playing chess or the recorder, listening to opera on their new hi-fi, tennis and swimming at the Y. He'd actually like it. For a brief, unendurably intense moment she detested him.

'But,' said Charlie, anxious not to give the impression that he had been unhappy in his garden apartment, 'we'll miss it here, it's very comfortable, nice neighbours, you can walk into town . . .'

'That's why we're here,' said Addie. 'Is it the same as Frankie's?'

'The same?'

'You know, same layout, same kitchen, same everything.'

The implication was not lost.

'Oh no, each apartment is different is some way or another. We first tenants got to choose our own appliances and could modify the floor plan if we got in early enough . . .'

Addie rose from her seat, carefully avoiding the two cartons full of dishware at her feet, pushed under the dining-room table.

'Can we have a quick look round?'

It didn't take long, the Silbers anxious at the state of things: pictures removed from the walls left rectangles on the exposed paintwork, piles of blankets and bedding crammed into black garbage bags, the desolate air that makes any soon-to-be-abandoned home dreary and unwelcoming.

Addie walked through quickly, aware of her hosts' embarrassment, anxious to spend just enough time not to be rude and get out of there. Anyway, it *was* exactly the same as Frankie's, same floor plan, two crumby bedrooms, the larger perhaps ten by twelve feet, the other tighter and squarer, adequate for the kids. Small bathroom with bath and shower above, basic kitchen, basic appliances. More or less what she was used to in Alexandria, though preferable: lighter, slightly larger, more attractive yards. Better parking.

She tried to imagine what D.H. Lawrence might have said about it, but even he would have been speechless.

'That went well, I think.' Ben guided the car out of its parking place, checked the mirror twice and pulled away smoothly. 'Yes,' he added, agreeing with himself. 'Nice people, pleasant apartment. Nice development. We can be happy here. Buy a house in a couple years, once I get established.'

He didn't expect an answer and didn't get one. They drove back to the bungalow in silence. It was hot in the car, baking, he wiped his forehead with the back of his hand, transferred the stickiness onto his pants.

Liar! She thought to herself. *Goddamn liar.* His attempt to be positive infuriated her. He knew as well as she did that it was a disaster, way worse even than Alexandria.

When they pulled up behind the Caddy in the driveway, Addie got out quickly, pausing only to say, 'I'm sorry, I can't do it. I won't. You'll have to find some other way.' She didn't slam the door, closed it delicately and firmly. Purposefully.

Ben looked at her back as she retreated, went into the porch and closed that door too. *Enough with the closing doors!* Pretty soon he'd be back in Alexandria, blessedly free of

Addie's balkiness – opening a door not closing one, and receiving a welcome the warmth of which made him tingle in anticipation. It had been a guilty secret for too long, only he wasn't guilty about it any more. Might as well enjoy it while he still could . . .

They had arrived back East in 1948, when Jake was five and Becca one, when Ben got his job working on the Rural Electrification Projects for the Department of Justice. The young couple looked at apartments in DC, but nothing other than tiny one-bedroom units were affordable, and reluctantly found a halfway decent two-bedroom apartment in Alexandria, from which Ben could commute and in which Addie could fester.

She negotiated an agreement with her anxious-to-placate husband in which they spent Saturdays, when they weren't all too exhausted or cranky, exploring the new city. Unlike Addie, Ben was unimpressed by the many monuments to America's glorious slave-owning past and imperial present: the grandeur of American power revolted him. The Pentagon! The White House! The Senate! Lovely architecture, but so what? The glorious playground of hypocrites and bloated capitalists. Addie was happy, on a sunny afternoon, to walk round the Washington Monument or Lincoln Memorial with Jake, perhaps go to the Smithsonian, and would allow Ben to go off for an hour or two (with the baby carriage) to his favourite haunt, the Washington Cooperative Bookshop on 17th St NW.

He'd never encountered anything like it before: a shop, an inventory, a programme of events so Left-ward leaning that it was amazing it hadn't fallen over (two years later it did), with a stock of socialist and Communist books and tracts, plus well-chosen new books on various subjects – all offered at discount prices to members of the Cooperative. Ben was soon on first name terms not merely with the staff but with many of the friendly browsers, believers and fanatics, not one of whom even glanced at his gorgeous baby companion.

On the noticeboard was a copy of the in-house publication, *The Bookshopper,* advertising the annual picnic in Rock Creek Park. In July, as always. It was supposed to be great fun. The Cooperative cultivated a family feel, had events and special areas for children, concerts, lectures. The members and their families were more congenial, more his types than anyone in Justice. He could go to a lecture or two, perhaps a concert. He'd smiled at the very thought and resolved to say nothing.

He'd heard the rumours, of course. Since 1941, when the membership list of the bookshop had been seized by Federal agents, there had been constant surveillance. At last year's picnic an inappropriately chic woman, claiming to be a journalist, was taking pictures of many of the revellers, then asking their names and jobs. None had been willing to divulge much, but it had rather spoiled the atmosphere. A number of families left early.

As he'd leafed through the magazines, Ben was being watched, quite openly stared at, by a casually well-dressed man in his thirties, clean-shaven, slim and bright eyed – not one of the regulars! – who met his eye and gave the briefest of nods, as if to say *'We know who you are. If I were you I'd put that down.'* Ben had, frightened not so much by the cool hostility of the glance as by its apparent knowingness. It was directed at *him*. At Ben Grossman. He'd tried not to let his shiver of apprehension show. He had nothing to fear from the Senator himself, who didn't squash vermin personally, but the nice-looking young man could make Ben's life more than miserable.

There was regular surveillance of thc bookshop's premises, after all it was a hotbed of Reds, a meeting place for Commies anxious to subvert democracy, Christianity and the American way. Nobody could read that much propaganda and come out unsullied; in fact, they went in sullied and came out filthy.

The spies in disguise were easy enough to spot. No G-Men shiny suits, no hats, no ties. They'd been told to wear slacks and sweaters to blend in, look round the inventory in an interested fashion, make a note of who was there and what was said. So they donned their pressed and pleated trousers, button-down white cotton shirts with V-neck wool sweaters, put on their shiny black shoes and lurked. The rest of the clientele, dressed in baggy flannels, loose fitting casual shirts, with long hair, often bearded, unselfconsciously scruffy, looked with amused disdain on their preppy interlopers, teased them, made speeches in favour of revolution: made themselves and their fellow travellers as easy to pick off, and to dispatch, as apples on a tree.

In the midst of this dangerous hothouse, Ben would avoid political discourse – after all he was a member of both devils' parties – and devote himself to choosing his reading matter for the weeks to come. He made it a point to come most weekends; if Eleanor Roosevelt could lecture there, surely he could buy some books?

It was at the Cooperative Bookshop that Ben first encountered George Orwell's unprepossessing little book of fiction – hardly a novel, more an extended fairy tale or allegory – entitled *Animal Farm*. There was a small pile of them on the table. The book had aroused more – and more heated – debate and discussion than any novel since the war. The hardliners deplored its anti-Stalinism, its all too easy rejection of a mis-described autocracy, branded its author a bourgeois, worse than a bourgeois, an aristocrat who went to Eton, *encore les barricades,* they intoned gleefully. But for leftists like Ben, who knew Stalinism to be as brutal, arbitrary and cruel as Nazism, Orwell's finger was pointed in the correct direction.

From this time, Ben re-described himself as a socialist and in the 1948 election had refused to choose between one meretricious candidate (Dewey) and a slightly less unappealing one (Truman). Instead he voted for Norman Thomas of the American Socialist Party and felt himself richer, fuller, more upright for having done so. It was a romantic gesture, and a futile one according to Addie, who was scornful and dismissive. Why waste a vote on a loser?

Hadn't they both supported FDR? And if FDR was a fancy pants, spoiled and privileged, no one was going to offer America a better palliative than the New Deal, and they (Communists though they may have been) were sensible enough to support it. The New Deal was the only deal for the poor, the disenfranchised and the downtrodden, though that category, in the early 1930s, included a great many people who, if they could be called workers, were workers in the banks and markets, in big (or mostly small) businesses.

One afternoon, while he was in law school, Ben had treated himself to a modest lunch in Horn and Hardart's Automat on Chestnut Street. He loved the banks of little shuttered windows that raised up when you inserted the correct change to reveal a piece of pie, some French fries, a grilled fish. It was like a playground, and every time he put his nickels and dimes or quarters in, and that window popped open, he gave a sigh of delight. Like a kid, really, all kids loved the Automat, everyone did. If you looked around it was hard to locate, even in those straitened times, anyone who didn't grin when his window popped up.

As he began eating his chicken pot pie and mashed

potato, an impoverished man sat next to him, his clothes soiled, smelling of days and nights on the streets. It was winter, but he had no coat, his nose was red and runny, his hair unkempt, veins lined what had once been rather a handsome face. As Ben watched, he went to a window and put in a nickel to buy a plate of rolls, then took the bottle of ketchup on the table and poured it all over the bread, getting his vegetables for the day, filling himself up as best he could. Ben watched him. When he finished he leant over to the poor fellow, who was mopping up some extra ketchup with the last piece of bread, and said, 'I wonder if I might give you this?', offering a quarter.

The man nodded, both yes and thank you, and put out his hand. Ben put the quarter in it gently and left quickly, no sense protracting such a painful scene.

He rarely told the story, which he feared would sound self-aggrandising, as if it were about him, his virtuousness. It wasn't, it was about the poor man. A quarter was a decent amount of money, those days: he knew the man would divide it into nickels, to get himself through the next couple of days.

Becca came running up the path, grabbed her hand, pulled.

'Addie! Come see! We made a fort!'

'What sort of fort?' She was glad of the diversion, pleased to be tugged away to examine this happy new structure.

'A fort, a fort! In the back. Jake and I made it, it took all morning. And we filled it with . . .' She thought for a second. 'You know, food and candy and drinks and stuff . . . providers.'

'Provisions?'

'We can sit in there and nobody can see us because we keep the fort door open away from the house, so it's a hideout!'

'Well,' said Addie, 'a hideout is just what I'm looking for. Lead the way!'

They had draped a blanket from the cedar chest between the two hydrangea bushes, and placed two chairs on opposite sides to widen the internal space, draped another blanket between those. Inside, Jake was reading a comic and eating a peach, the juice slopping down his T-shirt.

'Addie!' he said. 'Come in, you're allowed. I'm the General, so I give you permission.'

'The General, eh? And what is Becca?'

He paused.

'She's the Not General.'

'Yeah,' said Becca proudly. Being the Not General was almost as good as being the General. It was a title, unexalted perhaps, but not, to her ear, nothing. It was to her mother's.

'Surely you can do better than that? Maybe Becca can be the Sergeant? That's a good job, it means she is in your army too.'

'Army?' said Jake. 'What army?'

Addie pulled the edge of the blanket aside, leant over and came in. It was surprisingly roomy, enough space to sit comfortably, almost to lie down. They'd even brought their pillows in from the bedroom. She folded one, lay on her side, sighed.

'It's lovely in here. Aren't you smart? Can I be in the army too?'

Becca gave a shriek of delight.

'YES! Please! You can be Sergeant as well!' She paused for a moment and rummaged around in the gloom.

'Do you want some potato chips?' she asked.

In the kitchen Perle was making lunch, dusting something with flour which made the front of her apron almost as powdered as her face. She looked like a plump, square apparition; Ben almost expected her to begin hoo-ing and flapping her arms as he entered the room. In spite of her domesticity, which she wore like a disguise, there was something incipiently frightening about Perle, unexplained, latent, dangerous. The powdering suited her, she looked just right as a ghost, spooky.

'How did it go?' she asked, still kneading a ball of dough.

He looked round the room, helped himself to a nectarine from the bowl on the kitchen counter.

'It was OK. We had coffee and cake with Michelle and Frankie, then we had it again with the Silbers. Nice folks. Then we looked at their apartment.'

'And? How is it?'

'Just what we expected. Same as all of them, I guess. Perfectly adequate. We'll be just fine there.'

'I hope so,' said Perle, trying to sound convinced. 'I do hope so. Where's Addie?'

'I dunno, she disappeared round the back. I looked but I couldn't see her.'

There was a pause.

'I'm making a nice going away lunch for you,' Perle said. 'Chicken noodle soup with matzo balls, and some chopped liver and rye bread.'

'And pickles?'

'Of course pickles!' She paused for a moment. 'If I can find them, they seem to have disappeared.'

Of course nothing disappears, things just shift about, and the jar of pickles had migrated to a corner of the fort, which was slightly odd, because neither of the children liked them. But you could never tell which guest might arrive, and not everyone was as indifferent to pickles as they were.

Addie loved them. She would cut them into bite-sized pieces and mix them with sour cream, as an accompaniment to lunch, sometimes just as a sustaining snack. The kids hadn't, thank God, absconded with the sour cream, but she was quite happy, lying there on her side, to unscrew the jar and help herself to a pickle. Two pickles, she put one in her left hand and ate the first with her right. Screwed the lid on firmly.

'Ah,' she said, 'what else could anyone want? It's perfect here! Shall we have a little rest?'

Addie lay on her side on the uneven scrubby grass, her hip uncomfortable against a protruding knob of earth; the heat was intense in the enclosed space – it was eighty-three outside already – stifling, the air almost unbreathable. In front of her a tiny grasshopper hopped and leapt in the scorched grass; she closed her eyes, lest he jump into one of them. The sweat rolled down her back, soaking her blouse. She laughed to herself, what a sight she'd be when they re-emerged.

The kids lay down beside her and pretended to sleep, just like they did with Poppa.

'Do we get a quarter if we're quiet?'

'No.'

'That's unfair,' said Becca. 'Poppa gives us a quarter.'

'I know, but I won't . . . I'll give you a dollar.'

There was a considered pause before Becca giggled and came up with the line.

'A dollar is junk!'

Their cousin Deborah, a few years older than Becca, had disgraced herself with this sentiment at a Seder at the Greenbergs', when the children were offered a dollar to find the afikomen, and little Debs had scorned it, showing off in front of her cousins. Everyone was shocked, not so much at the naked greedy outspokenness as by the fact that Deb, a withdrawn little girl, immature for her age, rather inclined to hold on to her mother's skirts, should have said anything at all. It wasn't entirely clear why she'd made a fuss, but it was rather a good one: she put her hands on her hips, raised her voice, surprised and then embarrassed her parents, who quickly shushed her up, though without raising the stakes.

A dollar certainly wasn't junk to Becca, nor indeed to the more affluent Jake, who hunted round the living and dining rooms assiduously, hoping to find the hidden piece of matzo. When she didn't think it would be noticed, Bernice Greenberg caught Becca's eye and gestured downwards towards the sofa. Becca knelt and looked underneath. There it was!

'I get the dollar! I get it!' said Becca, proudly delivering the matzo to her aunt.

'You see,' said Bernice to her pouting daughter as she handed over the bill, 'a dollar isn't junk at all! Look how happy Becca is!'

She'd be happy to get another dollar just now, in the darkness of the fort, so settled down and closed her eyes, trying to think of what to think of. How to spend the dollar! They could go to Woolworth's. You could get a lot of neat stuff there. Cute bracelets with coloured jewels, rings with real diamonds, sets of pick-up-sticks, all kinds of candy.

'Do we get one each?' asked Jake. 'It's not fair!'

'Life isn't. But you get one too, OK? Now shut up, won't you?'

He rolled over on his side and thought about baseball cards. For a dollar he could buy twenty packs!

'Addie?' It was Becca's littlest voice. 'Can you tell us a story, like sometimes when we go to bed? Then I won't fidget, and I'll get sleepy and when I wake up I'll get a dollar.'

'Once upon a time . . .'

'Can it be a scary one?' asked Jake.

'Not too scary!'

'OK, just scary enough. Once upon a time there was an ogre, who was horrible and ugly, with a hairy face, and he was roaming the land, frightening people. Sometimes he made them join his army, but sometimes they ran away, if they were brave. Well, there was this family, a mother and her two children . . .'

'Where was the father?'

'Shhh. He was away at work, so they had to look after themselves. And one day they heard footsteps – CLUMP! CLUMP! – heading their way, and a ferocious loud voice saying, I AM COMING TO GET YOU! And they knew that if they didn't find someplace to hide, his hands with terrible claws would grab them by the ankles and capture them . . .'

Addie paused, slowly reached across the grass and grabbed Becca's ankle.

'Addie! I knew you were going to do that! I heard you! Anyway, I'm not scared of stupid ogres!'

'You should be. And the reason you're not is because you know how to escape from one.'

'I do?'

'Course you do,' said Jake.

'So just as the ogre was coming into view, the family ran into the woods and built a fort! It was the best fort ever because it was camouflaged, covered with brown blankets, with leaves and sticks on top. And they remembered to bring their box of provisions, so they had enough to stay in there for days, till the ogre was gone. They had Cokes, and candy, and cupcakes and a whole salami and bread. And as long as they were totally quiet, that ogre could never find them. And sure enough, in a few days he went away, cursing, and yelled into the air, I WILL GET YOU NEXT TIME!'

'Did he?'

'Never! They outsmarted him, didn't they?'

There was a pause. It was a pretty good story, just scary

enough. The children settled down and Addie had a fleeting yearning to tuck them in, kiss them goodnight.

'Addie,' said Jake. 'Are we moving?'

'Yes,' she said gently. 'I guess we are.'

'Do we have to?'

'We do. I don't want to either. But we'll build a bigger and better sort of fort, and you'll see, it'll be fine.'

There was a long silence.

'When?' Becca said.

'I don't know. Maybe later in the summer, maybe not. It's a bit complicated. But whenever we move I promise it'll be fine. Maybe we could live near Frankie and the girls, wouldn't that be neat?'

'Yeah!' said Becca.

'No!' said the boy.

It must have been – what? Fifteen minutes? A surprisingly long time, suspended in quiet contemplation, hardly aware of where they were, breathing together, Addie thought to herself whimsically, as if they were one organism. She hadn't felt so close to the children since they were babies, still part of her. Closer, really. They weren't so needy just this moment with her, not sucking at her. She grimaced.

Poppa's voice from the porch surprised her.

'Addie! Jake! Becca! Lunch is ready! Come and get it!'

Lunch would be welcome, they'd had a rest and a respite, were obscurely aware that something unusual had happened between them, welcome, hard to describe, comforting. None of them wanted to get up, they felt safe in their overheated hideaway.

'Do we have to?'

'I guess so,' said Addie. 'Time to get back to the real world. It's too bad, we liked it here. Let's do it again!'

She raised herself up and pulled the blanket open.

'Hold your horses!' she shouted. 'We'll be right there!'

'Can we have our dollars now?' asked Becca.

They crawled out of the fort, brushed themselves down as best they could, picked the grass out of their hair, disassembled their little retreat, folded the blankets, gathered up the provisions, took one of the chairs up to the house, promising to come back for the other one.

When they came into the dining room, no one asked where they'd been, sensing some quiet self-sufficiency that they respected, without knowing, quite, what it was that was being protected. In any case, Ben was already in the driveway, putting his overnight bag and briefcase in the car, getting ready to leave as soon as lunch was finished. If he made good time – and the roads were usually clear on Sunday afternoon, didn't jam up until later – he'd be home at suppertime.

Not that there would be any dinner, though there was food in the fridge. He was in no mood to cook. He had his specialties – spaghetti and meatballs, coq au vin, goulash – but they were all for the family, not just for himself. He liked cooking with the kids, who joined in with an unexpected enthusiasm, perhaps because their mother would have been uninterested in their abilities as sous chefs. No, he'd stop on the way, get some fuel for self and vehicle, arrive home, maybe put an opera on and go back to his book. He was reading a life of Dickens and deciding that he didn't like him very much. Not because he was a womaniser, but because he was a hypocrite.

'You ready to go, Bubby?' asked Addie, taking his arm. She only called him this fondly, and he was startled by how relieved he felt, had feared a confrontation before leaving, something strident and ugly. But she was curiously, mysteriously, pacified.

He gave her a hug.

'I'll miss you, you know!'

'You won't,' she said.

They walked to the car, soup finished, matzo balls dispatched – Perle made them large and heavy, the way her daughter liked them, you could cut them into pieces with your spoon, slurp them down with some rice. Perle insisted on making a couple of sandwiches for Ben's trip home and put them into wax paper, added a couple of the rediscovered warm pickles, wrapped them in a paper bag.

'Take these,' she said. 'You'll want a little nosh.'

Ben reached for the kids, who were standing by their mother. He pushed his arms out for an enveloping hug, which they entered with an unexpected reluctance. Not hostile, exactly, but not connected in the usual way. Usually they loved sentimental goodbyes, would shed a tear, make a bit of a fuss. He loved that. And all of a sudden they weren't, quite, there. Not there. It wasn't at all clear to him where they'd gone.

'I'll miss you, my darlings,' he said, surprised by the emotion in his voice. 'I'll write you some lovely letters, and then I'll come back in a few weeks. I can't wait for that!'

They joined him in his hug, one under each arm, aware they'd let him down, though unsure how, or why.

They waved as he backed down the driveway, and his arm resting on the door flapped in response. At the bottom the car turned and he was gone.

They stood there for a moment, as fixed as a family photograph, Perle and Maurice like statues at the rear, formal and unsmiling, Addie with the children, arms round their shoulders. They all looked as if something was momentously finished, as people do after a funeral or a bris. Satisfied rather than happy: *That's done now, thank God for that. It went all right, didn't it?*

Addie leant over and whispered to the children.

'You two go and play for a while, I'm going to have a nap.'

They understood the code: go outdoors, make no noise! Addie often slept in the afternoon, fitfully, anxious for the enveloping unconsciousness, but rarely finding it. Always sensitive to noise, any sound might wake her, and she would rise furiously to shout, 'Will you be quiet! Don't you know I'm sleeping? *Can't you have a little consideration!*'

The children were scalded by the venom in her tone, simultaneously guilty that they had caused such offence, but also aware that the reaction hardly fitted the crime.

'See you later,' she said, giving both a hug, before re-entering the bungalow and heading for the medicine chest to pop a Miltown. Dr Greaves had warned her against occasional use, wanted her to take two a day regularly, but she found them more helpful in ones. Perhaps her underlying depression didn't ease as she (and the doctor) had wished, but she was used to it. But when she was as anxious as she was now, this afternoon, this hour, it gave some relief. She washed the pill down with a full glass of water and lay on the children's bed, and though her mind kept turning over drowsily, she was asleep within a few minutes.

The children had already split up, in tacit recognition of the fact that they were less likely to make noise if they were on their own. Poppa had gone back to the garage, Granny to read on the porch, under the shade of the umbrella. The bungalow baked in the blue shimmering July heat, still and timeless, as if at peace.

Jake tiptoed into the living room to pick up his book, tiptoed out again, and headed for the fence at the rear of the house, which had one slat missing (fancy that!), providing a space on which he could put his foot and lever himself up onto the roof. Avoiding the right-hand side of the house, which went over the kids' bedroom, he made his way to the pitched roof, lay down, took off his T-shirt and rolled it up, put his head on it. But it was too hot, the tar shingles almost melting in the heat – they felt sticky – and though he liked to lie in the afternoon sun, this was intolerable. He made his way back, considered and rejected a visit to Poppa, who was sawing away in the garage, put his book in the front porch, decided to go for a walk down the lane to see if David was in. Usually he'd be at the beach in the afternoons, maybe Jake might walk there by himself? He'd never done so, but neither could he recall that it was forbidden. He set off, feeling decidedly more cheerful.

Becca had already ensconced herself in the sub-cellar, which was cooler than anywhere else in or about the house, though smelly and damp. She'd been frightened the first time she went down there with Jake, but his efforts to make it seem scary and haunted had the opposite effect. She rather liked being brave, it was a new sensation. She had left a blanket and cushion down there, and occasionally popped in for a little, not nap exactly, she was way too old for naps, just for a little rest, to close her eyes, like she did at the fort. Maybe think some more about spending her newly earned riches?

It was great having a fort, safe from the monster, safe with Addie. She snuggled down. All of a sudden she felt small, not small like a baby, more like she wasn't there at all, small like nothing, something like that. It was pleasant, a safe sort of feeling. If anyone looked into the cellar they wouldn't spot her, she wouldn't be there at all.

The afternoon drifted by. Jake wished he'd remembered to put on his swimsuit before leaving, but David's mom had an extra one in the car that he could use.

'Does your mom know you're here on your own?' she asked, as he changed clumsily behind a towel, the way he'd seen girls do sometimes.

'Sure. My dad just left in the car. He's going home, so I walked here.'

'Well, that's just peachy. We're going to have another swim, we already had lunch.'

He dropped the towel and emerged in the slightly damp swimsuit. It was an ugly rusty colour, like the edge of Poppa's saw. He'd never seen David in it. It didn't matter.

'Thanks, Mrs D,' he said, as he got into the back seat next to his friend.

It was Perle, as ever, who first felt the emptiness, the absences. Addie was still sleeping, you could hear her characteristic noise, somewhere between a snore and a bit of heavy breathing with a whistle attached. Morrie was in the garage. Ben had left hours ago. She walked round the side of the house to avoid making noise, scanning the yard in all directions. No sign of the kids on the swing, or in the hammock. Jake wasn't on the roof: he thought he was hiding up there, but you could spot his feet if you stood in the right spot below him.

She was fond of a cup of tea in the afternoon, perhaps with a cookie, or two, if no one was looking. Who cared, really? She claimed that she was watching her weight, but what she mostly watched was her stomach filling up and out. She did the requisite alterations, if necessary made new clothes, occasionally bought something pretty in the city, but at her age no one looked at her that way any more, or any way really. Might as well be invisible, and fat. Stout. Full-figured. Last year she'd taken down the full-length mirror from the wall beside her dressing table and put it on the side wall of the bathroom, saw herself less that way, and in the antiseptic fluorescent light, hardly her at all. Maurice never noticed the change, or perhaps, divining its cause, had been tactfully silent about it, though that didn't sound much like him. She'd damn near twisted her shoulder moving the mirror. It was surprising how heavy it was and how hard to lift onto the new hooks.

She went quietly into the kitchen and put the kettle on the gas hob. It would make a noise that Addie could hear in the bedroom – the wall between kitchen and bedroom ended two feet from the ceiling, for some reason no one could fathom. Maurice kept promising to fix it, to add the missing section, but never got round to it. Anyway, it was a way of checking on the children when they went to bed, to make sure they weren't fighting or just talking too much instead of sleeping.

Anyway, if Addie was woken by the steaming kettle, too bad. The kids might have been scared of her, Ben too was intimidated, but her mother certainly was not! Addie had kvetched her life away, from child to grown woman, demanding, self-referring, petulant. So she'd wake up? Too bad. The house doesn't have to stop because you want a nap, does it?

She was thinking these ungenerous thoughts – *May God forgive me,* she whispered, *my very own daughter* – because she was worried. It was too quiet, there was an emptiness in the air, not the sort that Ben left, he never filled it in the first place. No, something was wrong.

Very wrong. She knew it. It was the same emptiness they'd all felt when she was a child, living in the city, when cousin Moshe disappeared. The boy had a habit – he must have been about ten at the time, Jake's age, they even looked alike – of going for walks round the neighbourhood; kids did that in the city all the time. He would come to the apartment with the Brody girls after school, and be looked after until Simon and Molly came to pick him up at six-fifteen. They had a small accountancy business in an equally small office on the Lower East Side. Simon and Molly Cohen, the gilt letters on the office door proclaimed, though she modestly insisted that it was he who was the accountant and asked for her name to be removed. He wouldn't hear of it. They were a team!

He had qualified as an accountant at night school, and Molly already had basic secretarial skills; they'd met at the Adult Education Institute, started seeing each other. 'And here we are,' Simon would say with pleasure. 'I take care of the numbers and she takes care of the letters!' They weren't going to get rich, but were honest, reliable, and above all inexpensive; they did the tax returns for a host of immigrant families. 'Ve make a living,' Simon would say, shrugging his shoulders, mocking a Yiddish accent.

And they had their boy, their only child, their pride and joy. Molly had been thirty-eight when he was born, a difficult if exalted entry into the world, and the process left her unable to have another. It didn't matter, they exclaimed, Moshe was enough to fill an entire family. He wasn't the apple of their eyes, he was their eyes themselves, through him they looked at the world and rejoiced that it was good.

One afternoon, having his glass of milk and three cookies, Moshe announced he was going to go out, perhaps to the park to play on the swings. Did anyone want to come? But the girls were already busying themselves, preparing dinner, and so the boy put on his jacket, it was getting cool in the early autumn evenings, and stepped out the door. He knew to be back by six, at the latest. Better, by five-thirty. But he frequently went out, the apartment was too small and noisy with the sounds of too many women. Shrieking and giggling, arguing and declaiming, the air full of laughter and discord.

The locals all knew Moshe. Nice kid, real friendly, beaming, kind of hopped when he walked, always in a hurry. None of them had seen him. They asked, then they asked again, then the police asked and asked again.

Perle was only six at the time. She adored Moshe, who

was uncommonly kind to her, would even play with dolls, sometimes take her hand and go out for an ice cream. Though Perle was not allowed to go out on her own – God forbid! – he was encouraged to take her, he was an entirely trustworthy boy: kept her hand in his, looked both ways, and then again as they crossed the street, made sure that she was warmly dressed and that her hat was pulled tight and her mittens didn't fall off. But on this day – on *that* day – she didn't feel like going out, didn't even answer when he invited her. *Didn't even answer.*

Perle spent the rest of her life, or so it seemed to her, trying to forget what happened in the next days, the panicky anxiety that escalated to terror by the moment, the comings and goings of police, volunteers, the rabbi and members of the *shul*, teachers from the school. The doorbell rang and rang, and eventually they stopped answering, the police in the apartment could do that, send the well-wishers away, accept the cakes and proffered casseroles, as the family huddled in the bedrooms, paralysed with fear.

On the third morning he still hadn't come home.

On the third evening they found his body in the river.

What came next even she couldn't forget. Though the details faded, the sight of Moshe's poor body in the open coffin, his parents – her parents, everyone – crushed by grief, diminished to the point of non-being, unable to do anything except wail – became ineradicably part of her internal world. Moshe's dead white face, his body dressed in a blue suit purchased for his last occasion: it was more a part of her inner world than the beaming baby Frankie, or the beautiful needy face of toddler Addie. Gorgeous children, so alive and so fragile.

She'd buried it, really she had. Did not dwell on it, did not think of it. Really, she didn't. Had never even spoken of it to Maurice, though she was certain he knew. He was kind enough never to broach the subject. Moshe Cohen. Everyone knew, it was such a small and inward-looking community, and in some dread way it thrived on tragedy, had endured so much that loss was its lifeblood, its animating principle, something to share and to suffer together.

You could say many things about the world, good things that warmed the heart, remember the births, the Seders, the family growing up, going on holidays, these times at the bungalow, remember them all and kvell. You could thank God and immerse yourself in his world, but you could never trust it. Or him.

And where in the name of God were the children? Maurice was busy in the garage and said he hadn't seen the boy. She did a quick search of the available hangouts and hideouts, eventually locating Becca asleep in the cellar next to the washing machine – whatever was she doing there? She could have shaken her, though herself shaking with relief.

'Where is Jake?' she demanded. It sounded harsh, perhaps a little hysterical, and it frightened the girl.

'I don't know! I didn't do anything! He went away!'

She jerked Becca up with her arm, propelled her forcibly up the stairs.

'Went away? Went away! What do you mean?' She was shouting now, her voice brought Addie from the house, rubbing her eyes

'What's the matter? What is going on?'

Perle didn't answer. *Went away! He went away!*

What were the last words he'd said to her? Did she answer?

'When did he go? Where was he going?'

Becca started to cry, hunched her shoulders, turned away sobbing.

'I don't know! I don't know anything!'

The more the child sobbed, and the more hysterical her grandmother became – why this crazy over-reaction? – the cooler Addie felt, the more in charge. What a fuss they were making!

'Hold your horses,' she said firmly. 'Will someone tell me what's going on?'

Becca stuttered out the story, as Perle paced the grass, went to the rear, looked up into the trees in case he had climbed one, under the hydrangeas, round the boundary fences and into the neighbours' yard.

'Jake! Jake!' She was shouting. *Jake!*

'Mother! Come back here, listen to this . . .'

Perle came back, wringing her apron in front of her.

'Becca says that after lunch they split up, and she saw Jake walking down the lane . . .'

'Where was he going? Did he say?'

'No, he didn't. Let's walk together down the lane, and we can ask the neighbours. He might have popped down to see if David could play.'

'I don't think David is here, he's . . .'

'Let's all calm down and go together, he's probably there. I'm sure there's nothing to worry about.'

Perle pretended to agree, if only to calm down Becca, who was still crying by her side. From the garage they could hear sounds of hammering, but it would have been unwise to enlist Maurice's help. He wouldn't have been worried at all. Boys were like that, always wandering off, should be like that, boys. And women? Always fussing, always like that, women.

'After all, if he's not there we can always call the police.'

He wasn't, no one answered the protracted knocking, banging really, at the front door. Perle found that it was unlocked, as was usual in Harbor Heights Park, so she stuck her head in and gave a few hearty but anxious yoo-hoos.

As they were deciding where to look next, which neighbour to ask, and as Perle's mind swirled round the obvious and terrible possibilities, a station wagon pulled into the driveway, and in a moment the boys, David and Jake, tumbled out, happy and brown, pictures of buoyant health and optimism.

'Hi, everybody,' the boy said, 'what're you doing here?'

It was soon made clear to him that they had, as he put it to himself calmly, missed him, and strolled round to find him. Well, here he was. So why was Granny red-faced with fury, glaring at him, and Becca wiping her nose on her wrist? As for Addie, she just gave him a hug and said, 'Never mind, here you are then.'

'Never mind what?'

It was enough to set Perle off.

'How dare you!' She grabbed hold of his shirt and pulled him towards her. 'Going off without telling anyone, we were frantic with worry. Never do that again! Never!'

She may have pinched him. Perhaps it was inadvertent. But he pulled his arm away with a screech of 'Ow!', rubbing at his shoulder, which did, to be fair, have a red mark on it.

'You pinched me! You pinched me!'

'You need more than a pinch, you wicked boy! Frightening us half to death. You need a spanking. If only your father was still here!'

It was so absurd that the boy stopped rubbing and stared at the red-faced old woman. Addie could hardly suppress a smirk. *Spanked?* Theirs was the least spanky household in the universe, her children the offspring of Freud and Dr Spock, corporal punishment as unknown to them as fasting at Ramadan.

*

There was a man. In the summer he slept in the local park, in a hidey-hole under some bushes. He had a black garbage bag with stuff in it. The police would chase him away, but he always came back. The local children would giggle and peer into the bush, keeping a safe distance. Sometimes the man would come out, leafy and beardy, filthy with leaves and soil, uncoil himself, shaking his fist.

'Little pishers, get the hell out of here!' he would bellow, and they'd run away. There were grown-ups about, so they felt safe, really, just excited and just the right amount trembly. It was a game.

On that first evening, Moshe reported missing only an hour ago, the police went round to the park, but the man wasn't there. They knew him, but not his name. He wouldn't tell them, looked puzzled and belligerent when asked, as if they had no right to know, or perhaps he couldn't remember. Bushman! He was a local character of a sort and no one had yet established whether he was just grumpy, or dangerous. So far, merely the former to an extreme degree. There was something not right about him, wonky. Nobody could say for sure, but he had broken no laws, save for the habitual loitering. They'd grown used to him, he was part of the community, on the fringes, lurking.

The next afternoon he showed up with his black bag and began to lay out his blankets when the three policemen moved in. He looked up with alarm, never more than one, never more. And they had never looked like this. One of them had his hand on the holstered gun at his side.

'Hey, Bushman,' he said loudly and firmly, 'put your hands up and don't make a move!'

He moved backwards, slowly, and raised his hands.

'Where were you last night?'

He didn't answer. His stock of words had diminished and

he was terrified of the police. The police could mean jail, and jail meant you were locked in, he couldn't bear that, would clutch the bars and wail to be let out.

He didn't answer, and was manhandled into a car and taken to the local station for questioning. Men in suits, that was an even worse sign. They showed him a picture of Moshe. He looked at it intently, and nodded his head up and down, back and forth.

'You know him?'

He looked away, shrugged. Looked up, frightened. 'No.'

'What do you mean, no? He comes to the park, he's seen you! When did you last see him?'

They got nothing out of him. Nothing connected him to the disappearance, there were no witnesses who could establish he'd been in the park the day before, no signs of Moshe under the bush. No blood, nothing.

He was a wonderful suspect; it would have been so agreeable if they could have caught him out, some admission, some slip of the tongue, but as the hours passed the man retracted and withdrew until there were no responses save for tiny whispers of breath, hardly any signs of life. They held him in the cells for a couple of days; he screamed until he fell asleep, and on the third day they released him.

No evidence, they said, shrugging their shoulders regretfully.

The man was never seen in the park again, and no suspect as likely ever emerged. Moshe's body had neither bruising nor signs of struggle. He surely hadn't committed suicide. Could he have been playing by the river and perhaps fallen in? There was a slippery pavement, a low fence. He could have fallen over, and once in the water a high wall would have prohibited any escape.

It was preposterous. Impossible. Unthinkable, but not as unthinkable as what might have happened.

Either that – not that, surely not that – and if not, someone, perhaps someone from the community, someone they knew? Him? Or him? Or even, God forbid, him? It was impossible, it could have been one of them, and they could look no one in the face. A few months later Simon and Molly moved downtown where they knew no one, a morose childless couple. They returned to the office after a time, had to make a living, but dropped their old clients without even a shrug of apology, rebuilt their practice but never their lives.

They should never have left him after school like that. It was their fault. Perle believed that it was hers, too.

By now, Ben was in New Jersey, heading south less sedately than he had planned, surprisingly anxious not so much to get home as to put an increasing distance between himself and his family, the bungalow, Harbor Heights Park, Huntington, Long Island. All of it, all of them. It was only after the first hour that he felt he could breathe normally, after a few deep breathing exercises that he'd learned for swimming the crawl. Slowly in, hold, slowly out, and again, keeping the rhythm.

You couldn't get a decent martini on the flat and featureless roads south, with their occasional diners and infrequent bars. God knows what that might lead to, if he found the right bartender, and perhaps some congenial company. Should have pilfered a couple of Addie's Miltowns, that would have done it.

After passing through the stinking conurbations of northern New Jersey and heading south, he might turn left and head for one of the surprisingly rural spots, with lakes and woods, even go a little further to a beach. Maybe have a swim? The water, though it flowed along the coast of the industrial shores, was less polluted than that of the Long Island Sound. He had a bathing suit, could change and have a proper swim for once, without the subliminal worry of a turd in the nose.

He'd taught himself to swim when he was an undergraduate at Penn. He'd always liked the idea of the water, but no matter how hard he tried down at the university pool, no matter how he worked at controlling his breathing, he could never manage more than three lengths without panting and having to stop, side-stroke his way back to the shallow end, feeling defeated and rather stupid, as elderly faculty members made their slow way up and down, up and down, doing their interminable daily lengths.

He was not a quitter. He'd learned Latin and French, though he had no facility for languages, had taught himself to play the piano, a bit, knew what results practice could bring. And then, one Thursday afternoon, nothing special about the day or his feelings or condition, nothing different at all, he got in the pool, swam his three lengths, felt just peachy, and exultantly swam fifteen more. It was no fluke. For the rest of his time at Penn he swam most afternoons, faster and more elegantly than the superannuated professors chuffing along behind him. He always did exactly eighteen lengths, a memorial to something rather wonderful, though he could not say quite what had happened. It was a lesson of a crucial sort, and he promised himself that he would abide by it: *Keep swimming.*

But not today. It would take a couple of hours to get to the beach and back, and if there was something wonderfully free in the thought of doing it all by himself, just for himself, he was aware too that he'd be lonely, miss the kids and the camaraderie, feel . . . well, a bit sad. Best get home.

He rejected Perle's offering of sandwiches, and stopped for a quick late lunch at Howard Johnson's, took his time, checked in the lobby to see if they had a public phone, and that he had enough change. Ordered his meal, then spent ten minutes on the phone. When he returned the food had just been placed on the table before him, and he slid into the booth hungrily, feeling calmer now, excited even, as if at the start of a new adventure. Of course it was the end of an old one, if you could call that an adventure.

You've got a lot of decisions to make, don't you? She'd said that again, been saying it for a while, but she was wrong. He'd made his decisions, it was now only a matter of timing. Not what or even how, only when.

God knows he'd waited long enough. For years he had feared the dread knock on the door, the order to clear his desk, the questions, insinuations and accusations, a long paper trail that would render him unemployable for the foreseeable future. *Card-carrying?* How stupid, like being a member of the YMCA!

Ben Grossman was insufficiently important to be made an example of, hauled before HUAC like the writers and Hollywood moguls, required to squirm and to betray friends. In his fantasies, he would have welcomed a chance sit upright in a chair surrounded by hostile interrogators, relished the opportunity to take a stand. In bed at night, unable to sleep, he composed speeches in defence of himself, of the freedom of the individual, that sounded to his half-conscious ears and mind as elegant as Lincoln, and as apposite.

To his surprise and relief, it hadn't happened. He had survived, but there was neither relief nor pleasure in it. He'd had enough. He was going to quit because it was insupportable working for, and within, a government that not merely tolerated the rise of Fascism but supported it institutionally, in the House and Senate, that had a president so frightened to stand up for what was right that it had begun to appear – could this be possible? – that the Beast himself was slouching to the White House to be born.

It made Ben furious, the passivity and compliance at the highest levels. Eisenhower grandly announced that 'nothing would probably please him – McCarthy – more than to get the publicity that would be generated by a public repudiation by the President', proclaiming instead, *'I will not get in the gutter with that guy.'*

'Oh, terrific,' Ben spluttered, 'how genteel! But if you want to kill a rat, where would you look except in the gutter?'

No, he would no longer be part of that. It was immoral, ignoble, unsupportable to be implicated in the undermining of the state from above, from within. It made him feel a rat too. For the Beast was right: there *was* a tangible threat to democracy and the American way. He was it, and Ben near as damn it worked for him. It was time to go because his nostrils could no longer bear the ordure and pollution. Some part of that foul smell was coming from him. He was a G-Man, one of them.

If something is inevitable, choose it, make it your own. No one and nobody was going to destroy him, or his family. It was time to hunker together in their wagon while the Indians circled, see them off, regroup, move on. To the new frontier? *Huntington!*

Why not? But it seemed absurd to Addie, and sterile: she was a city girl, talking already of New York, or Philadelphia (talk about regressive!) or even staying in DC. Refusing to see what was in front of her eyes. If he was going to build a private practice – the thought of joining a big law firm was unappetising, too much like what he already knew – it would have to be where they had contacts. Too many desperate lawyers in New York, too few clients. No, Huntington would do nicely, would have to do. They knew people there and would know more soon enough. Move in, move on.

He finished his fried clams, ate the last of the coleslaw, topped the final french fry with ketchup: he managed his meals so that he took a bite at a time of each of the constituents, ending up, satisfyingly, with a final mouthful of each. Addie teased him about being so obsessional at the table, but it puzzled him that others did not do the same. It was the best way.

When he got home, the apartment felt abandoned. He turned on the lights, opened the windows and drapes, the air looked stale and yellow, dust motes floated. He walked round rubbing his hands, as if to say, *Well, well, what do we have here*, which only elicited the answer, *Not a lot, nobody, nothing.* He was surprised to feel so, for he had often spent time in Alexandria on his own, the family off to the bungalow, he more or less commuting between DC and Huntington. He'd always looked forward to the weeks of peaceful self-determination, the quiet, the opportunity just to be . . . himself. Perhaps to write? Yet this time it was different, and the desolation that he sensed was a projection, not out there, but in himself, his chest and lungs, heart, mind.

He fiddled in his pocket for his cigarettes, lit one and sat down in his Eames chair under the window, put his feet up, took a deep drag, felt better, got up in a few minutes to make himself a martini. He kept the bottle of Gordon's in the freezer, so as not to have to dilute his cocktail with ice. Swirled vermouth in his glass, just to make it a bit smoother, emptied it out, added the gin with a double twist of squeezed lemon peel, sat down, lit another cigarette.

Nothing to decide. Just a matter of making plans.

And writing a letter, it would make him feel better, and

show Addie (and the kids) that he was still with them in spirit, still there, really.

Dear Addie,
I got back just fine, the traffic was light, and I stopped in that new Howard Johnson's just outside Wilmington. Can't get enough of those fried clams! I thought of the kids, sitting there reading my newspaper, how much they like the HoJo burgers. And thought, too, of our ride up to the bungalow, the fun and songs and teasing, how jolly it was, and how much I will miss that, and all of you for the coming weeks!

I thought the visit to Michelle and Frankie went just fine, and hope so much that the new (almost new) apartment is sufficiently enticing to reconcile you to the move.

Try to keep calm and to enjoy the summer. The bungalow is lovely really, and the beach, and Heckscher Park, maybe even an occasional trip into the city to the Natural History Museum or the zoo? They'd love that. And if Michelle or your mother get on your nerves – by which I mean, when they do – do try to withdraw, define some impenetrable space, breathe deeply, count to ten. Or a hundred.

Anyhow, I think I can get away in three weeks or so, and am looking forward to it already!

Love to the kids, tell them I will write a special letter just for them – for each of them – and love to you of course, and as ever,

Ben

He read it over to himself, not quite satisfied, but it was fit for purpose, so he folded it, fetched an envelope and three cent stamp from the secretaire desk, addressed it and headed out the door to put it in the mailbox. It should be there on Tuesday, they'd all be so pleased that he was thinking of them.

Returning home after the short walk, the air in the apartment seemed refreshed, less yellow and dusty, almost welcoming. He'd have almost three weeks. It was worth another martini, to celebrate. Feeling mellow and sleepy, he had a quick shower and was in bed just before nine, on top of the covers in the heat, naked. He considered jerking off, but none of his usual images appeared and he hadn't the energy or wit to summon new ones. He was a bit dull like that. Anyway it was time to sleep, best be fresh for the morning.

Addie dropped the kids and Perle at Brown's Beach – Becca recalcitrant and cranky, Jake in his own world, already scanning the water for his friends – and drove down the road a mile or so, less than a mile, a minute, to join Sally Morris at the tiny beach that served the residents of the development on the hill above. It had no facilities save a floating raft to swim out to, and if you wanted a drink or something to eat, you had to bring it yourself. This was good: it meant that families tended to go down the road, where the sand was better and there was a ready supply of hotdogs, Cokes and ice cream to pacify the children, and slow them down. Whereas at Sally's beach – as far as Addie knew, it didn't have a name – a few indolent adults roasted on the sand, swam in their stately breast strokes to the raft, tried to climb up its slippery ladder, soon swam back.

The women laid a blanket at the rear of the beach close enough to the road to catch a bit of the shade from the trees, poured themselves some iced tea from the Thermos, happy to be together, free from domestic responsibilities. Sally was long reconciled to her childlessness, had indeed come to treasure it, when she looked at the lives of her friends and the strangleholds their children had over them. No, no thanks! It had been a trial and a long ache, but now it seemed a blessing.

'So, how's it going, are you settling in all right? Is your mother being . . . well, you know, your mother?'

Addie laughed, lay back on her blanket, adjusted a folded towel under her head. Sally was her only friend in Huntington, always available, non-judgmental, waspish, funny. They claimed to have the same view of the world, though neither could have articulated, quite, what it consisted of, though disappointment was writ large at the centre. Wry disappointment, perhaps, but neither woman felt she had entered the promised land of her girlhood dreams. Nobody does, they acknowledged, nobody does. Everyone is disappointed, but not everyone is both angry and funny at the same time, in similar ways. It was common ground, they were proud of it.

'Never mind about her,' Addie said. 'But have a look at this, will you?'

She reached into her bag and took out Ben's letter, which had arrived that morning, handed it over. Sally read it quickly and looked up over the rim of her sunglasses.

'*Nu*?'

Addie sat up, took it back and crumpled it up before depositing it angrily in her bag.

'Have you ever heard such condescending bullshit? I'm so furious I almost called him at his office!'

'Bad idea,' said Sally firmly. 'Very bad idea. Anyway, what's so terrible about it? Bit boring, yeah, I get that. Not engaged.

Dutiful. But it's sweet he wrote as soon as he got home. Harold would never do that!'

Addie was fascinated by her friend's marriage, so unlike any she'd encountered, the opposite of a Lawrentian passion. If she'd been a novelist it would have been her subject, it was a great story, there was something so touching and pathetic about it.

Harold was no match for his wife's wit or incisiveness, her openness to experience, which didn't stop her not quite *loving* him, but being a devoted, and fond, wife. He had the kind of sweet nature that masks vacuity – it didn't take long to sense the emptiness within – but his had been a hard life. He'd been born with a harelip and had been subjected to a lifetime of surgical procedures designed first to eradicate, then to ameliorate, his disfigurement. They worked to a small degree, but no one meeting him for the first time failed to be startled, and no one would have guessed that he had previously looked even worse.

It was the single fact, that harelip, that first drew Sally to him, and which she found if not attractive certainly not unattractive either. Viewed from the right angle and with the right attitude, Harold looked like he was turning up his lip – not in a sneer or a smirk (the usual descriptions) but with a look of wry amusement: it looked . . . well, intelligent, whimsical. Sexy even.

Sally was a brilliant student, could have gone to Yale or Radcliffe, with all those perfect blonde girls, but chose Hunter instead, in the sad belief that the many Jewish girls there were uglier than *shiksas.* She would blend in with the flabby, frizzy-haired, baggy-eyed and hook-nosed.

Her father supported the choice of college in his usual tepid manner, nice to be amongst one's own, he supposed. Having no sense of humour, he read joke books and memorised the best ones, unfailingly lame. He was not a practising Jew: *I don't have to practise, I'm very good at it.* It made her wince: *I'm not very observant, I'm sort of Jew-ish.*

Harold, whom she met at a Freshman Mixer, was first a friend, then her first lover, recognised quickly as her destiny. One of her college acquaintances, seeing them together, suggested to another – who reported it back to Sally – that it was a hare-brained relationship. She and Harold ran away and got married the next week, came back to school and never mentioned it, not even to their parents for some months. The parents, all four of them, were relieved. *Thank God for that!* If they'd missed the show of a wedding, at least there had been one.

It had been a satisfactory arrangement, the best she was likely to find, lucky really. Life was drab, but it was the best she could get, being her. She'd been jealous of Addie, perhaps envious was a better word, ever since they'd met at the beach some five or six years ago. Addie was not merely beautiful, she was, well, sort of exotic, with her dark eyes, improbable cheekbones, gorgeous hair, wavy and perfect, and she never had to do anything to it!

Addie went back to her bag, unscrunched the yellow letter, looked at it with disdain.

'What I can't work out,' she said, 'is whether he's deluded, or being hostile?' (She loved the term 'hostility', which she'd picked up in graduate school in a seminar on passive aggression.)

'Not sure I'm following you . . .'

'This crap about what a jolly car trip to the bungalow, like some family out of a Betty Crocker commercial: see the happy family, smiling together, eating their goddamn cake! Ben knows perfectly well – I think he does, please God he does, God help me if he doesn't – that it was a nightmare, awful, really terrible, with him pretending and joking and singing stupid songs, teasing the kids and goading me, and setting them against me . . .'

'Stop! Stop! You're allowed to breathe, you know.'

'He does it on purpose, this misrepresentation, he does it to deny my unhappiness, to goad me, to make him the good guy and me a sourpuss!'

Sally started to laugh.

'But Addie,' she said, 'you are a sourpuss!'

Addie laughed as well, heartily, stopped talking, drank some iced tea, wiped her pristine, beautiful lip with her fingers.

'Goddamn right, I am.'

She lay back and closed her eyes, as if in acknowledgement of a complete truth. But a moment later she sat up and continued.

'OK, we have to leave DC, we have to. We are agreed about that, it's insupportable. But why do we have to come to Huntington? I'm a city girl, I've only ever lived in cities: New York, Philly, St Louis, DC. City life is the only life that gives women a chance! And anyway, I don't want to be near, anywhere near, my mother and that goddamn Michelle and her uterine utopia.'

'I agree. Harold and I like coming here for the summer, and for weekends sometimes, but I'd die without Manhattan, shrivel up and die. After all, what is there *to do* here?'

'Beside bitching on the beach, you mean?'

'Yeah, besides that.'

'I'd go mad here. Without a job. It's been too long. Any more time goes by and I will have lost the will to work. Or to live.'

'Wait a minute, hang on! I saw something . . . was it *Newsday*? Or *The Long Islander*? I can't remember, but it was something about the Long Island school districts hiring school social workers. Not now, but sometime soon. Some sort of worthy programme with a lot of state funding . . .'

Addie shuddered. 'Not for me, not for me. I don't like children, even when they're happy and well adjusted. The idea of working with miserable ones makes my skin crawl.'

Sally looked slightly shocked, turned away, tried to hide it.

'You seem to like yours well enough . . .'

'Of course I do, of course I do. I make an exception for family.' She thought for a moment. 'Most family.' She was obviously thinking of Michelle's eldest, a scowling and petulant child called Jenny, who needed her own personal social worker. Instead Jenny got Michelle, her own personal slave. The child took no pleasure in her mother's docile desire to please, ran roughshod over her.

'Darling, no one likes children. Anyone who claims to "adore" children, without consideration of which one, and in what way, is a sentimental idiot. And a liar. Children are the ultimate advertisement for original sin.'

'Agreed. So why are you telling me about this schleppy job? I thought we were friends.'

'All social work is schleppy! Nobody said you'd enjoy it. Plumbers don't have to like shit, do they?'

'You know why I did it? Parental pressure. I wanted to do a training in clinical psychology and become a therapist, but Maurice wouldn't hear of it, wouldn't pay for it. "One more year," he said, "and you're on your own."'

Sally took her hand, as if in sympathy, but mostly just to slow her down; she knew the signs, a little more of this and Addie would implode, start to cry or to rant. She was always moved by the spectacle of her own unhappiness.

'Self-interest, my dear. Think self-interestedly.' It was

hardly necessary to give this advice to Addie, who usually did. But she wasn't focusing properly, needed to be directed. 'So we're agreed. It was a bad choice of career, all social work jobs are miserable, but some are more miserable than others . . .'

'Like those with children!'

'Do shut up. The key to this is that it is *school* social work.'

There was a pause. Addie was trying to think but nothing happened in her head. So what if it was in a school?

Sally waved her hand in the air, turned it round and round as if stirring a pot.

'What is unusual about schools?'

No response, Addie was starting to look both irritated and bored. *What's the difference between a duck?*

'When are schools open? When do teachers actually work, if you could call it work? Why is it so *easy* to be a teacher?'

'Is it? I think it's a miserable job.'

'Of course, everyone knows that. But it's a *short* job. Home every day by four, great holidays, and best of all: summers off! If a factory worker did those hours they'd think they were in heaven!'

'Oh . . . You're right, OK, I can see that. But it would make me feel exploited, like a whore, renting myself out to do someone else's dirty stuff. No way, not doing it!'

'Sourpuss! If you don't want to feel like a whore you're in the wrong line of work. And if you cannot abide working with children, why not apply for a job at Family Service League? They're expanding. I know one of the women on the board, I could put you in touch . . .'

Addie nodded, submitting.

'Thanks,' she said. 'I need to get some work, it's been a dreadful few years.'

'Anyway, you know the best thing you could do now?

To calm down? Go soak your head! Come on, I'll race you out to the raft!'

Addie turned down the offer – the only thing worse than feeling hot and cross would be feeling wet and cross. Anyway, a quick look at her watch confirmed that she was already late for picking up Perle and the kids at Brown's Beach.

'Gotta go. Love you,' she said, blowing an air kiss and heading up to the road.

'She vomited.'

Perle made the announcement with a kind of relish, as if the arrival of an unexpected virus or bacterium was a confirmation of her entire view of life. Becca was lying on the blanket, a towel over her to keep off the sun, looking pale.

'What did she eat?' Addie didn't have much confidence in the fly-blown overcooked burgers and hotdogs at the beach café, but would never have prohibited their consumption, rather liked the odd burger herself, and if an occasional tummy ache or spot of diarrhoea followed, well, that was a price worth paying. There were enough things to worry about, things you could see, without worrying about germs. Invisible! What germs?

Perle, of course, wouldn't countenance beach food, always brought a basket of sandwiches, cool drinks and vegetables sliced into bite-sized bits: cucumbers, peppers, small tomatoes, carrots. The children refused to eat them, called them rabbit food, so she ate too many herself, to show how delicious they were, and ended up with a stomach ache worse than that produced by the hotdogs.

'Nothing, not even a drink. I tried to get some liquid in her. We've been waiting for you for over an hour, would have walked home if the little one could have made it. And it is so hot!'

Perle wiped her forehead dramatically. It was in the nineties, again, the hottest July for many years, and they had to make a constant effort to keep the children from overheating. In the yard the hose was running most of the time while they squealed and squirted each other; other times they went to the beach and stayed in the water. Not that it was cool enough, even, to be refreshing. The sun darkened their skins quickly, they looked like brown little animals with white tushies where the sun didn't shine.

'Hold on a second! I was only due to pick you up at three . . .'

'Exactly!' Perle said. 'You're late, as usual.'

'Mother,' said Addie, 'it's only a quarter after.'

Perle nodded at this confirmation of her disappointment.

'Can I go home now?' asked Becca weakly, rising slowly from the sand. 'I feel sick.' Addie leant over and put her hand on the child's forehead, left it there.

'No way to tell in the sun, she's hot anyway,' said Perle scornfully. 'We can take her temperature when we get home.'

Becca winced. 'No! You don't need to. I just want to rest!'

Addie was gathering up the beach stuff, folding the blankets and towels, putting the paper plates and cups back in the picnic hamper, waving to a reluctant Jake in the water, urging him back to the beach.

'She'll be fine,' she said, dismissively. 'It's only psychosomatic.' She thought almost all illnesses were generated by the mind, just forms of attention-seeking, not worth taking seriously, except when she had one.

On their arrival at the bungalow Perle set off with grim measured tread in search of the thermometer and jar of Vaseline. She adored making a medical intervention: applying Mercurochrome, dispersing aspirins, putting on Band-Aids, mopping brows, rubbing in ointments and creams, squeezing pimples and pustules, removing splinters, inserting enema tubes or thermometers. Reluctance in her patients only confirmed how necessary her ministrations were.

One year, when Jake was starting to shed his baby teeth, he had one very loose in the front of his mouth, which he kept worrying with his finger, making it looser and looser, but still moored in its setting. It made Perle furious to see him so reluctant to face the dental music, and if she could have tied him down and removed it with pliers would happily have done so. As it was, she convinced the reluctant boy, with offers of various treats (and a dollar) to use the tested procedure – though never tested by her, or him – of putting thread round the tooth, attaching the other end to a doorknob and closing the door sharply. At first it didn't work because he merely moved towards the door as it was closing. Then it didn't work because the thread came loose. Then it didn't work because the thread bit into his gum, the tooth stayed fixed, and copious blood and screams were released. She found the process, all things considered, rather satisfying, all that bleeding to see to. Two days later the tooth fell out of its own free will.

Becca was shepherded into the bedroom, laid on her stomach, swimsuit pulled aside. But rolling onto her side in evasive action, she saw her brother lurking in the corner.

'Addie! Make him go away!'

'Jake!' she admonished. 'What did I tell you about this?'

Yes, she had a temperature of 101.4, was given an aspirin and a lot of water, and put to bed, sweating and miserable, but glad soon to be on her own. Granny fussed about for a time, tucked her in, interrogated her on any other symptoms: Headache? A little. Tummy ache? A little. Sore throat? Yes. Anything else? Becca considered.

'I'm tired. I want to sleep.' Which she did for four hours, until the next aspirin was due.

Dear Ben,
Thanks for your letter, which arrived this morning. I'm glad your trip home was so enjoyable. I'd quite like one myself! Not much new here, in only two days, but Becca seems to have caught some sort of bug and is in bed with a temperature. If it doesn't go down tomorrow I'll take her to the paediatrician, what's his name, that nice Jonathan . . . Rose, was it? The one you thought I flirted with. I didn't, but he should see her, you have to be careful these days. Not that doctors can do much good. I'm sure there's nothing to worry about.

My mother is driving me crazy clucking round her sick granddaughter, making a fuss, enjoying herself. She likes to feel indispensable, and God knows I'm no clucker myself. Anyway illness only confirms her view of the human condition. She keeps popping into the bedroom to make sure Becca is still asleep, straightens her blankets in an attempt – not at all unconscious! – to wake her, so the poor child can see how her Granny dotes on her, and her mother doesn't.

The kids miss you, with your good cheer and funny riddles and goofy songs. They keep humming Sam Hall, all the time, it's starting to drive me crazy. Crazier. Damn his eyes.

I envy you the peace and quiet, and hope you get some writing done.

I don't know what to say about the Silbers' apartment. I know you were trying to be positive.

I'm not. Neither are you, not really. It's as awful as ours. Does it have to be Huntington? Does it? It's terrible to raise children in a wasteland like this, with nothing to see or do or visit or be educated by. No theatres, no museums, no department stores, no bookshops – cities have decent schools full of interesting children, of different backgrounds, different races even. I love it when we go into DC and there are faces and people from all round the world, brown and yellow and white, it's so thrilling and rich, and so good for the kids to see. Cities are the great invention of mankind, the triumph of civilisation! Why abandon them in favour of this? The only brown faces you see on Long Island are workers and maids, gardeners, busboys. It's monochrome, racially and morally. It teaches children all the wrong lessons!

I'll write some more, maybe tomorrow, and get this in the mail this afternoon. I'm starting to feel sick too, thinking about this. And that's what I have to do, isn't it, think about it until I'm ill? You too, wade through the sick feeling and come out the other side? Only: where is that?

Addie

She noticed that she hadn't signed off with 'Love', though it hadn't been withheld intentionally. Of course he would think it had. Perhaps he'd be right? She looked at the bottom of the page and found room to put something fond, and personal. It would fit just fine, but after some thought she left it as it was.

Anyway, with Becca sick she ought to call him, needed to. She hated the telephone, inhuman, mechanical, it distorted both voice and person, and though she would make calls if necessary she tried to avoid it. Michelle, unsurprisingly, was always on the phone to her many friends with babies. How was this one doing, or that? Colic? Teething? Who was pregnant again, who had her period, as if the menstrual cycle was the key creative process of human life.

Addie shuddered. She hated her periods, couldn't bear being on the rag, felt physically and emotionally cramped every month, had pre-menstrual tension so severe that she often had to take a few days off, stuff herself with tranquilisers and shun human company. Ugh.

Michelle loved it, all that stuff, basked in it, talked to her young mother-friends incessantly. *Pregnant! Again? Lucky you!*

That was what the phone was for, that *narishkeit*. But calling Ben, after dinner was over, that wasn't personal, that was business, family business. If she had something to say, real and in her own voice, she'd write another letter. She picked up the phone reluctantly and dialled the number. The phone in the apartment rang several times, ten times, rang some more before she put it down. Past eight and he was not home yet? Or come home and gone out?

Never mind. If the little one was worse in the morning, after the doctor came, then she'd ring Ben at his office. The receptionist at the department office was always frosty if she rang asking for him, asked if it was an emergency. No personal calls were allowed.

In the night Becca was restless, crying out in her sleep, troubled by nightmares, querulous, damp, unsettled. Addie came to her several times with a bowl of cold water and a washcloth, with which she gently removed the perspiration caused by the fever and the night humidity. The air was cloying, painful to inhale, hardly fit to sustain life; it burbled in the lungs, unwilling to release oxygen as well as water, hostile.

'I had a bad dream!' Becca said.

'I'm sorry, darling. It's just a dream, they go away cos they're not real, are they? I bet you don't even remember it!'

'I do so!' She scrunched up her face. 'It had a dog.'

'Well, that's nothing to worry about then, is it? We like doggies!'

'It wasn't a doggie. It was a dog!'

She took the cloth and ran it slowly over Becca's legs, treasuring and inventorising the finely wrought structure of flesh and bone, the smoothness, the predictable regularity, went down to her feet and ankles, renewed the cooling moisture, tested the tiny, moving toes, so perfectly formed, so adorable, the arch of the foot, the sole as soft as it had ever been, since her tiny days in the crib. So perfect, so perfectly formed, so utterly satisfying. So reassuring. Becca gave herself up to the ministration, sighed with pleasure, a little gurgle at the back of her throat, began to go back to sleep, content for this one perfect moment to have her mother's love, entire, unambiguous, hers alone.

The next morning her temperature had gone up to 102 and her sore throat had worsened. Jonathan Rose said he would prefer to come to see her at home – why was that? – they should expect him in the late afternoon, sometime after his office closed at four. In the meantime it was best to give her plenty of liquids, perhaps some soup to keep her strength up.

It was unspoken: even Perle, who had a whole universe of disasters floating in the forefront of her imaginings, could hardly allow herself silently to acknowledge this fear. In the morning Maurice, dressed in suit and tie on his way into the city, sat at Becca's bedside and held her hand as she drifted in and out of consciousness.

He lifted the bedclothes and examined her moist limbs anxiously, arms, legs, sheened in sweat but otherwise as they should be. Perle handed him a washcloth she'd dipped in cold water and he placed it delicately on the child's forehead, rubbed it round slightly, then lifted it to do the same to her cheeks, lips, chin. Becca twisted her head to the side, no. Hurt, he took it away, put it on the bedside table and sat looking rather helpless, uncertain what to do. He was impatient by nature, and if he was going to be involved he needed to do something, not just sit and wait, for what?

Perle touched him on the shoulder, urging him up, and out, and on his way.

He looked at her, his face pale, sweating already in the morning heat, his pupils slightly dilated.

'You don't know what this does to me,' he said.

She didn't reply. In a few moments he was gone, and soon she heard the engine of the car start up. He had no business that she knew of in the city, he hadn't mentioned anything; she had a hunch – she always regarded her hunches as shrewd – that he was going to see their friend, Meyer Levy, a *macher* who worked at Beth Israel. Just for a visit, maybe a drink, he'd say, nothing special, catch up on things, have a chat.

In the living room Addie was sitting, staring out the window. 'It's ridiculous, I know, it's stupid. *What are the chances?* Ben always says that. Million to one, millions, even now with this outbreak . . .'

Perle sat down next to her. 'Well, somebody gets it. Lots of somebodies, *Khas-vesholem*.'

Jake had been forbidden in the kids' bedroom, slept on a camp bed next to Addie, had already helped himself to an ice cream instead of cereal. No one noticed.

'I want to see Becca,' he said, his tone petulant, aggressive and frightened at once. 'I could read to her.' He sucked on his ice cream as if it were a comfort blanket. Transitional object was the term. Transition from what to what, via the Good Humor man?

'Why can't I?'

Addie rose and gave him a quick hug, not too fiercely, reassuring.

'We don't know if it's contagious, don't want you to catch it too,' she said. 'Best wait until the doctor comes, then we will know what it is. I think it's just a touch of strep throat, you know, like you had last year?'

'Is she going to be OK?' he asked.

'Of course she is, darling, of course. It's nothing.'

Perle was rummaging in a lower drawer of the desk, pulling out an assortment of yellowing files, neatly labelled in her regular, reassuring hand. She selected one and took it outside to the porch, where Addie could just see her emptying the contents onto the table. Newspaper and magazine articles, from the look of them, cut out, stapled.

Addie went to the kitchen to pour two glasses of cold tea from the pitcher in the refrigerator, added some ice and a sprig of mint, and went outside to join her mother, placing the glass beside her as she perused a newspaper article.

Perle nodded her thanks.

'It's from the *Times* a month or two ago,' she began.

'Mother, I don't want to know. It makes things worse. I wish you'd put those damn things away, they're poisonous, they do no good.'

'It's best to know, maybe we can learn something . . .'

'If we could do something, Dr Jonathan would have told us.'

'You never know, I remember reading this and it said

something about the early stages. You remember Marion and Herschel had a boy? About Becca's age . . .'

'*Have* a boy, Mother! *Have!* His name is Isaac!'

'You should see him now, God forbid. Their lives are over.'

When Jonathan Rose arrived at a quarter of five, Becca was much the same, but Perle and Addie were a lot worse. They greeted him anxiously, trying to stay calm, but to a doctor's eye – to anyone's eye – they were in a barely controlled state of hysteria. He'd seen a lot of it recently in the parents of young children.

They ushered him through the kitchen.

'You'd like maybe a cup of nice tea?' Perle asked, without her usual enthusiasm.

'No, thank you,' he said. 'Let's have a look at the patient.'

He pulled up a chair by the side of the bed, wishing that the women would leave him with the little girl, who had clearly been infected by their hovering anxiety.

'Becca,' said Addie, 'it's the doctor to see you. You remember Dr Rose?'

Becca looked up, her face red and feverish, fear in her eyes. The last time she'd been to his office he'd given her a shot . . . something, some word . . . it made you not get a disease. She hated it, cried and tried to pull away, but he pinned her firmly but gently to the examining table and pushed the needle into her tushy. She'd howled.

And here he was again, with his black bag. Full of things to stick into you: into your mouth, or your bottom. She hated him.

He had a nice voice, quiet, and a friendly smile. He put his hand to her forehead, left it for a moment, looked at Addie. Lovely eyes, lovely smile.

'101.2 two hours ago,' she said. 'Much the same.'

'You're giving her aspirin and plenty of water?'

'Of course.'

He opened his bag and took out a tongue depressor.

'This will help me look at that sore throat,' he said. 'Open wide.' Becca did, a bit, and then more as the stick entered her mouth; he pushed it back and she gagged, pulled away.

'Let's try again,' he said comfortably. 'No hurry. Just open as wide as you can, I want to see if your throat is red. Does it hurt?'

She nodded, opened her mouth ostentatiously, improbably wide, a good girl.

He bent to shine his pointy little light into the back of her mouth. The back of his neck was covered in fine black hairs, silken almost, not nearly so thick as those on his head, mired in the wet like those tiny veins in the leaf of a tree.

'Ah yes, I can see it now. That must hurt!'

The girl nodded bravely, solemn.

'Addie gives me ice to suck,' she said.

Addie? He looked over at her, hovering by his side, so close they might have touched had it not been so humid, might have stuck together, almost. *Addie?* Why? Huntington kids were 'mom' and 'dad' kids, none of this first-name nonsense.

She saw the thought cross his face. The hell with it, let him figure it out, thought he was so smart. Anyway, him with his fancy Jonathan. Not John or Johnny, oh no, God forbid. *Jonathan*. She didn't say anything, nor did she withdraw the proximity of her hip to his shoulder, moved forward slightly, touched.

'Well,' he said, 'I'm going to write a prescription for some antibiotics. You should pick them up first thing in the morning. That should cure it in a few days.'

'It?' said Addie.

'Just a touch of strep throat, nothing to worry about. It's been going around.'

She'd known it, really, but the relief into which she was submerged, like a cold current, was unexpected, welcome, rather startling. Strep throat! Thank God, if there was a God, may he be thanked. No! There was. Thanks be to God! She paused, guilty. What would Marion and Herschel have said? Or Isaac? Abandoned as they were, helpless and suffering.

'I think I'd like that cup of tea now, if it's still on offer,' Jonathan said, turning to Perle, who beamed at him as if he were the Messiah.

'With maybe a piece of cake? Some strudel? I made it just this morning.'

'Irresistible!' he said, turning the full force of his charm on to her, holding her eye, referring no doubt to the strudel but perhaps, who knows, maybe to herself as well. Such a gentleman! She wondered if he was married. He must be, what woman wouldn't have such a man? She blushed, simpered, straightened her dress, left the room on unsteady feet.

Addie was already leaving the room, stopping only to give Becca a quick hug, tuck her in. She'd forgotten how oily Jonathan was, his silly faith in his own attractiveness. In fact, he was supremely unattractive, merely an actor. Like most doctors. No, that was wrong, most of them didn't bother to act. Like most lawyers then.

As they sat under the awning, she felt a terrible weakness and started to cry gently but inexorably, not sobbing, but her eyes filling and refilling, and she had nothing to stem the flow but her sleeve, which she used unselfconsciously. She could feel him yearning to put his arm around her for comfort, perhaps something else, more.

'Here we are then!' said Perle gaily. *Gaily?* She sounded near as damn it gay, but gay was not in her register. *Coquettishly,* could that be it? Your humble servant, sir, eyes-down curtsey, blush, simper.

If you'd put a tongue depressor down her throat, Addie would have vomited. Jonathan basked, still, dangerous, showed his teeth.

'How delicious it looks,' he said. 'Thank you! And I am so sorry you have had this scare, everyone is on tenterhooks these days, half my visits now are from frightened parents with perfectly normal, normally ill, children . . .'

Addie was still wiping her eyes, and Perle handed her a napkin from the tray. Poured cups of tea, handed round slices of cake.

'Have you had many . . . you know . . . cases yourself, in your practice?'

'A couple,' he said. 'It's frightful.'

He clearly wanted to end there, was unwilling, perhaps unable, to say more.

'But,' said Perle, 'you doctors see everything. This is so different?'

She knew it was. He knew. He knew she knew. He gave in.

'No. This is like nothing I have experienced. It's a plague. Like something out of a Hieronymus Bosch picture of souls in torment . . .' He looked up, afraid the allusion might be missed. 'You know, the sixteenth-century Dutch painter . . .'

Perle looked blank but impressed, satisfied to be given such a scholarly allusion.

'Fifteenth-century,' said Addie.

He continued, irritated but undeterred. 'Like a visitation from a malign being who twists and distorts and deforms – you would hardly believe what this disease can do – and there is nothing, literally nothing, to stop its progress once it is established, or to alleviate the pain, minimise the self-loathing that deformity brings with it . . .'

His eyes, those gorgeous brown sympathetic doctor's eyes, brown with a touch of hazel, had misted up. He had seen too much, assimilated it only partially, unprepared by his medical training or internship for a visitation of this magnitude and malignity.

He would not wipe his eye, nor accept the proffered napkin, just sat, wished to say no more, had exposed himself too thoroughly, foolishly, risen to the bait.

'How can we help keep the children from being exposed?'

'Well,' he said, finishing his large bite of strudel, wiping the stickiness from his upper lip, 'you live in Harbor Heights Park. Which beach do you use?'

'Brown's Beach,' said Perle.

'I'm surprised to hear it. You should – may I speak frankly? – you really should know better. There have been stories in *The Long Islander*, and we know the water is polluted, and that infection is caused by faeces in the water supply. That beach should have been closed years ago!'

Addie and Perle lowered their eyes, ashamed but not compliant.

'The authorities have tested the water,' Addie said. 'There was a report. And we only allow the children to swim at high tide. So far no one has been infected!'

'So far,' he said, more sternly than he had a right, presumptuous really, but they had been thoroughly frightened and were fully aware that if Becca had caught polio Brown's Beach might have been responsible. *She* would have been. *And* her mother.

'Well,' said Jonathan, finishing his tea and pastry more quickly than strictly necessary, 'I must be going, thanks for the hospitality.'

He rose from the table and turned to the two women, who were in the process of standing up.

'If it were my children,' he said, 'I wouldn't let them within a hundred yards of that cesspool!'

They knew, they knew. But most days they didn't have a car, and the beach was only a ten-minute walk up and down the hill. There was nowhere else to go. And the town council and medical authorities had tested the water. It was safe!

So why were they so frightened, and so guilty?

Sensing this perhaps, and unwilling to leave the bruising atmosphere that he had created, Jonathan paused before taking his leave. A bit audaciously perhaps, certainly unexpectedly, he took Addie's hand in a manner ill-suited to shaking and said, 'In a couple of days I'd like to see her again . . .' Was there a pause, a slight hesitation before *her*? He meant *you*, surely if imperceptibly.

'Perhaps you might come by the office on Thursday, just to keep me up to date? Becca should be on the mend by then, but if not do bring her as well.'

Next to her Perle was standing still, nodding idiotically, as if in approval of a coming betrothal.

'I'll give you a call,' said Addie, detaching her hand. 'It was good of you to come.'

It wasn't, of course, it was his job, though he could have insisted that mother and child come to his office.

Maurice returned a couple of hours later, delayed by rush-hour traffic on Northern State, bustling and bursting with good news.

'It's nothing,' he said. 'The girl! Nothing to be alarmed about!'

'Your dinner's on the table,' said Perle. 'We already ate.'

He wondered what he'd done wrong this time.

Addie had been coming to the bungalow for many years, even before the children were born, but she'd never got to know the village very well. She could navigate between the high spots, up and down Main Street, and onto New York Avenue: the supermarket, the delicatessen, baker's, butcher's, one or two shops for basic things, the pharmacy – but it surprised her that there were so many roads, so complexly intertwined. She laughed at the description. So many? Five? Six? Complexly? Intertwined? What a dope she was, how lacking any sense of direction. Ben used to joke that when they had a new apartment it took a week for her to find the kitchen. When, occasionally, she had to drive in DC she invariably left an extra hour to find her way, correct it, ask directions, consult a map (she wasn't very good at maps, too much plot and not enough character) before arriving, usually a bit ahead of time, sometimes late. Once or twice she just turned around and went home. She got lost then, too.

She looked at the note in her hand. *Huntington Paediatric Practice* and an address somewhere on Green Street. That was off Main, according to her local map, quite a large road running to the left as you went up the hill. She'd only been there once and had no memory of where it was. She'd passed Green Street many times but never learned its name or turned up it; it might as well have been Timbuctoo. Unsure of whether or not she would actually go, or if she did whether she would find it in time, she'd called to enquire about their opening times and a haughty receptionist asked if she needed to make an appointment.

No, I'm casing the joint for drugs, she wanted to say. *I'm addicted to aspirins, can't get enough of the little darlings.*

'No, that's not necessary. I just need to know when you close.'

'Four o'clock,' came the voice, even cooler and more distant. 'Sharp.'

At four-fifteen Addie was outside the front gate, trying to look relaxed and natural, as if just walking by, which she did several times, in each case keeping an eye on the door. Jonathan's maroon Buick was parked by the side of the white shingled house, which before its conversion might have housed a small family. The rooms were painted in warm colours, light yellow, pink and sky blue, with pictures for children of all ages; toys and games were kept in a box by the sofa, a table was set up for children to draw or crayon on. It was welcoming, and the timid children and concerned parents who availed themselves of it must have felt reassured. Until they met Mrs Downing, looming behind the reception desk. Every childhood space has to have a dragon. It said little for Jonathan's attentiveness that he hadn't slayed his.

Just past four-thirty, as Addie walked back towards the house from the Main Street end, he appeared at the door, closed it gently and trod down the steps. His right hand combed through his hair, not so much to rearrange it – it was short and neat – but in a gesture of weariness. God knows what he'd seen that day. She thought of his voice when he'd described the crippled children, his distress that he could do nothing to cure or to ameliorate such suffering. Had he seen one today? Or perhaps just a child with leukaemia? Too bad: not enough strep throats to go around.

She halted by a picket fence fifty yards away, shrank back slightly, gave herself a sharp pinch on her fleshy upper arm. It hurt, but propelled her forward. Why would pain and an incipient bruise do that?

He was about to get into his car as she walked up the drive, uncertain what sort of noise or language might catch his attention in a natural way. A cough? A cheery hello? But he heard the sound of her shoes against the drive and turned, caught her eye, paused, didn't say anything, let her come to him.

She suppressed her quick response – *Christ, you're good*

at this, you've done this before – in favour of a nod, a shy smile and hello.

'So sorry to bother you. Have you got a minute?'

She was a few feet away now, standing still.

'Of course.' There was a pause that was a couple of beats too long. 'And tell me, how is . . .' He stopped to think for a moment – *was he putting her in her place? What place?* – 'Becca? Better now, I hope.' He paused. 'Presume.'

Presume! What presumption! He was as uneasy as she was, had reverted to being a doctor, formal but – she could see it in his stance, the slight lean forward, the too insistent eye contact – incipiently available.

'Becca. Better, she's getting better now.'

He nodded.

'Thanks to you, Mother and I were so grateful for your help.'

'Lovely woman, your Mother. Makes great strudel! How is she?'

'Fine, just fine, for a while . . . She'll find something else to fret about!'

He laughed.

'Look,' he said, touching her upper arm just where it hurt. 'I don't have anywhere special to go. Would you like to come into the office and have a coffee? Or perhaps something stronger?'

She drew away.

'Not just now, I have to get away. I'll be missed . . . But perhaps some other time?'

'I'd like that very much,' he said.

She had an impulse to shake hands, to find a way to touch him as he had touched her, pat him on the shoulder perhaps, but turned and retreated down the drive. Her legs were working, just.

She didn't look back at him until she had turned onto the sidewalk. He was standing still, looking after her.

She walked back to Main Street, turned left and crossed the street towards the supermarket (and the dreaded Nathan Hale Drive), thinking to get some cough drops for Becca, something soothing for her throat, maybe those root beer ones, when she was startled by a hand on her shoulder.

'Addie! What are you doing here?'

What was she doing there, indeed, she hardly knew. The uncertainty must have passed across her features, or perhaps something more telling, evasiveness perhaps, or humiliation?

Michelle looked at her more closely, put the brake on the baby carriage, checked that baby Charlotte was asleep, her little darling, her best, with her captivating smile, a good sleeper, a wonderful feeder, just looking at her made Michelle yearn to offer a breast, all those babies being fed that disgusting formula, it was shocking!

Addie knew Michelle breastfed the girls, had often seen her in her own apartment, or in a shaded recess at the bungalow when the men weren't around, or knew enough to withdraw, had seen her unbutton her blouse, pull her bra aside, release the enormous breast, place the engorged brown nipple into the hungry mouth, baby and mother intensely satisfied, smiling into each other's eyes. It was disgusting.

Addie looked odd, flushed and anxious. Michelle was unused to that, usually felt immediately on the defensive around her sister-in-law, but now for some unaccountable reason she was in the ascendency. She didn't know, quite, how to press home this advantage, was unsure whether it was right to do so with Becca still sick in bed at the bungalow, Ben in Washington, Addie marooned with her parents. Michelle wouldn't have minded so, was always happy to spend days at the bungalow and beach with the kids, but she had a home to go back to, a loving husband and growing family.

She'd read an article once – was it in *Reader's Digest*? – that only children were confident and assertive, not having had to fight for attention with needy siblings. But her childhood experience was just the opposite, she'd felt taken for granted, and if she was to get any attention, had to clear a space, make herself agreeable, assert, quietly, her value in the household. She should have been adored – if she were a boy she would have been! – but her parents were simply too busy scratching a living in their small shoe shop in Long Island City to pay her much mind. Except, of course, that she could help out, and from her earliest days they regarded her as one of the staff. She could dust, sweep up after the shop closed, stock the shelves where she could reach high enough. Unpaid, of course, without holidays or rights. But of course, for her parents too, there were no holidays and no rights, and if they were paid, by themselves, it was never enough.

A functionary whose existence was defined by the needs of others, she had no right to an education. Though studious by nature, anxious to learn, to please, to excel, she was withdrawn from school at fifteen to work full time behind the counter, sometimes helping ladies to fit too-small shoes on their too-large feet. It was her fate, if she acceded to it, but she did not. If she was not going to be granted an education, she would have an even better thing, a husband. She kept an eye out. She was a pretty girl, always slightly overdressed and made up, to her mother's consternation, but who knew on which day Mr Right, or even Mr Pretty Good, might pass through the shop door?

Her parents, their cramped shop and tiny apartment, were like metaphors from which she longed to escape. Not in some worthy way to better herself – though she ardently wished to do so – but simply *to get the hell out of there.* That was how she had put it, it was accurate, a bit risqué, a bit dismissive. Modern. She said it to herself every day, a mantra to keep her going, *I have to get the hell out of here*, and felt both proud and ashamed as she did so.

It is only those who lack a college education who feel how important it is to have one, how wonderful an opportunity. Addie took hers for granted: two college educations, hardly referred to the experiences at all, was often rude about her former teachers, unwilling to acknowledge the gift she had been given. Maurice had paid through the nose for it, he always did. There was no evidence so far as Michelle could see that Addie was grateful. It was her due. She wore her education effortlessly, and Michelle, however much she tried, could not suppress her envy, nor her sense of inferiority. In Addie's presence she felt ignorant, though she knew she read more, and more deeply, than her sister-in-law. Yes, in spite of the babies, was more attuned to the spirit of the age, kept up with the news, read the latest novels when she could sneak an hour before sleep. And lovemaking.

'Is Becca any better?' she asked.

'Maybe a little. She's been pretty miserable.'

'Poor thing. But those antibiotics are like a miracle, she'll soon be on the mend.'

Michelle had called and talked to Perle – Addie pleaded a headache and wouldn't come to the phone – and was up on the news. Family, family was what mattered, and she rang each morning to get updates.

'I gather Jonathan Rose called by . . .'

Addie nodded. Michelle never missed a trick, without a change of inflection she nevertheless made it sound as if a doctor's visit was a form of flirtation, of courtship.

'He's *very* attentive,' she said. 'Not many doctors make

home visits these days, they like you to come to them, no matter how sick you are . . .'

'It's a matter of what the disease might be,' said Addie darkly, unwilling to shift from medical to personal grounds. 'These days you have to be so careful, it's like a plague.'

Michelle shuddered, looked at Charlotte asleep beside her, banished the invasive image.

'You're right, of course. And anyway, who wouldn't welcome a visit from the dashing Dr Rose?' She paused for a moment, for too long. 'I saw you walking down Green Street. Did you go to his office?'

Had she winked? It was intolerable. Had Perle noticed something, conveyed it over the phone with a grunt of amused disapproval? If not a wink, some sort of smirk then. Michelle's face made an unusual set of grimaces and infoldings, as if she were sucking two lemons at once.

'You have to watch him, that one, he's a bit of a devil . . .'

'I don't know what you're talking about. I've only met him a couple of times, last summer when Jake hurt his thumb, and before that when Becca had the flu. He was very helpful, very competent we thought. Ben likes him.'

'*Everybody* likes him, he knows it, he courts it, ingratiates himself, craves admiration, needs to be doted on. Ever since his divorce . . .'

'He's divorced?'

'Couple of years ago. She's lovely, they had a couple of little ones, and she caught him . . . you know? Seeing another woman? I guess it's like an occupational hazard. He spends his days with anxious young mothers, harassed and exhausted, who feel as attractive as yesterday's leftovers, and there he is, right in their faces, an arm on the shoulder, warmth, eye contact . . . Like shooting fish in a barrel, isn't that the expression?'

She was looking Addie right in the face, would not withdraw her glance. She knew.

Addie tried to still her humiliation, give nothing away, but she blushed easily and was not a good or natural liar.

A fish! A barrel! How utterly demeaning to think of herself swimming in circles waiting for the shot to ring out, the splash of the bullet, belly turned up. So what would he do with her then, eat her with horseradish? Stupid metaphor, stupid goddamn woman!

'I'm so sorry we haven't been able to visit,' said Michelle, 'but it's best to keep the children apart until Becca isn't contagious any more. Perhaps you'd like to come to supper with us one night? Tomorrow maybe?' She paused. 'Maybe I could invite the Silbers for a drink. I gather you haven't been in touch with them, what with one thing and another. They understand, I told them what's been going on.'

The Silbers! Addie had quite forgotten about them. Was it rude not to have been in touch, as Michelle was suggesting? Why? They had shown them the apartment, indicated when it might be available. They'd been told that a decision was in the offing but that it was complicated and might take a while. Presumably if Addie and Ben didn't snap up their damn apartment some other dopes would?

Addie declined the invitation to supper – ugh! – promised to call the Silbers, waved an insincere goodbye with her index finger, turned her back and headed down the hill towards her car, if only she could remember where it was.

She'd learned one thing, though. Jonathan Rose was attractive, she wanted him but would not and could not have him, and that her inner organs were intact and functioning. It came as something of a relief. Huntington was too small, she had no privacy even to make a phone call, though, come to think of it, she might sneak to Sally's to make the calls. But then her friend would know, and though she wouldn't be disapproving, quite, she would be interested, which was worse. And Michelle would find out, God knows how, but sure as shooting. No. No Jonathan Rose, best keep him as a figure of temptation and a reminder that she still had the old black magic, if only she could find someone to share it with.

Dear Ben,
Well, it's been a bit of a business here. Becca has strep throat and has been in bed for a couple of days – I called you one night but you weren't in, or not answering the phone – and the doctor came and prescribed antibiotics, which are starting to work. My mother got hysterical as soon as the little one got a fever – it came on at the beach – kept rubbing and examining her arms and legs, preparing them for the iron lung. It made me furious, but I got infected by it too, and by the time that oleaginous Dr Rose came we were both a little overwrought. It's all settled down now.

I bumped into Michelle in the village today and she intimated – a bit aggressively, I thought – that the Silbers have been sitting by their goddamn telephone waiting for us to confirm that we want their goddamn apartment. Well – surprise! – I don't! They are moving at the end of August, and it is too much, too soon. This is not a decision we can rush, and I don't believe for a moment – as I keep saying and keep saying – that Huntington is the right place for us, or for raising children, whatever the hordes of new suburbanites might think. It's dull, it's ingrown, it's provincial, it is infected by relatives. Please, please, I beg of you, please keep an open mind on this.

I know I keep saying this. I'm sorry. I don't so much mind being a bore, but I don't want to turn into a nag. And of course I know that the decision is more up to you than me, really, because you have to find the best place to set up a practice and make a living.

Sally says that the local schools are going to be hiring more social workers in the coming year or two. I can hardly bear to think of it. I know you will see this as confirmation that Long Island is the right choice for us, and I find myself feeling that too, damn it. It would just be so nice, so utterly wonderful, to be at work again, having my own place and earning my own money, even if it is with my head down the social work toilet. I won't drown, anyhow there's other job possibilities. I'm looking into them, just in case . . .

I knew I shouldn't have told you about this, but I can't be bothered to tear this up and start again. So try not to have renewed hope in your heart, or to be thinking positive thoughts, not about this place.

There is no need for children to move school at the start of a new year, they can join a class at any time. I checked. So whether it is here (ugh) or somewhere else (hooray) there is no hurry save that generated at the DC end. How is that going? I feel a bit starved for news, or conversation, my mother clucks round Becca, strokes her, caters to Jake, spends her time in the kitchen. I hardly see Maurice, who makes himself scarce, either in the city or the garage, banging away. Banging away? Get it? I made a pun!

I want to know what you are thinking and feeling. Do write me an extra good letter, like you can and used to.

Love

Addie

PS I wrote two letters in a row! You owe me big time!

Becca, being six years old, had never read *The Magic Mountain,* though she would have wondered from the title if it were some sort of children's book. But unversed as she was in the ways of Swiss sanatoria and tubercular patients, she nevertheless did a reasonable impression of a delicate child taking the air, anxious not to exert herself, breathing slowly and evenly, waited on hand and foot, lest her infection deepen and a crisis occur. Doing nothing, elegantly. On her first day out of bed she put on her best dress, a sun hat with blue daisies against a yellow ground, and shuffled her way slowly onto the porch, demanding a glass of lemonade with ice. She rested on a recliner, pulled the awning so that no sun got in her eyes, closed them, lay back, it felt wonderful. Her throat wasn't so sore any more, but she didn't tell anyone, swallowed gingerly, gave little coughs, wiped her mouth delicately with a hankie.

Perle was amused by Becca's *invalid* persona – a term Ben later played with, with much self-slaying – invalid! In-valid! – which infuriated Addie. When told about the sensitive patient episode, which only lasted a day or two,

Ben could only come up with one background possibility. That December he had read the children *A Christmas Carol* and the pathetic figure of Tiny Tim had moved Becca to tears, which, though they were undoubtedly forced, nevertheless dribbled down her cheeks.

'He's so sad!' she intoned.

'He's not, he's stupid,' said Jake, who was not a sentimental little boy, and whose current hero was the new heavyweight champion, Rocky Marciano. 'He's not as big as the other ones, but he's the toughest! Nobody can beat him!' One of the smaller boys in his class – indeed, several of the girls towered over him – he was wiry and pugnacious, with a quick temper, the kind of boy who would have enjoyed a bit of biffing and boffing, except that his first experience of fisticuffs had been unfortunate. He now limited his aggression to his mouth, though his vocabulary was limited. Burgundy Farm regarded cursing as vulgar and aggressive, and didn't so much ban as discourage it, however much they promoted the ideal of the free child. When, in a rage over being denied something or other, he once called Ben a 'basted', his father, instead of taking umbrage or being amused, merely corrected his pronunciation. 'Bastard,' he said. 'You pronounce it "bastard".' Jake didn't believe him. Neddy said 'basted' when they played in the streets. Neddy said a lot of words. He could fight, too.

On the first days of Becca's illness, when Perle and Addie thought it best that the kids be separated, Jake was fretful and restless, wanting to go into the bedroom to see his sister. Becca would have liked that, so he lurked by the door, books in hand, until shooed away by Perle. When the fever lifted, and Becca was preening delicately on the porch, the desire to serve her, or even to be with her, had passed. She couldn't understand it. She wasn't yet a strong reader and confined herself to comics, of which she had a large number. She particularly liked *Peanuts,* had the book and read the strip in the newspaper every day. It was about kids her age. She loved Charlie Brown, he was so nice, but that Lucy was horrible.

That afternoon, to her surprise and delight, Jake came in with a book that had cartoons in it, a real book in a real cover that looked like it was for grown-ups. He took the limp *Peanuts* paperback from her hand, put it on the table by her side. 'Put that silly book away, it's only for kids!'

'I am a kid!' she said, but weakly, as if without conviction. If Jake had something better she'd be interested. He sat beside her and opened his book, which was filled with cartoons in heavy black ink, not like *Peanuts* or *Sluggo*. Sometimes with a lot of writing as well.

'These are in the newspaper too,' Jake said, anxious to establish their importance. 'They're about politics!' Becca looked a bit blank. 'You know, like the government and what's happening that gets on TV.' He had dog-eared a couple of the pages, though he knew he wasn't supposed to. He could always fold them back, no one would notice. If they did, he didn't do it, nobody could prove he had.

In the first few cartoons there was a man with a beard who looked ugly. The cartoon was making fun of him because he was a bad man.

'That's Senator McCarthy,' said Jake. 'He's the reason we're moving.'

Becca had already forgotten the discussion in the dream-world of the fort, put it out of her mind. They were *really* moving! When? And why was that ugly man making them?

She peered at the picture carefully. He looked like that man on TV sometimes, on the news, surrounded by other men all in suits and ties, having meetings. Nobody seemed to be having a good time.

'How come he can make us move?'

'Because he is hunting Communists, and he says there's lots of them in the government, and they are against America. He's a big fat schmo!'

By the time he'd finished his explanation, including the astonishing information that Ben was a Communist – that must be wrong, Communists were bad, really really bad! – Becca was turning away, not in tears but in shock. That ugly man hated Ben, and Ben was going to run away. With Addie and her and Jake. To Huntington. What if they found him there and took him away?

She put her hands over her ears and closed her eyes. Where was Granny when she really needed her? Or Addie, even?

'Go away!' she said. 'I hate you!'

He was already turning to another page.

'If you think that's scary, look at this!'

He had opened to one of Herblock's cartoons featuring Mike the Atomic Bomb, a towering personage with the legs of a man, a huge sausage-shaped body and a leering expression, with whiskers like that bad Senator (he loved big bombs!) and a funny topknot on his head. He was enormous: people only came up to his knees, he leant over and threatened them, they cowered.

'Just look at this, it's funny!' said Jake.

She couldn't resist, opened her eyes, turned back round, studied the picture. The big creature had a bunch of little bombs in his hand and a cuckoo clock with a horrible bird looking out. He was pointing to the time.

'He's so ugly. Who is he?'

'He's called Mike.'

'Mike?'

'He's a bomb, the biggest one. He's an atomic bomb.'

Becca knew about bombs, sort of. On *Looney Tunes* sometimes one of the bad guys had a bomb, like on *Tom and Jerry*: it was round and had a string with fire on its top and in big white letters it said BOMB. Then it went BOOM! and there was smoke and then everything started again. Bombs couldn't hurt you, they were funny.

Becca looked at him again, fascinated by the picture without understanding it, quite.

'We dropped one of him on the Japs,' said Jake. 'Twice! Killed millions of them, they were totally blown up, nothing left, not even any bones! Then they surrendered, pronto!'

This was too much to take in, and Becca didn't wish to hear any more. She got up from her chair with surprising speed and agility, and turned into the house, pausing only to ask, 'Who'll look after us when Ben's in jail?'

3

'Will you read it to me?'

She didn't expect an answer, or get one.

'You're so private about your writing. I don't understand. You're not shy, and you certainly don't lack self-confidence!'

She'd been impressed, impressed and appalled, when Ben told her the story of how he'd got his first job, just out of law school. Asked by a prospective employer to provide a reference from one of his professors, he had approached the Dean of the law school, with whom he'd taken two classes.

'I'm too busy,' said the Dean, winking. 'Why don't you write it yourself, and I'll sign it?'

'Gosh,' she'd said. 'What'd you do?'

'What would you have done?'

'Me? I'd have refused.'

'Why?'

'Aside from the fact that it's unethical, I wouldn't have been able to do it. It's impossible to be objective about yourself.'

He'd laughed and shook her by the arm. 'Objective? Is that what you think references are? Nonsense. They are advertisements for yourself, and you have to make sure that whoever provides one does just that. Sells you!'

'So what did you write?'

'I wrote the best goddamn reference anyone ever had. I said Ben Grossman is an exemplary student and person. That he was Phi Beta Kappa, chairman of the Philomathean Society, editor of the *Law Review* . . .'

'Shameless!' she'd said, shaking her head.

'So far it's true! I then went on to say that I was an outstanding student with a first-class, highly cultured mind, would make an exemplary lawyer, combined virtues of intellect and high moral purpose in a way unparalleled in the Dean's experience . . .'

'Jesus!'

'And then I added some really complimentary stuff! I forget most of it.'

'Did the Dean even read it?'

'Of course, he had to sign at the bottom. He read it quite carefully, even added a comma in one place, then signed it with a flourish. "Good for you!" he said. "Just what I thought you'd do, quite right, that should do it!"'

She considered the story, stretched her arms and rolled over in the bed.

'What's that word you use, you know, that means unmitigated gall?'

'Chutzpah!'

'Plenty of that, it's amazing!' She rolled over on top of him to demonstrate her admiration, her sexual intensity all the more appealing to him in that it was silent, save a final, not entirely ladylike grunt. A considerable contrast, and a welcome one. He didn't make much of a fuss about coming either, just an orgasm after all, not exactly oceanic.

He rubbed her naked arm, resting on his side, his head on the pillow, soothed to silence by their lovemaking.

'I need to talk about your writing,' she said. 'I feel as if it's a sort of barrier between us, that if you could share . . .'

'It's private, that's all. Leave it, Rhoda, please leave it.'

'One of your compartments, is it? Everything in its place, nothing slopping over the boundaries, each area sacrosanct. For someone who wants to love you, who does love you, you never come together, never form a whole.'

He saw that this was right, for it was what he intended, what protected and nourished him. 'I know.' He should have said he was sorry to have excluded her, but he wasn't.

She'd had the same answer before, the same tepid response, and knew that was all she'd get.

'But do you share it, you know . . .'

'Not any more.'

In fact, though he would not admit it to her, even his writing was compartmentalised. She knew a little about the unpublished novel, and the short story that had been published in *Story* magazine, been impressed that he was keeping company, if only on that one occasion, with real writers, famous ones. What he didn't tell her was that he also wrote popular articles simply to make some money, full of faux wisdom and shoulder-shrugging cuteness. He'd had one published in *Your Life,* a sub-*Reader's Digest* rag, entitled 'Let's Not Pretend'. It ended with a folksiness that had made him wince until the cheque arrived: 'Most of us have a long, long way to go. But no one has ever crossed the ocean without first leaving the shore. As one dope to another – *Bon voyage!*'

Such articles were surprisingly hard to write, he'd had too many rejected, and could hardly tell why some were deemed better than others. You just had to keep trying, like fishing with six hooks, one would catch a fish.

'Let's Not Pretend' – why would he tell her about that? It made him ashamed. And proud too, ashamed and proud. She thought of him as the high-brow author of that piece he'd published in *Story* magazine, claimed even to remember it. Probably even went back to it after they'd met and she became interested in him. Though it had been published six years earlier, the gloomy tale of marital discord might have suggested to her that there was, as it were, an opening available. (Or, she giggled at the thought, an opening unavailable?) On rereading 'Track Shoes', Rhoda was struck by how obviously autobiographical it was: the story was virtually a cry for help.

The marriage at its centre, between Bob and Helen Goodrich, is sterile, undermined by her unhappiness, hostility and promiscuous flirtatiousness (perhaps something more). Sexless, virtually.

'That night, Helen was sleepy. When Helen was sleepy, the little Louis Quinze table between the two beds stood guard over no-man's land . . . How long since they had even—? Quite a while . . . Good thing one of them could sleep.'

Two beds? No *man's* land? Poor Ben, married to such a frigid bitch, what a sorry situation! The story turns on the Goodrichs' argument about Helen's unjust treatment of their older son, who had caused the younger one to hurt himself falling off a bike. Helen punishes him by withdrawing permission to run in the hundred-yard dash at the weekend picnic, a race he is sure to win. His father had bought him a pair of track shoes to help him to victory.

Helen asserts her right to make household decisions, clearly favouring the younger child. What's done is done, unjust and irrevocable. The story ends, as if inevitably, with that ghastly wife enticing him into her bed, and he following abjectly, abandoning his moral high ground for the low terrain of the bedroom.

But the story, Rhoda recognised, was more than an

expression of desperation, it was finely wrought, knew when to hold back and when to let go, entranced and involved the reader. Ben was a real writer, and *Story* was a great magazine!

'Didn't they publish Shirley Jackson and H.E. Bates and Tennessee Williams and . . .'

'And,' he said, 'Langston Hughes, and Peter De Vries.'

'Enough! Why didn't you do more?'

'I tried. But kids came, Addie is pretty demanding, and DC came, and I didn't have the time.'

'Real writers always have time!' she said, as if she knew what she was talking about.

'Perhaps I didn't have the heart then,' he said. 'Enough already.'

She paused, having crossed a line. Contrite.

'Time, you need time . . .'

He laughed, as if what she was suggesting was pure fantasy, the hanging gardens of Babylon. To have time to write!

He'd tried, half-heartedly. Sat in his office at the typewriter, hunting for the right words, stalled, the blank page mocking him, made as few pecks as a replete chicken, pushed the typewriter away and closed its case. Hunt and not peck. Even when it was going badly, though, nothing was more important than this, he reassured himself: making the words matter.

Lawyers should be like that, they should be wordsmiths too, like proper authors, writing succinct briefs, arguing cases compellingly. It was one of the reasons he'd gone to law school at Penn, edited the *Law Review*, joined the Department of Justice lawyers arguing the cases for rural electrification and the development of hydroelectric power in Tennessee. To make a difference, and to make it crisply and compellingly. He wanted his briefs to bear a personal stamp. *That must be Grossman,* he wanted to hear his colleagues say as they examined his arguments, and his exposition, enviously.

Most lawyers were prolix, their prose impenetrable and jargon-laden, the absence of proper punctuation enough to bring a tear to the eye. For every Clarence Darrow, there were ten thousand illiterate shysters and incompetent dogsbodies droning on. It made his ears hurt and his heart ache.

At an Appellate Court in Tennessee, arguing what should have been a straightforward government case, he treated the judge as if he were an attentive reader, as Hemingway would have regarded his, keeping his language simple but exact, compelling attention. He had traipsed through small courts like this for years, arguing a case that should have been obvious! Rural electrification was essential, it had improved lives that were still mired in the primitive deprivations of the nineteenth century. Thanks to the federal government projects, there would be electrical outlets in every room, and hence lighting even in the night-times, indoor toilets, electrical pumps for water. Telephones to keep in touch with each other! But even in communities that had begun to profit from the bringing of the light – that was what the Rural Electrification Act of 1936 accomplished! – there was still resistance. Country people did not like federal intervention, they could look after themselves! That they had failed to do so was hardly the point, it was not up to the government to tell them what to do!

Ben was used to explaining this patiently, and in detail. It was so obvious to him – it was obvious to anyone with half a brain. But he had trained himself – perhaps not altogether successfully – not to talk down to the people he encountered in small-town courts. All he had to do, after all, was to explain. The government wanted to improve people's lives! He listed the many benefits, one by one. Small local businesses could not provide such changes, it took vast amounts of money. The government was anxious to provide loans and create jobs, create huge projects that would bring the light into the darkness. The New Deal was a great deal!

'That was an elegant presentation,' drawled the judge in his summing up, looking at this Grossman directly and unsympathetically, eyes hooded like a water moccasin from a Southern swamp. During the trial, he had continually referred to Ben by his full title, 'Chief of the Consulting Section of the Electrifications Operation Division', which he drew out languorously, syllable by syllable, until it seemed meaningless nonsense.

'Like some lines from *Jabberwocky*,' thought Ben, at first amused by the ploy, because he thought it was a fatuous title too. The more unwieldy an organisation is, the dumber its job descriptions and demarcations. But by now Ben had heard his title numerous times and it caused him nothing but the irritation it was designed to elicit.

'Veh elegant . . . Ah'm gonna rule against you.'

It was the absence of the 'but' that gave the game away: Grossman – not the name of a proper American! – was a Yankee Jewboy big shot who thought he could hornswoggle a bunch of rednecks. He lost because his argument was elegant, not in spite of it.

The hell with it, with them. Let them sink back into the darkness. Better to be a writer, a proper writer, to write short stories, be brief, not write briefs. But there was no sense forcing it: trust your unconscious and it will come. Right?

'You know,' Rhoda said tentatively, taking his hand, 'I

don't tell this to everyone, no one really, I'm sort of ashamed of it, but . . .'

He had no idea what was coming, felt apprehensive. Was she married? She was evasive about her past, had alluded briefly to a privileged childhood in Santa Barbara, California, but gave few details about her family, though she claimed to be close to them, mentioned occasional boyfriends and lovers but didn't give details. When he solicited more information – a sign, to him, of interest and desire for increased intimacy – she would draw away and say, 'I don't want to talk about all of that. It's boring. I only care about what I am now, what we have now.'

This attitude, unusual enough in his experience, piqued his interest. Indeed, that may have been its purpose: to self-present as a woman of mystery who came into his life fully formed, without antecedents or personal history. Santa Barbara? Boring. Brothers and sisters, yes, three, lovely people, adored them. No more. Life at Stanford? Tolerable enough, bit rich.

She never finished the sentence, left it hanging: something to reveal . . . *What?* Never mind, it would come sometime, or not, maybe it was nothing. He had no more right to press her than she, him.

She was whoever she chose to be, came fully furnished with reading, knowledge, opinions and was well-travelled – had spent a number of summers, or perhaps it was years, in Europe, spoke fluent French and tolerable Italian, hated the idea of saying even a single word of German (though she could). Some of these journeys featured a companion, male, about whom she said almost nothing and wouldn't be drawn. His name was Jean Paul.

Ben thought about Jean Paul occasionally, though the less he knew, the less he wanted to know. A boyfriend, presumably. Or perhaps a husband, now estranged? Or deceased? Who gave a damn?

They'd lived in Rome together, she working for a small Italian publisher, in 'a nice apartment' in some piazza or other. He was expected to recognise the name, God knows why, he'd never even been to Europe, knew nothing of Italy save some reading of Dante, fat lot of good that did. He was – he knew he was, there was no way round it – unsophisticated. Compared to her. So was everybody else. When she talked of Italian neo-realist films, of Visconti and Rossellini, of novelists like Svevo and Calvino, or the hill towns round Rome, trips to the Amalfi Coast, he faded into silent incomprehension, felt envy, felt patronised. She didn't mean to, said she was sorry, simply had this, at least, to share. Italy was far enough away, but it was too far for him.

It was all he was going to get; closer to home she closed up entirely.

'I'm bored with this woman of mystery persona,' he'd said once, as they were walking down a corridor from their offices towards the elevators. 'I am longing to know you. I'm a writer, I need to fill in the blanks.'

'Blanks? I prefer creating them, especially in *this* world!' She'd looked round, motioned to him to look behind him, took his head in her hands and turned it to the side.

'What do you see?'

He was puzzled. No elephants, no raging fire, nothing out of the ordinary.

'See?' he asked. Thought for a moment. *See? Seeing is what I do, what I am here for, the part of me that I give a damn about. To notice things that go unnoticed, unrecorded. To be one on whom nothing is lost.*

What do I see?

He closed his eyes, that was how you saw things, recollected in tranquillity. Sort of a party trick.

'OK: offices painted the same drab colour as a hospital corridor, mushroom/beige/taupe, nothing on the walls except government-issue photographs of TVA projects and a few badly framed diplomas from indifferent law schools, worn and chipped wooden furniture, pre-war, linoleum floors that smell of oil and industrial polish, disembodied drones like the workers in *Nineteen Eighty-Four,* badly dressed, eyes down, no sounds of laughter, an air of quiet desperation with floating dust motes . . . I could go on, you want more? I got plenty!'

'Please God, no!'

'OK, glad to have satisfied.' There had been a pause. She hadn't said anything, just stood there in front of the elevator, not pushing the Down button.

'Oh. OK then, what do you see?'

'Men,' she'd said.

He looked round, the corridor was bare, the office doors closed.

Rhoda waved her hand, dismissing the emptiness as chimerical. What she saw was a place replete, inhabited by the usual antagonists.

'I can see them, smell them, if it weren't an inappropriate metaphor I would tell you I can taste them, everywhere, every hour, they take up all the space, breathe all the air, and the more I am here and with them, the more I need to enfold and protect myself . . .'

'You mean men are the enemy?'

'No, that's too strong. I dunno, maybe they are? But this is hostile territory and if men are not my enemy they are not my friend either. Generically I mean, I don't mean you!' She took his hand, but it was only a gesture and he rather resented it. 'Come on! I am relentlessly monitored, observed, distrusted and desired. Ignored or stalked. I've been here for six months and no one comes to my office for a chat or to discuss a case – and I'm smarter than most of them, I have to be or I wouldn't be here at all. No one knows who I am or where I come from . . .'

'I don't either! You don't give much away . . .'

'Why should I? Half of them – of you – notice my tits and ass more than me, *me*. And the other half are too shy to leer, but I can feel the impulse as they avert their eyes. I get arms on the arm, arms round the shoulder, pats on the back, which would be on the ass except they know I'd deck them. And when I draw away, draw back, I can hear them thinking *ice maiden, frigid bitch, dyke*. Fun! Hours of fun! I hate most of the pathetic bastards and I don't show it. Shouldn't have told you really, but you're you, I guess . . .'

Ben had never thought about this, at least with regard to women. Negroes, yes: you didn't see a lot of them in government service, unless they were the cleaning staff. It was DC after all. The South. Fancy that! He'd ended up whistling Dixie!

'Do you actually feel discriminated against?'

'How many women lawyers are there in this department?' she'd asked.

'I don't know.'

'How many women lawyers work for the federal government?'

'I don't know that either.'

'Neither do I. So I asked, here and there, everywhere I could think of. And you know what? Either nobody knows, or perhaps they won't tell. But one thing is for sure: hardly any. One day I walked round the building counting. Lawyers only, not associates, administrators or secretaries or cleaners – proper lawyers. Only saw seven, maybe less, with one or two it was hard to tell. And hundreds of men. Lawyer-men.'

'You should be very proud of yourself then, shouldn't you?'

She shrugged. 'I guess so. Maybe. What I actually feel is mildly ashamed.'

Again he'd been puzzled.

'Why is that?'

'I don't know,' she'd said. 'I don't want to talk about it.' She'd stepped forward and pressed the Down button firmly. It came on, yellow, insistent, round and bright as a sun.

In the enclosed space, heading downwards slowly, he always feared that this time, today, might be the one that it stopped, shuddered, gave up the ghost, and he would begin to panic at the very thought, aware that he would soon claw at the doors, then weep, then cry . . . Many days he took the steps, even when it was hot.

'So,' he said, sitting propped on the pillows, daring to raise the question. 'What is it you're so ashamed about? You're not married, are you?' Though that might have been a relief, a solution really.

She laughed and shook her head.

'God forbid! It's just this . . .' She paused, moments of self-revelation unusual for her, and discomfiting. 'I have some money. My grandparents left it to me. And I'll have a lot more, a trust fund that matures when I'm thirty-five. I don't really need to work, not much anyway. I have enough to get on with. And you know what?'

'What?'

'I've hardly spent a penny of it, just keep it in the stock

market, even reinvest the dividends. I always told myself I would wait until something necessitated it, and now . . .'

'Now?'

'It does. You do. I'd like to invest in you, in us. Let them all move to that bungalow place, they'll be fine there! You stay in DC, write, I can stay on in my job. It's perfect. It's what you want.'

It was hardly a disinterested offer, though lightly made, entirely in her interests rather than his. He wasn't tempted, was he?

'Stop it!' he said, cross. 'I'm not for sale!'

'I'm sorry. Let's get up,' she said. 'We can go round to the trattoria for supper, then maybe come back for a nightcap, and who knows what?'

'That'd be nice, I'd like that.' He sat up and walked across the room to the shower, knowing how lucky he was on this enveloping humid evening, knowing too that it could not last, that one thing was about to slop over into another.

'Mere anarchy,' he thought wryly, 'is about to loose itself upon my world. And there's nothing I can do to avoid it.' He wondered for a moment what was so mere about it.

The restaurant was only five minutes away, tucked under a faded awning on a row of shops set just off the road. There was no need to make a reservation. They walked in and sat themselves down at a table in the window. Their usual.

'I love this place.'

She looked round, smiling, waved to the owner behind the cash register. His eyes lit up and an extravagant smile distorted his features.

'Well,' Ben said, 'it's awfully modest, but the food is OK and it's convenient.'

'No, I mean I like it. I like the lack of pretension, the

checked tablecloths, these funny lamps with candles, the old cutlery, these fat glasses and heavy plates . . .'

'Sometimes I wish I could take you somewhere good!'

'You mean fancy, don't you?'

He paused.

'I guess so. Like my father-in-law sometimes takes me to, you know, the 21 Club or one of those places in New York.'

She laughed.

'Do you actually enjoy it?'

He considered for a moment.

'Actually, I hate it! I always feel out of place, as if everyone is patronising me. I suspect that's why Mo – Addie's father – takes me there. He is always glad-handing the waiters, showing me how at ease he is, making me feel a rube.'

'I bet he's not confident at all. You don't need to do that if you are.'

She sounded as if she knew what she was talking about.

'I saw him there once, at one of those places . . .'

'Him? Who do you mean?'

'The Prince of Darkness himself.'

'McCarthy?'

'Who else?'

Ben shuddered.

'I cannot bear the sight and sound of him, it makes me nauseous. He's disgusting! My kids have a name for him, whenever they hear him on television or on the radio.'

'What's that?'

'They chant it together, and go on and on. It makes us all laugh. "JOE! JOE! THE BIG FAT SCHMO! JOE! JOE . . ." You get the idea.'

She laughed. 'The Big Fat Schmo! It's perfect, he would hate that so much, he cannot bear being ridiculed.'

She paused for a moment, reflecting.

'You have no idea how disgusting he is . . .'

'What do you mean?'

'I mean, physically. Repellent, scrofulous, skin like a hairy reptile. You can smell him from a yard away.'

Ben was rather taken aback.

'How do you know this? Don't tell me . . .'

She had the sense not to be offended. After all, she was being provocative.

'I sat next to him at dinner once.'

'At dinner? Where?

'The Colony.'

'Never heard of it. In DC?'

'Fancy new place, decked out to look like a place in Paris. Pathetic, pretentious food. You feel ill for a week after you eat there, all that cream and butter. And they flock to it, all the men in suits who want to make themselves feel important.'

'So, how'd you get there?'

She laughed.

'With a man in a suit, naturally. And at the table next to us was the Senator with a couple of his cronies. You could hardly believe it – the maitre d' was appalled – but he ordered two steaks, well done – charred! – with a bottle of ketchup. It made the whole restaurant stink.'

'Have you met him personally?'

'No, I see him in the street sometimes. Have you?'

Ben winced.

'I have never even seen him, but in his absence he is still one of the major characters in the story of my life – he surrounds and defines it. Like that London smog last year, he makes it hurt to breathe and impossible to see clearly, to find your way . . .'

She shook her head vigorously.

'He's of no real importance, and anyway his day has come and gone. He may be a schmo, fair enough, but he is only a symptom of what is wrong with this country. The witch-hunts were going on long before he was elected – they are why he was elected – and they will go on after he is gone. The problem with America is not McCarthy, it's Americans. The public has an insatiable need for someone to blame!'

'And for someone to fix it!'

Yes, the Senator's days were waning, you could sense that, but the national misery would go on and on.

There was no need to look at the menu, or to order. The usual. Over her spaghetti alle a vongole, emboldened by a couple of glasses of Soave, she risked a return to their post-coital conversation. His recurrent silences, if anything exacerbated by their sexual happiness, had originally been a source of attraction; and then of satisfaction to her. At last a man who wasn't desperately anxious to please, who was complete and replete in himself, didn't send a thank you note after making love, who asked little and demanded nothing.

Of course he had no right to do either, and she felt that the imperative to a reciprocal passivity ought to apply to herself as well. She knew what she was getting into, and for. It came as no surprise, but it couldn't go on.

She reached across the table and took his hand, held it, increased her grip as he tried gently to withdraw.

'It doesn't have be like this,' she said. 'You know it doesn't. Why not choose the life you were made for? And the woman?'

He squeezed her hand back, unresigned to having to hurt her. He couldn't bear being a source of pain to another, it was one of his major weaknesses, and his many prevarications and evasions were simply ways of avoiding an unpleasant emotional confrontation, a scene. When he'd been an undergraduate he'd had a few girlfriends, and it was never he who broke off the relationship, he couldn't bear the tears and recriminations, being the cause of such unhappiness. So he withdrew, behaved badly in measures, and created the conditions under which he would be rejected.

They saw through it, most of them, knew they'd been rejected by someone without the backbone simply to say: *No, sorry but no, it's better this way, anyway it's what I need.* Nothing so difficult about that, was there? He couldn't do it.

She knew this, and was not going to be manipulated by it.

'You have choices, you know? Why not choose freedom and happiness, be a writer, not a crappy lawyer? Why not commit to the delight we have taken in each other? You know it's better, much better!'

'But . . .'

'No buts. We've been through this too many times! Twenty per cent of marriages end in divorce. Children might suffer at first, a little, but children are survivors, they recover.'

She knew nothing of children, had hardly encountered any, had a couple of fugitive nieces in California whom she hadn't seen for years. Encountering a child in a park or museum, or worse in its home, she would shy away as if from contagion, breathe carefully, sidle away . . .

In a foolish moment he had once asked her if she might want children, there was plenty of time, perhaps with the right man. (Not him!)

'There's enough goddamn children already,' she said firmly. 'This whole country is filled with children, little ones *and* big ones, Chucks or Busters, nicknames that make them all sound the same, add a "-y" to every one. And every one of them infantilised and entitled, empty-headed, it's no wonder they are so biddable, easy fodder for anyone who can convince them he is a leader. They are natural pickings for demagogues and Fascists. In no time at all, this country . . .'

'Oh, do shut up,' said Ben, trying to sound light and fond, and failing. 'You have no idea what you are talking about.'

He had turned away.

'I bet your friends call you Benny, admit it, don't they?'

'They don't,' he said firmly.

She shook her head at what was no doubt a lie. She was in danger of losing him.

'The money issues can be handled, you can pay child support, we'd have enough money, plenty really. And can I say one more thing?'

It was incomprehensible, this nonsense. Twenty per cent? Where did she get that figure? Made it up probably . . . He hardly knew any couples who had divorced, one or two who had married too early at Penn, otherwise . . . He thought for a minute. No one, nobody. Divorces happened, he knew of them the way he knew about Bulgaria. But not to Jews. Divorces were for the *goyem*, for the rich, the ostentatiously unfaithful, terminally entitled, the psychotic and psychopathic . . .

It was clear that Ben was pursuing a hostile line of thought, the silence had gone on too long.

'I do love you,' she said. 'I do. Doesn't that count?'

He felt himself thinking, 'For what?' as if she'd made a point that could turn a case; she was good at that, sharp in court, head-turning not merely because she was so striking to look at but also to hear.

She'd been determined to remain calm and loving, knew how easily he could slide away, but she was drinking more than she was eating, and could hear her tone morph into the stridency that embarrassed her and made him cringe.

'It's toxic,' he said. 'Polluted.'

She stood up abruptly, shaking the table, the glasses wobbled but settled down.

'*Toxic? Polluted?* How dare you!'

He didn't mean that, it, her, them. It was useless to explain.

'For someone so smart,' she said bitterly, 'you're as emotionally stupid as a chimpanzee. Worse!'

He stared into his glass, drank it down.

'See you around,' she said, turning her back on him, not abruptly but with a studied calm that suggested just how furious she was.

Back in his apartment, earlier than expected, as comprehensively shaken as the martini before him, iced, sour with onions, he sat down at the kitchen table to write a letter on his yellow legal stationery. The paper directed him, slowed his breathing, helped him to calm down, to try to think straight, marshal his arguments, be brief.

He hoped – no, he rather assumed – that she'd respond to the yellow pages and the fine lines in the same way he did. Pavlovian, the reverse of Pavlovian. See a legal pad and you stopped slobbering.

> Darling,
> I am so sorry, so sorry indeed that I hardly know what to say.
> We've been through this, and I don't see why it is necessary to go through it again. I won't.

I feel desolate that my shorthand reference to toxicity and pollution might be taken, in any way, as a metaphor that defines or affects us. We care for each other, deeply.

But, of course, it does. The toxicity and pollution are what we breathe, and what fails to sustain us, the shit in the air and on the streets. I have no future here, we both know that, and so we have no future together. If I had any faith in the organ or the metaphor I would say it breaks my heart.

But Order 10450 was the final straw. They've given themselves the power to persecute anyone and anybody, not just for being a Red – they were on that road already (and I was, and in my heart I still am) – but now anyone who seems to their beetle gaze morally compromised, or dangerous. Like me. May they rot in hell!

I can't live like this, and if the air in Huntington is not uncontaminated it is not befouled like it is here in DC. I have a family, and I have obligations to them, to locate them in some space that is not toxic for us all, to protect the love that I have for them. For the children, of course. And for Addie? She is my wife, the mother of my children, I have chosen her and she me.

And so, so. So sorry, so desperately sorry to hurt you. But this shouldn't go on, should it? It's been too wonderful, but it has to stop sometime.

Love,

Ben

He put the pen down, finished his martini, chewed the onions carefully so that the sour taste filled his mouth. He'd done version after version, and in the end it sounded that little bit equivocal. Well, why shouldn't it? *He* was. The first draft had 'can't go on' rather than the later 'shouldn't'. He had added the 'Love' at the end, reluctantly. It would have seemed unbearably cold otherwise. But surely she would get the message? He went to bed without brushing his teeth.

In the morning, groggy with sleeplessness, head throbbing, he arrived at the office half an hour early, before she would get in, and slipped the note under her door. That was all very well, but in twenty-five minutes she would enter her office across the hall, read the note, ignore him and his entire geographical location studiedly and keep clear of him for as much of the day as was possible, a strategy it was impossible to sustain. But what else could he have done? At least this way she could be allowed to end it once and for all.

It wasn't *his* attractiveness that had drawn them together first for corridor chats, shared cigarettes in his office or sometimes (which was more intimate) hers, then coffee, then walks and long talks, then, well, it was inevitable. If it hadn't have been him, it would have been one of the others.

Rhoda made a striking first impression, there were few enough women lawyers in the department, none so chic, so memorable. Unlike the many secretaries she didn't wear dresses that looked like advertisements for flower shops, was slim and free enough to dispense with a girdle. She loathed them, the slick sweaty pressing confinement, the sense of being packaged. 'My pussy has a right to breathe!' she said to him, assuming it would shock, pleased that it didn't. He loved that. If it had been allowed at work, she would have dressed much like the men, in dark suits and cotton shirts. Maybe even a tie. She sometimes went to parties dressed like that, which caused some comment, and insinuation that she was a lesbian, especially from the many men whose advances were summarily dismissed, hardly even noticed. *Oh, were you flirting with me? Is that what it was?*

Ben got lucky, his office was opposite hers, he saw her every coming and going. She saw his. And if he wasn't Rock Hudson he was amiable and bright and funny, and his tongue wasn't hanging out. Things progressed slowly but inexorably, until one day, over hoagies on a park bench, she tried to draw back from what was inevitable.

'Look,' she said, taking his arm, displacing a few onions and shreds of lettuce, 'you need to know I don't fool around with married men.'

'Thank God for that!' he said. 'Neither do I.' He started to giggle, and was immediately encouraged by her protracted guffaw – perhaps she was about to change her policy?

'Where'd you say you're from?'

'Philadelphia!' She knew that, he was miffed that she'd forgotten.

'I thought so. You've eaten too many of those cheesy steaks! That's one of the oldest lines in the book!'

'Was it? How mortifying! I thought I was making it up!'

'You and every guy who's ever come on to me . . .'

'That would be a lot?'

'Look at me! Buckets full!'

And then they were in bed, that very evening, and for months after when they could, resolved to be careful, to make things last, knowing they could not, would not. Did not.

He needed to write a letter to Addie, an extra big one, packed with lies, and evasions, false heartiness and true concern. Becca had been ill, he could start with that.

Addie dear,

Two letters! I'm quite overwhelmed, and touched, and apprehensive about meeting the high standards you have set. To be frank, it's been difficult here. It's not just the State Department that is at risk, it gets in the news, but the rest of us are under surveillance as well. Arnold W. finally got a position with a firm in Maryland, small and leftist and utterly inconsequential. Pays a pittance. You know Betsy left him? She took the boys, couldn't stand the heat any more. He's utterly desolate.

The game has changed, now all they have to do is claim you are morally unfit, and they have no need to specify how or why. I am morally unfit by their standards, and proud of it. But it is an insidious business and I wonder how we can tell the children why we are moving? Jake is already on edge, and the little one is catching his anxiety. She tends to somatise, her sore throat is the result of this.

He put the pen down, not wearily but firmly, as if combatting some enemy. *Let's not pretend.* The letter oozed insincerity – that was to be expected, it was inevitable – but it was the wrong sort, it was crap, it pained him to re-read it. Addie would see through it, most of it anyway, and though it was shadowed by Rhoda she would, please God, be imperceptible. He crumpled the yellow page into a ball, tightened it, closed one eye and aimed for the wastepaper basket on the other side of the room, missed. Crumpled another sheet, a clean new one, tightened and rounded the ball, squinted again, cocked his wrist as if for a free throw, tossed the paper delicately and precisely. Missed again. Tried again, missed again, gave up.

Dear Addie –
I feel a bit embarrassed, owing you two letters, to be writing only this note, because I am just off to the office and things are hotting up. I spend hour after hour meeting folks – friends and colleagues, yup, but also the few (relatively) sympathetic administrators, trying to get clear how best to make my escape.

I guess we will have to hammer out details when I come. Only two weeks now! Perhaps the Silbers' is too soon, but we have to settle on something. I cannot see a way round Huntington, sorry, I wish I could. I need to make some money after I pass the Bar and Huntington will be best. We have quite a lot of contacts already, more through Maurice and Frankie – and I can join things and meet new people: the Arts Council, tennis club, even the *shul*. Temple Beth El, is it, the one on Park Avenue? Mind you, half the congregation will be lawyers.

I feel terrible asking your father for a few more sandwiches for the months that I will need to study. I have no idea how he can afford it.

Sorry to be so business-like. I feel swamped, and emotionally clogged. You'll get more and better from me when I get there. Can't wait!

Glad Becks is better, and Jake is OK. I am concerned at how they are going to respond to moving, but we'll just say it is a great new opportunity for us all. Exciting! Kids hate change, but they accommodate it easily enough in time. You and I will too. DC palls. It stinks.

Love, as ever,

Ben

He addressed an envelope using his typewriter: Adele Grossman, Harbor Heights Park, Lane L, Huntington, NY. He liked that, so rural and unimaginative, as if it were the best that some hick Long Island town board could think of. L for what? *Luck* (Bad). Of course there were Lachrymose, Laughable, Loser, Lunatic . . .

He was satisfied with the tone of the letter, best to keep things cool, though their emotional carpets were bulging with swept-under issues. There wasn't much choice really, but to write: the phone in the bungalow right there in the middle of the living room, any conversation could be heard round the house. Anyway, Addie was a quick correspondent and her return letters were likely enough to set an agenda, and extend the process of making choices and decisions.

In emotionally demanding times, it was his invariable habit to get down to work, review case law, begin constructing arguments, lose himself in the minutiae that he used to find stimulating. But, now, why? He was leaving, about to resign before the forces of darkness banged on his door to fire him for his multiple personality and political disorders. The cases were no longer his – never had been really – and, from the increasing distance suggested by his escape, it was impossible to give a damn.

He brought his books to the office, best to lock the door, lean back in his office chair and read. He had abandoned Dickens, that little rat, and returned to Proust, to a second and even more satisfying reading of *À la recherche du temps perdu*. Three weeks to wallow in the luxurious prose, to lose himself amongst his aristocratic friends.

When Rhoda first sighted him opening his much thumbed copy of *Swann's Way*, she teased him about swanking it, trying to impress her, only she wasn't that sort of girl. She didn't give a damn about Proust, never read a word, nor did she care about Ben's other heroes, about Joyce or Eliot, Frost or Wallace Stevens. *Modernism*. She sneered.

'If you want to be so modern, why not read what is exciting today, not yesterday? You're studious, not engaged, you're not excited by new voices!'

He was rather hurt by this, apparently disadvantaged by being so East Coast. She'd been at college in San Francisco, majoring in English before going to Stanford Law, and she'd immersed herself in the new poets. *Read these,* she'd insisted, placing a handful of pamphlets and little paperbacks aggressively before him. Kenneth Rexroth he'd heard of, not most of the others. Sloppy rubbish, most of it.

He said so. 'I read an article in the *New York Times* about this, didn't I? Maybe last year. Beatniks, was it?'

'Beatniks! Some fatuous journalist bigging himself up by inventing a name. There are no Beatniks! Never were, never will be.'

'That's a relief then,' said Ben.

'Why?' she asked.

'There's enough bullshit in the world already.'

4

On his sixty-second birthday Poppa Maurice didn't have a fall. He insisted on that. Though they had found him on the garage floor, his forehead bloodied, half-conscious and only barely able to stand, he said that he had tripped over a wire – *what wire? where?* – and banged his head. What he had was an *accident,* a category that he approved of. Men had accidents, not falls – old people had those. He was a man not an old person. All men need is a band aid, four aspirins and a glass of water, and a little rest, then they are fine.

He wasn't, and he knew it, and Perle suspected it. She'd discovered the phial of pills tucked behind the socks in Maurice's dresser. Stupid hiding place! Who put the socks in there anyway? She made a note of the contents and immediately rang Cousin Hattie's son Barry the Doctor, an internist in Brooklyn, who was always happy to allay her anxiety. Anxiety was his specialty. There was a lot of it about, he prescribed for it whenever anyone asked, dispensed more Miltown than penicillin, and it did more good. Informed about the pills, he confirmed that Maurice had a treatable heart condition. Perle followed Barry's sage counsel and kept her own. And as ever, kept an eye out, both eyes.

For the last three and a half years Maurice had been making regular visits to Beth Israel in the city, where his atrial fibrillation was monitored. With medication and adequate exercise, his condition had not worsened, and his cardiologist continued to prophesy, if not to guarantee, a long life. It might, he said, be good at least to cut back on the smoking. Though there was no conclusive evidence that it was bad for you, his clinical experience left him in no doubt that it was. Whether this was related to, or exacerbated, Maurice's recurrent bouts of dizziness was unclear. But what was there to lose?

Cigarettes, that's what. Maurice made his promises, he was a first-class promiser, and continued to smoke a pack and a half a day. That wasn't so bad; it might easily have been two packs, it was when he was younger, when he went to clubs and speakeasies, so that saved ten cigarettes a day right away, 3,650 a year. That must be good for you.

Perle and Addie had planned a party to celebrate his birthday, wondered now whether to call round and cancel, say that Maurice had a headache, or the flu, something or other. Perle knew this would be wise, but Maurice had no need of wisdom, he wanted a party. His party, in his honour, though what honour accrued from a *farkakte* birthday of a man of sixty-two was unclear. But company, good food, a few beers, being the centre of attention, some laughs, some smutty jokes about not being so young any more (hard enough to get up, much less get it up): it was the stuff of life, he adored it as much as Perle would have hated it.

But by the mid-afternoon he was still fast asleep, unusual for him and rather a worrying sign. Might he have a concussion? Perle called Barry on the phone, and got a return call when he was between patients, explained the situation.

'Could be,' Barry said, without much concern. 'Did he have double vision? Dizziness? A bad headache?'

No and no, maybe a little.

'Well, tell you what, when he gets up make sure he is steady on his feet, test his memory – ask him questions about baseball, maybe – check his vision, see if the headache is any worse. If it's all OK it's just a bump, nothing to worry about . . .'

'Baseball, what do I know from baseball?'

'Ask the boy, he'll know. And call me if anything still seems amiss, I can get him admitted to Huntington Hospital.'

Gratefully Perle sent love to his family, hung up and sought out Jake. Best not to alarm the boy – what did he know from a concussion? – so she just asked, in an innocent voice, to be told some things about the Yankees, that was Poppa's team, wasn't it?

Jake looked puzzled.

'What things, Granny?'

'Anything. I don't know. When do they play?'

Jake looked excited. 'Tonight! There's a great home game tonight, it's Whitey Ford against Early Wynn, a real pitcher's duel.'

Perle wrote this down carefully, unsure what an early win might consist of.

'Can we have the TV on even if it's the party?' the boy asked eagerly.

Now there was an idea! If it was such a big-shot game, Maurice would be sad to miss it, and perhaps it would be adequate compensation for the cancellation of the party. Party schmarty, they could always reschedule it at short notice, nobody went anywhere in the summer, most sat around wishing for the phone to ring, maybe a little action.

Yes, that was right. As Jake looked on with big eyes, she

rang Martha, Momshe, Michelle – such a lot of Ms, she'd never noticed! – a couple of the other wives, to say that Morrie was feeling ill – nothing to worry about! – and that they would have to reschedule.

When Addie and Becca got home from town, Perle told them about the accident and that she had cancelled the party. Addie looked relieved, remembered herself, and asked after her father.

'He'll be fine,' said Perle. 'He's having a nap.'

The nap had already lasted three hours, which was not a good sign, though when she went to the bedroom, she found Maurice sitting on the side of the bed wearily.

'You're up? That's good. How are you feeling?' She stooped to put an ice pack against the growing bump – there would be a real bruise in a day or two – and took his hand, adjusted it to hold the pack firmly on his forehead.

How was he feeling? He was wondering that himself. Paused to consider, took a quick organic inventory. Put a finger gingerly on the Band-Aid on his forehead.

'I'm not used to sleeping in the afternoon . . . Know what, it makes you feel worse!'

'How worse?'

'Groggy, like you can't wake up. Not refreshed, more tired.' He didn't mention the throbbing headache, no need to cause alarm, he could take some more aspirins once he got rid of Perle.

'Can I ask you some questions?'

It was always a bad sign when Perle asked questions.

'Sure, but I want to get up, have a shower, might perk me up . . .'

She put three fingers in front of her face. She'd read that in a magazine.

'How many fingers?'

'What?' He hadn't read the magazine. Was she worried she'd lost a finger? Why? He looked for signs of blood, or maybe a tell-tale stump.

'No need to worry,' he said with a laugh. 'You haven't lost any.'

'How many!'

'Three.' He started to get up, but she placed a hand on his shoulder to restrain him briefly.

'When are the Yankees playing?'

Now this really was alarming. Perle might well have misplaced a finger or two, but to evince an interest in the Yanks was a sign of something mentally amiss. He peered at her intently.

'I think it's you we need to worry about,' he said.

'Please. Maurice. Just answer the question, and one or two more, then I will know you're all right . . .'

'Tonight.'

'Who's the pitcher?'

The pitcher? Who's pitching?

'Whitey Ford.'

'Who else?'

Else?

'Early Wynn.'

She took her hand from his shoulder and bent over to kiss his forehead, which was sufficiently unusual to confirm that she was seriously disturbed.

She laughed, full of relief. (*Very* seriously disturbed.)

'Well,' she said. 'I have some good news and some bad news.' She loved that phrase, and the bad news was always her favourite, the headline leader.

He knew how to play this one. 'Start with the bad.'

'I talked to the doctor – you know Barry from Brooklyn Heights? – and he said you might have a concussion, but I know you don't because you don't have the symptoms. But he said it would be best to cancel the party, so I have. Nobody minds, they all send love, and we will reschedule . . .'

He tried to summon some anger, irritation even, but in truth he was relieved. The fall had shaken him up, and the idea of drinking and schmoozing didn't appeal a bit.

'You should have consulted me. It's up to me.'

'No, it isn't! And anyhow, I didn't know how long you would sleep.'

He was unwilling to acknowledge the good sense of this, but ceased to complain. 'And, *nu*, the good news?'

'You can watch your fancy-pants game with Jake, Addie will let him stay up. It starts at eight.'

Fancy pants was a good name for the Yankees. He smiled, he loved those pinstripes, made them look like big businessmen at work. And they were, the best in the business.

He got up, pressed Perle's hand and headed for the shower.

Please God, please, she thought. *Please, he doesn't have another fall.*

She'd made a birthday dinner for him, his favourite: steak cooked well done – he didn't put ketchup on it, like Frankie, just A1 sauce – baked potato, corn on the cob, a wedge of iceberg lettuce with Russian dressing, some pickles. He declined a beer, which was unusual, but ate a large slice of birthday cake. A good appetite! A good sign!

He and Jake arrived at the TV just before eight, twisted the aerial so that the interference wasn't too bad, loaded bowls of popcorn and pretzels, opened a real beer for Poppa, you can't have baseball without beer, and for Jake root beer because you got to *root, root, root* for the home team, only the Senators were his real team. Poppa knew that, he didn't mind.

Jake's secret was that he had another home team, not the

Yankees – Ben said they looked like Republicans! – but the Dodgers. Ben said the Dodgers were real people. It wasn't clear what that meant. Sort of like real workers, Ben explained. It wasn't clear what that meant either. But both of them liked that the Dodgers had Negro players, and the Yankees didn't have any. They were prejudiced.

Jake had asked Poppa about this.

'It's not prejudice,' he said. 'They're just not ready yet. There's one or two good Negroes under consideration. One's a catcher, he can come in after Yogi. We just have to be patient.'

Ben had been listening.

'That's what they say about prejudice everywhere, don't you worry if you have no civil rights or human dignity, just be patient! Morrie, you should know better!'

Morrie knew better, better than to be drawn on such a subject. What he cared about, most, was winning. Of course it would be good if Negroes had civil rights, even better if one of them could hit .300 and thirty home runs for the Yanks. Now that'd be civil rights, in spades!

'I know, I know,' he said, 'all things come in time.'

They'd argued about the subject before. Maurice was . . . what word could Ben use to describe him? A bigot? Too strong, even with the *Schwarze* business. Maurice came from a culture that did not deal with the coloured, it employed them; he never met one socially. Negroes were coming, there was no doubt about that, but like the Yankees, Maurice was prepared to wait for the good ones. Not many of them about.

In the meantime, the all-white Yankees in the pinstripes were doing just fine. By the bottom of the sixth, Jake was asleep in his chair and Maurice felt his eyes closing too. The Yanks had just gone ahead 4–0, and Whitey was pitching up a storm, game over really, they didn't blow leads like that, that was why they had won exactly twice as many games as they'd lost. 'A win percentage of .667,' said Jake, who loved baseball statistics, could quote them not merely about modern players but about Ty Cobb (*lifetime average .366: Best ever!*), Rogers Hornsby (*batted .424 in 1924: Highest ever!*), *Cy Young* (*won 511 games: Most ever!*). Maurice was very proud of the boy. What a memory!

One moment Maurice was watching Phil Rizzuto's double knock in the fourth run, then he was being shaken gently by the shoulder. The TV had been turned off. Jake was standing up, groggy and ready for bed, while Addie looked at her father with concern in her eyes.

'Dad, you were sleeping.'

'Why not? Been a long day, just a bit tired.' He stood up, stretched and yawned. 'Let's turn it off and turn in.' His head was throbbing insistently, though Perle had renewed the ice pack several times.

Addie helped him from the rocking chair. He didn't resist.

He slept late the next morning, the sleep of the dead, no dreams, no movement, not even getting up for a pee. Lying beside him, sleeping only intermittently, Perle would occasionally shake him by the shoulder, wipe his brow with a washcloth, insist he take a sip of water, enquire if he wanted the ice pack. He shook his head irritably and a moment later was unconscious once more. She woke him up regularly, that's what you were supposed to do.

When he hadn't woken by ten, she rang the doctor again and was advised to wake Maurice, get him dressed and take him immediately to the ER at Huntington Hospital.

'Do I need to call an ambulance?' she asked.

'Not if he's awake and ambulatory.'

'He is, but he's not right, not himself.'

'Get him there this morning.'

Maurice resisted going, though the combined forces of Addie and Perle, and the hovering children, were adequate persuasion. He got showered, took four aspirins, had a quick shave. The smoothing of the lather on his face – he didn't use one of those new-fangled pressure cans – was soothing, and he was careful, feeling as ill as he did, not to cut himself. His only concession to modernity was that he had abandoned his old straight razor in favour of the new Gillette super-speed, with a double-edged disposable blade, which was almost as efficient, and harder to cut yourself with. The children loved watching him mixing the lather, putting it on, taking it off with smooth and precise strokes (not so smooth or precise today). And after, he would wash his face, put a hot cloth on it, then tip the bottle of Old Spice into his hand, rub his palms together and put it on his face and neck, going 'BRRRR!' and shaking his head to make them laugh.

Then he would put a few dabs of the shaving cream on their faces: they held their heads right back, stood still looking at the ceiling, closed their eyes.

'Don't move now!' Poppa would say seriously, and then he would draw the side of his Diners Club card down their cheeks, removing the lather. 'Eyes closed!' They screwed their little faces up, thrilled and frightened as the card scraped gently across their cheeks. Before they opened their eyes he would put some of the lather on his razor, to show them, before offering the bottle of Old Spice. They loved the smell, took some of the aftershave in their hands, put it on their faces – BRRRR! – shaking their heads.

When Addie smelled them, she would grab hold of Becca, laughing and lifting her up, sniffing her neck greedily, tickling her. 'You smell like Natalie Wood!' she'd say. Becca liked that, Natalie Wood was a Star, that was even what her movie was called, her picture was on front of the Shore Movie Theatre on Wall Street. Becca had bangs just like her, she looked like her and she smelled like her too!

Their father was a shaving bore. He'd bought a Remington electric and loved how much simpler shaving had become, faster too. No fun for the kids there, nor would he use aftershave of any kind. He felt it made men smell like tarts, but wouldn't have said so to Becca or Jake, nor to Maurice or Frankie, both of whom did.

Maurice was soon in the car, with Addie behind the steering wheel, the kids staying with Perle, who was torn between bringing them along to the hospital – *no, not that* – and the fact that Addie would then have to drive Maurice on her own. *Please God, she doesn't get lost!* She issued a set of instructions, wrote down what Barry the Doctor had said and got a promise that Addie would ring from the payphone as soon as Morrie got out, though it was only a ten-minute trip back to the bungalow.

'Don't worry so,' Maurice said. 'We'll be home in a jiffy, it's no big deal.'

It wasn't. It was a disaster. Not the concussion, not *that* – he was sure he had one, he'd had them before, got conked on the noggin more than once playing ball, saw double for a week, could hardly stand up, next week he was behind the plate again as if nothing had happened. Occupational hazard, nothing to worry about. But what there was to worry about was that he didn't have a week this time, he wasn't on holiday, had been going to the city most days and knew that the coming few days were going to be . . . what was the word, something not too dramatic? Not *important*. Not *crucial*. Maybe, just maybe, the right word was *critical,* as a heart attack is critical?

He shook his head, it hurt. Nah, he'd been in plenty of jams before, knew the ropes, always came out smelling of roses and dollar bills. He'd been expecting this one. So, they wanted to raise the prices, cut his margins, take a bit of the business? What did he expect? It was amazing, a real tribute to his . . . he hesitated to think of it as genius, no, his smarts, that was the sandlot word.

Molly and Sol had found him out early, well before the war. The off-the-books racket, making and selling clothes on his own. They summoned him to a meeting. *You can't serve two masters, you can't steal part of the business!* They had a good mind to fire him.

'Go ahead,' said Maurice. 'Silly thing to do. If you want to get on a high horse, remember it hurts if you fall off . . .'

Sol had glared at him. He was in his sixties, the business was declining, large manufacturing firms could undersell him, and his clothes no longer looked as fresh and modern as, say . . . Maurice's. Maurice had the unmitigated gall, even, to use some of his boss's designers (who thought Sol and Molly behind the times) to make snazzy new clothes, and he then used some of their own fabricators to make them up! Talk about chutzpah!

All off the books, all cash. Maurice bought his materials from a reliable guy called Sal in Little Italy, near the Bowery, and had them made into cheap but fashionable lines by ladies who worked from home and were paid in cash. When he sold the garments on, it was all cash as well. To all intents and purposes, his little sideline was invisible – it was hardly a big business, netted him maybe $2,000 in a good year.

He was vulnerable, of course. Someone might rat him out to the IRS, but it would be hard to prove much. Even Sol and Molly could, they were that mad, but what did they have to gain by ruining him? He was their best salesman, brought in more than the schleppers combined, without him they were *farkakte*, and they knew it.

He'd abandoned a potential career as a lawyer, all the tedium of having to pass the Bar (instead of going into one), hanging out a shingle, settling down to the stultifying details of closings and divorces, for the relatively easy life of the rag trade. He was a natural salesman, people basked in his warmth – Morrie, he was called, fondly.

A salesman's number one product is himself. And most have no natural geniality, shake hands too firmly, grimace instead of smiling, speak in oleaginous tones. And in their eyes the tell-tale desperation. They treat you as if you were an old friend and you're not. You're a potential customer and if you're not buying their product it's because you're not buying them.

Sometimes, sitting on the B train that took him downtown to his office, he would muse about sales pitches, coups of a sort no one but he would have contemplated. *And this, Mrs Eskimo – may I call you Mrs E? – is just the right air-conditioner for your igloo! Don't you worry about the cold air coming out, it's cold in there already. But this is conditioned air, it is purified and cleansed, it will protect your children from germs and infections!*

He needed his employers, and they needed him. His extra off-the-books income bought the bungalow, the Caddies, the sandwiches, Frankie's new office, Addie and Ben's furniture and school tuition for the children. And now he was going to have to support them for months while Ben studied for the Bar.

Fine, he could do that, was already putting some money away. Then one day he got the call. It was Salvatore.

'Morrie! How ya doin', pal?'

He was always 'pal' when something was amiss.

'Hey, Sal, what's up?'

It seemed there was a bit of a problem. Sal's suppliers were letting him down, raising their prices, it was highway robbery!

Maurice was very sorry indeed to hear it.

'*Nu*?' Sal knew from '*nu*' the way Maurice knew from *Pisan*.

'Long and short of it, Morrie, prices gotta go up . . .'

'Yeah, yeah. How much?'

'Double. Starting now, starting the money you owe me already. Double it.'

He'd been expecting it for years, planned for it: but not for this catastrophic rise. What can you do? You do business with the devil, he will bite your ass, keep biting it, and if you don't pay he drags you down. And your family. They'd suckered him with artificially low prices, maybe 25 per cent less than anywhere else, good credit terms, some nice food and booze, offered a girl here and there.

They weren't a goodwill shop, it had to end. He'd already had a few modest price rises, knowing them to be a foretaste of something bigger to come, as the ground war against the Japs had presaged the big bombs. He'd planned for that, maybe up by 50 per cent. So now he would be paying more than if he took his business elsewhere, and he knew better than even to think of that. They had him over a barrel, and if they decided to roll it, that'd be that. He'd rather be in the hands of the IRS, he'd run rings round them. But these guys?

'I think we need to talk about this, Sal. I haven't planned for it. I'll come see you next week, work something out.'

'Always love seeing you, Morrie, we'll go out, have a nice lunch at Mama Leone's. On me. It'll be swell to see ya.'

He'd spent the time in his garage since then, working out the figures, pretending he was fixing an iron that was on the fritz. Funny, Fritz was Frankie's nickname, brought it back from the war, at first Maurice hated it, Fritzes were Nazis. But somehow it stuck, though Perle would never use it.

Nothing lasts forever, he knew that, he'd been prudent, salted away a few bucks, could do with less income. But not just now. He could probably wheedle a week's respite out of Sal, who was a good enough guy until you crossed him. Tell him about the visit to the Emergency Room, put him off for a week or so, until the concussion eased.

But the heart condition wasn't going to ease, he wouldn't be able to work so hard, hustle for business – for two businesses; he would have to take it easy. Easier. But not yet. Next year maybe. Or maybe not. If he quit Sol and Molly's, they would go under, couldn't carry on without him; if he quit his sideline, Salvatore would be angry. Maybe not shoot-you-in-the-eye and rape-your-daughter angry, but (a phrase he used occasionally) 'very disappointed'.

Maurice had no desire to find out what this actually meant, or entailed – surely he was not indentured to Sal, he could retire, same as normal human beings, especially those with heart conditions? He was small beer, a small fish, no big deal. He always ironically described himself as 'a small man', by which he meant *not* a small man, but just now he felt one. Surely he'd earned some rest?

Mr Smarty Pants, Perle called him; she knew the score. But it hadn't stopped her taking the money and running the family. She knew they were compromised, like him she was used to it, had learned to cast a blind eye and shrug a shoulder, but the shrugged shoulder was also the one she'd been looking over all these years, and it was starting to hurt. Maybe she'd get to retire, too.

No one would have called Maurice an ironist. Salesmen can't afford to be. But this particular irony was not lost on him, not for one second: *Sal was doing to him what he had been doing to his own customers for thirty years.* Get them hooked, reel them in, make them dependent, raise the prices. What was that expression about being hoisted? He was! Did he deserve to be? No, not at all, no way, never. It was an outrage!

Of course it wasn't working, couldn't work, God knows why he thought it might, as if sending Rhoda that letter had resolved their problem, rather than simply delayed any resolution. In fact, made it more difficult. It was insulting, as if an emotional problem could be settled with a letter! They saw each other willy-nilly, coming into the building, in the hallways, in the elevator, nodded in what was intended to be a neutral manner to avoid making colleagues curious, but hardly exchanged a word.

It was horrible. The day after Ben's special delivery, he got a knock on the door, not aggressive, curiously muted, a couple of light taps, intimate even.

'Come in,' he said.

It was Rhoda. She stepped inside, closed the door, leant her back against it.

'Let's stop this,' she said. 'We need to talk.'

'You're right. But not now, not here.' She crossed to his desk and took his arm, and he defended himself from the reflex of pulling away, or of taking hers in his turn. It was impossible to know what to do, and how to do it.

'Why don't you come round tonight after work? I'll make something simple, open a bottle of something nice and let's see where all this leaves us . . .'

Us? Surely the point of his sad letter – pathetic, really, how do people write such things? – was that there is no Us, no longer can be an Us. And as soon as he thought this, he knew it was wrong, and mean-spirited, and anyway unrealistic. Of course there was and is an Us, there always is with former lovers and ex-friends, we do not erase intimacy, and when it morphs into something less intimate, it is nonetheless ineradicable. Something like that?

He was thinking like a writer, how to say things, find the right words, and had frozen as if some potency in her touch had rendered him speechless. What was he to say, save 'Give me a moment to think, I don't quite know what to say.'

He said it.

She was curiously calm, didn't press his arm, kept a carefully calibrated distance, did not presume upon their intimacy. Former intimacy perhaps? It was hard to tell what she might have been thinking.

'Come tonight at seven, you'll have collected yourself by then. You know my address, don't you?'

He did, though he had never been there, and he got a bit confused about Washington neighbourhoods, with all those indistinguishably named streets. He'd written her address in code in a pocket diary, if he could only find the diary and remember the code. Somewhere in Georgetown, but you couldn't tell if it was fancy. Not like Park Avenue, grand-sounding.

She'd been curiously reticent about inviting him – it was obvious they should go to her place for their occasional trysts, she lived alone – but she never suggested it. Not clear why not, nor did he ask her, hadn't the right. It was up to her to shovel the dirt over the details of her private life, so they had shared the occasional hours at modest hotels a discreet distance from their offices. She always insisted on paying, and after a while he gave up objecting, skimmed some of Morrie's cash, bought the lunches and dinners, kept his end up, just.

What was there to say, after all? A clean break was impossible, not with them working together as they did, might as well face a sloppy one. It broke every lawyerly bone in his body to acknowledge the sheer messiness of what he had gotten into, what he had created, but there you are. Not an open and shut case, there aren't many of them.

'OK,' he said. 'I'll see you later.'

After she turned and closed the door, he took a moment to regain not so much equilibrium as the power of locomotion itself. *Rooted to the spot* was the phrase that came to mind, though he rejected it fastidiously, and just stood there until his legs and brain reconnected, which they eventually did sufficiently for him to return to his desk and slump into a chair that was hardly designed for slumping. It was no wonder he had backache by the end of every day, had to take three aspirins to deal with the pain, resolved to buy a leather desk chair and bring it to the office, but it would have been frowned on as an indulgence. By himself as much as anyone. He was a wooden chair worker, he wasn't there to lounge about.

He knew very little about Georgetown, though it was only a couple of miles away, twenty-five minutes by streetcar, with one change, but itself as foreign as if another country, England perhaps, antique, genteel.

He smiled to himself, as the car swayed, at the vapid metaphor of classiness – England was a post-war dump, he knew that. But his knowledge of the most desirable borough of DC was equally vague and probably equally cliché-ridden. Rich people lived in Georgetown, old money in old houses, diplomats, senior members of the government, businessmen who looked like aristocrats and who frequented DC's gentlemen's clubs. He paused to think, but couldn't name any of them. Places where you were discreetly greeted at the door, deferred to in hushed tones, ushered upstairs to dining rooms, libraries, lounges with leather chairs . . .

God, it was pathetic, this inward reel of received ideas and clichés, but anything was better than thinking about the visit with Rhoda, now only ten minutes in the future. Five minutes. A juddering clanking stop and they were there. It would take him a few minutes to walk to her address, but he'd spin it out, he was early, as usual. Have a little walk, compose himself, gawp at the beautiful restraint of the federal architecture, stately, imposing, unenterable. And Rhoda lived in one of them! He'd known it, just – she once mentioned not Georgetown but the street on which she lived, and he had hurried to look it up on a map when they parted. Georgetown! Apartments were in short supply there, rents were astronomical in the best streets, and hers was on one of them. Her salary would hardly have covered the monthly outgoings.

The house was set off the street, with a tiny well-tended front garden full of shrubs, no flowers, and a set of steps up to the door. There was only one doorbell, which was odd, and he pressed it gingerly. A faint bell sounded inside, and he waited impatiently, certain that she was dragging it out, standing on the other side of the door counting to twenty.

She smiled as she opened the door, said nothing, stepped side, let him in, almost reprehensibly at ease, dressed casually in navy slacks and a rust-coloured angora sweater, no make-up, no scene setting, almost as if she hadn't been expecting him. She was that artful. Her raven hair, usually strand-for-strand perfect at work, had been swept back with her fingers after her shower, the effect loose, slightly louche. Crimson toenails proclaimed that her feet were bare, and perhaps something else. What? That she was casual and relaxed? Couldn't be bothered with shoes? Went with bare feet at home? Was offering herself with this partial disclosure, partial nakedness? She had lovely feet, he caressed them sometimes. Toes, nail polish, nudity. He made a resolution to transfer these observations to his pocket notebook, might be something there to use.

She was studiedly at ease. When she was tense, which was most of the time at the office, her jaw tightened and gave a tiny recurrent twitch that made him want to rub her shoulders and whisper reassuring words. No sign of that, no. Surely it was some sort of an act, it was inappropriate not to be anxious. Inhuman almost. He was.

Had there been music playing in the living room and candles glittering suggestively, a set table with dim lights and smells of food and perfume, he would have bolted. As it was, the room offered sanctuary, and he took it, removing his overcoat and hat, which she took and hung in the closet next to the entrance, in a manner both formal and incipiently friendly.

The living room was large and rectangular, the inner hallway leading to a set of steps along the right-hand side. The room surprised him, though he tried not to show it. He had expected something showy, rich, ornamental. Antique furniture, rosewood and walnut, Georgian, English. Things that proclaim things. Instead there were white leather chairs and a sofa, with steel legs, a coffee table and side table in glass and chrome, a shaggy white rug. And paintings. Paintings of a sort that he had seen in magazines, and sometimes in museums. He had no idea if their abstract exuberance was expensive or not, nor who the artists might be. Delighted to have a chance not to talk, he walked across the room, towards a large kitchen with an open double doorway revealing a dining table and chairs, stopped and looked intently at the picture above the white sofa, its swirling reds, oranges and greens, the half-revealed unexpected figuration of several nude figures, angular and contorted. It looked like a description of a state of mind, or at least as if it was supposed to look like a description of a state of mind. He was unsure if it worked, though the more he looked at it the more he felt some subtle kinship, almost as if she had placed it there to provoke him into such identification. He smirked to himself. What a narcissist I am, he thought, with a hint of pride and a touch of shame.

Rhoda had gone into the kitchen, opened a bottle of white wine and poured it into two glasses. Italian probably, she knew about such things, had tried to teach him, just a little. Soave Classico, something like that? He couldn't remember the names or, hardly, distinguish the tastes. But he sure enough needed a drink and took an ungentlemanly slurp, half-emptying the glass as if it were a shot of gin, shook his head with satisfaction, finished the rest and handed it back to her.

'More, please.'

She hadn't touched hers yet, avoided the obvious opportunity to make a wisecrack, simply turned and came back with his refilled glass.

'Do you want me to show you around?'

The wine had acted quickly, or perhaps he had merely anticipated his reaction, but he could feel a quickening relaxation, a desire to touch her arm, or put his round her shoulder. Friendly, not intimate, intended as a sign that they would get through this just fine, as long as they were careful and respectful.

'I'd like that, it's a lovely place.'

'Well,' she said, stepping aside, 'you can see most of the kitchen. Just a kitchen, not much to say.' There was, a lot, but men didn't give a damn about cupboards and finishes, floor surfaces and tiles, lighting fixtures, appliances and the latest gadgets. She saw him glance into the space, that his eyes did not attach themselves to anything but the table and chairs. He went in, passed his finger across the grain of the wood.

'Teak,' she said, 'from Denmark.'

He didn't comment, or understand, quite, turned his back and went into the living room. On the right-hand side was a door, which she opened.

'My bedroom.'

It was a high-ceilinged space, painted in white, with more pictures – still abstract but these confined to palettes of white, silver and grey, with touches of black – and a bed with a glistening silvery bedspread. Pillows, cushions. He felt himself drawing away, not from any suggestion of intimacy, but from the studied formality of the setting. It was no wonder she'd never suggested they make love in her place, he could hardly imagine getting in the mood in such a venue. Too cool to get hot.

'How nice. It's very beautiful and comfortable here, you have wonderful taste.'

She didn't respond. Ben had no idea what wonderful taste consisted of, she rather liked that about him, and was touched that he would pretend, in order to admire her.

'But can I ask one question?'

She nodded.

'Well, where's all the books? I expected shelf after shelf, knowing you.'

She stifled a little burst of laughter at the realisation that he thought that the revealed rooms were all that there were, that the staircase led to another apartment, or two.

'Oh, them,' she said, as if casually. 'They're upstairs, in the library. Do you want a look?'

The staircase was carpeted in fine green and purple stripes, as if itself a painting. If you looked at it your eyes began to wobble. He gripped the handrail. Metal, that was odd, in such an old house.

Off the revealed hallway, a gleaming white door led into a large chamber, shelved from floor to ceiling on opposite sides, filled with books to be sure, but also various statuettes, pieces of antique pottery, and a large number of framed photographs, none of them of people. Some landscapes, village scenes, from Italy presumably, nothing obviously personal, but obviously personal.

In the centre of the room was a large wooden table with an inset leather top in dark green, with gilt tooling at the edges – was it called a library table? – with two reclining leather desk chairs tucked in until their arms touched the protruding edge. At the far end of the table was a large Remington typewriter, alone, as if introducing itself, making some sort of statement, with another chair behind it. It presented itself as an object of contemplation, like that Dada urinal perhaps? Or some votive offering? It made him uncomfortable.

Rhoda had walked over to the window, her hips canted to the side, letting him make his way round the room, sniffing this or that, making it in some infinitesimal way his own.

He scanned the shelves, walked along them slowly, pulled an occasional title and examined it. The books were in three languages – French, Italian, English – at least three. Novels, poetry, travel books and guides, politics, psychology and philosophy, not organised or alphabetised, each simply placed when its time came, as if she of course would know where it was. A lot of them had that indefinable quality of having been read, had lost the first flush, though perhaps she bought them second-hand, or treated them negligently.

'Pretty impressive,' he said. 'Having this all to yourself . . . I can hardly take it in.'

He looked out the door into the hallway.

'What are those rooms?'

'Oh, a den, for watching TV, and another bedroom. There's two more upstairs and a couple of bathrooms.'

She might have sounded apologetic, perhaps should have been, but her tone was studiedly neutral, as if she were an indifferent realtor showing the property to a prospective client. A rich one.

'Shall we go downstairs and have something to eat?'

Something to eat? Perfect. Not *have dinner*, nothing so formal. A bite. *Agenbite of inwit*, he thought. Wonder if she'd get that one? Joyce.

Warm bread from the oven, several soft cheeses he could not name but could certainly smell, a tomato and red onion salad drizzled with olive oil, the bottle of white wine. They ate quietly, exchanging observations about the food – *Hey, these tomatoes actually have taste! Where'd you buy the wine?* – honouring the tone of the evening, until they had polished off the cheese, and she began to make coffee in some sort of fancy coffee maker. Espresso.

'Can I ask a question?' Ben had been curious about this for some time, never quite comfortable, hadn't brought it up. But Rhoda was so obviously intending to . . . what? Make a pitch, her pitch, marshal the arguments, make a case? 'I don't get it. You are younger than me, more attractive, you come from a world that leaves me breathless, as if I were an alien from another and lesser planet . . .'

She had no desire to deny it.

'Yes?'

'So, why me? I'm out of your league, below it, I've never even aspired to someone of your class, or caste, or wherever you come from or fit into. But girls like you don't settle for guys like me.'

She put a *shhh* finger to her lips, reached across and took his hand.

'God, you're dumb!'

'Dumb, what . . .'

'You don't even know, do you?'

'Know what?'

'That you're a legend, a goddamn legend. And I am a girl who is enormously seduced by intelligence.'

He made some modest modesty noises.

'Let me finish! I heard you in front of the Supreme Court, watched Justice Frankfurter nodding in admiration, felt proud merely to know that you were my colleague, that was before, you know . . .'

'Yes.'

'In the office they hardly talked about anything else for the next week. Ben this, Ben that . . . and you know what I think?'

'What?'

'You may be a legend, but you're the wrong sort of legend. Any highly-witted Jewish boy can argue a case, though maybe not as well as you. But who cares? You're not cut out to be a lawyer, you're too smart to be a lawyer.'

Even he could see what was coming, and he started to object.

'And don't you Clarence Darrow me. You're a writer!

So, write! Make a decent commitment to your own gifts. And speaking of gifts, you know what that was, don't you?'

He didn't.

'Upstairs. The room, the typewriter. Those are my gifts to you. A place to write, and time to do it.'

'I don't think—'

'Do be quiet, at least let me finish! There's more, something complete, where everything goes together. Did you think I was giving you a typewriter for your birthday? For Christ's sake, it all goes together. The place to write: your room, this house, a bed we will share, a life, together.'

He laughed at the sheer audacity of it, its cunning, its attractiveness.

'Have you even thought what this would mean? I leave Addie, I abandon my children, I have no means to support them or myself . . .'

'You know what?' she said sharply. 'You know what? Addie is a survivor, I will bet you five bucks she already has an eye on a suitable replacement for you. Your short story says so, and you cannot have made that up. And the children? You'll get to see them regularly, spoil them with presents. Track shoes. They'll survive, children go through wars, can adapt to most anything . . .'

Responding to his look of chagrin (which was good) and outrage (which was less promising), she put up a finger.

'Let me finish. All this would be accompanied by a loan – we can discuss how much – over three years, to let you meet your obligations. At the end of that time, however long, could be longer, depends how you are getting on, you can repay me with the advances and sales from your novels.'

He tried to rise from the chair, but was too exhausted, too drunk, too incredulous to respond. He slumped back into the enveloping leather.

'You're mad,' he said. 'Off your rocker. It's unthinkable.'

'Wanna bet?' she murmured. 'I'll see you tomorrow. Your place this time!'

He wanted to cool things down? Well, she could hot them up. A few nights together and he'd forget who Addie was!

'Something's going on.'

Addie adjusted her blanket and cradled her head on a folded beach towel, paused for a moment, blew a hovering fly away.

'I don't know what to do, but I have to do something. He almost never answers the phone, and when he does he sounds shifty. He hasn't written, even to the kids. It's not like him, he's usually slavishly punctilious.'

Sally grunted. 'I guess so. But you don't even know if something *is* going on, or if there is some innocent explanation . . .'

'Innocent? Innocent? He's a man. Sort of. But I'll find out. And in the meantime I will sharpen the knife.'

'Very funny! But look, Harold goes away on business all the time, stays in the city when I am here, sometimes forgets to call or is too busy. And he isn't fooling around . . .'

Addie hardly needed to observe that Harold was hardly a catch on the pick-'em-up and stick-'em-up scene, with his bashful ways and harelip, an unlikely partner for even the drunkest horny gal.

'Of course not,' she said. 'Harold's a gem.'

'Yeah, but so is Ben, you should remember that.'

'I do, or I did. I'm trying to remind myself. And failing.'

She wasn't jealous, not quite, had never regarded infidelity as high on the list of human sinfulness, had been tempted herself before her libido was lobotomised, and would have regarded an occasional indiscretion as a bit of fun – if she was lucky – not life-threatening, quite the opposite, a sign of life. No, what she detested was lying, and evasion. If Ben was having an affair – fancy word, a what? A fling? A thing? – why not come out and say so, instead of hiding and slithering and evading her? Say so! Then she could kill him, slowly. She would enjoy that.

The wine had turned red, how odd, he hadn't noticed her opening the new bottle, she must have done it when they moved into the living room. He put his glass to his lips, aware that he was that little bit woozy, drank, enjoyed the transition from the faint citrus acidity of that white to this heavily fruited deeper glassful. Fruit? Weren't you supposed to be able to roll the liquid round your mouth and come up with a string of constituent tastes? Blackberries? Redcurrants? Cherries? Like some demented greengrocer checking his stock. What nonsense. She'd tried to tutor him once, suggested, even, that the better reds had a less fruity taste and more of other flavours. Tobacco. Leather. Peat. Stone. Crap. He swirled it round again open-mindedly, swallowed, leant over and refilled his glass. He was unused to drinking so much wine, his vision fast becoming as unreliable as his emotions. Of which the major one was anger.

She'd set it up, that library and writing table, she'd set him up, all that casual wet-hair-no-shoes nonchalance, in the service of the final revelation, the gift. It was a gift that was not merely surprising, but surprisingly unwelcome; it signalled the unambiguous fact that she had no idea, no goddamn idea, none, none at all, of what a writer actually is. Of what he does.

That fat ugly typewriter perched on the library table was

merely a symbol, stripped of utility, more likely to inhibit than to encourage. What he needed was a kitchen table, some legal stationery and some pencils, peace, a couple of dry martinis, a bit of mess round him. Dishes, empty cups, unwashed plates. Addie was good at supplying those, better than Rhoda at setting a writerly stage, though unlike Rhoda she had no intention of doing so. She just hated washing dishes. He did that, eventually.

Rhoda's antiseptic library was not a writing place but a non-writer's idea of a writing place, a foolish, ill-informed archetype. And he had experienced it like a casually proffered insult; it startled him, he had no idea how to channel his distaste and disappointment, didn't even try. She meant well, she'd been shocked at his anger, though even she could hardly deny that she was trying, if not to buy – his horrid phrase – at least to entice him into a better life.

She was sorry, accepted and regretted her ham-fistedness, her inability to imagine what it was he actually did in the process of composition, her descent into good taste. If she had sanitised the creative process, it was only through ignorance, and it was beastly of him to be so ungenerous in response to her generosity, however misplaced. *Buy* him? What a thoroughly selfish response.

By the time his anger had drained somewhat, due to the dual effects of excessive catharsis and alcoholic daze, hers had flared into renewed life, the wine – they'd had a bottle each by now – enhancing rather than diminishing her emotion. Insults were hurled, names called, shoulders turned. If she'd had the energy or will to stand she would have thrown him out, but it was too late. He'd fallen asleep on his chair, his head lolling forward. She suspected drool, but didn't look. Nor had she the heart to call a cab and get him home.

She got up, shook herself like a sleepy dog and went

into her bedroom, lay on top of the silver bedspread and was soon asleep.

'When is he coming? Can we go to the station? I can't wait!'

Becca had missed Ben more than any of them, his ease and goofiness, the enveloping warmth of his love. She was thoroughly aware that she was his favourite. That if she had got the polio and died he would have been broken in a way that couldn't be fixed. If Addie or Jake died, he'd get over that, after a while, over them. But she was necessary to him, he made her feel that, know that.

'He's on the 11.25 train tomorrow morning, darling. You and Jake and I can pick him up at Huntington Station.'

'Can I wear my new dress?' Perle had taken the little one for a belated bit of shopping to celebrate her birthday, which had occurred at the end of June. The dress in question was not entirely pink, which her grandmother would have preferred, but it did have sprigs of pink flowers against a cream background. Becca had tried it on in the shop, sidled over to the mirror, turned round shyly looking over her shoulder. It looked lovely! And here was a chance to wear it!

'No!' The response came out too quickly, too vehemently. Before Addie could explain – which would have been impossible – or apologise, Becca had fled from the porch into her bedroom, slamming the door. Why did Addie have to ruin *everything*? She didn't notice Jake at the table at the back of the room, going through his box of baseball cards.

'What's the matter with you?' he asked, without looking up.

'Nothing, nothing.'

He could hear that she was crying, sniffling loudly, the prelude to sobs, but he didn't care. Girls were always making a fuss. Even Addie – moms made fusses too, he'd overheard her crying at night a couple of times recently – or might it have been Ruby? – could tell she was trying to keep it down. Granny and Poppa might have heard.

In a few minutes Addie tiptoed into the room and sat on the bed, waving Jake away with her finger. When he reluctantly left by the rear door, she put her hand on Becca's shoulder, for the girl had turned away and hunched up protectively.

'I'm so sorry, darling,' she said. 'I didn't mean to snap at you.'

'I only wanted to dress up for Ben. We haven't seen him for three weeks!' The words were muttered into the blanket.

'I know. I am sorry.'

'So can I?'

'Of course you can,' said Addie gently, 'and you know what?'

The child stopped sniffling and turned to look at her mother.

'What?'

'Let's all dress up! I can wear my pretty red dress that you like, and Jake can have pants and a button-up shirt and shoes, and won't we look great standing there on the platform when Ben walks down the steps from the train!'

Becca beamed.

'Can we, can we? That'd be so great! He'd love that!'

The last time they'd dressed up like that, as a family, was when they'd seen Ben's sister Sadie off from Idlewild last summer. On a plane going to London. They'd driven to the airport, got a bit lost and almost missed her before they called for the people to get on the plane. But they had fifteen minutes to have a hug and a squeeze, and Ben went to a machine and bought Sadie an insurance policy that meant they would get $50,000 if she died. It only cost $2! Sadie had laughed a little uneasily.

It wasn't clear why she should say thank you, but she did.

'But I am not going to die!' she reassured the children. 'You're more likely to die on a bus than on a plane!'

Becca took this in solemnly, resolving never again to go on a bus. When Sadie got to the going-off place – a gate, it was called – they all waved and she waved back gaily until she went through the door.

'That was a bit much, buying life insurance!' Addie said.

Ben laughed. 'We'll hope for the best!'

So he knew, Ben did. When a person went on a trip, or came home, you dressed up to meet them. And then they would give you presents!

It was quite right, Addie thought. The wisdom of children. She had intended dressing down, throwing on any old *schmatta*, studiedly unwilling to compete with whatever shadow figure she now presumed to be lurking in DC. But why, why make herself undesirable? Why not give him the full package, remind him what he was missing – and certainly would be missing in the three nights that would follow. *The red dress.* That'd do it, he'd be bemused and a little taken aback, it was a special dress, one of the few she had accepted from her father, shiny rayon, both free-flowing and figure-hugging, hard to understand how it could be both, showed off her assets perfectly. God knows why she liked it so much, it wasn't her at all really, she was hardly a party girl. But there was always the hope of a night in the city, theatre and a meal afterwards, glad rags on and then off, in some nice hotel . . .

The next morning they got themselves ready well ahead of time, Granny Perle perusing them with a puzzled look on her face as Jake reluctantly donned his best clothes, the little one preened in her peachy new dress, and Addie applied her make-up and lipstick.

'What's the big deal?' she asked. 'Going to a party?' She made going to a party sound disreputable, an activity likely to lead to nothing but trouble. Which, thought Addie, was just about right.

'Ben is coming back!' said Becca. 'And we are his greeters. We have to dress up.'

Perle smiled, that smile that meant she knew something was up, and certainly wasn't going to say so, nor fail to convey that she was on to it, whatever it was. Nothing good, that was clear. Addie looked strained, determined to be gay with the children.

She stood up from the dressing table, straightened her dress and looked at herself in the mirror, wiped a wisp of red lipstick from the corner of her mouth, put some perfume on her neck and wrists, looked again, approved ironically. Glad rags.

'Let's go, kids!' she said loudly. 'It's almost eleven.' The previous afternoon Jake had polished the Caddy and cleaned the insides; it had rarely looked so good, stately, like a limousine, with dressed-up rich people inside. Addie had joked that perhaps Poppa should drive, wearing a suit and a hat like a chauffeur. She had to explain what that was, which rather ruined the joke, and the idea. Anyway, none of them wanted him, he'd just be in the way, it was best just to be together, looking so wonderful, a surprise for Ben.

When he alighted from the train, Ben looked up and down the platform, and his eyes passed right over them as they stood, grouped like a photograph, some thirty feet down the track. He looked further down, and then slowly back, his eyes stopped, he paused with a puzzled look on his face, waved tentatively. The children ran to meet him, grabbed hold of his arms, as Addie walked to join them.

He looked puzzled, more than that, raddled somewhat, his hair askew under his hat, his tie at half mast, suit jacket over his arm, with his overnight bag in the other hand. As if he'd sat on the floor for the whole journey, dusty and soiled, blinking at the renewal of the light.

He shook himself slightly, readjusted his response and expectations, as if surprised by an unforeseen argument trying a case.

'Well,' he exclaimed, 'what a surprise this is!'

Becca giggled and squeezed his arm.

'It is a surprise! Welcome home!'

'Yeah, Ben,' said Jake, 'me too!

He looked at Addie, standing a couple of feet behind the children.

'Me too,' she said.

Jake grabbed the handle of Ben's small suitcase and gave a tug, commandeered it, and began a quick walk to the car. Becca took his hand, while Addie strolled alongside.

'My God,' he said, 'you all look terrific. What's the occasion?'

'You are!' said Becca. 'Cos you came home!'

'And you,' said Addie, looking at him closely, 'you look terrible. What's the matter?'

It was true enough: his outward rumpledness mirrored some inward collapse, or desolation. He had those bags under his eyes that indicate both lack of sleep and stress, had shaved badly and patches of hair showed along his chin, his colour reminded her of the belly of a whitefish. Instead of feeling concern, she felt a shiver of revulsion. Could these be the symptoms of late nights, too much drink, too much, too much . . .?

'Yeah,' he said. 'I know. Not been sleeping very well, I stay up all night worrying. And then I thought I could get a few hours' nap on the train – you know how I can hardly stay awake on trains – but it was full, and a woman with a screaming baby sat next to me. It was purgatorial!'

'You should have moved.'

'I tried. No seats anywhere, people in the aisles. I thought of standing but wasn't sure I could stay up straight . . .'

The requisite 'poor you' was not forthcoming.

'I called you on Wednesday night and there was no answer.'

'Oh, what time did you call?'

'Nine, and ten, and eleven . . .'

He paused, but not, she could observe, for thought, but for emphasis, as if his major concern was to deliver his lines convincingly. Looked round to see if the kids were listening, but Becca had run ahead to prepare the car for its royal passenger. She'd brought a silk cushion to put on his seat, he'd be so tired after his trip.

'Wednesday! It's rather embarrassing . . . I had a meeting late in the afternoon, talking to one of the personnel people about severance terms, and it was clear that something was up, only she wouldn't say. But it was a frosty atmosphere, and I couldn't get out of there fast enough. I went home and drank four martinis instead of eating, and I woke up early in the morning with a hideous hangover.'

'That's not like you. You can drink four martinis without a trace . . .'

'OK. I lied. I drank half a bottle of gin, with ice. And even I am not used to that.'

'Well, that explains it then,' said Addie, 'you didn't hear the phone, did you?'

'No,' said Ben, as they reached the car. 'And then last night I did it again. Fell asleep by eight. Did you call?'

'No.'

'Well, I am so sorry. This has got to stop. I can't go on like this.'

'You bet you can't,' said Addie, getting into the driver's seat.

Becca was holding the front door open for him, standing at attention, as if she wanted to salute. He slumped down and closed his eyes. The kids got in the back. Addie drove them home.

After one look at Ben, Perle did not press lunch on him, though it was laid out, just how he liked it. He'd been travelling since the early morning and said he was hungry, but he looked pale and exhausted. She rushed into the rear area to make up the bed, ushered him into the bathroom to shower and change, settled him down in the bed. Turned on the fan – it was already pushing ninety – and tiptoed out. He was immediately asleep. In the other room Addie and the kids had changed into the usual shorts and tops. The party was over.

At the table the family were soon eating listlessly, enervated by the heat and by some contracted emotion that rendered them speechless, though none could have said why, quite. Too tired to eat, or to talk. After they'd cleared the table, Mo went off to his workshop with Jake, Becca took her *Peanuts* book to bed, while Addie and Perle did the washing up, it was easier than asking Ruby, best leave her to stew and swelter in her little room.

'What's the matter with Ben?'

'Nothing, Mother. Just a couple of late nights, worrying about this and that, burning the midnight oil . . .'

'I've never seen him like this. Should we check his temperature? There's been a bug going round, Michelle told me about it, I think Jenny got it last week.'

'Mother! He's been in DC. They have their own bugs. He's just exhausted. We'll have an easy weekend, and he'll be better . . .'

There was a pause while Perle dried the plates and put the leftover food in the ice box.

'Addie,' she said tentatively, 'is everything all right?'

She knew it wasn't. Addie knew she knew. Perle knew that Addie knew she knew.

'Yes, Mother, everything is fine. Just fine.'

'Well,' said Perle, using one of her characteristic phrases, guaranteed to make Addie bridle. 'May I make a suggestion?'

'Nobody has ever been able to stop you . . .'

'He needs an easy weekend. Let's let him read, have a rest, listen to his music. We can make ourselves a bit scarce, make some lovely meals for him.'

'Mother! Stop!'

Over the next two days Ben sat in a deckchair on the porch and read. First he read comics to Becca, and then a Hardy Boys book to Jake, and then he'd earned the right to read to himself, which he did for hours, totally immersed.

It was not a book he was reading. It was something or other in a fat black folder with a lot of typed pages in it. None of them had ever seen it before. When he once got up for a pee, and left it by the side of his chair, Addie snuck over and opened it. The title page read *Nature's Priest* by Martin Brennan, *Part 1*. Though she knew what it was, she was nonetheless astonished to see it, had assumed it not merely abandoned but lost, or thrown away. Silly of her, really, writers – not that Ben was a writer, not a real one – never throw things away, just stuff them in boxes and put them in the closet, or an attic, perhaps the garage. Out of sight but obviously never entirely out of mind. Why had he disinterred it, why now?

No reason not to ask, was there? He had it right there, out in plain sight, was virtually asking to be interrogated about it.

She lifted it up when he returned.

'Ben, how come you're reading this? You haven't looked at it for at least ten years.'

'Haven't I?' he asked owlishly, taking it from her hand. 'What do you mean?'

He paused for a moment, did not meet her eye, reclaimed the folder from her hand.

'I guess it would be wrong to say I am haunted by it, nothing as dramatic as that, but it niggles at me. I worked so hard on it, for so long. It was my life, then, it was about my life then, and before then. A sort of autobiography in the form of a novel . . .'

'But publishers didn't want it!'

'They didn't, and they were right, I could see that even then, and even more strongly now I am looking at it again. After all these years I can see quite clearly what is wrong with it.'

Addie didn't like this, not one little bit. Why renew interest in a failed project just when they were going to move house, and Ben would have the stress of studying for the Bar, and setting up a practice? It was . . . what was the right word? It was regressive.

'Not good enough!'

'No,' he said, 'not quite that, but almost. Not good enough as it stands. And that is because it is a first draft, and though the writing is not bad – sometimes it's quite good, you know – the architecture is wrong. And the voice. But I think, even after all these years, that I know how to fix it. It will involve some . . .'

That 'will involve' was alarming. Very alarming.

'You cannot tell me that you are going back to this unpublishable stuff now, in the midst of everything. Are you mad?'

He offered a smile that was even more alarming.

'I'm quite good at doing a lot of things at the same time. I can put things into categories, give them their due when they're due, not let one thing slop over into another. I could do it if I wanted to enough . . .'

'Don't tell me, please don't tell me, that you are seriously considering this?'

'I'll tell you when I decide,' he said. 'You'll be the first to know.'

He sat down, placed the folder in both hands, located the right page and cast his eyes down. He didn't look up again for three hours, when dinner was ready.

At the table he ate quickly and ravenously, having had nothing since a roll and coffee at the station in DC early that morning. He seemed, to Addie's eyes, determined to keep his mouth full; the conversation flowed round him in a desultory way, relief that the heatwave might be ending, plans for the beach the next day, but he was unable to contribute, with a mouth full of chicken, or potatoes, cucumber salad, lima beans. A beer, swilling it down, virtually gargled, another beer. It was mildly disgusting, it was reprehensible. Addie knew the signs: when Ben was writing he ceased to talk, hardly responded to questions, abjured social and family life, woke in the night to make notes or clack away at the typewriter. Entirely self-absorbed, heedless, unreachable. Selfish. She knew what writing was, and what it did. Writing made you worse. It made Ben worse, it made her life worse. Writing stank.

And she wasn't having it, no, not now. Not anytime really. Rather be married to a lawyer even – bunch of paper-pushers and big liars, mouths for hire – than a goddamn writer. No, like it or not, Ben was a husband, and a father, he had responsibilities, and a family to take care of. She knew about writers, what they got up to and away with. Hemingway, Fitzgerald. Drinkers and fuckers. Even that creepy D.H. Lawrence (who was neither) ripping his pretty German wife away from her children, then sitting round kvetching and writing his stupid overheated books. Well, she was no Frieda Lawrence, big fat Kraut, and Ben was sure no DHL! It was time to take things in hand.

Over lunch on the Saturday afternoon following Ben's arrival, Maurice announced, with something of a mysterious air, that they would be going out to dinner. The children were both thrilled and puzzled.

'Why?' said Jake, who hated mysteries.

'Where?' asked Becca, who liked them, but not as much as she liked going to a restaurant. She adored menus, the longer the better. Would peruse every item, from appetisers to desserts, consider each, whether she liked it or not, before coming to a decision, which was quickly withdrawn, interrogated and eventually replaced with something else. It drove Jake crazy. Anyway, she usually ended up wanting whatever he wanted. Because if she ordered something else she would spend the whole meal regretting it, gazing at Jake's meatloaf enviously. With ketchup!

'It's a surprise,' said Maurice, making his biggest wink with his right eye, and a lesser but not negligible one with his left. He could wiggle his ears, too.

'Where? Say where!' said Becca. A Chinese restaurant

was a dire possibility, she hated them, would only order spare ribs and rice, though she carefully considered everything from Moo Goo Gai Pan (*horrible name! yuck!*) to sweet and sour pork (*no way!*).

Poppa paused for a moment. The kids leant forward. Ben and Addie looked on with a degree of interest, unable to work out the occasion. Perle was forbearing: she didn't like eating from non-kosher kitchens, but would when it came to it.

'I reserved a table at Linck's,' he said. 'We need to leave by five-thirty.'

The children were exultant, the adults rather puzzled.

'How come, Poppa?'

'What are we celebrating, Morrie?'

He paused a little, gave a wry smile.

'My semi-retirement,' he said. 'I've decided I'm going to take it easy.'

Addie and Perle looked worried, Ben bemused, the kids didn't care.

Linck's! Linck's Log Cabin! It was the best place, everyone loved it, the children for its setting by the pond and rustic feel, plus a menu that had everything on it; the grown-ups because the food was good, the ambience welcoming and the prices reasonable.

Everything, anything you could possibly want? Jake winced, it would be intolerable waiting for his little sister to order. Maybe they ought to leave at five?

Linck's was not merely a local hotspot, people came from all over the Island. On the weekends there was a wait of over an hour for your table, but the cocktails were good, the waiters friendly and efficient. If you were a regular you were greeted by name and given a decent table away from the front desk, the kitchen or the toilets.

Maurice even had a regular waiter, Angelo, who would rush over to greet him – *Mr K!* – as he entered, and make sure that he was well looked after. Apparently the old man went to Linck's more than you would have supposed, or perhaps Angelo had an unusually retentive memory and found Maurice good company. They were like a party act together.

Maurice always ordered the same thing, which wasn't even on the menu, which made him feel special, and tickled Angelo because they had made it into a routine.

After he had handed out the menus, and waited a very long time while the little girl agonised over her choices, he eventually put his pad in his left hand and a pencil in his right. He took the ladies' orders first, then the children, who usually ordered the same thing, then Ben, whom he recognised with a formal nod, and finally Maurice, the climax of the whole show.

'And you, Mr K?'

'The usual! You know how I like it, Angelo!'

'Fit for the garbage, Mr K!'

'Fit for the garbage!'

The reference was not to the calf's liver, which was merely going to be well done, but to the accompanying onions – *extra* onions – which Maurice liked crispy black, calcified.

'I don't know how you can eat them, Mr K! Chef always wants to cook them normal like, and I stand over him, and every time he tries to lift up the frying pan, I ask him, "Are they fit for the garbage?" Not yet! He puts it back on! It breaks his heart!'

Maurice never tired of the story of the grieving chef, to whom he once tried to offer his compliments, but he was apparently too busy. It was Linck's, after all!

Angelo was an Italian, the chef was called Mario, a few

of the other waiters were Italians too. That was funny, because it wasn't an Italian restaurant, just a normal one with normal food: turkey or chicken, and roast beef, steaks and lobsters, the best hamburgers on the Island. No garlic in sight or smell.

Maurice looked round him and grimaced. He leant over and whispered to Ben, rubbing his nose. 'Not long for the world, this place.'

'Why? Is it in financial trouble? That would be hard to believe. It's full all the time.'

'Yeah,' said Maurice, 'lots of financial trouble, they can't pay the vig, got to be looked after, and the owners refuse to pay up or to sell.'

Vig? As in vigil? Vigilante? Vigilance?

Maurice rubbed his nose again. 'The vig? It means protection, protection money in case, God forbid, there should be an accident. I give it two years, maximum. It'll burn down. Fit for the garbage!'

Ben was both shocked and, to his dismay, rather impressed at the range of his father-in-law's knowledge. But of what? *Italians!* Could it be – he searched for the appropriate Italian name, failed to find it – the Mafia?

'How do you know?' he asked quietly, but Maurice was already getting ready for yet another of his party tricks.

'Who's got a quarter?' he asked, looking at the children.

They didn't, but he did.

'You ready?' he asked. 'This one is going straight through the table!' The kids had seen it all before, knew all his tricks and most of his routines, the onions, the quarter, the ashtray game. They never tired of any of them because Poppa Mo could make it exciting every time.

He took the quarter in his right hand and placed his fist in the middle of the table.

Leaning forward, he put his left arm under the table, ready to receive the miraculous transfer. He pushed his right fist, wriggled it about, made a moaning noise, pressed it again.

'Let us see, Grandpa!' said Jake, excited in spite of himself. 'Show us!'

Maurice lifted his left hand from under the table, opened his fingers. There was nothing in it, no quarter, nothing.

Becca grabbed his right hand and said, 'I bet it's still here!'

And it was. Maurice looked chagrined, red-faced and mortified, shook his head in disgrace.

'I did my best,' he said. 'It won't go . . .'

'It always goes!' shouted the kids.

'Can I help, Mr K?' Angelo had been watching, failing in his duties to the other tables. He proffered a silver dollar, heavy and impressive. The children strained to look, they'd never seen one. 'Try this,' he said. 'We polished the table this morning, a light coin won't go through . . .'

Maurice took the coin, nodded in appreciation, put it in his right hand, pressed it to the table, made his funny sounds, strained and looked towards the ceiling as if in prayer.

'I can feel something!' he said.

Even Ben and Addie were transfixed. So were the families on either side of them, everyone holding their breath as if at a real magic show.

He raised and opened his right hand. No silver dollar. There was a gasp of appreciation, everyone craned forward as he raised his left hand from under the table, kept the fist shut, placed it on the table, opened it slowly.

A silver dollar! There was a round of applause, he bowed his head in acknowledgement.

Becca was thrilled. A silver dollar was way better than a quarter! And Poppa gave it to her! He reached into his pocket as Jake started to protest and gave him one too.

Poppa does the best tricks with money!

At the end of the meal Maurice reached under his chair, brought out a bulging brown paper bag and handed it to Ben.

'This'll keep you going,' he said with a wink.

Ben took it, it was heavier than usual. This was surely going too far: in the light of what he was beginning to understand, *way* too far. And now was hardly the time!

'Morrie,' he said, 'thank you, thanks once again. But this time it is strictly a loan . . .'

'Loan? What loan?' said Maurice. 'Open it up!'

Ben unfolded the top, looked in. A puzzled look crossed his face as he lifted out . . . A sandwich! Examined it. It was stuffed not with cash but with roast beef. Lettuce, too. Was that a metaphor? He looked across at this father-in-law, who was chuckling at his own wit, and by the fact that only Addie and Ben could get the joke.

'I'm still hungry,' said Jake. 'Can we have it as a midnight feast?'

Angelo, who had slipped the wrapped sandwich under Maurice's chair, smiled at Jake, nodded amiably to Becca: 'You kids share it,' he said, 'it's a really good one.'

On the way to the car, Ben bearded Maurice, took his arm, slowed him down while the others walked over to the pond to feed the ducks the last of the rolls from the basket on the table. That was part of the fun of Linck's.

'Mo,' he said, 'stop. Slow down. What the hell is going on?'

His father-in-law looked at him.

'It's my fault, I'm sorry. Always with the jokes. Not so funny, right?'

'I have no idea what you're talking about,' said Ben.

Maurice looked at the ground for a moment. 'The wise guys are all over me . . .'

'Wise guys? What wise guys? You don't mean the goddamn Mafia, do you, with all this talk about the *vig* and burning down buildings? What have you gotten yourself into? Is this why you always have so much cash? I never . . .'

Mo took his arm to calm him.

'No, of course not the Mafia, for goodness' sake. Me? I'm a small man. But these days every goddamn dago acts like he's some big-shot gangster, thinks he can lean on you and you'll collapse . . .'

'Are they leaning on you?'

'Yes.'

'And are you collapsing?'

Mo paused and looked his son-in-law in the eye.

'What choice do I have?' he said. 'They're pushing and I haven't the strength to stand up to them any more. I'm over sixty, I have a dicky heart. I've tried to provide for everybody for too long.'

Could it be? Ben looked at him again, as he turned his back. Tears were forming in his eyes, he'd lost control of his voice, breathed a couple of times slowly, paused to light a cigarette. Took a deep draw, exhaled, took in more smoke.

'I'm so sorry,' he said, 'but that sandwich is almost the last of the Mohicans. I have enough cash just about to fill one more bag, then I can take out a mortgage on the bungalow while you pass the Bar. You can pay me back once you start your practice. I can find the money.'

'*I'll* find the money,' said Ben. 'Plenty of other things to worry about.'

As Ben was packing his bag the next morning, getting

ready to catch a midday train back to DC, Addie came in to remind him to take his painkillers for his shoulder.

'You left them in the bathroom,' she said. 'You should be more careful.'

'Thanks.'

He was sorry he'd given her so little over the weekend – all of them so little – hunkered down with his manuscript, reading diligently, lost. Even now, with the offending folder safely packed away, he could see new promise in it, knew where it had to go, where he had to go. He finished his packing – he folded his clothes obsessively, they never emerged with creases – looking intently into the small leather valise.

'So,' she said. 'What have you got on this week? Busy? Any trips or big meetings?'

It was kind of her to offer a subject so everyday, she usually didn't give a damn what he did at work, if anything unusual happened she could count on him to tell her about it.

'Nope, dull as dishwater. I have to tidy up some paperwork on outstanding cases, don't want to leave them in a mess. Otherwise, just the same old, and counting the days . . .'

'Will you promise me one thing?' she said, taking his arm, perhaps a little firmly.

He disengaged himself with a sideward step.

'Anything. What?'

'Enough with getting soused. It's dangerous, you already drink too much, and if you get into a habit of—'

'You're quite right,' he answered. 'I promise.'

'Are you sure?' asked Sally, more animated by the forthcoming drama than was seemly, prurient almost.

'Positive.'

'Why? Surely he didn't admit it?'

'Of course not! It was the way he acted, all weekend. He wasn't at all loving, even with Becca: first he'd be all over her, and she wrapped round him like ivy, then he'd disentangle her and withdraw. And then you could hardly get a word out of him. He just sat outside in a corner on the porch, reading that crappy novel that he wrote fifteen years ago.'

'Why?'

'He wants to go back to it! It's crazy! Something's up. There's a woman involved, sure as shooting.'

Sally looked puzzled.

'What would a woman have to do with some old novel of his?'

'I don't know, but I will soon enough.'

'Well,' said Sally, pretending a sophistication entirely foreign to her, 'he's a man . . .'

'No! The point is that he's not. Never has been, when he finds a woman he sticks like glue, even when they treat him as badly as I do.'

'Addie!'

'Well, as I sometimes do . . . My point is that he's not dick-driven. If either of us is, it's me!'

Sally laughed.

'But don't you see that's worse! He's not on the make. So she will have made him! Whoever she is, she's there, she's cunning, and she's available. Local!'

'What else is there? You can't fall in love with someone you don't see regularly.'

'Well, we don't know the neighbours except the old bag next door, who's not exactly a strawberry gumdrop. It'll be someone in the office.'

'Probable enough . . .'

'But here's the bad thing, the thing I can't quite get my mind round: what is she offering?'

'Oh, come on! It's sex, isn't it?'

'No. No way. He's not that easy, or that interested. There's something else going on, and only one way to find out.'

Sally thought for a while. 'We're talking more than letters or phone calls here . . .'

'Yup! I'm going tomorrow. Spin the kids and my folks some cockamamie bullshit about leases and agents, moving men, all that.'

'I'll bet your mother'll give you one of her piercing looks!'

'Two! She knows something's up, but would never ask. But I'm off first thing tomorrow.'

'You're not exactly going to catch him on the job, you know. It ain't that simple.'

Addie grinned like a wolf looking forward to encountering a sheep.

'Oh, he'll talk!'

'You sharpened the knife, right?'

If she caught a train at about ten, she could spend a couple of hours in the city before changing for a train to DC and catching a cab – *why the hell not!* – to Alexandria. Leave from Penn Station at two and she'd be in the apartment by six, plenty of time before he got home for his lonely (she hoped) supper.

She had an impulse to cross town and treat herself to a dozen oysters and a Bloody Mary at the Oyster Bar. A sentimental journey. When she was a senior at Hunter and going out with Ira, they would sometimes sneak downtown on the 6 train, to initiate a naughty afternoon, sitting at the bar, legs pressed together, with a dozen oysters (both of them from kosher homes!), a couple of Bloody Marys, looking forward to a drunken romp in his bedroom a few blocks east. On the way out of the station they'd stop in the whispering gallery under the four giant columns, stand at opposite corners and send each other suggestive messages, rather hoping to be overheard, proud to be lovers on their way to making love.

She'd had a certain amount of experience by the time she was twenty, but she was Ira's first, and he was initially overcome by shyness, but delight and enthusiasm followed soon and naturally enough. He was skinny, his body virtually hairless, his ribs and shoulders showed their bony definition, so slight that he shook and trembled when he made love. She found it curious, an exciting tribute. It took her a time to get him to abandon the sexual euphemism 'cutting the mustard', which was hardly flattering to a girl, though to Ira a metaphor that also suggested hotdogs and pastrami sandwiches was an expression of the strength of his appetites, and desire. He'd have adored the phrase 'hide the salami', had it been available.

Ira knew how to have fun, take a break, make a girl feel special. Addie still wore, sometimes, a gold-plated bracelet engraved on the inside 'Adele from Ira'. He'd hinted that it would be replaced, when the time was right – soon! – with something smaller and rounder, more important and enduring. When she wore the bracelet, even all these years later, she fancied she could feel the engraved letters caressing the skin on the inside of her wrist. Erotic, almost. She would twirl the bracelet round and round, up and down, sensuously.

Ira was a *macher* in the city administration now. Lived somewhere on the West Side, his number was in the phone book. Give him a call and say meet me at the Oyster Bar?

At the bar, on the stools on the left, where we sat and loved each other when we were just kids? She laughed at the very thought, not an amused laugh. How the time passed. He'd be married, likely enough, with some kids, he'd wanted four, two boys and two girls, as if you could buy them at Macy's. She had occasional strands of grey in her hair now, plenty of grey in her life. Was about to become a Long Island wife. When she'd seen off the unknown competitor, that was going to be her prize. A booby prize: she was the booby.

She hummed mournful songs to herself on the morning train as it laboured through Cold Spring Harbor, Syosset, Mineola, the drear wastes of Long Island, ugly, burgeoning and indistinguishable, hunched in a window seat, lighting one cigarette after another, crushing them out after a few draws. The kids had been clingy when she'd left, the little one with tears in her eyes, as if Addie had been going to Siberia and would never be seen again.

'Do you have to go, Addie?'

She'd tried to reassure her.

'I'll be back in a couple of days. Don't you worry.'

What a mess.

No stopover for nostalgia and oysters, and she wept all the way into Penn Station.

The train jolted to a stop in the tunnel of the Long Island Railway, Track 19, waking her for a bewildered moment, during which she stared into the ill-lit platform filled with hurrying people and had no idea where she was, or who. Sat for a moment, closed her eyes to catch her breath and regain her place in the order of things, looked up the aisle of the train, which was emptying quickly. Ah, yes: Addie. On the way to Washington DC, soon to catch the train upstairs at Penn Station.

She reached up into the luggage rack above the seat, grabbed the handle of her heavy purse, hoiked it down, hurting her shoulder when it took the weight – she didn't even know she had a sore shoulder, presumably it was an emerging metaphor – and stumbled her way down the aisle, hopped across the divide between the train and the platform, aware of nothing more than an urgent need for coffee. And maybe a muffin? Or a Danish? At last, something to look forward to.

She had over an hour before the next DC train, so sat comfortably on the station concourse, sipping her coffee, reading the *New York Times.* Senator Blackbeard was still at it, purging America's enemies, spurring HUAC into further persecutions of Communists and their sympathisers. Making people frightened. She was going to DC. He was there at the moment. She should have brought a gun, done something to be remembered by, and honoured. Or sharpened another knife?

She'd sworn to give up reading the papers, listening to the radio, watching the news. All news was bad news, disgusting, degrading, obscene. And she was addicted to it, as people are often drawn by horrors that both repel and fascinate: to fires, car crashes, public executions, places of mass murder.

The country was being taken over by Fascists who'd invented an imaginary enemy to terrify a gullible public into submission. Communists? What Communists? A few idealistic kids and beardy know-it-alls yearning for what cannot be achieved, and never had been. The only threat to the American way was from those defending it! Americans crave something to fear and a leader to protect them from it.

The next thing you knew one of them would be in the

White House, as good old H.L. Mencken had predicted thirty years ago: a moron.

Are you now or have you ever been . . .

'Yes, sir, I have, and I am proud of it. Go on, send me to jail. Or worse than that, exile me to Long Island for life . . .'

Before boarding the train she tossed the paper into a wastepaper bin. It meant she would have nothing to read for the next three and a half hours, but reading on trains made her feel nauseous, and the sway and noise affected her like a lullaby. She had slept badly since Ben left and had a long fraught night ahead of her. By the time the train had made its way out of the city, she was fast asleep.

You didn't have to be goddamn Sherlock Holmes to find the evidence. No need of a magnifying glass, tweezers, collection bags, sniffer dogs, traces of dirt or obscure footprints. Any amateur could have read this evidence and drawn the inevitable conclusion. Bed unmade, with pillows on both sides bearing the impressions of heads, one of them with long dark hair, the other with Ben's curly grey. A distinct smell of perfume on her (!) side. Chanel? Who could tell?

In the air a cigarette mustiness that was unfamiliar, powerful and peculiarly disgusting. In the wastepaper basket were a large number of butts, some of which were from Ben's Camels, the others – as an empty packet proclaimed – were a brand called Fatima, with a veiled Oriental femme fatale on the cover, which proclaimed Turkish cigarettes. Turkish delights. The real thing, presumably, or closer to the real thing than Ben's Camels. So, his lover was a pseudo-sophisticate, a show-off, leaving her traces of lurid red lipstick on her butts. Addie shrugged. And on his, likely enough.

No clothes on the floor, no make-up in the bathroom, no further traces, but what more did she need? Photos? She pulled off the bedspread, examined the sheets with the forensic intensity of a pathologist. There were bits of mucky stuff left through overuse and inattention, though whose effluvia was unknowable without recourse to a laboratory. Perhaps she could send his corpse there as well.

Who's been sleeping in my bed?

And in the kitchen: an empty bottle of red wine – she looked at it, Italian, who knew from Italian wine? – and two glasses with black dregs, no sign of food consumption, presumably they went out to eat, came home to drink some more and to make love. *Make love?* To *fuck*! It was what she had feared, and expected, but it was a God almighty shock nonetheless, taking her from conjecture to certainty. She stood still by the front door, stood and waited as if something were about to happen, and it didn't. Stood some more, still, as if waiting.

Waiting? That was what she had to do now. He would be home in an hour or so, she would wait. By the front door, so that the first thing he would see on entering the apartment was her, sitting there. She moved an armchair from the living room into the hallway, pulled the side table next to it, placed it just so, set down her cigarettes, ashtray and lighter, and went to the kitchen to fix herself a drink, Rye, bit of ginger ale, on the rocks. Why not bring the whole bottle, no need to get up and return to the kitchen? She didn't want him to come in and not see her, encounter her, hear her. It would scare the shit out of him; there was that to look forward to.

She sat, no need of anything to read, or to listen to, or even to think about. Stared at the door with an intensity that might have incinerated it, if it had any decency.

Concentrated, distilled into a purity of rage that was new to her and by no means disagreeable. Nothing overblown, or childishly reprehensible. No *throwing a tantrum.* No, it was righteous, it felt right, a feeling for which she had been waiting for a lifetime: the moment at which her sense of not having been given enough, of being abused, taken for granted, stepped on and over was at last *true*, not the neurotic petulance of a spoiled child who can never be given enough, or in the right way. Hah! This was not anger, it was fury, this was the real thing. If it didn't feel so overwhelmingly dreadful, it would have felt terrific.

The drink took the edge off, a second helped even more, one cigarette followed another. She felt a drowsy luxuriousness, sank into the soft upholstery, plumped her cushion, closed her eyes, opened them again to look at her watch. It was past seven, he was late. Important not to fall asleep, what sort of surprise would that be when he walked in, to find her collapsed in a drunken heap on a chair in the hallway? No moral high ground there. Brisk middle-aged lawyer finds dribbling drunken sot wife . . .

She refilled her glass, drank deeply, wishing it were a cocktail with orange slices and maraschino cherries, and was soon asleep once again. After some time – how could she know how long? – she woke abruptly, hearing voices in the hall, and the turning of a key in a lock. Two of them! She hadn't counted on that, planned for it, or composed the right speeches in her head. What a disaster, what a humiliation . . . But thank God it was only the neighbours across the hall. She looked at her watch. It was past nine. What if he didn't come home at all? Two hours later she abandoned her perch, and the half empty bottle of rye, moved the chair and table back into the living room, emptied the ashtray and went to sleep on the couch. She was never going to sleep in that bed again, the marital bed, never, the Salvation Army could have it. A besmirched bed, an adulterous bed, a bed of shame, her shame. And with such righteous thoughts she went back to sleep and did not wake till dawn. There was no sign of Ben.

Perhaps it was better this way? Unambiguous, leaving him no place to hide, no defence against the plunging of the knife. It was a thought that had sustained her, but the metaphor was getting out of control, she could now imagine said knife in her pocket book and plunging it into said adulterous husband's heart! She consoled herself with the thought that if the knife was not real the outrage certainly was, and by the time he'd felt the full force of it, he might be begging for a quick execution. Which would be too good for him, the rat. Better he should suffer and suffer some more, and come back to Long Island with what used to be his tail between what used to pass for his legs, begging for forgiveness, unforgiven.

She both loathed him and wanted him back, and how he might negotiate between these poles of rejection and acceptance (on her terms) was unclear. Who gave a damn? She didn't know either, how to balance her need to banish him from her sight and her heart, and her competing understanding that she needed him, still, as a father to her – and his – children. And goddamn it, as a husband to her. Nobody ever claimed husbands could be counted on, like dogs they strayed, even Ben the little dog, but she could whistle and he would return, longing for home and hearth.

Ugh. She was thinking like the dopey heroine of a dime-store novel, increasingly aware that the received ideas and categories available to her simply did not work. Romance, the end of romance. Love, the tribulations of love. Marriage, the challenges of marriage. *Let's Not Pretend. I'm a Dope.* What utter rot.

No, all that didn't matter. She didn't have the right words, and her rage was not going to produce them. What she had to do, simply, was to face him, and to make something happen. Quickly. On her terms.

She arrived at his office building just after nine-thirty, and if he was going to come in to work – he'd said he had no appointments outside the office – then he would already be there. He was always on time, usually early. She took the elevator to the fifth floor and walked down the empty corridor; it was always empty, as if they only unlocked the doors to the cages at set times. For lunch, perhaps, or to go home. How did they get out to go to the bathroom?

Room 520 was indistinguishable from all the others, none had bells or buzzers, nor even nameplates, you just had to knock. She didn't. Just opened the door, stepped inside, closed it behind her. He was sitting at the desk going through some papers and didn't look up immediately, as if used to the entry of someone who didn't need immediate acknowledgement. When he did look up, a few seconds later, an initial smile transformed into a rictus of astonishment and anxiety.

'Addie! What's wrong? What are you doing here?'

She didn't respond, just looked at him steadily and almost neutrally, as if unwilling to give something away, or perhaps in shock.

'Oh my God! What's happened?'

She could see the thought, his worst fear, cross his mind and register in his eyes and mouth: Becca was dead. The worst, the crippling, disabling catastrophe. And Addie had come to tell him in person; it would have been wrong to call on the phone.

She just stood there, locked eye to eye with him, unwilling to offer any reason for her presence. Just looked, and saw him gradually move through a process of thought: even if a disaster had occurred, how did she get to his office so early? She must have arrived last night.

Last night! Arrived at the apartment to tell him the terrible news – perhaps Mo had a heart attack? Or the boy had drowned? And Addie had waited in the apartment and he hadn't come home.

The apartment! With its dishevelled bedclothes potent testimony to another's presence, she would have seen that, smelled and interrogated it. For a moment he almost wished that there had been some sort of mishap on the Island, something bad but not catastrophic, not as catastrophic as this. Mo dying, or Perle.

He lowered his head in thought. Did he have two disasters to cope with or only one?

'For God's sake,' he begged. 'Talk to me! What's happened? Why are you here?' He pushed back his chair, ready to stand up.

It was better that he stay seated. If he stood he would soon tower over her, or make for the door. Better to trap him behind the desk.

Addie put her hand up, as if to restrain him, never losing his eye.

'How long has this been going on?' Her tone surprised her, the line delivered as neutrally as a pizza. It rather surprised her, and made her feel as if she were indisputably on the high ground.

'How long has what . . .' He trailed off. She wasn't going

to do his thinking for him, fill in the blanks, lay it out. She was too collected, too calm.

'Do you want to sit down?' There was a simple wooden chair on the other side of his desk. Sit down! What was she, some sort of associate, a student, someone anxious for counsel? She stayed where she was, refusing to drop her gaze, increasingly aware that it was too melodramatic, all this staring-down-I-won't-blink-first stuff, but unsure when to release him.

He lowered his eyes.

'Hold on, please,' he said, 'give me a minute to think, this is such a terrible surprise. I don't think . . .'

'You sure don't,' she said. 'Not one little bit.'

He was looking down at his desk, and his head seemed to bob in acknowledgement and contrition.

Not so fast, buddy boy, she thought. *This is going to go on for some time. Why the hell should I make it easy for you?*

He looked at her with his best tried-and-true beseeching look.

'I don't know what to say.'

'You'll think of something,' Addie said, 'we've got all day.'

If she hadn't been standing by the door, it would have opened easily and naturally. As it was, Rhoda had to give it a push, causing Addie to falter forward, while Rhoda, the pressure so suddenly released, stumbled into the room, almost knocking Addie over, like the slapstick choreography of a metaphor. The two women gathered themselves and looked at each other. It only took Addie a moment: the jet black hair, the smell, the familiarity of the entrance. The Turkish delight! It had to be, and one look at her face proved it. The dark-haired woman did not look frightened, chagrined even, merely surprised, and after that, quickly, quite composed.

'I've been hoping this might happen,' she said. 'I presume you are Addie?'

'That's right,' said Addie. 'And now it's time for you to get the hell out of here!'

'No,' said Rhoda. 'That's not going to happen. It won't solve anything. Now we are all here, we need to talk.'

'Like hell we do,' said Addie, taking Rhoda by the shoulders firmly and pushing her towards the door.

'No need to get rough,' said Rhoda in an infuriatingly calm voice. 'I can wait, if you insist. But when you two leave, I will leave with you, and whether you like it or not – either of you – we're going to have this out!'

She closed the door behind her with surprising gentleness, an example, presumably, of how calm she was, how patient, how considerate.

It was ludicrous, farcical. The Turkish delight lurking in the hall, the two of them confronting each other without anything to say, with too much to say. Same thing, was it? It would take a while, best to let it run and run, let little Miss Delight wet her pants lurking in the hallway.

'Do you love her?'

Ben seemed surprised both by the bluntness of the question and its appropriateness. Very Addie, surgical: locate the core and go for it. Nothing like a lawyer would do, they might – he would! – circle round, prepare, lay the foundations, get the facts right, put the points in order of priority, begin marshalling an argument. And what did he get? Like a thrust of a knife: *Do you love her?* Did he?

The timing was important. Too quick, and it would sound like a mere defensive reflex. Too considered, and it admitted the possibility that the answer was *yes.* He counted to three.

'No.'

'Well, you're hardly a sexual predator. What's this all about, then?'

'I'm not sure I know . . .' he began.

'We got plenty of time, she'll be asleep in the damn hallway before we get out of here.'

'It's complicated,' he said.

'Let's make it simpler,' she said. 'Do you love me?'

Two seconds.

'Yes.' Two more seconds. 'In my way. I don't think I am very good at it.'

She took this in with the contempt that he deserved, seemed almost to elicit.

'One more question. Do you want to see your children again?'

The air seemed to congeal with his fear. He leant back in his chair, took a deep breath, put his hand to his heart, rubbed his chest as if to assuage a stabbing pain. He was a lawyer. He knew that in all but the most extreme kinds of divorce custody was given to the mother, visitation rights to the father. He *would* see his children again, sometimes.

But he knew he wouldn't. By the time the process was finished, and their mother's rage had ignited their contempt, Jake and Becca would be withdrawn and distant, no longer his children. Hers. And in time, and probably not all that much time, someone else would be living with them, some man or other, and they would learn to think of him as their father. They were that young, that malleable, that anxious to please. That realistic. He would still be Ben, this new guy would be Dad.

In a spasm of guilt and anxiety he summoned their faces, to make them real, but nothing showed on the screen behind his eyes. The little one? He couldn't remember what Becca looked like! Couldn't hear her voice, recall her gestures and habits. She was going, she was already gone. No Jake either, not a trace. He could feel himself squinting, trying to see; it must have looked as if he were fighting back tears, or summoning them. No harm in that.

It took more than a count of two. A full minute must have passed, a very long time. Too long a time. If he had been clear about what case he needed to argue, he would have done so. Did he unequivocally want his family, the move to Long Island, the new life and law practice? All the things that had seemed so necessary and so right only a few weeks ago. *Yes*. That was exactly what he wanted, but the words would not release. He sat, looked stupid and indecisive, and could see the growing doubt and rage manifesting themselves on Addie's features. *Unwilling even to say he wanted his children!*

But if he registered her outrage, it was accompanied – he could see it in the set of her shoulders and the thoughtfulness in her eyes – by a growing unease. Perhaps this was more serious, more life-threatening than she had assumed; suppose she couldn't simply scoop him up and return him to his rightful place, like putting a dropped scoop of ice cream back in the cone, give him a hard time for a while, forgive him eventually? Suppose he actually was considering an alternative life?

How could he?

'Ben . . .' she said. That was a good sign. 'Ben, what is this really about? Who the hell is she? What does she want?'

'Me,' he said.

'You?' As if it were inconceivable.

'Me! She believes in me.'

'Believes in you?'

'Yes.'

'Oh, how wonderful. Like in God?'

Easy phrase, easy sarcasm, easy to deny. But there was

enough truth in it to give him pause, enough time to recollect Joyce's view of the artist as the god of creation, paring his fingernails . . . Yes, she believed in him like that, wanted not to worship but to enable and to extol.

'No,' he said.

She walked the few steps towards his desk and sat in the chair, aware that it ceded physical ascendency but she had oodles of ascendency to give away.

'You don't sound like you,' she said. 'Where'd you go? Where are you now?'

He started, of a sudden, to cry. Not fugitive tears tracking the lines of his cheeks, but sobs that might well be heard through a door in an office corridor. He didn't care, or think of that. The tearstorm had taken him unaware.

'I don't know,' he sobbed. 'I don't know who I am any more.'

She reached across the desk and pulled at his arm.

'Let's go,' she said, 'and talk, and you will remember who you are, and I will try to find a way to forgive you, if I can. And you will let go of all this *mishegas*!'

He stood up, compliant. If only it were as easy as that.

Addie opened the door, just a crack, and glanced out into the hallway, looked both ways, looked again. The Turkish delight was gone, she was smarter than Addie had given her credit for, unwilling to hang around outside the door like a dog – no, a bitch – waiting to get in. Had some pride, that one, she wouldn't give in so easily. There was trouble, more trouble, plenty of trouble ahead.

She stepped into the hall, leaving the door open for Ben to follow.

'I'll take the day off,' he said. 'I can leave a note on the door and tell the reception girl that I have to go home, won't be back till Monday.'

'Wrong,' said Addie, firmly. 'We are going directly to the train station and on to the bungalow. I am never spending another night in that apartment again.'

He looked startled, but didn't demur.

'And as for you coming back on Monday,' she added. 'I don't think so.'

5

'Rabbit food,' said Sal, pushing the vegetables across the table to Maurice. 'Can't stand the stuff.'

He waved imperiously, looking round the room. 'Hey, you! Take this stuff away!' He pointed to the salad and a puzzled busboy scooped it up. Not many customers rejected the fresh salad! By the time most of them were through with it there were only a few stems and sprouts, the odd leaf perhaps, huddled at the bottom of the wicker basket.

It was part of the Mama Leone's schtick that every table was loaded with an overflowing basket of garden produce – fresh lettuces and cucumbers, fat tasteless tomatoes, bunches of celery, carrots and radishes.

'It don't cost them much, and the tourists love it. Think they're getting something for nothing, only it's the other way round!' Sal laughed loudly at his own wit.

'What do you mean?'

'The tourists get half a buck's worth, and then they pay through the nose because they feel grateful for the generosity, poor schmucks. They come back again and again, recommend it to the other schmucks, never even notice that the prices are higher than other wop joints and the food's worse.'

Schmucks. Mo smiled at the Yiddish word on Sal's shiny lips, wet with the first glass of Chianti Classico. He probably thought it was just English.

'So you're one of the schmucks, too?'

'Nah. It's owned by my cousins. I don't get stuff cheap, I get it free. So order what you like! The steak pizzaiola's great!'

'You go ahead and order for the two of us, you know what's good.'

Sal smiled at this acknowledgement of his culinary expertise, but paused to ask, with unexpected sensitivity, 'You ain't kosher?'

'Not here, I'm not. Why miss all the fun?'

They raised their glasses into the air, clinked them gently, as if toasting their forthcoming business agreement. Morrie sipped his and avoided making a face. He only drank wine at Seders, that Mogen David was good stuff, but this Italian slop tasted like shoe leather. Sal emptied half the glass, as if drinking water, to quench his thirst.

When the teeming bowls of spaghetti arrived they ate in silence for a few minutes, slurping and chewing, bibs round their necks. Sal was too hard on the place, the food was great! If you could stuff it all in. No wonder Italians were even fatter than Jews!

Sal had been heavy-set as a young man, but in middle age he'd entered the spectrum between corpulent and obese. His shiny grey sharkskin suit was some years old, and too tight, the buttons of his not entirely fresh white shirt strained, and patches of hairy chest and stomach showed through. Though the restaurant was air-conditioned, almost too cool, Sal looked overheated. He always did, even in the winter.

By the time they'd finished the spaghetti Morrie was satisfied, replete, begging for mercy. And then the steak pizzaiola arrived, huge slabs of meat swimming in red sauce, together with potatoes fried in olive oil and plates of sautéed vegetables, enough to feed the Israeli army. Or the Italian army, if they had one. It probably got taken away from them after the war.

Maurice knew it was essential that he finish his food, had eaten sparingly the night before, abjured breakfast. When you eat with an Italian, eat like an Italian. Perle would have understood.

At last the waiter took their plates away, refilled the glasses, brushed the crumbs from the tablecloth, offered menus for choices of dessert. Sal ordered tiramisu, recommending it earnestly. Morrie managed to settle, just, for coffee.

'Espresso?'

'Regular.'

Eating precedes business in Italian culture, he surmised, while Jews can do both at once, talking with mouths full, gesticulating, bargaining, haggling. Fun, usually, sometimes less so. This wasn't likely to be.

'So, Morrie,' said Sal, as if casually, 'you understood what I said, right?'

Maurice acknowledged with a nod of the head that he had indeed.

'So. No problems. Right?' It didn't sound like a question.

Morrie dared to waggle a finger, pointed at Sal, waggled it some more. 'The golden goose,' he said. He took a sip of his regular coffee, like a regular sort of guy. 'The golden goose!' As if that settled the matter, and Sal might rise and shake his hand apologetically, having remembered how rare the species was.

'C'mon, Morrie, gimme a break,' said Sal, spreading his hands expressively. He'd become more Italian as the meal went on: the more he ate and the more wine he drank, the more he sounded like, well, a minor mafioso. Which he was not, as far as Morrie could tell. Just another wise guy.

'So, Sal, cut to the bottom line. What're we talking here?'

Sal took a red leather diary from his jacket pocket, put on his reading glasses and leafed through the pages. Put his finger to the page, looked up.

'As of today you owe me $1,130, near enough.'

Morrie nodded, quite right.

'And like I told ya, prices gotta go up. My suppliers are killing me . . .'

So Sal had to kill his customers, that was how it worked: the killing went on up and down the sales chain. That was called business.

After all, he'd done the same thing. A long time ago. Shrewder than most of the *machers* drinking and schtupping their nights away like animals, Maurice had come to the realisation early: These were good times! They were too good! He was smart enough to suspect a bubble, émigré Jews sniffed impending disasters, planned accordingly. If the disaster failed to materialise, that was terrific. If it did, best have a fully mature Plan B in the cupboard.

He did not, of course, foresee the catastrophe of 1929, or the years of deprivation to follow. But one thing was clear to him from the start: good times or bad times, there would always be big shots and hot shots, celebrities, sports stars, movie stars, politicians with deep pockets, old money that stuck, new money that could be made in difficult times. Especially in difficult times.

And all these folks, every one of them, would want to look good, put on their glad rags and take an equally snazzy girl to a club. No matter how bad things were, there was always money to be made. And Maurice had set himself early to making these contacts, pressing flesh, buying drinks, giving out his business cards, being an entertainer. *And supplying those clothes too cheaply.* He didn't need to make big money, not yet. First he got his customers addicted, supplied them at only tiny margins to himself. *Good old Morrie, let me introduce you to him. He's the best!* He could always raise his prices later, like a drug dealer.

And now good old Sal was doing it to him. The only question, now: was he dead, like that ex-golden goose, or just maimed? A leg removed perhaps? An animal that valuable you don't eat all at once.

'Make it reasonable,' said Mo. 'I can pass it on.'

'Course I will, we're old pals, ain't we?'

'Well, thank you,' said Maurice, knowing it to be premature. 'How much are we really talking here? Be a mensch!'

Sal closed his little red notebook and put it back in his pocket, took off his reading glasses, put them in their case, pocketed that as well. Took a sip of his espresso.

'What I said! *Double!* Including what you owe me. Double as well.'

'Sal!'

'You got thirty days,' said Sal, pushing his chair back, standing up. 'It's always great to see you, you take care.'

Morrie stood up with him, grabbed his arm, fought a humiliating desire to fall to his knees in supplication.

'Let me explain, Sal. It's a bad time, very bad. I have obligations. Family, you know. Family.'

Italians liked families. Same as Jews. *Family!*

Sal brushed his hand aside.

'I gotta go, stuff to do, people to see.'

At least he didn't say *people to do*. And with that he sauntered towards the door, pausing to talk to the middle-aged woman at the cash register, turning to wave goodbye in a manner easily mistaken for friendly.

Morrie collected himself slowly, finished his coffee.

No such thing as a free meal!

Before catching a train back to Huntington, Maurice stopped first at his stockbroker's and then at his bank. The situation was not good, but it was manageable. He could pay the $2,260 within thirty days, if he had to. Maybe he could talk the fat bastard down a little, or get more time to pay? He was hardly insolvent, and the prospect of giving out six or eight months of sandwiches to Ben and Addie was painful but not impossible. He would have to sell his few remaining stocks, raise a mortgage. It could be done.

Maurice was by nature optimistic, and by the time he boarded the train from the LIRR his native spirits had recovered. Perhaps this was a good thing after all. His little cottage industry had flourished under the conditions of Prohibition, and then the Depression, which was curious, or perhaps it was ironic. Who cared? Even during the war, with the boys away, many of the girls continued to have a good time, and there were always servicemen aplenty to party with. But now the party was over, and the girls had grown into women, had children of their own, and if they were looking for clothes it was not fancy duds but outfits suitable to suburban mothers. Matrons. Cheap dresses in cheap prints, crap really. Morrie tried to keep up – or down! – with the new tastes (you wouldn't call them fashions) but his income had diminished, his suppliers grown old and he no longer knew where to find his clients. Certainly not at the 21!

The girls were older, he was a lot older; they had lost heart, he had a dicky heart. The writing was not so much on the wall as emblazoned over the sky, as if left there in trails of vapour by some trick pilot: MORRIE IS FINISHED.

Pay the wop the money and walk away. He could stay with Molly and Sol, that was routine, and easy enough, and though they distrusted him they also needed him badly. He'd tell them he was no longer moonlighting, was theirs and theirs alone. They wouldn't believe him, not at first. Who cared? He'd still earn enough to pay his way, minus the sandwiches. Well, the kids would have to learn to stand on their own two feet; they'd had plenty of support, plenty to thank him for.

Not that they were all that thankful! Ben had spoken to him, after dinner at Linck's, as if he were some sort of mobster! Ungrateful *schnorrer*, with his morally superior airs. A big-shot Communist, right? To each according to his needs! And now he needed more money from his sandwich dispenser (lot of thanks he would have for that!) and was pretending he could raise it himself. What was he planning, to rob a damned bank?

But Addie needed the money, and it would have to be found, and not by that lousy husband of hers. He'd spend it.

The burst of optimism dissipated, and it was a weary and heartsore Mo who plodded down the pathway into the bungalow a few hours later. Perle watched him walking like an old man, she'd been waiting for this moment, though she didn't go to the door to greet him. When he entered she turned from the rocker and said in a tone he didn't recognise, 'You need to sit down. Take your tie and jacket off, and I'll get you a cold drink. A beer?'

He began to make himself comfortable. Took off his shoes, too. His slippers were next to the rocking chair. *Solicitous?* That was the word. And *gentle*, too. It was no wonder he didn't recognise it at first. He looked up as if to make sure that it was really Perle looking after him so tenderly, but she was opening a beer in the kitchen, clinking a glass.

'Mo,' she said, 'you look plain worn out. This can't go on. We need to have a talk.'

A talk? What the hell was she talking about?

The next thing he knew, she was sitting on the cedar chest. He put out his hand expecting the cold glass of beer, but instead got hers. He tried to withdraw, it was too hot for this sort of uncalled-for stuff, but she pressed his fingers.

'I don't want to lose you. I need you, we all need you. But this has got to stop!'

He could hardly meet her gaze.

'I have no idea . . .'

She squeezed his finger.

'Enough,' she said. 'Do you think I am stupid?'

He did, sometimes. Not exactly stupid, only not smart in the way he was. Perle was there, Perle was Perle. Her acuity was wasted on him, but her women friends regarded her as anything but dumb. *Smart as a whip, that one.*

He removed his hand, took a long schlook of beer, wiped his mouth with his wrist.

'What are you talking about?' he asked, and as he asked it, knew the answer. She knew *everything.* God knows how.

'You cannot go on like this, Mo. Schlepping your stuff round the city, the clubs, the girls, the shady contacts. Those crappy Italians!'

He nodded.

'So they're after you at last? I'm not surprised. You saw it coming?'

He nodded again.

'I thought I had a little more time, then I could give it up.'

She smiled like an experienced mobster.

'Yeah, yeah, I guess everyone thinks that . . . How much do you owe them? Who? That putz Sal?'

'Yeah.' He looked weary and defeated, so exhausted that not even her prescience aroused his curiosity. She knew. So what? Big deal.

'How much?'

'Couple of grand. It'll be OK, I can just about find it . . .'

'I'll pay it,' said Perle, standing up and retreating to the kitchen. 'Finish your beer and I'll get dinner ready.'

There were a great many reasons, compelling reasons, for Ben to resist the precipitous and humiliating exit from DC. As he sat next to a silent Addie on the streetcar on the way to Union Station, he enumerated them to himself. He hadn't had time to pack. Hadn't told his colleagues that he was taking the rest of the day off. Hadn't packed the necessary papers and briefs for next week's work. Not to mention hadn't found a way to tell Rhoda what was going on.

The alternatives to these humiliations and inconveniences great and small would have been either to refuse to go (consequences unbearable) or to at least have gone back to the apartment to pack (consequences intolerable). So here he was sitting like a naughty and recalcitrant child at his mother's side, paying the price of his misdemeanour. Felony, rather.

On the train to Penn Station they sat in silence, smoking and reading their newspapers, both aware that, for the time being, this was all that was left to them by way of marital connection. At some point they would have to talk, but for the foreseeable future what they would have to do is pretend. They ought at least to make up some story to tell the folks and the kids. They could call ahead from the Long Island Railroad.

'OK,' said Addie, lighting another cigarette with the butt of her last one, 'here's what we are going to do.'

It was up to her.

'We will say we have agreed' – she looked at him like some sort of recalcitrant specimen, a balky llama perhaps, something formerly useful, cute even, but now cowed and biddable – 'that you are going to look after the kids for the weekend . . .'

He looked at her quizzically.

'. . . because I cannot bear to be anywhere near you. I'll stay at the folks' apartment in the city, then come back when you are ready to go back to Alexandria.'

'But what am I to tell them?'

'You're a first-class liar, you'll think of something.' She hunched away from him as if from a putrid smell, then turned and took the sleeve of his jacket and tugged it slightly, redirecting his gaze towards her, making sure he was listening.

'That gives you four weeks to pack it up. Resign, negotiate whatever severance terms you can, give the shortest notice you can, get some document that says you have left of your own free will.'

'That is not . . .'

'No lawyerly points! Just do whatever you can to make yourself look less bad. And here's the other thing: I will never set foot in that apartment again. You can pack it up, get rid of the bed, the sheets and pillow cases, put my things in some suitcases, do what you can. I'm not sniffing the foul air in there ever again.'

He looked surprised, his eyes narrowed slightly, forehead wrinkled.

'Sure, see her again. Say goodbye, forever. Have a weepy farewell, feel sorry for yourselves. I don't give a damn. But if you ever contact her again after that it is going to get nasty.'

He had no doubt about that.

There were compensations, she supposed. She'd been betrayed and could hardly find the means or even motive to contemplate forgiving him. Not yet anyway. But on the far horizon was the image of the children and the sanctity – no, hardly that – but the impulsion of the ongoing family. Did she want to raise the children on her own? God forbid.

Might she parlay her ascendency into a change of terms? To insist on a move not to dreary Long Island but to Manhattan! Could Ben refuse that now? He would trot out the usual excuses: they didn't have connections in the city to start a practice, she would find it harder to find work, costs of living and accommodation were high and standards low, it was an uncongenial place to raise children, they had no close family there . . . blah, blah, blah. But when you added them up, however reluctantly, counted them on your fingers, it made sense: people didn't move into the cities these days but out of them, into the open spaces, new houses, burgeoning opportunities.

She had a whole weekend to reflect, to rediscover the city, walk the streets, sit in the park and look at the ducks, window shop, maybe buy something pretty to perk herself up, mooch around the museums, maybe call an old friend or two.

Maybe call – *might this be possible?* – maybe call Ira.

Before she left the bungalow Addie had given her mother strict instructions not to be strict.

'I'm only going to be away for a night or two, but the kids are feeling a bit fragile, so it would be best if you just give in to them, spoil them a bit. No confrontations, no rules, just have fun!' She was aware, saying so, that it was like encouraging a rhinoceros to be frisky.

A bit fragile? What do children know from 'fragile'? (Perle loathed that word!) Children don't like change? Too bad. What, so they had to move to Huntington? It would be good for them, much better than that boring Alexandria. They'd love it once they got used to it!

Just have fun? That was Morrie's territory and he was going to be at work in the city during the days. Perle and the children had never been alone together, just the three of them, for more than a few hours at the beach. Spoil them a little? They could hardly be more spoiled. No, what she was going to do was provide a *structure*. That meant some rules, for once. Mealtimes, bedtimes, reading times, less television times. It would be good for them, make them less restless and self-engrossed. If only she had not two days but two months, at the end there would be some improvement. She nodded to herself, with the satisfaction of a prison guard imposing a curfew.

The children weren't entirely happy with their advice either. Addie told them that they would have fun with Granny – *who couldn't see through that lie?* – and that they should just do whatever they felt like doing – *or that one?*

Becca climbed onto her mother's lap, clung to her, took a piece of her skirt into her hands and rolled it up, put it into her mouth. Sucked it, snuffled, wiped her nose with her sleeve. Addie could have sworn her eyes rolled back into her head. Classic regressive behaviour, indulge it for a few minutes, dial up the warmth then dial it down again, count to a hundred and slowly detach. Change the subject, distract. Reclaim the six-year-old from the two-year-old.

It was classic, and it worked almost too easily. After the required two minutes, Addie detached herself slowly and said, 'Let's go smell the cedar chest.' It surprised the little girl, who looked up immediately, the languor draining from her eyes, surprised and engaged. Addie liked cedar chests too!

'Can we?' she said urgently, as if invited to indulge a forbidden activity, like swimming after eating a hotdog. She rose and hurried off. Addie made sure to follow in her footsteps; it was an important moment. Becca gestured towards the rocker: 'You can sit here,' she said, for at her height she could just lean her neck into the chest. They both readied themselves, leant forwards, took a deep sniff.

'I told you,' said Becca, sniffing again. 'Isn't it just the best?'

'Divine!' said Addie. 'Better than flowers!'

A few minutes later, sniffing abandoned and sniffles abated, the taxi drove up the drive. Addie picked up her purse from under the dining table, opened the screen door and went out with Becca and Perle, who looked about her anxiously.

'He's just off having a sulk, making a point,' said Addie. 'Just leave him, he'll come round . . .'

Perle was not good at just leaving things, much less *him*, and started back into the bungalow.

Addie walked to the taxi, where the driver had opened the door for her. 'Goodbye, Mother, thanks so much! See you in a couple of days.' She gave Becca a final hug, closed the door and was off.

'Wanna come smell the cedar chest with me, Granny?' asked Becca.

Perle took the little girl's outstretched hand.

'I'd like that a lot,' she said. 'Then we'll have some lunch. Shall we eat on the porch?'

When Perle was determined to take control, she would say, 'May I make a suggestion?' This was not a question, nor was the forthcoming suggestion a suggestion. It would not have countenanced the answer *no.* Anyone saying no would have regretted it immediately, though no one could predict the duration of her potential resentment because no one had ever declined to hear a suggestion, or to follow one.

Jake hated suggestions.

'When I was a little girl, only five years old, I had a big move. I will tell you about it so that you can learn something.'

Perle rarely talked about herself, nor did she refer to the many tribulations of her childhood. Not to the children. Their childhoods had to be shielded from the details of hers. 'Not in front of *die kinder*' was the maxim, and now was the time to break it. It would be good for them. It would see them right, and serve them right.

'My family came to America on a big horrible boat, seven of us going to New York. And do you know what? When we arrived none of us spoke even a word of English!'

She winced at the memory. How could the children understand such things? They didn't. Jake was both uncomprehending and disapproving.

'That's stupid going there if you couldn't even talk the language.'

'We didn't have any choice.'

'Same as us then,' said Jake triumphantly, delighted to find such easy common ground. 'You were forced to move! How did you like it?'

'It didn't matter if I did or I didn't. None of us liked it. We were frightened and miserable. But even we children knew that what we were going to was better than what we were leaving!'

She paused to allow the obvious question. It wasn't forthcoming. She would tell them anyway. Yes, in front of *die kinder*, how else would they learn?

'In my village . . .'

'Was it in the old country, Granny? Same as Poppa's?'

'Well, it was in a different place, but yes, it was like Poppa's . . . And there were very bad men. They were called Cossacks.'

'What's a Cossack, Granny?'

'A very bad man. And they would come on horses. Gangs of them, they were horrible killers, like wolves, only worse.'

'Why?'

'Because at least a wolf eats what it kills.'

'But who did the Cossacks kill?'

'Our families and our friends . . .'

'Why?'

'Because we were Jewish. Cossacks hate Jews.'

'Well, Jews would hate Cossacks, too! So why didn't they kill them back?'

Jake should have been wide-eyed and frightened, but it was too far away, too long ago, nothing to do with him and the threatened exile to Huntington.

'They tried. But the Cossacks had big swords and horses. They could just do what they wanted. They were horrible. The best thing to do was run away.'

'Didn't everybody run away?'

'Some of us did. My family ran away to America. We had to leave as soon as we could, we left everything behind, the rest of our family, our parents and grannies, all our cousins and friends. And our house.'

'Are they still there?'

'The house might be. It was a nice, big house.'

The children looked at her politely, wondering where all this was going, why it was of the slightest importance to them.

'Understand this. *It wasn't up to me when we left.* Parents decide if you need to move and when you need to move, and parents decide what is good and right for the family and for the children. It is not up to the children. They're *children*!' The term was now invested with contempt.

'Yeah, well, maybe you were just dumb. Anyway, I'm not going!'

Becca looked both ways, choosing her side. Jake could do most damage.

'Yeah,' she said. 'I'm not going too!'

'Oh,' said Perle, 'what a good plan! You'll stay in Alexandria, will you?'

'Yes! We will!'

'Where will you live, under a bush? What will you eat? Berries?'

Jake paused to consider.

'We'll live at Neddy's,' he said.

'Yeah!' said Becca. 'At Neddy's! We can live with him!'

Becca had never met Neddy, though she'd once or twice spotted Jake playing catch with somebody he said was Neddy – if it was him, how would she know? – and she sometimes doubted his existence. Maybe he was an imaginary friend. She had one of those when she was little, her name was Hattie because she wore funny hats; they used to play dolls in her bedroom and talk and giggle and eat gumdrops. One day she stopped coming. Becca wondered where she was now, maybe she had an imaginary friend herself? That would be funny. But where would they meet and how would they get gumdrops?

After Granny waddled off, looking satisfied, Jake took Becca by the hand, which was unusual, and led her outside.

'You know we can't live with Neddy, don't you?'

'I guess.'

'So here's what is going to happen. We need to think

about it. Addie went away. We might not even see her any more . . .'

Becca was staring at him, her eyes wider than wide.

'We won't?'

'Maybe not. It means they are getting divorced. You know that, don't you?'

'What's divorced?'

'It's when your mom and dad don't live together any more, and they have to share out all the stuff. Including the kids!'

This was too much to take in. Becca had retracted, pulled her shoulders in and up, chin down.

Her voice had diminished, too.

'How do they share us?'

'Well,' said Jake, attempting a judicious tone, 'we have to choose . . .'

'Choose what, what do we have to choose?' Becca was crying now, her face trembling, freckles displaced.

'Which one of them to go with. Because when there is a divorce you go to a judge and the judge asks the children which parent they want to go live with. So you have to decide.'

Becca considered for a moment.

'What're you going to do?'

Jake had thought about this.

'Ben!' he said. 'I am going to stay in Alexandria, and Ben will get a different job. It's so unfair that he is going to lose his job just because he is a Communist! Communists are good, they want a better world for everybody!'

Becca wasn't listening, knew nothing of Communists, save that the horrible man hated them.

'So I have to choose?'

'Yes.'

'When?'

'Soon, I think soon. School starts soon, so if you are staying with Addie here at the bungalow you'll have to get your stuff and move it here.'

Becca set her face.

'That's what I'll do then. I'll stay here.'

Jake looked surprised.

'Addie needs me,' said Becca. 'It's only fair if each parent gets one kid.'

Jake gave her a hug.

'I'll miss you,' he said. He'd never said anything as nice as that to her before.

'I'll miss you too!'

It would be OK living with Addie, it would. Addie was fun sometimes, not just silly like Ben. One night when Ben was in Washington and Granny and Poppa Mo had gone out, Addie had turned out all the lights in the bungalow and, before the kids could turn on the switches, she would jump out and scream, 'BOO!' Becca hid behind the couch, laughing and crying, begging for the light to be turned on. But soon Jake was with her, taking her hand in the darkness.

'We're going to get you back!' he shouted in the direction of his mother's voice, as if bravely. 'We're coming to get you!'

Addie shrieked, 'No! No!' and they could hear her stumbling and holding on to the furniture as she went out the back door. She made her way down the yard to the swings, to hide behind the tree, while the children stalked her in the dark, lit only by pale moonlight and the intermittent flashes of the fireflies.

'We're coming to get you!' shouted Becca. 'Woo! Woo!'

Addie was clutching herself, laughing and crying, and then laughing harder. 'I'm wetting! I'm wetting!'

'Boo!' screamed Jake.

'Woo!' yelled Becca.

That was so great. After they went into the bungalow and turned on all the lights, wiped their eyes and made hot chocolate. Addie found the marshmallows and put one on the top of each hot mug. It melted and got all gooey.

You couldn't play that game with Ben. He'd be too scared.

You couldn't make a fort with him either.

They parted ways at the concourse of the Long Island Railroad, where Addie insisted on escorting Ben onto the Huntington train. Not that he would have had the gumption, or even the energy, to make a surreptitious getaway back to DC: she had told him what to do, and he would do it, somnolently. He'd have time to make up some damn story or other – Addie shopping in the city, or maybe having a few days off with a college friend? No one would believe it, and it didn't matter. What would they do, give him the third degree, make him confess? No, they'd look askance, Mo would draw him aside to ask what was up, he would shrug and smile and deny and pacify and play with the kids. It would be good for him to see them. The thought of any impending loss of their centrality in his life froze his soul, what a fool he'd been.

He had never kidded himself that he loved Rhoda, not really, but she had perfect pitch, had made the perfect pitch. All the way up from DC, sitting silently on the train, unable to talk with Addie because of the frozen air between them and the proximity of others in the adjoining seats, he had been thinking of redrafting his novel. It could be so much better, he'd been too young, got the authorial voice wrong, started in the wrong place. It could be rectified. It could be good. *Nature's Priest*? Have to reconsider the title as well. What could he have been thinking, precocious Jewish boy from Philadelphia swanning about like Wordsworth in a yellow field of flowers? Hardly! Where'd that come from? *Nature*? *Priest*? Hogwash.

Best to let it go, he'd have to, he already had. It had been written fifteen years ago, was an embarrassment really, without any of the polish and restraint of his short stories. He had enough of those – twelve or thirteen – to make a small volume. Not all were as good as 'Track Shoes', but he could renew interest in them, take them one at a time, polish them up while studying for the Bar. It was just a matter of discipline; after all, they had been written when Jake was a baby and he had been working full time. Get up early, write for a couple of hours, move on to other (and lesser) things.

He nodded his head, comforted by the thought. If he could salvage that, and find a way to navigate Addie's hurt and anger – they would abate, she'd calm down, she didn't have any better choices than he did. It was just a matter of time, really. Unpleasant time perhaps, but Rhoda might turn out to have been a benefactor after all. If he'd learned anything from his political past it was this: bide your time, stick to your beliefs, take the long view. Not that it had worked, not yet anyway. How the hell long a view do you have to take?

At ten after four an exhausted Maurice stepped onto the platform at Huntington Station and trudged wearily round to his parked car, which started first time for once. An hour and twenty-seven minutes later a bewildered Ben arrived at that same platform, walked across the tracks and hailed a taxi. 'Harbor Heights Park,' he said, as if it were one of the minor circles of hell, for the eternally bruised and anxious. The taxi driver nodded, kept silent, seemed to understand.

At much the same time, Addie, having deposited her few belongings in the apartment on West 86th Street and poured herself a whisky, was contemplating making a phone call to Ira's office. It was daunting, and she feared a reflexive rejection, but she was cramped with loneliness and had no one to turn to. She still had former friends in the city, girls from college, now wives. No sense talking to them.

The switchboard girl announced 'Mayor's Office' – Ira was some sort of high-up associate, Deputy Chief of Staff perhaps? – and Addie could just about utter the words 'Ira Gellhorn?'

'Excuse me?'

'May I speak to Ira Gellhorn?'

'Hold on a moment, please . . .'

And please God he would have left for the afternoon, or be in a meeting, or be ill, or on holidays, or anywhere, anywhere but about to be on the phone, on the phone to her . . .

'Hello. Ira Gellhorn . . .' It was his voice, of course it was, and it had that old diffidence that, when he introduced himself, always ended on a rising tone, as if asking a question, or wondering whether he was, in fact, himself: *Ira Gellhorn?*

Before making the call she'd planned for this very moment, how to say the next few words in such a way as to be recognised quickly, nothing worse than the possible (and not unlikely) pause, followed by 'Adele who?'

The pause was already lengthening.

'Hello,' he said, beginning to doubt there was anyone on the line.

'Ira,' she said, her voice holding remarkably well, no letting it quaver or he wouldn't recognise it.

'Ira, it's Adele . . . Adele Kaufmann.'

'Adele!'

The tone was surprised but not hostile, and the pause that followed contemplative. She could hear a faint humming sound, though whether it came from the line or Ira's lips was unclear.

'Sorry to surprise you like this, out of the blue. I didn't even know I was going to call you until I . . .'

'My God!' he said. 'It's been such a long time . . .'

In the following pause they were both recalling – it took no effort – the last time they had seen each other, on the corner of 67th Street near Hunter College, on the day after graduation. She'd broken off the relationship a few weeks earlier, prior to leaving the city to go to Philadelphia, and had only run into him after clearing her possessions from her locker and heading for the subway for the last time.

Her announcement that it was over, and that she needed to move on, had taken him by surprise, though she had tried to ease him into it. At first he thought – how foolish was that? – that she was teasing, and when it became clear that she meant it, that it was over, he had broken into tears and rushed off. A supplicatory note followed, and another, but she thought it wise not to answer. And then there they were, on that corner, and his tears were still flowing. She'd given him a quick, fierce hug, not at all sure that she wanted to leave him but certain that she should.

'Goodbye, darling Ira,' she'd said.

And now here he was, or there he was in some drab office with a good view, remembering as she was remembering, clearly uncertain how to proceed, or if.

'Adele,' he said, 'I have someone in the office with me,

and a meeting to finish. Can I call you back in an hour or so?'

She was relieved, it would give both of them time to draft a script, find a way to . . . to what? To exchange histories, fill in the fifteen-year gap? Or even to do so in person, not over the phone? Was he married now, might he have children? Probably. Stupid goddamn thing to do, calling him up out of the blue like this. Unkind, preposterous.

'Yes, yes, of course. No problem at all. Good idea. I'll be here . . .'

He laughed, he had a lovely laugh with warmth in it that included you.

'I don't know where you are. Or what your phone number is.'

She laughed too – less, well, self-conscious.

'Oh, me. I'm in the city. For the weekend. In my parents' apartment on West 86th.' She gave him the phone number, slowly, and repeated it in case he got it wrong.

'I got it,' he said. 'I'll get back to you.'

She replaced the receiver in the cradle gently, unwilling to break the ensuing silence, took a full swallow from her Scotch and water; she could already feel the effects, sank into the cushiony armchair, took a deep breath.

'What have I done?' she asked. 'What am I doing?' The possibility, still unlikely, that she might meet once again with her old boyfriend, who had adored her, that possibility seemed now dreadful, undesirable, embarrassing. What was she to do, and to say? Pretend everything was just dandy and she was in the city shopping for the weekend? Or tell him everything, simultaneously revealing the desperation that led her to call him and how little that call had anything to do with him, now, the adult incarnation, the husband

and father (probably? Maybe not?) that had nothing to do with her, and would want nothing to do with her. A chill of humiliation spread from her spine onto the top of her skull and down the neural pathways of her arms. She shuddered. My God, what a fool she was making of herself! She couldn't even remember what he looked like, hadn't kept any pictures. He was gone, a ghost with a voice.

The best thing would be to go out, go for a walk in the park, let the time pass, maybe have a cup of tea at the café? Let him call, let the phone ring unanswered. He wouldn't try again and she'd be relieved not to have to bumble her way through the next call.

In the bathroom she washed her face and tidied her hair with her fingers – she looked frightful! – made sure she had the keys in her purse, went out into the hallway and closed the door firmly, rang the bell for the elevator. In a few moments she had passed through the deserted lobby and turned left onto 86th Street, only a few moments from Central Park, warm in the sun, delighted by the whoosh of traffic and the honking of the cars, the accelerating stink of the buses, the pigeons on the sidewalk, people in their summer clothes, sauntering rather than rushing, making room for one another even at the close of the working day, happy to put their faces up to the sun, to feel warm. New Yorkers!

And this, this warmth and energy, the buzz and hum of endless possibility, this was bad for children? It had been good for her, nurtured her, made her alive and alert and curious about the world. The city did that, it made you into you, not into some cookie-cutter facsimile of a person, some suburbanite. Someone real, and substantial.

You want nature, you want trees and ponds and rocks and sunlight filtered through the leaves? Go to New York

City! As she walked she could feel the exhaustion lifting, looked round with pleasure, watched the squirrels scamper, delighted that she wouldn't recognise a single person, that no one would come up, unwelcome, as Michelle had, to examine her and find her wanting. In the city you could know people, lots of people, but entirely on your own terms. In the city you were free.

If the kids were here she could have taken them to feed the ducks, popped into the zoo, gone on the subway to the Automat for dinner. Maybe caught an early evening movie? Or they might, in some alternative life, have been Ira's children, their children, together, and she would live in Manhattan in a nice apartment on the West Side, and have a job and her fancy husband. Go to the opera, see the latest plays, keep up with the art gallery exhibitions. Go to films, try the new restaurants. Take the kids to look at the monkeys and laugh, and cry.

She was crying now, there in the park, remembering Ira, the funny little things, even the things about which she had been scornful at the time. How his hair stuck out, how skinny he was – the first time she saw him naked she awarded him the Nobelly Prize. He loved that. They'd been so young. Why does one have to decide everything important when one is still a child?

Ira adored Yankee Stadium, he said he felt at home there, though he had no idea what he meant by that. He had many friends who were Yankee fans, yet he always went on his own. He would have made an exception for Adele, but she had no interest in baseball: baseball players were roughnecks, she wouldn't be caught dead in the same park as one. So Ira would bring a book, sit in the bleachers to read and watch the game, eat a hotdog and drink a beer.

His hero was Lou Gehrig, who, if his playing wasn't on

the titanic scale of Babe Ruth, was better than him in every other respect. 'A true gentleman,' Ira would say. 'A good family man.' But he cheered as loudly as the rest of them every time the Babe rounded the bases.

He signalled his allegiance to the Yanks by wearing one of their baggy blue caps with NY in white on the front, which meant you could always spot him in a crowd, a sporting eccentric. He had perfect manners, would never have worn it inside, but outdoors it was his trademark. No, he'd say, his uniform. Addie hated it.

'You look like some retarded kid!' she'd say, and beg him to take it off. 'It's the very opposite of exciting.'

He knew exactly what she was implying, considered for a moment and left it on. She came round, eventually. If he was patient enough, she might even come round to the stadium, too.

He'd gone to a game, once, with her father, as devoted a Yankee fan as Ira, though inclined to overestimate the Babe, who was a friend of his.

'Great fellow, the Babe,' Maurice would say. 'Knows how to have a good time.'

That they had come to the game together was a tacit acknowledgement that Ira, already like one of the family, was soon to become one. He was ideal son-in-law material, was going to Columbia law school next year, solid and reliable. Bit funny-looking with all that curly hair, like Harpo Marx, same goofy grin, though he didn't cut your tie in two. Maurice would have liked that, the big pair of scissors, snip! Bit of fun. The boy was too serious, always studying, but he'd grow out of all that. His father-in-law could teach him the ways of the world, not all that college stuff, take him to some swell joints.

Perle knew when to keep her mouth shut, and how to

bide her time, but she was already naming her grandchildren. It was about time: Adele was twenty-two, most of her friends already engaged or married, several with babies on the way. Perle was constructing guest lists for the wedding and seating plans for the dinner. She and Morrie hadn't yet met Ira's parents – didn't even know their names! – but when she suggested to Adele that they invite them over for a meal, the idea was brusquely rejected.

'When I am ready for that, I'll let you know,' she said.

'But Adele . . .'

'And I'm not, not by a long way. Leave it, please.'

Perle did, no sense making a scene, but she went on making her lists, thinking about a caterer, planning menus. This summer would have been a good time, right after graduation – that was when so many of them tied the knot. But no announcement from the kids was forthcoming.

Morrie was better at this than she was, less inclined to plan and to scheme, just warm and welcoming. He and Ira would sit over a beer and talk baseball, animated and happy in each other's company, a more natural fit – Perle sighed ruefully – than Ira and Adele were. But men were like that, they liked to be with other men, understood each other, talked the same language, laughed at whatever it was they were always laughing at. She shrugged. Women too, women were like that as well. If it wasn't such a mucky (and sterile) business, humans should marry within their own sex.

During the last month of their senior year, Ira spent some time in the diamond district midtown on the West Side, hondeling with the Hassids about rings, learning to distinguish qualities and sizes, discussing various mounts. He knew he should consult Adele about her taste – maybe she hated diamonds? – but he wanted it to be a surprise, perfect, memorable.

It was. Not a surprise, a shock. Before he had even closed the deal on a one-carat beauty in a platinum setting she had said 'we need to talk', a phrase likely to strike fear into any lover's heart. His was immediately seized, ceased to beat. Her face confirmed the seriousness of what was to come.

'Ira,' she said, 'darling Ira . . .' She had never called him darling, was not fond of terms of endearment, of honey bunch, sweetie, snookums. She was standing too close to him, her voice lowered. It was intolerable, right out there in the street. If she had something serious to say, why not say it in private? Was she afraid of his remonstration, or the excesses of his grief? He was a sensitive boy and cried easily and sometimes loudly; he was rather proud of that, it was a sign of refined sensibility.

Adele rarely cried, was certainly not crying now, and in spite of the unusual term of endearment was neither warm nor dear. There was something clenched in her, she took his arm too firmly, pulled him towards her as if for an embrace, pushed him back slightly.

'I am so sorry,' she said.

'I don't understand!'

'I can't go on seeing you. I'm so sorry.'

He'd had no idea. Thought things were just fine, finer all the time, heading inexorably towards the conclusion towards which fine things headed: the ring, the celebrations, the *chuppah*, the apartment, the children, the life. Surely she didn't mean it?

He couldn't respond, and seemed unable to process what she was saying. All over? Why? How? They were jostled by passers-by, exposed, humiliated. Anyway, his voice was gone. He stood there, looking at her. Hung his head, began to cry.

She clasped his hand, firmly and quickly.

'I'm so sorry. But it's for the best, you'll see . . .'

He managed a stifled *NO*.

She had already turned, said goodbye, was walking down Lexington Avenue, quickly.

She did not respond to a further series of pleading and impassioned letters demanding to know her reasons, decided it would be better for him if it was a clean break. It certainly was better for her, what was she supposed to do? Reconsider? Negotiate? It didn't matter what her reasons were, and she couldn't have adumbrated them with any clarity. She loved Ira, had loved him, he was her best friend, they laughed and understood each other. No, it wasn't Ira. It was marriage. She felt the insistent shoulders of her parents impelling her into a wedding that she had no desire for, whatsoever. She felt family-bullied, culturally bullied. She was twenty-two, on the cusp of spinsterhood. So what? The mere fact that she loved Ira wasn't sufficient to make her want to marry him, or anyone. What she wanted was to leave the city, get some proper professional training and embark on a life that was her own, not a mere dependence on a husband and (shudder) a bunch of babies.

She didn't think of this as a reasonable decision, or a brave one. It was the only possible choice, if she was to become the person about whom she had been dreaming: independent, worthy of respect. And if Ira had to be sacrificed – poor dear Ira – then he did. He'd get over it, marry someone more in keeping with what he needed, a home-and-baby maker. He'd be just fine.

Addie paused, kicked at some leaves on the pathway, walked round the pond, wondering. Was he just fine? What would he look like now, still skinny and frizzy? He'd surely have abandoned that dumb Yankees cap, though perhaps he still wore it on the weekends when no one was looking, like those funny men who dress up in their wives' clothes.

Had he found that archetypal accommodating woman, with an easy nature and fruitful womb? A Michelle? How disgusting, please God he'd done better than that! She looked at her watch: forty minutes had gone by. She turned back down the path and hurried towards 86th Street. If she was lucky, she'd have time to catch his call.

Ben's arrival, by himself in a taxi, had caused a storm of incomprehension at the bungalow. The children were predictably ecstatic for the requisite thirty seconds of leg-hugging and hand-holding and lifting up and kissing, but on being put down again enquired about their missing mother.

'Where's Addie? Is she still in Alexandria? How come she didn't come back?'

Ben had his story ready and prefaced it with a friendly chuckle.

'Well, you know what Addie's like! No sooner had we got into the city and off the train than she decided she had some shopping to do and headed directly for Bloomingdale's! She had that look on her face . . .'

He looked down at Becca, who nodded enthusiastically.

'I'm going to buy a new dress!'

'More than one, I suspect,' said her father. 'She said she was going to stay in the city overnight and shop till she drops!'

Jake looked sceptical, not so much at the explanation – he couldn't conceive of an alternative – but at the activity. Shopping was stupid.

Standing to the side, in front of the house, Morrie and Perle exchanged one of those looks that tacitly acknowledged that something was up and agreed to say nothing about it. When the kids released their father, they each gave him a hug and Maurice insisted on carrying his briefcase into the bungalow. Why didn't he have more luggage? That was odd.

'It's great to see you!' he said, a little too emphatically.

It wasn't dinnertime quite yet. They gave him time to shower and change, mix a drink and sit on the porch, collect himself after the long journey. The children hovered for a while but soon wandered off to play in the hammock, one wrapping themselves in while the other swung it round and round. It made Granny crazy when they did that, they were sure to hurt themselves! Maurice was reading the paper in the living room, Perle was in the kitchen, as if each of them, the adults and the children, had agreed that it was time to be quiet and to leave each other be.

The next morning, after coffee and toast, Ben asked if he could use the phone.

'Use the phone? Of course you can? Why do you need to ask?'

He'd never felt entirely comfortable at the bungalow, didn't treat it as if it were his own, make himself snacks, turn on the radio or television, borrow the newspaper, take a shower, use the telephone. These things, this place, belonged to them, and if Addie rightly felt comfortable in availing herself of every facility, he certainly did not.

I wonder why that is? he thought. Why he had never settled during his Huntington visits, never felt as if it were home? Well, soon enough it would be, it was time to see to that. Either he could pussyfoot around, negotiate with his wife, wheedle and ingratiate, or he could do something positive, on his own, right now.

He consulted his pocket address book, took up the phone and dialled. After four rings it was picked up by Harriet

Silber, breathlessly, as if she had been running, afraid to miss the call. How far could someone run in that *ferschleptah* apartment anyway? The phone was right there, ten steps away from anywhere. What the hell else could she have been doing?

'Harriet? Hello, it's Ben.'

There was an uncomprehending pause.

'Ben Grossman, you know, Addie's husband. We came to look at the apartment . . .'

'Oh yes, I remember . . .'

The tone wasn't chilly, quite, but Harriet had clearly been expecting this call for some time, if only as a matter of courtesy. She was anxious to get the lease resolved before they moved to Great Neck, though they hadn't yet tried to find anyone else. Michelle had been so sure that Ben and Addie would be *thrilled* to take over the apartment. Some *thrilled*!

'Look,' said Ben, 'I am so sorry we've been slow getting back to you . . .'

'Yes. Of course . . .'

'. . . but as you know it has been a very hectic time, rather . . . complicated, if you could put it like that.'

You could. She knew the story.

'But I think we are seeing our way clear now, and I can confirm . . .' There was a brief pause while he asked himself if he could indeed confirm anything at all. 'I can confirm that we are definitely interested.'

'That's a relief,' said Harriet, 'and Michelle and Frankie will be delighted! It's a perfect solution for you all!'

'Perfect,' said Ben, 'just perfect. Could I come round this afternoon to have a final look and to discuss details?'

'Sure. I'll see you both then.'

'Oh, it'll just be me, Addie's in the city doing some shopping.'

There was an interrogative pause, which he didn't interrupt.

'Would three o'clock be all right?' he asked.

'Perfect, see you then.' Harriet hung up, perhaps a little quickly.

At two-thirty he asked Morrie if he could borrow the car to go into town.

'Don't ask! Stop with the asking already! What's mine is yours!'

'Thanks, Mo, I appreciate it.'

Maurice passed him the keys.

'Doing some shopping?'

'Yup, few things to pick up. Anything I can get while I'm in the village?'

He could sense that Maurice, who seemed at a loose end, was about to suggest they go together, thinking it would give them a chance to talk for a few minutes, man to man. Something was up. And knowing his daughter as he did, he suspected it might be trouble. Ben had never spent a night at the bungalow on his own, and the story about Addie doing some shopping didn't cut any ice with him. No, something was up.

'I think I might get a haircut while I'm out,' said Ben. It was a good excuse, it would take a half-hour, maybe more, if there was a wait on a Saturday afternoon. You don't take your father-in-law to the barber's with you.

'Oh, OK. You do that. I'll see you later. You want me to arrange a game of pinochle tonight? I could get Popshe and Sam. Or maybe Frankie might play.'

'That'd be great, Mo, let's do that.'

His father-in-law smiled at the thought.

'You better go to the bank too,' he said. 'You're going to need some money!'

*

She could hear the phone ringing as she opened the door, rushed across the room and picked it up, trying to keep her voice neutral, as if answering a call from the beauty parlour.

'Hello?'

'Hi. It's me.'

'Thanks for calling back.'

'Why wouldn't I? It's been a long time.'

It wasn't clear to Addie, nor perhaps to Ira himself, what this meant. That after fifteen years it's good to catch up with an old friend? Old? Friend? More than that, surely, and both of them knew it.

The pause had gone on long enough. Pregnant, did they call it? What would be would be.

'Let's cut to the chase, can we? I have such fond memories of those times . . . I'd love to know what has happened to you.'

He laughed.

'Lots! And you?'

'Lots!'

The next pause signalled: *We're not getting anywhere, are we?*

'Look,' said Addie, 'I don't know how you're fixed these days, how you live, who with. Anything, nothing. But I am in the city, and I am free for a drink tonight, or anytime tomorrow. What do you think?'

'I'd like that. I think I would. And I am leaving work in an hour or so, let's meet.'

'Great! Where?' She knew better than to suggest the Oyster Bar, but hoped he would. That would be the sign she was waiting for, the signal.

'I work up at 88th on the East Side.' She knew he worked at Gracie Mansion, Mayor Impellitteri's residence, and that he would not say so. Perhaps he was embarrassed to be serving a relative non-entity who was rumoured to have Mafia connections, who was a former law clerk to a schmuck: Supreme Court Justice Peter Schmuck.

'How funny, I am staying right across the park on 86th and Central Park West.'

'If you could bear to come to my side of town, there's a bar and grill on Lexington between 64th and 65th. Donoghue's. It's simple and friendly. Good drinks.'

'I think I'll walk across the park. I need to clear my head. So I'll see you there at seven-thirtyish,' said Addie. 'Don't worry if you're a bit late, I'll have the paper.'

'See you then,' he said. His voice sounded relieved. Perhaps because the call was over. Or perhaps because they were going to meet? Both, presumably, she thought. Both, I hope.

Was it significant that the meeting place was just a few blocks south on Lexington from Hunter College, almost within sight of the corner on which they'd said goodbye?

Of all the joints, she thought, why'd he choose this one? It must be significant, but what did it signify?

She had no intention of walking across the park, was just buying time to see if she could put herself together. She walked into the bedroom and studied her image in the mirror on the back of the door. My God! A drunken, broken night, that frightful scene, the ghastly silent train journey. Her face looked as if it had been soaked in detergent, blotchy, sagging, irrecoverably miserable. And she was going to see Ira in an hour and a half! Why had she agreed to that? How could she? She didn't even have a change of clothes, even of underwear, hadn't seen any need to bring an overnight bag, all her stuff was in the apartment. Which she would never again set foot in.

She ran a bath and undressed reluctantly, discarding her rumpled skirt and blouse, looked at herself in the mirror once again, naked. Looked away. How would Ira remember her? What could he possibly think of this exhausted, saggy-eyed, floppy-titted, greying middle-aged incarnation of that pretty girl?

Best to call it off. She walked to the phone, began to dial, put it down, went back to the bathroom and turned off the taps, dressed again, went out the door. There was a clothing shop on Amsterdam, at 85th, was it? Somewhere round there. A five-minute walk, nice shop with a green-striped awning. She bought everything she needed, and then some more. Pretty satin underwear, a skimpy new bra that sent a clear message. She deserved a treat. And if she was unlikely to look like a treat, at least she wouldn't look a walking disaster.

She walked home with her bags, started the bath again, lay down to soak. What was she so anxious about after all? It wasn't like they were going to rent a suite at the Waldorf Astoria. Just a drink with an old friend . . .

Perle didn't have much in the way of make-up, but Addie had her own powder compact, lipstick and mascara, and found an old jar of Max Factor Pan-Cake Make-up, designed to make you look like a Hollywood star. Addie was shocked to see it. Her mother! She would have been less surprised to find a gun.

By the time she was dressed and done up, her second visit to the mirror was more reassuring than her first. If she didn't entirely like what she saw, the emerging lines and wrinkles, the loss of skin tone, the baggy eyes and lank hair, she knew that Ira would. He'd never had much of an eye for detail. And he sounded excited to hear from her, hear her voice again. He had loved her.

And she, him.

*

Harriet Silber was not there, and Charlie Silber was not happy. He opened the door to the apartment, waved Ben towards the living room, indicated which chair he might take. Ben took it.

'To tell you the truth, Ben,' said Charlie in a tone just short of lawyerly, 'we are a little disappointed not to have heard from you. In fact, we have people wanting the apartment – you know the Wassermans, Teddy and Ellie? – but we've been waiting to hear from you. In fact, on Monday we were going to offer it to them . . .'

Ben nodded in a manner suitably apologetic.

'. . . unless this visit is to agree to take on the lease, and to arrange a date to sign the papers and to firm up the details?'

Ben still didn't say anything. Sometimes, as any lawyer knows, it's best to let the opposition talk themselves out, make a mistake. *Opposition? Mistake?* What was he thinking? If there was any opposition it wasn't the poor sad Silbers, and if any mistake was being made it was his.

But Charlie was finished, nonplussed that Ben was so unforthcoming. What was the matter with the fellow? Where was his pretty wife? Something fishy was going on, he could smell it.

'I gather Addie is in the city? So have you and she agreed, and can we all now agree?' He'd warmed up a little, talking, slowly and sympathetically, as to a retarded child.

'Yes,' said Ben, not altogether firmly but in a clear enough voice. 'Yes, we have. If you can draw up the papers with the management, we can sign them as soon as they are ready. Or' – he paused for a moment, things were going to get a bit tricky – 'Addie can sign them. I will be in Alexandria, serving out my month's notice and getting the apartment packed up for the moving men. We hope to be able to come sometime in September. If the kids need to start school before we move, we can always stay at the bungalow with Addie's folks.'

It sounded slightly odd to Charlie, but he had no reason to doubt Ben's word, only his sanity. It wasn't hot enough to be sweating that profusely, and his picking at the dead skin on his hands was not only compulsive but disgusting. Flakes appeared on the carpet as regular as light snow.

Ben stood up, collecting himself, gave a wry grin. 'Well,' he said, 'nothing ventured, nothing gained. I'm sure we will be happy here.'

On the evidence to date Charlie was by no means certain they would, but it wasn't his look out. Great Neck was, and the last bridge had been crossed. Harriet would be delighted to hear it.

Two, Addie reflected happily, was just the perfect number. Just the two of them, at Donoghue's. To-day, a two-some, what a to-do. Two Bloody Marys, just right, today as yesterday, blessed be the Lord. Two made them both warm and giggly and connected, risk a third and they would end up in bed, only separately, ready for sleep. Best keep it at two, order a strip steak for dinner, medium rare, some mashed potatoes and gravy, maybe some cabbage. Irish places always stewed it to mush so it dissolved in your mouth, but with a comforting flavour and smell, like day-old baby food in a nursery.

They had drinks at the bar, but the after-work clientele was egregiously gregarious and invasive. Had they come in before? Did they work locally? Ordering the second Bloody Mary, they spotted an emptying banquette towards the rear and installed themselves on the red leather seats, designed for maximum discomfort, straight-backed and unyielding, so you wouldn't be tempted to stay and stay. They didn't mind. Their knees touched under the table, they raised their glasses, touched them together. Clunk, not ping. Heavy glasses, used to multiple toasts. Shall we toast ourselves, our meeting again? They laughed. Their talk was starting to flow now, thank God, it had been a little stiff at first, neither of them relaxed – why should they be? – not quite knowing how to get over those first few minutes, before the first drink took hold. Or, Addie had to admit to herself, her second, if you counted the one in the apartment.

'Have you seen *The Crucible* yet?' Ira asked. 'It's extraordinary!'

Making conversation, a bit sad. Addie hadn't been to the theatre in years and, though she'd read the reviews of Miller's new play, she didn't know anyone who had seen it.

'No,' she said, 'I'm not sure I even want to. I don't trust these allegories – is that what you call them? You know, when a thing gets used to represent another thing? We have our own witch trials here and now, why should I give a damn about a bunch of hysterical pilgrims?'

'But that's just the point! This kind of hysteria has deep roots in the American psyche . . .'

She waved her cigarette in the air, leaving plumes of smoke.

'Gimme a break! The American psyche? Whose psyche? Mine? Yours? A farmer in Kansas? A redneck in Arkansas? There's no such thing. There's no such thing as America . . .'

He shook his head, weary and dismissive. She sensed him hunching away from her and had an acute recognition that if she carried on she would lose him.

'But anyway,' she said as gaily as she could muster, 'I guess I'll see it. I'm a big fan of his, and I adore Willy Loman. I just worry that he has gone too far this time, and that before he knows it he'll be on trial before those HUAC vampires, defending himself!'

'I'm sure that is just what he is intending,' said Ira, recovering himself and re-joining her.

Addie lit another cigarette off the butt of her dying one, pulled the ashtray close.

'I wish you wouldn't!' Ira said.

'Why not?' She lit up and took a deep drag, exhaled, not exactly in his direction.

'Please. Since I stopped, the smoke makes me feel sick and makes my clothes smell.'

So what? her expression said. *Big wussy!*

'Besides, they are bad for you!'

Addie held hers in front of her face and looked at it enquiringly.

'Bad for you? How?'

'They make you cough, can't be good for your lungs . . .'

'Not mine! Couldn't live without them!'

'Ask your doctor,' Ira said tartly. 'And do please put it out. It was OK sitting at the bar, close to the door. Surely you can make it through a meal without one? Maybe you could just concentrate on me!'

Put that way, Addie found herself acceding and concentrated on him ferociously. He squirmed and laughed. She needed a cigarette.

He was different, it was unreasonable to suppose he would have been just the same; he was better, grown into himself, had put on some weight, looked great in a well-cut suit and striped tie, no stupid baseball cap with frizzy hair sticking out. Less hair altogether, he'd be pretty bald in a few more years, just as his father had been. No hat at all, it wouldn't have suited him.

She remembered him, and them; it was impossible not to.

'What are you smiling about?' he asked, aware that there was something he was being left out of.

She'd been thinking, how could a girl not, of making love with him, those sultry afternoons in his apartment.

'What?' he said again, as she rubbed her finger round the rim of the cocktail glass and put it into her mouth, excluding him, seeming to retract.

'Just thinking . . .'

'What, thinking what?' He smiled too, perhaps catching on. He got it, sort of.

He'd been forthcoming, though there seemed little enough to forthcome about. A successful but not meteoric three years at Columbia Law, a slow rise in the ranks of the lawyer/politico spectrum, the cushy but unsatisfying job in the Mayor's office, perhaps something better if a decent Democrat won the mayoralty election next year and kept him on.

'Yeah, yeah,' said Addie teasingly, as if dismissively, 'get on to the real stuff!'

He knew what she meant, but his real stuff wasn't all that interesting either. He waved his hand. 'I'll bet yours is better!' he said. He knew she'd got her Masters at Penn, but then she'd disappeared from the radar. What happened in those years? Husband? Children?

She resented the fact that he didn't ask, first, about her work. Career? Professional life? His account of himself left matters of relationships trailing in second place behind career advancement.

'It's been difficult,' she said. 'I was so politically active when I was at Penn . . .'

He looked up from the rim of his glass, surprised.

'Politically active, you? I wouldn't have guessed that. How come?' The implication was also clear: following the lead of some guy, no doubt, politics at second-hand, commitments too. She was never that sort of girl, thought entirely individualistically: psychology, therapy, social work. Picking up the wrongs and the wronged one by one, applying bandages but never staunching the bleeding.

'It was exciting. It made me feel alive . . .'

'But now?'

'Less alive, I guess.'

How much should she tell him, how little? She couldn't blurt out the whole story, it would make her new contact with him seem as pathetic and regressive as no doubt it was. Best keep him in the dark. Best avoid personal matters, both of them, for a time.

Maybe a third Bloody Mary might just be tolerable. They were eating a heavy meal, all that food would sop up the alcohol. She didn't feel drunk after two, just heady and a little excited. She raised her hand and waved to the waitress, pointed to her glass. Ira, surprised, pointed to his as well.

'Virgin,' he said.

'Fallen,' said Addie. The waitress looked at her blankly.

'Real!' explained Addie. 'Spicy!'

The waitress looked at Ira, the lightweight.

'You spicy too?' she asked.

'Nope,' said Ira a little ruefully.

'Coming up!' said the waitress.

The third drink quickly imbibed, Addie got the short story from Ira. An ex-wife, no kids. A few relationships, some lasting a few years. Not seeing anyone at the moment. Didn't mind, not too much, so much work to do in his job.

And her? What brought her to town?

Addie hesitated almost too long, suppressing a strong desire just to blurt out the whole sorry story, the hell with it, it would chase him out the door pronto.

'Doing some shopping, as I said, just for the weekend. My husband Ben and the kids are on the Island at my folks' bungalow . . .'

A look of fond reminiscence entered his eyes and he bowed his head.

'How are they?'

'Same as ever, I guess, getting on a bit. My dad's as young and vital as ever . . .'

Ira smiled.

'I loved him, you know.'

'Yes. Everybody does!'

Why'd she say that? It diminished his attachment, made him seem just another of Morrie's casual admirers. He'd been more than that, a lot more.

He lowered his eyes.

Addie put her hand over his.

'I'm so sorry, stupid me, always putting my foot in my mouth. Of course you loved him, and he loved you, he wanted . . .'

He took his hand away, slowly.

'I know he did.'

There was a pause as they recollected themselves, reconnected, carried on.

'Anyway, Ben's just up for the weekend, works for the government as a lawyer, so you can guess . . .'

Ira's eyes met hers, and held.

'I'm sorry, it must be hard.'

'Very! We have to leave DC, make a new life. The kids are only ten and six, they'll adapt, but Ben will have to pass the Bar, start a practice. And I'll try to find work, it's been a while . . .'

'Where will you move to?'

She paused for a long time, yearning for a cigarette to extend her thinking time.

'Probably the city,' she said. 'I'm going to look for an apartment, I've been going through the real estate section in the *Times*, not sure we can afford anything halfway decent . . . But this is the only place where I feel like myself!'

'I'm not sure what you mean.'

She paused for a moment, wiped her mouth unnecessarily.

'I dunno. But when I look at the lives most women lead, it makes me sick . . .'

He looked doubtful, or perhaps it was disapproving. He'd had ample experience of Addie's rage for self-determination, and what had it led to? Was she happier now than she would have been with him? *In the city!*

'It'll be nice to have you back in town, and I'd like to meet Ben. I'm sure . . .'

'You wouldn't,' she said. 'And I don't want you to, things have gone dead between us, all this pressure has more or less squeezed the last juice out of the orange. Or do I mean lemon? Anyway, there's nothing left except raising the children together, pursuing our own ends.'

Pursuing *her* own ends? Did that mean what it might have implied? Was that why she'd got back in contact, to see if he was available, if only on a part-time basis?

If it did, he was, probably he was, going to have to think about it . . . Why not?

After his haircut – he had to return shorn, to justify the lie – Ben looked at his watch, and decided that ten of five wasn't too early for a drink at Finnegan's on Wall Street, where he and Mo sometimes had lunch and a beer, watched the baseball on the TV behind the bar, stayed out till the enemies squawked. Came home happy, laughing, not having been missed at all. The bungalow was a steadier ship without men in it.

He ordered a martini on the rocks with a twist, found a table in the corner and, twirling his finger round the rim, contemplated not so much what he had just done – the audacity of which surprised and rather frightened him, when he wasn't admiring it – but how he might get away with it. Addie would be home by Sunday afternoon. She would have to be told. Why not? She might detest the very smell of him for the moment, but she'd get over it, she'd have to. And wasn't he providing what was best for the family? She'd reluctantly agreed to just that only a week ago, how could she fail to see that he had acted in all their interests, provided the platform on which they might re-establish themselves and move on?

By the time he'd downed the second martini, he was secure in his self-belief and increasingly angry that Addie would be unable, or unwilling, to see sense. OK, he'd made a mistake, people do sometimes. And sometimes, often, good things come of such incidents. It was only an incident after all, had only lasted a few months, during which he had known it would not last, nor should it. Rhoda had played her cards as well as possible, not very subtly but compellingly, offered him what she presumed he wanted and needed. But they both knew he had the winning hand, and it was called children. He would explain that to Addie, maybe even add something about her, she would understand.

No. She wouldn't. He looked round the dimly lit room, filled with afternoon drunks, a hunched and bulky one who was blowing smoke rings from a large cigar, watching them rise, then blowing another through it as it expanded. A few late lunchers, or perhaps they were early dinners-ers, were spotted round the tables. Ben noticed a payphone on the rear wall, with no one at the table beneath and a cord long enough to talk while staying seated. He picked up his drink, nodded to the barman and relocated himself, searched his pocket for change, found a few quarters. It would be enough for a ten-minute call, that would be plenty. It would be heartless simply to disappear, leaving Rhoda lounging round the building hoping for a glimpse of him as he was towed away like a broken-down car. Anyway, in a few days, on his return to the office, there she'd be. It was impossible to contemplate reconnecting like that, in a hallway. Not that there was a connection still, not really.

The operator directed the call to her office and the phone rang four times before she picked up, as if she knew it would be him and didn't want to seem anxious.

'Lo,' she said, unusually. She usually made a formal response, gave her full name, sometimes even her title.

'Rhoda? It's me.'

'Oh, it's you. All of a sudden you don't even have a name?'

This wasn't going to be easy, but at least she hadn't hung up, recognising, as he had, that even this stilted call was likely to be better than any alternative.

'I just wanted to say . . .' – *Just wanted to say?* For Christ's sake! So say it already – '. . . that I am so sorry. That was a terrible scene, wasn't it? I'm in Huntington now, but I will be coming back to DC in the next day or two, not quite sure when . . .'

'You mean, when she lets you.'

'But I will certainly be in the office by Tuesday, say. I

have a lot to catch up on, a lot of things to do, it's a bit of a nightmare.'

'Are you asking for some sort of permission? Or just giving me your itinerary?'

He looked round the bar. Smoke rings were gathering round the ceiling, it was hard to breathe, hard even to see. He sniffed, closed his eyes.

'Look, Rhoda. All I am asking is to see you, to talk. There's no sense ending up this way. Can we have a drink after work on Tuesday?'

'Oh, you'll be allowed to see me? What a treat.'

A sudden anger approached and threatened to overtake him. She had no right to such contempt. They'd had a fling, she'd pretty much initiated it, it was going nowhere, it was over. Why make a goddamn fuss?

'I don't need this,' he said, intending to be firm, sounding loud. For someone who never raised his voice, it was surprisingly strident and had attracted the attention of Bill the bartender and the corpulent ring-blower, who turned and looked at him quizzically. Things happened at Finnegan's, if you kept an ear out. Nobody spent a prolonged time there because they were happy, only because they were hoping to be so after a few drinks.

'Rhoda, it's up to you. Tuesday, say at six? I'll be ready. If you're not, fine, I will go home. And I won't be asking again.'

He put the phone down gently, rather proud of himself. He'd had a good afternoon: arranged things neatly. The lease for the apartment. The fare-ye-well with Rhoda. And he still had two quarters left. Efficient, and cheap. He took out his cigarettes, lit one delicately, leaned so far back in the chair that it teetered. The folks at the bar looked at him admiringly, he thought. A real man's man.

The thought lasted a second or two, quickly replaced by its lurking shadow: *How pathetic: what a goddamn mess.*

Dinner was on the table when he got back to the bungalow. Some meal or other was always on the table, the table was never empty. How did that figure? Were they supposed to be eating all the time? Yet he was grateful, for food did not prompt but prohibit conversation. He was rather pleased to have a reason not to talk. He chewed slowly twenty times, as some magazine had suggested, good for the digestion – his certainly needed all the help it could get, the heartburn had been particularly severe the last few weeks. He was practically keeping the Tums company in business, ought to buy shares.

Everyone was looking at him. The kids, heads down, gazing upwards under their eyelashes, frightened to say anything lest he get up and leave the room.

Maurice, unable to tolerate silence of any duration, remarked that the haircut looked good. 'Got those curls at the back of his neck, didn't they, Perle?'

Unable to see, Perle got up from her chair and walked behind Ben, peered sceptically.

'They did, but Ben is always so well-groomed.'

Which was to say – as she reclaimed her dining chair – that he hadn't needed a haircut at all, and who did he think she was, some sort of dope? And why did his breath smell of mints? Ben didn't even like mints, never had one, even after dinner.

Something was up, sure as shooting, and she was going to find out, no sense them all sitting round like bumps on a log. She'd already helped the children, taught them something about life, how to get things in perspective. They'd be better for it, you could tell; they were a bit more thoughtful, not so restless. Taking things in.

She'd helped Maurice too, set him straight. She smiled a smile of self-satisfaction, which felt funny on her face, she wasn't used to them. It was a good thing no one was looking, they'd have thought she was choking on an orange fruit slice. Mo had been surprised, chagrined, felt out-something . . . manoeuvred? Or maybe just outplayed, as if in a game of canasta. Snap!

It was like that story Ben told him about. Dead, something Dead. 'It's by Joyce,' he'd said, and paused, soliciting the ignorant response 'Joyce who?' Mo had stayed shtum. The story was about a wise guy who thinks he's superior to everyone in his family, but who discovers at the end that he's just another schmuck. He ends up staring out of the window at the snow. In Ireland, was it? Doesn't matter, yeah it was. Joyce, James Joyce. Pretty smart guy.

He was a schmuck too, Mo the big shot with his sandwiches, the centre of all the attention. And Perle was right, all it did was make them take him for granted, and resent it when he didn't deliver, as if he were an inefficient delicatessen.

'Enough already,' she'd said firmly. 'It is bad for them. They need to stand on their own two feet, it's about time. Already Frankie resents Ben and Addie, he wants more for his new offices! When's it going to end?'

He didn't pause, he'd made up his mind, or she had.

'Now!' said Mo. 'It's over.'

'Thank God for that,' said Perle, dangerously close to hugging him. 'Now they can just love you because you're you.' He had refused her offer – of a loan, she'd insisted – to pay off Sal from some money she'd salted away when her mother died, and invested wisely. Never said a word. Still wouldn't say how much she had. Enough.

It astonished him to know so little, and to have been

known so much. He should have been ashamed, but he was unfamiliar with the feeling.

He shrugged his shoulder. 'I'm a small man,' he said.

Just another schmuck. No better than the others, no worse. Just me.

And as for Ben? You just had to corner him, pin him down, offer a few words of wisdom. He was teachable, Mr Smarty Pants, if you knew how. Addie didn't. Perle paused for a moment, went into reverse. Where was Addie anyway? Shopping in the city. What *mishegas*! And why wasn't she back yet? How long does it take to buy a dress?

Perle shook her head and aimed a significant look in Morrie's direction. *I am moving into action.* But he was eating latkes obliviously, his mouth dripping a blob of sour cream at the corner. He wiped it with the side of his wrist, didn't even look round to see if anyone was looking, didn't care if they were. Only a man would do that; women used napkins or handkerchiefs, women were civilised. Not a term she would ever have applied to men, though they had their virtues, only Perle couldn't remember, just at the moment, what they were.

She'd leave the dishes for the girl to unset and wash, she was lazy this one, it would be good for her to do more, mooning about in her room most of the time, you hardly knew she was there, and when she came out, surly and unresponsive. 'Time to send her home!' Perle thought. 'Causes more problems than she solves.'

She suggested coffee to Ben, offered to bring it out to him, but unusually he declined, though he took his place on the corner lounger pacifically enough. If you looked him in the eye, which he resisted, he was a bit glassy. He could hold his drink, that one, had plenty of practice, but you could always see it in his eyes. Drunk, near enough drunk, ate too much to try sop it up, try to get away with it.

It didn't take an Einstein, did it?

'Ben,' she said, 'can I make a suggestion?'

He knew better than to flinch, or make a funny face. *Here they come*, he thought. *Perles of wisdom*.

'Of course.'

'Well,' she said, 'it's obvious something is up. I think you ought to talk about it. Get it out in the open.'

'Well, Mother . . .' he began. He seldom called Perle 'mother' and when he did what was intended was the opposite of intimacy. The term made things formal, unaccustomed, stilted. She was *not* his mother. Not that he called his mother 'mother' either. He rarely called her at all.

'. . . as you know, we are under a lot of pressure – about work, where to live, when to move, how to make a living – all at the same time, and there's not much time to make the right decisions. Things at work are very delicate, and it's a strain.'

He knew better than to play the Red card, which would not elicit sympathy: when Perle thought of Russia, she thought of Cossacks dressed in red, with sabres for killing. Russia was the homeland of vile oppressors, not of the intellectual saviours of mankind. What *narishkeit*: Communism! Ben was too young to understand.

'I guess we're all showing it, the kids . . .'

'Don't you worry about them,' said Perle firmly. 'They know they have to move, they won't be any trouble at all.'

Ben looked at her quizzically. First he'd heard of it. They'd been nothing but obstreperous when talk of moving had been raised. Last he heard they were planning to live with that schlepper Neddy.

'But,' Perle continued, 'I am worried about you and Addie.

She's gone off. I don't believe this shopping malarkey for a minute. So tell me what's going on. Where is she?'

'At your apartment, like I said. Call her up if you don't believe it.'

'I did,' said Perle grimly. 'Believe you me. Three times. No answer.'

Ben was not entirely surprised to hear it, though he didn't know where she might go. She was unlikely to be mooning about that tiny, depressing apartment.

'And,' said Perle, firmly, pointing a finger as if accusingly, 'please tell me when she is coming home?'

'I don't know,' said Ben.

Late on Sunday morning the phone rang and Becca beat everyone to it.

'Hello, this is Becca speaking.'

She listened for a few moments, and smiled, a big one.

'That's great, Addie,' she said. 'I missed you!'

She listened for a moment to the reciprocal missing-you-too response.

'Do you want to talk to Ben?'

He was directly behind her, reached out his hand, put the receiver to his ear, listened.

'I'll see you then,' he said, and hung up.

They were all clustered round.

'She'll be at the station at 12.47,' he said. 'I will pick her up.'

Becca held on to his arm excitedly.

'Can we come?' she said.

'I don't think so,' said Ben. 'You'll see her when we get back to the bungalow.'

In fact, Addie was arriving at twelve-thirty. The extra minutes would give them time to talk before she arrived home to a heroine's welcome. Why is it that the worse you behave, the better you get treated? Something of the prodigal daughter about it. No wonder Frankie resented her so.

Morrie looked at him steadily, fished in his pocket, proffered the keys to the Caddy without comment. He knew the LIRR timetable backwards. There was no train due at 12.47, Ben was buying time.

When the train pulled into the platform, and Addie disembarked from one of the front coaches and walked down the platform towards him, Ben's immediate response was: 'That isn't her!' It was, of course, same face, same body, same gait, recognisable outfit: Addie. But not Addie, something added, the walk quicker, even assertive, her head held higher than usual, anxious to hold his eye, she looked like a lawyer coming to a meeting with an attorney for the opposition.

When she got to him he almost expected her to hold out her hand to shake, but instead got a perfunctory nod.

'Hiya,' she said. 'Thanks for picking me up.'

Thanks? For picking her up? Why wouldn't he, unless she was some sort of stranger? Stranger: that was what she was, not herself, something else, something . . . more perhaps? Other?

All the collected calm that he had manufactured, working on himself as he drove to the station, was fractured. She had, with those few unwelcoming words, taken the ascendency, dictated whatever agenda was going to follow.

He stood in front of her stupidly.

'Hiya,' he said.

They walked down the platform to the parking lot, he unlocked the Caddy, opened the door for her, closed it after she sat down, traversed the car, breathing steadily and deeply, got into the driver's seat. *The driver's seat*. That was where she was. He should have given her the goddamn keys.

'Let's go for a walk,' she said. 'Maybe in Heckscher Park?'

'Sure,' he said.

It seemed to carry some sort of risk, to utter the next words, and neither of them spoke during the ten-minute ride to the park, Addie staring intently out of the window, as if taking in strange sights, Ben breathing as studiedly as a swami attaining a higher plane of consciousness. It didn't work, but at least he wasn't hyperventilating.

He parked, turned off the car and got out to open her door for her, as if she were a visiting dignitary. *On her dignity*, was that the phrase? Formal, withheld, superior.

My God, was it possible, could it be possible that she had decided to leave him? Could she do that, would she? Her bearing announced that she had nothing to do with this chauffeur who had collected her, and would have nothing to do with him when he dropped her off at last and went back to his work, to collect someone else.

She took a few steps away from him, looking at the trees, stretched and yawned, as if tired, or bored, and began strolling towards the pond, without looking back to see if he was following. He followed.

She was walking quickly, as if on reaching the pond she was going to throw herself in, or perhaps wait until he caught up and throw him in. She stopped at the water's edge. A family of ducks pottered across the water quacking excitedly, looking up imploringly, sensing bread. She waved her hand dismissively. *Scram, ducks*.

Catching her up, Ben stood by her side, wishing he had some bread or something to say.

'*Nu*?' he said.

'Yeah,' she shrugged.

'What'd you do in the city? Bought something nice, I hope . . .'

Good Lord, he knew he was trying to ingratiate himself, so cut himself off, made a flipping gesture with his hand as if discarding some pellets of bread. The ducks looked hopeful, then disappointed, quacked.

'I got back early . . .' Addie began.

Early? Early for what?

'. . . so that you could make connections to get back to DC . . . To Alexandria.' DC was where that woman was. 'There's a train from Huntington just past four-thirty that makes a good connection. You'll be back in plenty of time.'

He was rather shocked.

'What's the hurry?' he said. 'The kids will be upset, won't they?'

'Not at all! Tomorrow is Monday. It's a working day. For those of you who actually work. You need to be there in your office.'

'I thought maybe I'd go back on Tuesday. That would give us a chance to gather ourselves, have a longer talk tomorrow, do something with the kids in the morning . . .'

She gave herself a little shake, as if insects were all over her, tiny shocks and itches coming from their transit across her skin, shook herself again.

'That is not going to happen. I am not sleeping with you, the very idea makes me ill. Go back to Alexandria, do what you need to do . . .'

Need to do? Was she suggesting that if he slept with anyone it should be Rhoda? Surely not. Must be 'need to do' as in: give notice of quitting the job, finish up whatever paperwork and personal work needed finishing, get his internal house in order and external apartment packed, get ready to move. And then, when they were in the new apartment, where was he going to sleep? In a basket, like a dog?

Best keep shtum, anything he said now, anything at all, would aggravate her and the situation.

'OK,' he said compliantly. 'We can have a nice lunch with the family and then Morrie can take me to the train with the kids . . .'

'Good. And one more thing.'

'What's that?'

'We're moving to New York.'

He made another, more forceful flipping gesture, the ducks moved in expectantly.

'No, I'm sorry,' he said. 'No, we're not!'

She'd made the announcement to provoke him and it worked.

But she was aware, saying it, having made her faux announcement, that she didn't mean it, not entirely, perhaps didn't mean it at all. The long evening with Ira, which ended with too warm a hug and the quickly rejected possibility of taking a cab together somewhere with a bed in it, had only confirmed what she knew already. When Ira asked for her phone number, just prior to leaving the bar, she'd hesitated, and he'd reacted quickly and irritably.

'I'm not doing this again,' he said. 'Once was more than enough, either this is . . .'

'Is what?' asked Addie. 'Is what? We came out for a drink. You chose to come. It has been good to see you again, almost too good. But what is the point of you having my number?'

'First of all, you have mine. It's in the book, and yours isn't, and I'm not calling you at the goddamn bungalow. But the real point is that you simply cannot once again enter my life and then disappear.'

'I am not *entering your life*! And I did not disappear! You knew I was at Penn!'

'Sure, Adele, how wonderful! I could call Information

and ask for Adele Kaufmann at the University of Pennsylvania. And after you left there, for a phone number anywhere in the world . . .'

She went quiet, knowing he was right, and not knowing what she ought or wished or needed to do. Ira was not the answer to her problems, nor was a quick roll in the hay likely to make things better. It wouldn't help. Nothing was the answer to her problems. She gave Ira a quick hug and got into a taxi, without giving him a number.

She slept heavily and woke up late, groggy and hungover. She rarely drank too much, that was Ben's forte, he could hold his booze, rarely suffered afterwards. When she didn't respect her limits – two drinks maximum – she paid for it. She soaked for a long time in the bath, took a few aspirins, laid her head back, tried to think.

She'd been a fool, that was for sure. But what sort of fool? For not following her inclinations – could she call it her heart? – and getting into bed with Ira? Following up, following through. Doing it. And having done it – it would have been so sweet, made her feel a girl again – done what? It, again?

There was no room for Ira in her life. No room in her life at all, no air to breathe, no satisfying emotional choices to be made. That stupid Groucho show that Ben loved so much: *You Bet Your Life*? She'd bet hers. And lost.

How was she to keep in touch with Ira, or he with her? She had no room of her own, no office, no sanctuary. No privacy. She was a function of her marriage, controlled by it, not in control of her life, as Ben – damn him! – was of his. *Her phone number?* Fat chance!

Out of the bath, dry, her head and stomach settling down, she picked up the phone and called Ira's office. (She didn't have his home number, he hadn't offered that!)

She did so not knowing why, or what she wanted to say, but she needed at least to say she was sorry and that, perhaps, they might try again. *Try what? When, where, how, why?* She almost put the phone down when his secretary answered.

She asked for Ira, there was a pause. Who was it calling, please?

The secretary knew.

'Adele Kaufmann.'

'Ah yes,' she said. 'He is away for a few days. I will tell him you called.'

She turned her back on the ducks, and on Ben again, leaving him to enjoy the residue of his momentary assertiveness, and walked back to the car. He stayed for a few moments at the side of the pond, communing with the importuning ducks. Nice little family, they were, simple beings with simple needs. He wished he had some crusts of bread.

The chauffeur took her back to the bungalow in silence, but honked as he entered Lane L. By the time the car was at the top of the driveway, the kids were clambering round, clasping the door handles before it had even come to rest. Becca on the driver's side, Jake opening Addie's door. They looked more than delighted, Ben thought. They looked relieved. All together again.

Soon holding Addie's hand, Becca asked, 'Did you bring us a present?'

Addie looked pleased. 'You bet I did!'

She fished round in her bag and pulled out two buttons, with pins at the back. 'I got them at Union Station. They were selling like hotcakes. I think I got the last two!' She pressed them into the kids' hands. Ben moved round, looked with interest, began to laugh.

Jake grabbed his and pinned it to his T-shirt.

'Thanks, Addie, that's so cool! You're the best! A kid at school has a button but it just says "JOE MUST GO" and that's stupid because it could be any JOE, even Joe DiMaggio!'

Becca was still studying hers. Ben read it out to her.

'What's a Fuehrer?' she asked, pronouncing it 'Fewer'.

'Hitler, stupid! It's Hitler!' Jake reached out for the pin, but Becca wouldn't let go.

'I don't get it.'

Ben lifted her up, put his arms round her in a bear hug.

'It means that we don't want a bad man like McCarthy bossing us around like he was Hitler . . .'

Becca considered this for a moment.

'I don't!' she said. 'I'm going to keep mine in the bedroom and pin it on Teddo!'

What a dumb idea, her brother could be seen thinking. Ben put a finger to his lips.

'Ben,' Jake said, 'I'm not taking mine off until that hairy creep gets lost. Or somebody kills him! I wish he was dead. He's a big fat schmo!'

Ben looked at his son proudly.

'He sure is!' he said.

At last Becca caught on.

'JOE! JOE!' she yelled, dancing round the grass.

'THE BIG FAT SCHMO!' Jake added, twirling round, holding his sister's hands.

'JOE! JOE! THE BIG FAT SCHMO!'

In a moment Ben and then Addie had joined in.

'JOE! JOE!' they chanted, waving their hands.

'THE BIG FAT SCHMO!' the kids responded.

They laughed, all of them.

Though they were used to their father's comings and goings from occasional weekends at the bungalow, the children were clingy when Ben got into the car to leave. Once again they asked if they could come along, and once again were told no. It was a bad sign. Addie and Ben 'need to talk', they were told. *So what? They always talk when we are there. What's so special about talking now?*

Perle had accompanied them into the driveway, shhhed them up and led them to the freezer. 'Let's have an ice cream, shall we?' she said, itself a bad sign. Ice cream between meals gave you a stomach ache.

There were a number of afternoon trains, so there was no hurry getting to the station. Ben couldn't get on the train, he knew, until he broke his news to Addie, weathered the ensuing storm and got her agreement to signing the lease with the Silbers. Her announcement that they would be moving to the city was sheer bravado, he knew that. It was an attitude that couldn't abide, but might take time to abate, for it accompanied her current anger. As long as he stayed toxic, she might hold on to this idiotic counter-move. But how to bring her round?

'Before I go,' he said, in a tone intended to be neither compliant nor aggressive, in a friendly but business-like voice, 'we need to make some decisions. Time is pressing . . .'

'We can talk when you get back to Alexandria,' she said. 'It's not a good time now.'

'And it'll be better then? Let's be realistic.'

She bridled, turned from looking at the road ahead, glared.

'Going to lecture me, are you? On making realistic plans? On putting the family first? On thinking what is good for the children? On how to lead an exemplary moral life!'

He tried to take her hand, and failed.

'I am so sorry. I was weak and stupid. I promise you it is over and will never happen again . . . And weren't we all happy and together singing JOE! JOE! – that is what is real, that is!'

She shook her hand as if it had flies on it.

'Once a thing like this happens, all bets are off. You did it once, you could do it again!'

He paused, thought it worth taking a risk.

'Surely you have been tempted sometimes? We're still young and attractive – especially you – family life wears you down. You remember "Track Shoes", don't you?'

'The one where it's me that has the affair and you're the good one?'

'That wasn't us!'

'Yeah! Yeah! And of course you are right. I get tempted same as you. Only difference is that I don't act on it!'

He laughed bitterly.

'Only because you don't have the opportunity, the time or the place. Don't you keep masturbating your wrist with that goddamn bracelet Ira gave you? That is unfaithful too, and distressing. Don't be a hypocrite!'

She pulled over onto the side of the road, a block before the station, and turned off the car.

'Get out! I've had enough of this, enough of you!'

Ben turned in his seat and looked at her steadily.

'I'm starting to feel the same. But we'll get over it. We have to.'

She didn't respond.

'Before I go, though, there is one thing I have to tell you. Yesterday I went to see Charlie Silber . . .'

'You what? Why would you—'

'. . . and I told him that we will take the apartment and that you would be in touch with them in the next couple of days to sign the lease.'

He turned away from Addie, put his hand on the doorknob, turned it and got out of the car, closed the door again and leaned in the open window.

He bent lower to get a full view. Addie was sitting stiffly, her hands gripping the wheel, immobile, staring out the window.

'I am so sorry to have caused this,' he said. She didn't respond. 'We can work it out, just bear with me, please. With us. With all of us. I'll call from Alexandria tomorrow and start doing what needs to be done. There's nothing left to discuss really, just things to do. Leave it to me, no need for you to come down, I quite understand that. Perhaps you could explain to the kids, they'll be a bit puzzled . . .'

That got her attention.

'No! You explain it to the children. You caused this. They know something is up, they've been acting out. Becca is withdrawn, Jake moons about and won't look up from his book. So why don't you write them one of your charming letters with illustrations, reassuring them that everything is going to be all right? You might even tell them about Daddy's little adventure . . .'

He'd turned away by then, begun walking towards the station. He had a train to catch.

6

Elementary schools smell of disinfectant: too many little ones unable to get to the toilet quickly enough. Jake sniffed and made a face.

'It stinks in here!'

'It's just chemicals from the cleaning,' Addie said. 'Nothing to worry about, you'll get used to it.'

It would take time, she knew that, for a boy used to the open spaces, clean air and green fields of his progressive school, with only wholesome farmyard smells in the air, to adapt to the cramped and insalubrious conditions of this suburban dump. She looked up, casing the joint, a large three-storey brick building suggesting a reform school not a haven for little ones. She had a sharp desire to take his hand and light out for the territory, anywhere but here. What right had she to inflict this on her children?

Mind you, Becca had been OK on her induction – came along, held hands, biddable and only slightly anxious. Miss Saul, her new teacher, stooped down to child level to give her new charge a hug.

'Aren't you lovely!' she said. 'Are you called Rebecca, then?'

'No, Becca.'

'That's a nice name. I will introduce you to the others

in a minute, and I'm sure they will be pleased to meet you. It's a very happy class!'

There'd been only a slight sign of sniffles as Addie left, turning at the door as she did, but Miss Saul was firmly in control and Becca had already gathered herself, was standing up straight as Granny Perle had recommended, not looking down at the floor. She looked a nice little girl, the other kids would surely take to her.

But Jake had more problems. He was too mature, really, for elementary school, this one anyway, advanced in reading and writing and mathematics. He would do just fine academically, but he was too – Addie hesitated to use the term – too *sophisticated* for this suburban environment of conformists and cultural dimwits.

Too strong-willed as well. She had tried bribery – a dollar! two dollars! – to make him take off his 'McCARTHY FOR FUEHRER' button, and failed.

'I am not taking it off till he is gone!'

And so it was a balky, fastidious and politically engaged ten-year-old who was introduced to his formidable teacher, Miss Connolly, a stout besuited middle-aged Irish spinster – lesbian, sniffed Addie, can't fool me – of distinctly conservative leanings. She liked her fifth graders well-dressed, well-behaved and full of patriotic fervour for their great country, lustily pledging their allegiances to the flag, belting out 'America the Beautiful' at Assembly.

Miss Connolly bent down in a stately manner, which took some time, and peered at Jake's button. He stood still, thrust his chest out proudly.

'And what is this?' enquired Miss Connolly in a voice heard right across the halls.

'It's a button,' said Jake. 'Because I hate McCarthy. He's a big fat schmo!'

'*Senator* McCarthy!' said an outraged Miss Connolly. 'And you are to take it off this very moment!'

'I don't have to.' He had prepared himself for this in conversations with Ben, who was inclined to support his son's political allegiances, though he no longer shared them. He had tried to explain about Stalin, who was as bad as Hitler, and why he had abandoned the party himself, but the boy argued that just because a bad man came along it didn't mean Communism was a bad idea! Suppose McCarthy got to be president, would that mean democracy was a bad idea? *Fair point,* thought Ben proudly, *a lot of very smart people think like that too.*

Miss Connolly stood up straight, her face reddening.

'I beg your pardon!' She reached out to grab him by the sleeve of his shirt, but Addie (tactfully, she thought) drew the boy away.

'I don't have to,' said Jake, his voice quivering only a little. 'I have a right. It is called freedom of speech! It is protected by the First—'

'You insolent boy!' This time Miss Connolly succeeded in collaring him. 'Come with me to the principal's office!'

'Good,' said Jake bravely. Addie stood beside him, speechless at his courage.

'I think,' Addie said, 'that you will find he is right, that freedom of ex—'

'Then you,' said Miss Connolly, 'are as misguided as he is. There is no "freedom of speech" in Woodbury Avenue Elementary School. What a preposterous idea!' She looked at the boy sternly, then at his equally misguided mother with contempt.

'Is this boy some sort of Communist sympathiser then? Is that what this horrible button signifies?'

'Yes,' said Jake. 'I am. Communists are good people,

they want fairness for everybody. *To each according to his needs!*'

Miss Connolly was not going to be lectured on subversive politics by a ten-year-old.

'Come with me,' she said, turning with a stately air and heading down the hall. Addie followed compliantly, but Jake, amazingly, seemed to be enjoying himself. She felt proud, watching him standing up for himself. Miss Connolly was a formidable woman, and a principal an archetypal menace. And here was Jake, taking them on! They'd done a good job with that one, Ben and she. Good parenting, that was!

Mr Burkett stood up and came from behind his desk as Miss Connolly barged in, tugging Jake in her wake. It looked, thought Addie with a wry smile, like a scene from a Marx Brothers film, with Margaret Dumont dominating some weedy man. For Mr Burkett was hardly formidable. Dressed in a rumpled seersucker suit that had seen better days, the principal was slight, a trifle dandruffy and obviously disliked confrontations. He looked at Miss Connolly briefly, unwilling to meet her eye, turned to Addie and said, 'Ah, you must be Mrs Grossman, I've just been reading your application forms for Jacob and Rebecca. We are so glad to have them, even if it is a few days late. Quite useful, otherwise they could get lost in the rush of the first few days of term. Thank you for coming in—'

A red-faced Miss Connolly interrupted him.

'This insolent boy, Principal Burkett—'

'Ah yes, thank you, Miss Connolly. You may go now.'

Miss Connolly spluttered, drew herself up, opened her mouth . . .

'Thank you, Miss Connolly. Please shut the door on your way out.'

Miss Connolly did, more firmly than was strictly necessary.

Mr Burkett turned to Jake.

'Jacob,' he said, 'Miss Connolly is an excellent teacher, I'm sure you'll get on. She sometimes seems a bit fierce, but she has a heart of gold. And you know what?' He looked down at the papers on his desk. 'She lives in the Garden Apartments too, just like you!'

'I'm called Jake,' said the boy, unwilling to contemplate living next to a female incarnation of Mike the Atomic Bomb.

'Jake, then,' said the smiling principal, who rose to shake his hand, held it for an extra second while reading his political button. Addie smiled back. He was OK, Mr Burkett, reasonable.

'I see you have just moved to Huntington,' he said. 'Where have you come from?'

'Alexandria, my husband was an attorney with the Department of Justice, and he will be setting up an office in Huntington after he passes the Bar.'

Mr Burkett screwed his forehead into a thinking shape, making the inevitable computation. Lawyer leaving DC hastily, a late application for the school, child with an anti-McCarthy button, wife a social worker with (he looked down again) Family Service League. Good organisation, growing every year, he often had families who needed their services.

An archetypal leftist family. No wonder Miss Connolly had turned against them. She thought Senator McCarthy was insufficiently vigilant in his pursuit of such people. Silly woman really, but a good teacher.

'I hope the move went smoothly, it can be such a trial, especially for the children. And hard on your husband, having to pass the Bar. I always think it is absurd, how each state has its own qualifying examination. It must be stressful for him, and humiliating.'

Addie smiled warmly. Such a nice man, who'd have thought it? Principals were often ex-gym teachers, muscle-bound klutzes. And this guy, she looked at him closely, was more a piano teacher than a gym teacher.

'For all of us! We haven't even moved yet. We are living with my parents in Harbor Heights Park while we redecorate the apartment. Our stuff arrives next Monday.'

Mr Burkett looked up from the paper, satisfied that all was in order.

'We do have one problem, Jacob – I'm sorry, Jake – and that is your button. I am afraid it will have to come off, you can't wear it in school.' He turned to Addie. 'Perhaps you could take it home with you?'

Addie shook her head. 'He thinks it is freedom of speech.'

'It is!' said Jake. 'It's the First Amendment!'

'Let me explain what the rules are here – because they are the same at all schools,' said Mr Burkett. (He had clearly never heard of Burgundy Farm Country Day School.) 'We encourage our pupils to express themselves, that is what a democracy is all about. But there have to be limits, and one of those limits is that we do not allow offensive or provocative language—'

'But . . .' interrupted Jake.

Mr Burkett raised a finger gently to shush him.

'For instance, we do not allow cursing. And more importantly, we do not allow children to say things that would be offensive to other children: suppose one of the white pupils called a Negro a "nigger"? That is a bad word and would cause pain, and it is not allowed in this school . . .'

Jake raised his hand.

'Yes, Jacob?'

'Jake! My button isn't calling anybody a name except McCarthy. And Hitler, I guess. It isn't horrible, it's good, and right!'

'You may well think so,' said Mr Burkett, 'and you certainly may proclaim it with your button when you are not in this school. But we do not allow political demonstrations of any kind . . .'

Jake was ready for that one.

'What about "I LIKE IKE"?' he said.

'Even that button,' said the principal. 'Next thing you know an "I LIKE ADLAI" button would show up, and we'd have disagreements, maybe even fisticuffs in the playground.'

He laughed. He clearly didn't mean that, but he was implacable.

'Be a good boy, then, and take it off. Then I can show you to Miss Connolly's classroom and perhaps the two of you can start again?'

'She started it!' said Jake.

'Then you can finish it,' said Mr Burkett. 'I will help you.'

Jake sat still in his chair, considering. Unpinned the button and gave it to Addie, who put it into her purse.

'Excellent,' said Mr Burkett. 'Thank you for being so reasonable. Perhaps you'd both like to come with me?'

Ben arrived to pick the kids up from school, having been briefed by Addie about the saga of the Brave Red Boy, hoping that it had been resolved without escalation. That Miss Connolly sounded a formidable old bat, and she apparently lived round the corner. *Oy vey.* He tried to clear his mind from the reconsideration of a story he'd written early in 1946, quite promising really, shook his head like a sheepdog in the rain, popped out of the car and wandered into the playground with the other parents. The kids would be out in five minutes.

The fact that he didn't recognise a single parental face didn't bother him. He would in time, and in more time he would be representing some of these folks as they bought houses, had accidents, divorced their spouses. It was a bit more common now, divorce, and there was good money in it. Yet he liked the idea of being a mediator – even when it meant there would be less fees – encouraging warring partners to take a deep breath, listen to each other, remember what it was that had united them, recall their vows and commitments to their families. He would be good at that: reasonable, benevolent, clear-minded. People liked him immediately. They would at Temple Beth El, too, which he would soon join, and where he was told there was an absence of competent leadership. Step right up: more acquaintances, more friends, more contacts, more clients. More money.

He could master the relevant material for the Bar, he reckoned, in five or six months – his memory was still sharp and he had every incentive – then set up an office in the centre of town. There were suites available above some of the older shops on New York Avenue. Addie would be starting her job at Family Service League at the beginning of October, so there would soon be enough coming in to pay back her father. *No more sandwiches!*

He attracted one or two bemused glances and hesitant smiles as he loitered with the other parents outside the exit from which the kids would soon flow. He didn't realise how paint-spattered he was, could see it on his shirtsleeves and hands, but had no idea that there was blue paint in his hair and on his cheek. He looked, in his old check shirt and dirty chinos, like some sort of workman. A painter and decorator? Good ones were hard to find. He noticed one or two of the woman eyeing him thoughtfully. At first he thought it was because they fancied him, but it seemed they only fancied his services. He smiled, there was a joke lurking there somewhere.

When the bell rang a flood of kids, in a surprising number of sizes and shapes, poured out of the not-wide-enough door, laughing and pushing, trying to locate their waiting parents. Jake was near the front, caught Ben's eye immediately and rushed over.

'Not so fast, could you go back and make sure Becca is OK?'

She was one of the little ones, she might get a bit lost and confused. But before Jake could turn, there she was, grabbing his hand, a huge smile on her face.

'It's brilliant!' she exclaimed. 'I have a new friend, she's nice, she's going to come to the new apartment to play . . . And I have the best teacher!'

Jake pulled at Ben's other arm.

'I don't!' he said.

'So I gather, Addie told me all about it. Did it get any better as the day went on?'

'I guess. She doesn't like me. And I already know everything they're studying, it's so dumb . . .'

'I'm sure there will be things for you to learn, but maybe they don't all come at once?'

Jake looked doubtful.

'It'll be boring!'

'Well,' said Ben, 'why don't the two of you come get in the car and I'll show you something that isn't boring!'

'What? What!' said Becca. 'Tell us now!'

'You'll see.'

*

In the apartment there were dust motes floating in the air, it was so bright with all the lights on and the windows wide open, helping to fumigate and let the paint dry. Poppa Mo was standing on a ladder, which Addie was holding quite unnecessarily, filling in the holes in the wall that those Silbers had left, where the nails for putting up all the pictures were. Every wall had multiple holes and grey shadows where a horrible painting had been. As a housewarming present Harriet Silber had given them a particularly garish oil painting of the outside of the Garden Apartments, as if they needed to be reminded where they now lived. The picture was on the floor in the living room, its front to the wall. They could put it in a closet and hang it if the Silbers came to visit.

'Come this way!' said Ben. 'Poppa and I only just finished it, so you could see it after school, don't touch the walls!' He led them into their bedroom, with windows facing to the rear of the building, which had been decorated in a pleasing mid-blue colour, the result of hours of negotiation between the children, some tears and an eventual colouristic reconciliation.

Becca looked round, wide-eyed. Jake gave one of his little smiles.

'It's neat,' he said. 'Thanks!'

Becca nodded, said 'Thanks!' in a quiet voice, already wondering which side of the room her bed would be on and where she could hang her picture. At their last visit to the museum, she'd bought – or Addie had bought for her – a beautiful picture of a little girl, all swirly blue and yellow and green, by a painter from France, she loved him. And Jake got a silly picture that was just funny shapes, he'd be allowed to put his up too. The pictures didn't go together at all, but it didn't matter, Ben said. They just had different taste. Taste meant what you liked or didn't like.

'Don't forget to thank Poppa, too!'

They turned and went back to the living room. Poppa hardly looked down, concentrating, but Addie risked letting go of the ladder to give them a hug.

'So how was school?' she asked, in what was intended to be a casual tone. She'd been worried about this day for weeks; the kids were not used to a public school system, had been raised in a permissive environment. She had Jake's button ready to hand and pinned it to his shirt. He smiled at her, ran his fingers over its face, happy that it had returned to its rightful place in the world.

'It was great!' said Becca.

'It was OK,' said Jake.

That was good enough, the most that could have been expected. She breathed a sigh, relief.

'Did you hear that, Poppa?' she asked, re-taking her hold on the ladder.

'Mmm, good,' he said, without turning round. 'Jake, come and help me.'

There were sounds coming from the kitchen, and Becca popped down the hall to see who was there. It was exciting, getting ready to move, and there was Granny Perle – she had to look twice, she'd never seen Granny in old pants and a baggy blouse, looking altogether not Granny – but there she was on a stepladder, washing out the insides of a kitchen cabinet, bending low to dunk her cloth in a bowl of soapy water, wringing it out, starting again.

'Please, Granny! Can I help?'

Perle looked down at the little one, beaming up at her, so anxious to please, and an uncharacteristically broad smile passed her features. It was wonderful that the family were moving to Huntington, she would see them much more now, such a *brocheh*.

'Of course you can, darling. Let me show you.' She descended the two steps of the ladder and showed Becca the rag, dunked it in the water – 'It's a bit hot, you be careful!' – and wrung it out.

'When I hand it down to you, you can do this and hand it back, that will be such a big help!'

Addie was in what Harriet had referred to as the Master Bedroom, whether because that was its name on some brochure or because she was a pretentious nitwit. Addie rather inclined towards the latter, and the idea of Charlie Silber as a Master made her sneer. She was thinking these ungenerous thoughts as she surveyed the walls of what was certainly the larger of the two bedrooms – was the smaller one called the Servant Bedroom? – with increasing irritation and disdain. Harriet had used this private space to hang an unusually large number of her daubs, plus an even larger number of Scotch-taped drawings and cards. The walls, once a jade green, when stripped of their contents were shabby, mildewed, pitted, full of holes (now filled) where nails had been.

On the floor was an open can of Super Kem-Tone Miracle Wall Finish, which the instructions claimed could cover even a dark shade in a single coat. Addie looked at the antagonistic surfaces sceptically, hoping for a fair fight.

'Two,' she thought. 'It'll take two to cover all that *schmutz*!'

They'd brought Poppa's Roller-Koaters; it could be finished by the end of the weekend. Shasta White walls looking like new, all that foul underlying mess now invisible, still there but covered over. Brilliant! White-washed!

The white was Ben's idea. Nobody had white bedroom walls, but they could, like a fresh start! She had acceded reluctantly, would have gone dark green given a choice. It would have covered the *schmutz* more easily and more thoroughly. She found herself humming the tune that had taken possession of her mind. It wouldn't go away.

Covering up the schmutz!
Covering up the schmutz!
We shall come rejoicing,
Covering up the schmutz!

The white paint would see them out before the grime reasserted itself, but it would come back, sure as sure could be. *Schmutz* is like that.

Ben smiled, it was good to see Addie happy again.

A can was opened on a trestle table which they'd covered with an old sheet. She poured some into a tray, thinly, and covered her roller, shook it to make sure it didn't dribble, and applied it to the wall. Stepped back, took a hard look. *It will take a lot of effort, but it'll be worth it!*

Ben stepped in, watching her without being seen. Addie in purposive and positive mood was an awesome sight. He stepped across to join her.

'Hey, lady, you got another holy roller?'

'Sure do. Look under the sheets!'

He took it, rolled it into the paint and joined his wife. After an hour and a half they had painted two walls, and Ben put his roller down gingerly, rubbing his aching shoulder. Addie came up behind him, put her hand over his.

'Let me,' she said.

He was surprised, gave in immediately, bent over the stepladder so she could get a grip, dig in with her fingers. She was surprisingly good at massage, either for relief or simple pleasure: particularly good when it was both . . . He sighed. She'd hardly touched him since he had come back from Alexandria, his many practical and emotional chores completed. They'd slept together for the last few nights, but all contact was inadvertent, embarrassed, slighting. They hadn't talked: when she picked him up, Addie said, 'Let's just get on with it,' and they were doing so. He knew where he stood, but not how securely.

He reached back and put his hand over hers.

'I missed you so much,' he said. He'd said so many times on the phone from the old apartment. Most days he had called when he got home from work: she thought he was trying to show that he was alone, not with Rhoda, big deal, but after a week or so it was clear that he was calling so regularly because he really did miss her and wanted to be forgiven. Rhoda was finished, she could tell it from his voice, which sounded, well, normal again. Unburdened, unevasive. Like Ben, again, almost. She wasn't entirely sure that she welcomed him back.

And now, spattered with paint, leaning onto a stepladder, squeezed and kneaded, he felt – a joke coming on! – squeezed and needed. He knew better than to say so.

She hunched and scrunched her shoulders, gave a low moan.

'My God, I ache. I'm not used to all this.'

He nodded. He wasn't either. He moved to reciprocate her massage, but she evaded him. Enough already. Too much.

'I'm going to have a shower,' she said. 'I brought soap and towels, and a change of clothes.'

He looked at his watch.

'Do we have time before dinner?'

'Who gives a damn? I'm not going over to Little Miss Honeysuckle's smelling like a Cossack's armpit!'

He smiled and nodded, as if his permission was required.

She locked the door, surveying the bathroom suite with

distaste. She hated turquoise – American Standard called it Claire de Lune, for Christ's sake! – and the sink and tub were already streaked with age, or worse. She averted her eyes from the toilet bowl – Poppa Mo called it the crapper – turning down its lid fastidiously.

Dropping her sweaty clothes on the floor, she turned on the shower and stepped into the tub. There was a powerful flow, better than she was used to, sufficient to wash away her tears almost at source. As if that were possible. She needed to staunch the flow or Michelle would spot the signs, try to catch her eye and smile in commiseration, and triumph.

As she emerged, freshly clad but still spattered with paint, combing her fingers through her wet hair, Perle and Becca had finished cleaning the kitchen drawers and cabinets. They only had the stove and icebox to finish; there would be time for that tomorrow. Perle checked her watch, stopped to wash her hands in the kitchen sink, dried them on an only slightly soiled towel, stood back to approve her handiwork, gave Becca an approving smile and looked out into the rest of the apartment.

'May I make a suggestion?' she said in a loud voice. The others stopped what they were doing and stood at attention.

Across the courtyard, Michelle had prepared a buffet of sliced brisket, potato salad and coleslaw, lettuce wedges, pickles and bottles of beer and soda. The plates were stacked on the kitchen counter, with enough cutlery for ten, baby Charlotte already asleep in the smaller bedroom.

Frankie looked round.

'Bit crowded,' he said, pursing his lips.

'We've had more. Remember the Seder last year, all those kids, must have been about fourteen altogether?'

He laughed, he was in a good enough mood, considering

his sister was moving in across the way. It didn't matter, it wouldn't matter. He couldn't wait to tell them why. From the living-room window he could see them emerging from the Silbers' apartment, raising their faces to the still hot sun, splattered with paint. He hoped it had dried by now.

He went to the front door and opened it, stood aside as the children rushed by, hugged his mother, who was looking as close to radiant as Perle could get – which was not very – clasped his father by the hand, put his other hand round his shoulders in a welcoming hug. Nodded to Addie without hostility, greeted Ben with a handshake. Six. All accounted for and ready for feeding. It was the least he and Michelle could do, he was almost enjoying it.

Michelle – she thought of everything! – had arranged a tablecloth on the sparse brown grass in front of their entrance and, after the four children had filled their paper plates, ushered them outdoors.

'Look,' she said, 'you get your own picnic! And I will get you a big jug of Kool-Aid and some plastic cups.'

The three little girls tittered with pleasure, but Jake looked down glumly, aware that an entreaty to join the adults would be turned down. But it was OK, he loved brisket with lots of ketchup, and could finish it quickly and rejoin the grown-ups. The girls looked at his button, Jenny reading it, Naomi spelling out the easy words. They made a face, knowing their father would disapprove. He didn't like McCarthy, but thought he was right; neither of them was clear what he was right about. It was something important.

At the dining table, which just about accommodated the six adults, Frankie was fanning out a set of colour brochures.

'We thought we might look at these,' he said, putting

one at the top, pointing to the cover illustration. 'They're only $18,500 and at 4.5 per cent mortgage that's less than $1,000 a year!' Michelle took it in her hand, looked at it warmly as if greeting an old friend and passed it to Perle, sitting opposite.

'Look, Mother,' she said. 'Just look! A Cape Cod, four bedrooms with a living room and a den, and a screened-in porch. Lovely back yard, with old trees. AND a big kitchen with all appliances, even a built-in dishwasher!'

'I thought you were the dishwasher,' said Frankie.

She smiled at the stale old joke.

'Not any more!'

'And it's just down the road from the school on Park Avenue, and three minutes from town! We've already looked at the lot, and the house will be ready in six months. We're putting a down-payment down this week!'

Addie had already taken the brochures and plans in hand and was perusing them carefully.

'Congratulations,' she said. 'It looks pretty nice.'

Ben was later to quiz her about this response.

'I thought,' he said, 'that you were going to remark that it is everything you never wanted.'

'It is! Or it was,' she said, with a shrug. 'And now I want one too. I certainly don't want a garden apartment! Isn't life funny?'

She paused. 'But NOT near them, please God.'

'I'll do what I can,' said Ben. 'And you know what? In twelve months or so, maybe a few months more, we'll be ready, we just have to tough it out at the Ex-Silbers'.' Neither of them was willing, yet, to call it their apartment.

'After all, the figures add up: once I am earning and we have your salary, we can buy a house and pay your father back.'

Addie nodded, gave him a not entirely gentle punch on the shoulder.

'Please,' she said. 'I'm sick of existing on sandwiches. Let's cook for ourselves!'

Ben laughed. By committing herself to the stupid sandwich metaphor – how he hated it, always had! – Addie seemed to proclaim herself a competent cook. He suppressed the impulse to laugh, and to point this out. But of course she was right. If she couldn't make a sandwich, she could make sandwiches, could help provide, ensure an easier transition into a new life. And whatever she thought and said, an *exciting* new life. He was looking forward to it.

'Let's tell Mo,' he said. 'Soon! We can look after ourselves.'

'We can,' said Addie, without a trace of self-congratulation. 'And after we get settled, and you open your new office, then perhaps you can get back to your writing . . .'

'It's nice of you to say that,' said Ben, 'but that it isn't going to happen.'

'I know it's hard to fit everything in, but I know how much it means to you. And you're good at fitting things in, do you remember when—'

Ben put his hand on her arm and squeezed, as if staunching a flow of blood.

'No, time is not the problem. The impulse is gone, it has been for a long time. I've held on to it because my idea of myself required the epithet "writer". It still does, really . . .'

'So?'

'So I need to change my idea of myself. After all, lawyer, father, husband, Huntingtonian, and all that will entail . . . It's enough already!'

There was a pause of a few moments as they both considered what this would mean.

'I am worried,' said Addie, 'that you will resent me. For making you give up your dream.'

Ben laughed, not entirely humourlessly.

'That's what dreams are for,' he said.

It was an unexpected renunciation, but, as Addie reflected on it, an entirely agreeable one. Ben could write, but he was not a writer. Thank God for that!

'There was a brochure for a development just off Mechanic Street – you know where that is? Just north of town, ten-minute walk to your office!'

'Office?'

'On New York Avenue. You know?'

'I don't yet.'

'You will,' she said. 'Shall we go look at the plots tomorrow? They start building soon, I think.'

They had the whole weekend to work on the apartment, get it finished before the furniture arrived on Monday. There would be time first thing Saturday morning to drive round with the kids, have a look at the possible new neighbourhood. Maybe go out for breakfast, all of a sudden the kids loved pancakes and bacon, that would be a sufficient incentive to get them out of bed early.

When the time came, and the two sleepyheads were ushered towards the car, Becca didn't want to go, turning back towards the house.

'What if we get lost?' she said.

'Don't you worry,' said Ben. 'I know the way!'

Not entirely reassured, the little one allowed herself to be corralled in the back seat with a scornful Jake.

'So what if we do?' he said.

They did. Somewhere just off Wall Street they made the wrong left turn and ended up peering at street signs, stopping to discuss where they might be.

'Look at the map!' said Becca urgently.

'Don't have one of Huntington,' said Ben. 'But don't you worry, we'll find it soon. This is the right neighbourhood.'

'What if it isn't?' said Becca anxiously, just as Ben gave a thumbs-up and turned up the hill towards Mechanic Street. At the top, there was a row of shabby old houses on the right, the kids peered at them anxiously – *poor people must live there.* They soon parked and looked onto a field on which frames for a large number of houses were visible.

'Let's walk round,' said Addie. 'This road' – she pointed to an unpaved track – 'is going to be called Brookside Drive, isn't that a nice name?'

Jake looked round. 'No,' he said, 'it's stupid. I don't see any brooks.'

'I don't too,' said Becca, wondering what a brook was. 'It's stupid.'

It was stupid, and ugly too. The trees had been cleared from the whole site and a baked reddish clay with tussocks of grass covered the desolate space: the frames for the houses looked like skeletons, a house graveyard.

Even Ben was depressed, looking at it, and resisted going further. Instead he retrieved the brochure, turned it over and bent down to show the artist's impression of the final development to the children.

'You see,' he said, 'it'll look great!'

They gave a cursory look. 'So where'll all those trees come from?' Jake cast an eye round the parched mud. 'Looks more like a desert to me.'

There was no sense arguing. Anyway, the boy was right. It did, and it was depressing.

'I'll tell you what,' Ben said, 'every few months we can come here and watch it come to life, the houses going up, the grass and trees planted. And then if we start to like it we might buy one, and if not we can look elsewhere. Huntington is full of new developments, they're springing up like mushrooms.'

The children listened sceptically – *what fun, living in a stupid mushroom!* – retreated to the car, got in and closed the door, looked up expectantly, visions of pancakes and maple syrup on their faces.

'OK,' said Addie, reading the signs. 'Breakfast time!'

'Can I make a suggestion?' Ben asked.

Everyone laughed.

'I have a new game,' he said. 'It'll be exciting, and we can all learn some things and get to know our new town.'

'What? What?' said Becca, smelling more rat than pancake.

'I just invented it,' said Ben. 'It has two names . . .'

'I'm not playing!' said Jake.

'It's called "My Turn, Your Turn",' said Ben. 'But it's also called "Lost and Found".'

Neither notion was compelling to a small, rebellious and hungry couple of kids.

'I don't want to play some dumb game with two stupid names. I want my breakfast!'

'Me too!'

Ben turned towards the back seat and smiled.

'We'll get breakfast on the way,' he said.

'The way to where?'

'Who knows?' laughed Ben. 'That'll be up to you three.'

Addie looked puzzled, Becca uncomprehending, Jake scornful.

He turned the car round at the dead end at the top of Mechanic Street and drove to the next intersection.

'We can start with Becca,' he said. 'Which way should I turn?'

Becca looked up and down the road, right and left. 'How should I know? I don't know where I am.'

'That's the point,' said Ben. 'We can discover parts of town we've never seen before. *We will get lost on purpose.* And you know what? We'll find our way home, sure enough!'

'I don't—' Becca began, just as Jake piped up.

'Left!' he said firmly. 'Go left!'

Ben turned, crossed the next intersection without asking, then stopped at the stop sign at the next.

'Right,' said Addie.

At the bottom of the hill was a junction with a big road. They stopped for the traffic, waiting for an opening.

'Left!' said Jake.

'It's not fair,' said Becca. 'He had two turns, and he always says left.'

Jake laughed. 'I'm a leftist,' he said, pointing to his button.

'Right!' said Becca.

'It sure is,' said her brother. He laughed louder. 'Grossman slays Grossman!'

Ben turned right and didn't ask again, heading away from town. After a few miles they could see water to their left and the entrance to a beach, which even at this early hour had a number of cars in the parking lot, umbrellas sprouting on the sand.

Becca looked out of her window longingly.

'Can we get out and go to the beach? We could paddle. Maybe they even have a food place!' And what they certainly would have, she knew, was a person who could tell them how to get back to Huntington.

By now they had passed the entrance to the parking lot.

'You should have said left,' said Jake, 'then we would have had to go in.'

'Go back! Go back!' said his sister, but was overruled. 'Back' was not a turn.

'It is,' said Becca, 'it's a U-turn!' Ben reckoned that was a fair point, but still didn't make one. Soon the beach was out of sight and there were no turns at all, just the empty road ahead, making them more lost.

Addie looked left out of her window, at a windswept landscape of sand dunes. 'Oh!' she exclaimed, 'guess what I just saw?'

'What?'

'A lion!'

The kids couldn't resist combing the landscape for lions, though they were pretty sure Long Island didn't have any. Alexandria certainly didn't, except in the zoo.

They peered out anyway.

'Where?' said Becca, just in case.

'You know what? I'm lyin',' said Addie.

Everyone groaned.

'Addie slays Addie!' she said, suddenly ashamed that like Ben she was using lousy puns to draw attention to herself, but away from her troubles. First it was him and his stupid mattababy. Now her, lyin' as well. What's a matta with *me*?

She shrugged her shoulders. Everything. Nothing. What choice did they have, really? You have to get on with things, they had to get on with each other, they would as best they could. It was what you did in a marriage: what, her parents were happy and in love? Or, worse example – or did she mean better? – Ben's parents, who could hardly stand the sight of each other, cramped together in their shabby shadowy apartment, silent, morose, lethargic, confined to their chairs and bedroom.

It was impossible. She was hardly cut out for raising children on her own: never mind the money and logistics, the claustrophobia would have smothered her. Of course her mother would want to help. That would make it worse. So, there she was. Ben was essential. And though she was attracted by the prospect of freezing him out, making him play bad puppy for the foreseeable future, who'd gain from that, starting her very own cold war? He was genuinely contrite. Perhaps, one day, not soon, she might be genuinely forgiving. In the meantime perhaps she should treat him like an uncongenial roommate – someone whom she hadn't chosen but had to get along with. Politeness, deference, distance. No intimacy, either emotional or physical. But roommates move out, and on, and she was stuck with Ben. And the children, bless them. Wedded to them all. That was a fact. *The facts of life*, her life. Best get on with it.

Anyway, couples who loved each other made her feel ill. Think of her brother and his soppy wife. All that schmaltzy cuddling. Yuck! Surely there was something better than love, something different, something grown-up? Love was for girl Addie and boy Ira, for children who didn't know anything. Wasn't it? Love was something you grew out of.

'Never mind about your stupid jokes,' said Becca. 'How are we going to get home now?'

She didn't look worried, just hungry.

'Yeah,' said her brother, 'we're totally lost. Becca is going to start to cry!'

'No, I'm not! I don't even care. No lion is going to eat me!'

Ben turned and gave an unnecessarily reassuring smile. 'We're not lost,' he said, 'we just don't know where we are yet. We will soon.'

He came to a crossroads and looked at Addie.

'Up to you,' he said fondly.

'Whichever way!' she said. 'It doesn't matter, does it? We'll get there sometime.'

Acknowledgements

Novels are often prefaced by an assertion that any resemblances between their characters and living persons is unintended. This is rarely true, but it helps prevent law suits.

A Long Island Story has many such resemblances, to both the dead and the living, because this novel is based on my childhood, and a great deal of what is done and said in it actually took place, or so it seems to me now. But 1953 is a long time ago, and though childhood memories have an unusual tenacity, I can't vouch for the literal accuracy of what is recorded here, nor does it matter very much. In the end, we make up our facts almost as comprehensively as our fictions.

In 1953, of course, I would have had no idea of what the inner lives and backstories of the adults in my life consisted of. Where they came from, what they yearned for, what regrets they harboured, what frustrations, what dreams. As one gets older some of these blanks are filled in, but never fully of course, nor would one want them to be.

I have wanted to write an account of this period in my childhood for almost fifty years but didn't know how to do it, quite. I tried it as a memoir, but it felt lifeless, and I twice abandoned the project. It was only when I realised – God knows why it took so long – that the best way to recover the truth of that time was in a work of fiction that I was able to get on with it.

I believe that the dead have rights, and am anxious that my fictional 'portrayals' of my parents and grandparents are fair and sympathetic in spirit. But this is not a memoir, and I have taken the liberties that all novelists take (for most novels have something drawn from 'real' life in them): where the demands of the facts and the needs of the story are in conflict, go with the story.

So I have made some things up. My father did not have the affair recorded here. And my grandfather was not a (loveable) shyster of the sort I have described. I don't think either of them would have minded much, if I explained. Novelists make things up.

There is the further possibility that this story may cause offence to the people, both inside my family and without, who are still with us. I am sorry about this, but not very. I have my own way of seeing and reconstructing the past, trying – both as a person and as a writer, if this distinction is makeable – to get my story whole, and compelling, and memorable: worth telling and worth reading. Other people would tell theirs in other ways.

As ever, I am grateful to so many people who help me to write. To my wife Belinda, for her exacting, loving counsel and support; to my sister Ruthie (Becca in this story), for wise advice about the development of the text, excellent memory, and acute proofreading; and as ever to my friend and literary agent Peter Straus. I am also indebted, again, to Rosalind Porter, for encouragement with an early draft, and to my nephew Matthew Greenberg, for his usual acuity and enthusiasm.

Once again I have had the pleasure and the privilege to work with the people at Canongate, whose belief in my work, and capacity to improve and to promote it, have meant everything to me in my late incarnation as a novelist: to Jamie Byng, of course, and to Francis Bickmore, but especially to my editor Jo Dingley, who sees things so clearly and helps me to improve them when it is necessary, and to copy editor Debs Warner, who has done an exemplary job helping me to tighten and to clarify.

I wrote most of this novel in our house in New Zealand, during the painful time when my beloved mother-in-law, Alison Kitchin, was dying. She was the first reader of this book, and looked forward to updates as soon as I could write them. I would print them out a few pages at a time, as they emerged. She was declining quickly, and I had to hurry. The last hundred pages of the first draft were written in about ten days, while she could still concentrate. We got it done, just, and at the end she laid it on the table next to her green reclining chair, Emma the one-eared cat on her lap, and pronounced it 'very enjoyable'.

This book is dedicated, too, to her memory.